# ⟨⟩ O9-BUB-762

ALSO AVAILABLE FROM LAUREL-LEAF BOOKS

HIS DARK MATERIALS: THE AMBER SPYGLASS
Philip Pullman

DEATHWATCH
Robb White

DOWNRIVER
Will Hobbs

DR. FRANKLIN'S ISLAND
Ann Halam

FIRST TEST
Tamora Pierce

RANSOM
Lois Duncan

THE
ORDER
OF
ODD-FISH

JAMES KENNEDY

THE
ORDER
OF
ODD-FISH

Copyright © 2008 by James Kennedy

All rights reserved. Published by Laurel-Leaf, an imprint of Random House Children's Books, a division of Random House, Inc., New York. Originally published in hardcover in the United States by Delacorte Press, an imprint of Random House Children's Books, a division of Random House, Inc., New York, in 2008.

Laurel-Leaf and the colophon are trademarks of Random House, Inc.

Visit us on the Web! www.randomhouse.com/teens

Educators and librarians, for a variety of teaching tools, visit us at www.randomhouse.com/teachers

Library of Congress Cataloging-in-Publication Data is available upon request.
ISBN 978-0-440-24065-5 (pbk.)

RL: 6.0

Printed in the United States of America

10 9 8 7 6 5 4 3 2 1

First Laurel-Leaf Edition

To Heather

ONE

THE desert was empty, as though a great drain had sucked the world underground. Every color, every sound had vanished, leaving nothing but flat sand and silence.

Except for the ruby palace. If you were blasting down the highway in the middle of the night, somewhere near Dust Creek, you probably wouldn't even see it. Or just blackness, a red flash in the distance, and then nothing. It was tucked away behind the mountains, alone and nearly forgotten, the old house of Lily Larouche.

From the highway the ruby palace sparkled silently. Come a couple of miles closer, though, and you could hear the buzz of voices—closer, and squeals of laughter, snatches of music, raucous shouts—Lily Larouche was throwing a party.

The last hundred yards and suddenly the ruby palace loomed all around, slumping and sprawling over acres of sand and weeds like a monstrous, glittering cake. Its garden swarmed with exotic flowers, vegetables of startling colors, and dark ponds with fat, ill-tempered toads; strings of lights were flung throughout the crooked trees, twinkling like fireflies, and torches flickered all along the stacked and twisting terraces.

Strange shapes moved in the shadows. A man dressed as an astronaut chatted with a devil. A gang of cavemen sipped fizzing cocktails. A Chinese emperor flirted with a robot, a pirate arm-wrestled a dinosaur, a giant worm danced with a refrigerator—it was Lily Larouche's Christmas costume party, and all her old friends had come.

A blossoming bush grew on the garden patio. At first the bush seemed ordinary; but then two green eyes flashed inside it, and stared. It was a thirteen-year-old girl, small and thin, with brown skin and black bobbed hair. Her name was Jo Larouche. She was Lily Larouche's niece. She also lived at the ruby palace, and she was spying.

"Where did he go?" Jo took a bite of her scrambled-egg sandwich and watched the party intensely. Jo never talked to Aunt Lily's friends, but she loved spying on them. They usually ignored her—but tonight's party was different.

Tonight someone was watching *her*.

A fat man was looking for her.

Jo's eyes darted over the crowd. The fat man had been wearing what looked like a military uniform, staring at her across the patio, tugging his beard and pointing at his stomach, rumbling something in a Russian accent. Jo had no idea what. One thing was for sure: the fat Russian was nobody she or Aunt Lily knew.

She couldn't see him anymore—maybe he had left. Good. She intended to enjoy tonight. Jo closed her eyes and inhaled the familiar smell of Aunt Lily's parties: the lemony smoke of tiki torches; the clashing, flowery perfumes; the warm musk of cigarettes . . .

She heard Aunt Lily's name.

Jo peered out of the bush. A couple of feet away, a woman disguised as an enormous eggplant was talking to a man dressed like a UFO.

"Did you see?" whispered the eggplant. "Lily's gone nuts again."

"Cracked as a crawdad, and worse every year," said the UFO. "The woman's going to hurt herself."

"It wouldn't be so bad if it weren't for the poor girl. Do you know, I've never even seen her?"

"I heard she's some kind of freak, actually," said the UFO. "Remember what the newspapers said about her being 'dangerous'?"

Jo crouched back and frowned. So Aunt Lily was causing trouble again. She wasn't surprised. But there was a chance Aunt Lily might go too far, get herself hurt. . . . Jo rocked back and forth, hesitating. No, she had to see what Aunt Lily was up to. She picked up her cocktail tray and crept out from the bush.

At once Jo was swallowed up in the party's shimmering confusion. Nobody noticed her in her plain black dress, but she preferred it that way. She hated attention.

Aunt Lily, on the other hand . . .

Jo scanned the crowd, biting her lip. It was true—Aunt Lily was getting worse. Jo remembered the party a couple of years ago, when Aunt Lily had dived, still in her cocktail dress, into the swimming pool; the year after that, when Aunt Lily had poured bleach into the champagne punch; last year, when Aunt Lily had kicked another old lady in the teeth. . . .

Where is she? Jo's head buzzed as the lights and noise of the party swirled around her. She turned back toward the palace; maybe she'd find her in—

Just then someone crashed into Jo, knocking her to the

ground, spilling her tray and breaking the cocktail glasses on the bricks. It was a boy dressed as a hedgehog, a lanky seventeen-year-old with greasy hair. "Watch it!" he snarled.

Jo looked up, shaken. "Hey, you ran into me."

"Tough. Who're you, anyway?" The hedgehog looked closer. "Oh, wait. You're *that* girl?"

Jo got to her feet. "What's that supposed to mean?"

"You don't look so dangerous to *me*," said the hedgehog with a smirk, and then he walked away.

Jo didn't have time for this; her heart was beating too hard, she had to find Aunt Lily—but she heard herself shout, "Hey! Get back here!"

"INDEED!" roared a voice behind her.

Jo turned, startled. It was the fat Russian again—where had he come from?—a lumbering, shaggy, harrumphing, absurdly dignified mastodon of a man, with twitching white whiskers and a gleaming uniform, swinging a great black cane.

"I will take it from here, Miss Larouche," he rumbled. "You, sir! Hedgehog! Turn around and apologize!"

"Mind your own business," said the hedgehog.

"APOLOGIZE!" said the Russian.

Jo looked from the Russian to the hedgehog with alarm. People were whispering and glancing over at them; the Russian was jabbing the hedgehog with his cane.

"You, sir, are disturbing my DIGESTION!" said the Russian.

"Hey! Stop that!" said the hedgehog.

"Do you understand what it means to disturb my digestion, sir?" said the Russian. "That even now, my stomach rumbles with contempt? That my kidneys flood with excruciating acids? That *my entire gastrointestinal tract* revolts at your ungentlemanly conduct?"

The hedgehog squinted. "Who cares about your stupid gastrointestinal—"

The Russian roared, swinging his cane—*crack!*—and the hedgehog howled, clutching his head, staggering backward.

"My digestion is not mocked!" boomed the Russian. "Nor will I stand idly by while Miss Larouche is insulted! You are banished, hedgehog! My digestion has spoken—BEGONE!"

The hedgehog wavered; the Russian advanced, waggling his cane; finally the hedgehog swore, and stumbled off into the darkness.

Jo glanced around, flustered. More and more guests were staring, and now the Russian was stooping down to her. "Miss Larouche! I hope—"

"Who *are* you?" said Jo.

"Who am . . . Oh! My apologies." The Russian bowed. "I am Anatoly Korsakov, colonel. I have been trying to speak with you. Where were you?"

"Um . . . in that bush."

"Brilliant. Excellent strategy. We have enemies everywhere." Colonel Korsakov nodded. "But you need not hide anymore, for I shall protect you! And what is more, Jo Larouche, I have it on unimpeachable authority that tonight you shall receive a gift!"

"Wait, wait!" said Jo. "How do you know who I am?"

"My digestion," said Colonel Korsakov. "It whispers secrets and instructions to me. And this very moment, Miss Larouche, my digestion advises us to be on guard. I have dispatched my partner, Sefino, to patrol the grounds for suspicious characters."

"You're the most suspicious character I've ever met."

"Really? Am I really?" murmured Colonel Korsakov. He frowned at the sky and counted paces across the garden. Then he drew a big X in the sand with his cane and stood back.

"Is that your costume?" said Jo. "The uniform?"

"What?" Korsakov looked confused. "No, no. These are my usual clothes."

"But this is a costume party."

"A costume . . . Oh! Yes, of course. I had forgotten." Korsakov fished out of his pocket some green cloth with a plastic flower sticking out of the top. He gravely placed it on his head.

"I am a daffodil," he murmured uncomfortably.

Colonel Korsakov shifted his tremendous bulk from foot to foot, the tiny flower bobbing atop his head, his eyes roving around uneasily, as if at any moment the other guests might jeer at him; but they didn't; but he and Jo were ignored.

"Do you want to come inside?" she said. "I have to find my aunt. I could make you a drink, if you want. . . ."

Korsakov's face brightened at this. He looked expectantly at the sky, then back at her. "For a little while, I suppose . . . Do you know how to mix a Flaming Khrushchev? No?"

The inside of Lily Larouche's palace was all red and gold. Crimson velvet curtains with gold embroidery hung in the windows, ancient and frayed; far above, hundreds of scarlet candles burned in gold chandeliers, dripping wax onto the shaggy carpet.

The party had moved inside and the dancing had begun. A squid glided across the dance floor, its tentacles wrapped around a dainty geisha. A table of centipedes in tuxedos played whist as a pack of witches and monkeys argued politics. A cigar-chomping penguin worked his way around the room, shaking hands and slapping people on the back. A vampire giggled obscenely in the corner.

Jo left Korsakov at the bar and pushed through the party, searching on tiptoe for Aunt Lily. Then she heard a crash, a man yowling in pain, and—she winced—Aunt Lily's cackle.

Jo wriggled through the crowd and found Aunt Lily dancing on a table near the Victrola, her dress nearly falling off her shoulders, flinging records at the guests. Everyone kept away from her, muttering and glaring.

"Jo! *There* you are!" said Aunt Lily, stumbling toward the edge of the table, waving a piece of broken record. "There has to be more dancing at this party!"

"Yes, yes, of course," said Jo, reaching up to help her down. "Really, Aunt Lily—easy! Don't you think it's time you got to bed?"

"*Bed?* Who's the mother here?" slurred Aunt Lily, with the dazed-but-dangerous look Jo knew too well. "I want more dancing. Why don't these people dance?"

"It's a mystery. By the way—careful!" Jo grabbed Aunt Lily's waist just in time to hold her up. "By the way, did you invite a big Russian guy to the party?"

"You say something, honey?" said Aunt Lily. "Now, if you played the organ, we might have a real hootenanny on our hands. . . . C'mon! What do you say?"

Jo opened her mouth to argue, then gave a tight little smile and nodded. Whenever Aunt Lily got like this, there was little she could do but go along for the ride. Aunt Lily leaned on Jo, giggling, as Jo led her away and sat her down on the sofa.

At least I've got Aunt Lily under control, Jo thought. *For now, anyway.*

Jo climbed up onto the organ, a baroque machine with five keyboards, fifty pedals, and hundreds of little dials and switches. As she started to play, she saw Colonel Korsakov shouldering his way through the crowd, the daffodil bouncing on his head, asking everyone for Worcestershire sauce. "You can't mix a proper Flaming Khrushchev without Worcestershire sauce!" he insisted to a skeptical bear. Jo waved at Korsakov and pointed him toward Aunt Lily; maybe she knew where the Worcestershire sauce was.

The story of Lily Larouche was well known.

She had been a famous actress long ago, with a reputation for strange behavior. The tabloids knew she was good for at least one sensational rumor per week:

LILY LAROUCHE THROWS RODENT AT STARLET

LILY LAROUCHE ARRESTED AGAIN
FOR RECKLESS HOT-AIR BALLOONING

HEARTSICK PRESIDENT SHAVES OFF OWN EYEBROWS
IN DESPERATE BID TO WIN LILY LAROUCHE'S LOVE

The rumors usually proved true. Lily Larouche *had* hurled a live rat at another actress who had insulted her. For many years, her red hot-air balloon *had* been a nuisance over Los Angeles, regularly disrupting air traffic. And Lily Larouche still had on her desk, floating in a jar of formaldehyde, the lonely eyebrows of President Eisenhower.

Then came the most mysterious headline:

LILY LAROUCHE DISAPPEARS!

She had vanished. Her notorious ruby palace, which for years had hosted the wildest parties in Hollywood, was empty. Nobody knew where she had gone.

Then, forty years later, there was a new headline:

LILY LAROUCHE RETURNS!
(WITH A "DANGEROUS" COMPANION)

Lily Larouche had awakened in her dusty bed, in her ruby palace. But she had no idea how she had got there. And she had no idea what she had been doing for the past forty years.

Then she heard a distant crying. She followed the sound to her laundry room—and there, inside the washing machine, she found a baby.

She also found a note:

This is Jo. Please take care of her.

But beware.

This is a DANGEROUS baby.

At this the tabloids swung into a twitter. Where was the baby from? How was she dangerous? What was she doing in Lily Larouche's washing machine? But there were no answers. And the baby, disappointingly, turned out to be ordinary. The public's interest eventually waned, and the incident was mostly forgotten.

It was now thirteen years later. Jo had grown up from the "dangerous" baby in the washing machine to the girl playing the organ. And she was still playing, watching the swinging crowd, when she saw something startling: Aunt Lily and Colonel Korsakov, dancing as though they'd known each other for years.

"But of course we've only met tonight," laughed Aunt Lily. She wore long red velvet gloves and a red dress with a plunging neckline. A diamond choker dangled trails of glittering stones down her neck; her lips were painted deep red; her hair was a brilliant white; her skin was deeply tanned and as wrinkled as a raisin. She was eighty-two years old.

Jo, Aunt Lily, and Colonel Korsakov were outside, lounging near the heart shaped pool. The party was winding down, and the last guests—a glittering silver dragon, a queasy-looking cowboy, an alligator in a bikini—milled about, reluctant to go home. An orange sunrise smoldered behind clouds, revealing a desert as empty and desolate as an alien planet.

Jo watched Aunt Lily flirt with Korsakov, her own eyes half closed. *But I've got to stay awake,* she yawned to herself. It was at this time of night that Aunt Lily was at her most reckless.

"So what brings you this far out in the desert?" asked Aunt Lily.

Korsakov looked around carefully. "A most secret and important business." He sipped his Flaming Khrushchev and nodded crisply at Jo. "I have come to bring Jo a gift. And I have come to protect her."

9

"*Protect* her?" snorted Aunt Lily.

"I didn't know I needed protecting," said Jo.

"What on earth from?" said Aunt Lily.

Korsakov gazed at Jo for a moment. "You *are* Jo Larouche, yes?" He rummaged in his pockets, extracted a sweaty wad of newspaper clippings, uncrumpled one, and looked at Jo again. "The . . . '*dangerous* baby'?"

Jo opened her mouth, but Aunt Lily cut her off.

"Balderdash," said Aunt Lily. "Whoever left that note was just having their little joke. The girl's as dangerous as a glass of milk. Lived with her for thirteen years, so I should know. Not a peep, not a pop."

Jo glared at Aunt Lily.

Colonel Korsakov looked disappointed—even the daffodil on his head seemed to droop a little—but then he rumbled, "Nonsense. I have it on excellent authority that Jo Larouche *is* dangerous—and that an *extremely* important item, an item that may even be unsafe in the wrong hands, will be delivered here tonight, to this very—"

But Korsakov never finished. A futuristic white sports car burst out of nowhere, skidded through the rosebushes, and spun to a stop in the sand. Its door flew open and the hedgehog leaped out, shouting, "All right, where is he? Let me at him!"

The boy, his hedgehog costume askew, spotted Korsakov and strode over to them.

Jo's eyes went wide. The boy had something black, gleaming—a pistol.

"Get up!" shouted the hedgehog, waving his gun at the old Russian.

Colonel Korsakov slowly rose.

"I'm—I'm a violent guy!" stammered the hedgehog.

Korsakov said, "You are an ass."

"What? Hey! What's that supposed to mean? Huh?" said the hedgehog. "Listen—"

"If I were you, sir, I would move from that spot," said Colonel

Korsakov. And Jo saw that the hedgehog was standing exactly on the X Korsakov had drawn in the sand.

"Is that a challenge?" shouted the hedgehog.

Jo couldn't move. She looked around—everyone else was frozen, too, even Aunt Lily. But Korsakov was silent, and seemingly calm.

This made the hedgehog even angrier. "You better apologize, old man, or I'll shoot!"

Korsakov sighed. "Then shoot me, for God's sake, or put your gun away. But please, move off that spot."

"I'm standing right here until you apologize."

"I strongly advise you to move from that spot."

"Not until you take back—"

"Sir! For your own safety—move away from that spot!"

"I'll give you three," squeaked the boy, the gun shaking in his hands. "One . . . two . . ."

"Don't shoot!" shouted Jo.

The hedgehog whirled, pointing his gun at Jo. "You again? Shut—"

And at that moment, several things happened.

There was a shrieking blast of wind that sent sand flying, paper lanterns swaying. A plane roared far above—and something fell from the sky, down into the garden, and down onto the hedgehog's head.

The hedgehog collapsed. His gun accidentally fired.

Something like a mountain threw itself in front of Jo. Her ears exploded, the world reeled, and then everything was silent except for a faint ringing in her ears.

Colonel Korsakov staggered backward, clutching his shoulder, about to topple. He had been shot.

But he managed to glance at his watch.

"Precisely on time."

Then he fell.

Jo scrambled back, just barely avoiding Korsakov as he thudded into the sand, and tripped over the thing that had fallen from the sky—a brown cardboard package, with these words written across the top:

TO: JO LAROUCHE
FROM: THE ORDER OF ODD-FISH

After that, everyone had the leisure to start screaming.

TWO

THERE was something ridiculous about the ruby palace by day. It looked tired, not exuberant; its concrete walls were cracked, its paint faded and stained. The debris of last night's party lay strewn about in the harsh daylight—ripped streamers, broken champagne glasses, burnt-out torches, and some guy's underwear floating in the pool.

It was a blisteringly hot Christmas. When Jo woke up she was already sweating. The palace's ancient air conditioner was churning at full blast, but Jo still felt uncomfortably hot—and nervous, what with a wounded Russian upstairs, groaning and rolling about on his creaky bed.

Jo opened her eyes and looked around her bedroom. The walls swooped away all around her, blanketed with fake gems, arching upward and drawing back together in the gloomy, cobwebby ceiling far above her head. Her little bed, plastic table, and scattered clothes were dwarfed inside the vast sparkling gaudiness, as if lost in a giant jeweled egg.

Who *was* Colonel Korsakov? Jo went to the bathroom, splashed cold water on her face, and squinted at herself in the mirror. In the morning light, she found it hard to believe Korsakov really existed. Still, she could hear him grunting and shifting upstairs; it made her uneasy, as if there were a wild rhinoceros in the house.

Jo padded out of the bathroom, glanced dully at the party-wrecked halls, and thought about the package that had fallen from the sky. The package with her name on it. And . . . the Order of Odd-Fish?

She hadn't opened it. She had left the package in Korsakov's room, almost wishing it would be gone the next day. But she couldn't help feeling the package was waiting. She almost felt like it was daring her.

In the meantime there was Christmas morning, and Aunt Lily's hangover, to deal with. Jo dragged the moaning, woozy Aunt Lily out of bed, got some coffee into her, and helped her hobble downstairs to the darkened ballroom.

As usual on Christmas morning, Jo and Aunt Lily opened their gifts in front of their battered aluminum Christmas tree, listened to carols crackling on the AM radio, and had a huge breakfast of bacon, eggs, and pancakes. They couldn't buy proper presents for each other this far out in the desert, so every year they rummaged through Aunt Lily's storage rooms for forgotten trinkets and exchanged those instead. This year Aunt Lily gave Jo a fake gold sarcophagus, a prop from a mummy movie she'd once starred in. Jo gave Aunt Lily a giant stuffed octopus she'd found rotting away in the attic, origin unknown.

Ordinarily Aunt Lily would've been delighted by the octopus, but this morning she was a wreck.

"Oh, why do I do the things I do?" she groaned, holding an ice pack to her head and fumbling with an antique shoebox-sized remote control. "Jo, could you—Jo?"

"What?"

"You mind if I turn on the Belgian Prankster?"

Jo grimaced. "Do we *have* to watch the Belgian Prankster?"

"Please, Jo—ooh, I feel like somebody turned on a blender inside me. You know? I think the Belgian Prankster's in Denmark this week. Do you think, could I just . . . ?"

"Okay, okay!" Jo could never resist Aunt Lily's wheedling.

Aunt Lily clicked the remote and the television slowly came to life. A goggled man in furs was rampaging around the streets of Copenhagen on a dogsled, chasing screaming Danes. "The Belgian Prankster!" said Aunt Lily, and her eyes glazed.

Jo lay in the sarcophagus, her eyes closed, and tried to block out the yammering of the Belgian Prankster. She was expected at work in an hour, but there was still some time to relax after her exhausting late night. The inside of the mummy's coffin, lined with black velvet cushions, was surprisingly comfortable. Lying in it, she felt pleasantly dead.

Still, the dim quiet of the house by day, after last night's wild noise and glittering lights, made her gloomy. She had a headache. The television was shrill, frantic, too loud. And the Belgian Prankster . . .

"Hey, Jo?"

Jo opened her eyes.

"That package—why haven't you opened it?" said Aunt Lily.

Jo turned over. "I don't know. I don't feel like it's mine."

"Of course it's yours," said Aunt Lily. "Had your name on it, anyway, huh?"

Jo frowned. "It also said something about fish . . . have you ever heard of that? The Order of Odd-Fish?"

Aunt Lily didn't answer at first. After a moment Jo twisted up out of the sarcophagus and looked at her. Aunt Lily seemed to be concentrating very hard, puzzled and frustrated.

"I don't know," she said at last. "I think I *have* heard of an Order of Odd-Fish, somewhere. But I can't . . . it must've been a long time ago."

Something about the words *Order of Odd-Fish* disturbed Aunt Lily; Jo could tell. Her eyes darkened, and her usual liveliness faltered. Jo and Aunt Lily sat silently in the crumbling ballroom's gloom, and even though Jo was sweating in the heat, she shivered.

"I do want to open that package," said Jo. "But didn't Colonel Korsakov say it would be unsafe in the wrong hands?"

Aunt Lily perked up. "Korsakov? What does he know about safe? The fool threw himself in front of a flying bullet. He's lucky it just nicked him."

"You could say he saved my life."

"It was his fault there was any shooting in the first place. I'd kick him out of the house if he weren't so darned cute." Aunt Lily turned back to the TV. The Belgian Prankster was pouring tons of cottage cheese down the streets of Copenhagen, burying his fleeing victims; the audience roared with delight. Aunt Lily started to get distracted. "Well, if you do open it, let me know."

"I won't open it until he wakes up," said Jo.

"Suit yourself."

"Maybe I'll take a bath," said Jo.

"Whatever."

Jo's bathroom, like everything else at Lily Larouche's palace, was a gilded wreck of red and gold marble, kaleidoscopic mirrors, and frenzied geometric mosaics, dimly lit by dozens of spicy smoking candles sprouting from a brass chandelier so mammoth and ornate it seemed like a fiery flying city. Jo lay soaking in the ivory bathtub, the silence broken only by the distant chatter of the television, and thought about Aunt Lily.

When Jo was small, she had believed Aunt Lily was the most fascinating woman in the world. But nowadays Aunt Lily was just exasperating. The more Aunt Lily aged, the more childlike she became; soon Jo found that *she* had become the real parent of their little family.

Jo loved Aunt Lily, but it was hard taking care of her. And she had little help. There was Dust Creek, where Jo worked as a waitress, but everyone who lived there was old, almost dead. Every Christmas Aunt Lily threw a costume ball for her old Hollywood friends, but otherwise the ruby palace had few visitors apart from Hoagland Shanks, the local handyman. He showed up once a week to shuffle around the palace, supposedly repairing this or that, but mostly he just stared off into the distance and mumbled about different kinds of pie he liked.

There's got to be more to life than this, thought Jo, sliding deeper into the warm pink foam. *I can't spend the rest of my life squirreled away in this old house. But where can I go?*

She went nowhere. Jo spent her days prowling the red dusty hallways, looking for new ways to kill time—practicing the antique organ, riding her bicycle awkwardly around the blazing golden ballroom, or just lying on the roof, staring out into the desert night sky.

More than anything, that note from the washing machine—that word, *dangerous*—teased her, pricked her curiosity. She still had the note. She was secretly proud of it; she liked the idea of being "dangerous." Sometimes Jo thought that if she was *really* dangerous, she would run away—just steal one of Aunt Lily's cars, drive to the city, and see what the world was really like. The idea excited her. It sounded like the kind of stunt Aunt Lily might've pulled when she was young.

So why don't I do it? thought Jo, frustrated. *What's holding me back?*

It was almost time for Jo to go to work. She got out of her bath, dried off, and changed into her waitress uniform—a pink, itchy polyester dress that didn't really fit—and went to check on Colonel Korsakov.

She knocked on his door. No answer. Jo hesitated, then cautiously tiptoed into the darkened room.

Korsakov lay on the sagging bed, snoring and snorting, his stomach heaving under his pajamas like an unsteady mountain of jelly. Jo stared in a kind of awe. Korsakov was somehow even more colossal than she remembered—like an exuberantly portly walrus.

On his bedside table sat the package from the sky.

The back of Jo's neck tingled. She reached out, touched the package . . . no, she couldn't open it. She would wait for him to wake up. All his talk about "unsafe in the wrong hands"—Jo had never thought of her hands as wrong, but she had never thought of them as particularly right, either. And yet . . .

She took the package.

The room was silent. Even the snoring Korsakov was momentarily still. And before Jo knew it, she had broken open the lid, sifted through wadded-up newspapers, and grasped the thing inside.

Jo stared at it. It was a black box, made of intricately carved wood and decorated with silver designs. A faint jingling came from within. She put her ear on it and heard something like a tiny alien orchestra: gurgling chimes, the cry and echo of horns, murmuring beeps and bloops . . .

Jo turned the box over. A silver crank stuck out the side. What would happen if . . . ? She touched it and her hand trembled; she felt fluttery, as though she were on a roller coaster that was right at the top, just about to take the first plunge.

An angry voice broke Jo's trance.

"It's unbelievable! The dirty rag! *Shameless!*"

Jo dropped the box in shock.

A giant cockroach had walked into the room, three feet tall, wearing a purple velvet suit with a silk shirt, cravat, and bowler hat. A green carnation was fixed in its buttonhole. The cockroach clutched a newspaper with four arms, reading it through a monocle. Jo backed away, but the insect barely acknowledged her.

"Libel! Scandal! Outrage!" said the cockroach. "I suppose *you,* too, would like to hear the latest slander about me?"

"What?" said Jo weakly.

"Oh, listen to this!" said the insect, flourishing the newspaper and reading aloud: "*Intoxicating evening at Christmas costume ball . . . Shootings, canings, and bludgeonings from the sky enlivened the evening, as well as the irrepressible SEFINO . . . Sefino, who dresses with that desperately flamboyant chic depraved cockroaches so effortlessly achieve! Nor did it take long for the enterprising gentleman to find someone to bind him palp to thorax, and subject him to delicious humiliations in the cellar.*" He hurled the newspaper across the room. "What on earth! *Really!*"

Jo managed to stammer, "Who . . . what are you doing here?"

"A youthful indiscretion," continued the insect, waggling his finger. "A dreadful nightclub in Cairo—an excess of gin— a frightful glass chandelier that, I maintain, *was improperly installed*—it could've happened to anyone, don't you think? Or do you?"

"Um . . . it could've happened to anyone?"

"You have good sense. I can tell. We'll get along smashingly," said the cockroach. "You *are* Jo Larouche, aren't you? I'm Sefino, of course. And it's all very well for *you. You* aren't hounded night and day by these . . . these *jackals!* Chatterbox indeed. Will I never be rid of these rumor-mongering muckrakers?"

Jo gawked at the insect. She had no idea what to do. Shout for Aunt Lily? But what help would she be?

Sefino ambled over to Colonel Korsakov and poked him. "Korsakov got himself shot again, eh? Not surprised. The man's hobby is getting shot. He has a positive talent for it."

"You know Korsakov?" said Jo hopefully.

"Know him? He's my partner! Have mercy on us all," said Sefino. "Thirteen years of working with a man who has philosophical debates with his digestion! Often I'll be talking with him and then I realize he isn't responding to me at all, but chattering away with his precious intestines. Oh, Korsakov is *off his nut*—don't believe a word he says."

"No, I'll believe the giant talking cockroach instead."

"That's too sweet of you. Maybe you can talk some sense into that damnable Chatterbox, the howling cad, what? *I shall write a letter to the editor,*" he exclaimed, rummaging through his numerous pockets with all six legs at once (quite a sight). "You wouldn't have any stationery, would you? You do take dictation? There's a girl." Sefino cleared his throat. "Dear Chatterbox . . . no, strike that . . . Dear *Eldritch Snitch*. I slap you with the satin glove of righteous wrath! From what noxious nest of nattering nincompoopery do you release your rancorous roosters of rumor . . ."

Just then Jo heard Aunt Lily creaking up the stairs. She had an alarming thought—if Aunt Lily saw a three-foot-tall talking cockroach in her house, could she handle the shock? Jo looked around wildly. Maybe she should hide the insect, or—

The door opened, and Aunt Lily shuffled in with a breakfast tray. "Ah! I see you've met Sefino."

"What!" Jo stuttered. "You . . . you know him?"

"Oh, yes!" said Aunt Lily brightly. "Found him in the basement while you were in the bath. Poor dear was tied up, hanging from the ceiling. Now that's the sign of a good party! I mean, if you're into that kind of thing."

Sefino narrowed his eyes. "*Madam.* As I explained, I was not tied up in your cellar for salacious amusement. My enemies—"

"Now, now." Aunt Lily patted Sefino's head. "You don't have to make excuses to me."

The insect wiggled his antennae, stamped his feet, and turned about in circles of barely suppressed rage; finally, with majestic dignity, Sefino cleared his throat, and was about to say something quite cutting, when he was interrupted by Colonel Korsakov.

"Harrumph! Hum! Ooog," rumbled Korsakov, opening his eyes in confusion. But then he saw Sefino, and recognized Jo and Aunt Lily, and settled back weakly. "Breakfast . . . ?"

"Right here!" said Aunt Lily, and bustled around Korsakov,

plumping his pillow and setting the tray in front of him. The old Russian heaved himself up, grunted thanks, and immediately started in on a heap of bacon, eggs, toast, and sausages.

Jo had just about had enough.

"Am I the only one who thinks something strange is going on?" she nearly shouted. "Aunt Lily! There's a huge talking cockroach standing there! Aren't you surprised at all?"

"Yes, yes . . . I know, it's strange, but . . ." Aunt Lily closed her eyes. "Somehow he reminds me of . . . You know, Korsakov and Sefino are both familiar. I've met them somewhere before."

"I didn't wish to seem overly forward, Ms. Larouche," said Colonel Korsakov, his mouth full of eggs. "But I, too, feel I have seen you before."

"And Ms. Larouche does not seem, ah . . . *entirely* unknown to me," admitted Sefino with distaste. "Though I am quite sure I don't know why."

"Then why are you here?" said Jo.

"An excellent question," said Colonel Korsakov, helping himself to more bacon. "But first Sefino and I must address a more pressing matter: *why* was I *shot?*"

Sefino looked offended. "Surely you don't blame *me*—"

"I do!" said Colonel Korsakov, accusing him with a sausage.

"I was waylaid! Shanghaied! Bound with ropes and left for dead! I shouted for hours and no one came—except for one of Chatterbox's lackeys, to snap some photos for the morning edition." Sefino flung the newspaper at Colonel Korsakov. It was called the *Eldritch Snitch*, and the front page had a humiliating photo of Sefino tied up and hanging upside down in the ruby palace's basement. Jo was startled to see her own basement on the front page of a newspaper.

"Had you come to my aid in time," said Korsakov, buttering a slice of toast, "I would not have been shot."

"Oh, *do come on*," exhaled Sefino. "The proper question is, why do you *always* get shot?"

"What!"

"Come clean about it already. You're never so happy as when you have a nice fresh bullet lodged in your belly."

"I never!" roared Korsakov between bites.

"You seek it out!" raged Sefino. "You deliberately enrage armed lunatics! You *love* getting shot; admit it!"

Korsakov flung down his toast. "Boiling Brezhnevs! I refuse to sit here and——"

Jo broke in. "Hey! You still haven't told us what you're doing here!"

"Yes, yes . . . you're right, of course. Explanations are in order." Colonel Korsakov gave a final glare at Sefino. "We'll tell you what we know—which isn't much, I'm afraid. Sefino and I, you see, we are wanderers."

"We meander, we drift," said Sefino.

"We have been known to ramble."

"I once gallivanted," said Sefino wistfully.

"Gallivanting has occurred," said Korsakov, frowning. "But throughout all our travels, we have faithfully obeyed one inflexible principle—the iron logic of my digestion."

"Guess whose idea," said Sefino.

"No matter what far-flung corner of the earth my digestion has indicated," rumbled Korsakov, gaining steam, "we have gone there. No matter what outrageous task my digestion has suggested, we have done it. I have submitted to the stern authority of my kidney; I have harkened to the wild, squishy poetry of my intestines; I have trembled at the invincible wisdom of my rectum. Is this not so, Sefino?"

"I have nothing to add."

"And thus," continued Korsakov, "when my digestion instructed me to steal that black box and deliver it to you, courtesy of the 'Order of Odd-Fish'—an organization, incidentally, of which I'd never heard—I did not hesitate to execute the order."

Jo picked up the black box. "Wait, you *stole* this?"

Sefino interrupted, "Naturally, Korsakov's digestion didn't bother to inform us what that box actually *is*. Looks harmless? I should say not. The day we stole it, that infernal machine sprouted jets of flame and escaped from us, incinerating my *entire collection* of powdered wigs."

Korsakov stifled a smile. "Yes, a tragedy. At any rate, my digestion has been tracking that box's movements. And thus we knew it would fall in your garden last night."

"But . . . you stole this?" said Jo. "From where?"

"Oh, you'll enjoy this," said Sefino. "Listen carefully, Jo, for some classic Korsakov flimflummery. Even I——"

"The box belonged to a certain Mr. Ken Kiang," harrumphed Korsakov, drowning out Sefino. "A Chinese millionaire, a collector of curiosities, and a ruthless and powerful man. I admit that by bringing this box to you, I have put you in some danger."

"In fact, considerable danger," said Sefino.

"Catastrophic, almost certainly fatal danger," agreed Korsakov. "But my digestion is not to be questioned! Indeed, my digestion has a great work before it, a mighty destiny to fulfill; you may doubt it, but I believe the fate of the world hinges upon some future act of my digestion! Therefore, when my pyloric valve bellowed, in a voice mighty enough to shake the very walls of my gastroesophageal region, that I must, first, steal that box from Ken Kiang; second, deliver it to you; and third, protect you——"

"Protect me?" said Jo. "From what?"

"Why, Ken Kiang himself. The man has been chasing us ever since we stole it. Sooner or later he is bound to track us here and wreak a horrible, violent, outrageous vengeance." Korsakov popped an entire Danish in his mouth. "But there is no need to worry, for everything is going according to my digestion's will. The submucosal glands of my jejunum are positively tingling."

"The what of your what?" said Jo.

Sefino sighed loudly. "Don't even try, Jo, it's pure rot from beginning to end. To listen to it for thirteen years is not unlike having needles slowly shoved into one's eyes."

Jo gave a little start. "Thirteen years?"

"Another mystery," said Korsakov. "Neither Sefino nor I remember anything from before thirteen years ago. I vaguely recall, perhaps fifty years ago, I was a KGB agent . . . then I went away, to a city somewhere. After that it becomes dim."

Sefino said, "And so for thirteen years we've wandered the earth, not knowing what we're supposed to be doing. Korsakov promised me that his digestion would lead us to an answer. Thirteen years later, needless to say, I am disappointed."

Aunt Lily said, "But . . . I don't remember anything before thirteen years ago, either."

"And I'm thirteen years old," said Jo.

There was a stunned silence. Colonel Korsakov, Sefino, Aunt Lily, and Jo all stared at one another. It was as though some huge invisible thing had floated into the room, prickly and electric; for a moment nobody even breathed.

"Well," said Colonel Korsakov slowly. "That certainly is remarkable."

"I fear," said Sefino, "that this is the beginning of a long, complicated headache."

Aunt Lily snapped up. "I knew it! I knew there was a reason I liked you, Korsakov. Jo—give me that box!"

There was energy in Aunt Lily's voice that Jo had never heard before. She handed the black box to Aunt Lily, who immediately curled up with it on the floor, poking and shaking it.

"Wait, wait!" Korsakov rasped, waving at Aunt Lily. "Please, before you fiddle with that box, I must insist—do not touch that crank."

Aunt Lily's hand hovered over the crank. "Why not?"

"Er . . . I'm not sure," admitted Korsakov, mopping his brow. "But my digestive juices swirl most excruciatingly every time anyone's hand approaches it."

"If only for that reason," muttered Sefino, "turn that crank for all it's worth."

"I remember this box," said Aunt Lily. "I think . . . I *built* it."

She turned it over and tapped the bottom three times. With a tiny puff of dust it popped open. Aunt Lily jumped a little, and Jo sat up curiously. Something was rattling around inside. Aunt Lily carefully removed a silver ring from the box. Then she took out a gold ring. Jo leaned forward. Both rings had tiny carvings of fish, with jeweled eyes and tiny scales.

"Let me see!" said Jo, drawing closer.

Aunt Lily didn't seem to hear her. She examined the rings, shaking her head, and whispered, "This ring . . . it has my name engraved on the inside."

"No way!" said Jo. "And the other one?"

Aunt Lily stared at Jo, suddenly clutching the silver ring to her chest. Her eyes clouded over, and she seemed lost, confused; but finally she exhaled and handed Jo the ring.

The name *Jo Hazelwood* was engraved on the band.

"Hazelwood? Who's Hazelwood?" Jo became excited. "Aunt Lily! Is that my real—"

"I don't know," said Aunt Lily in a small voice.

"Have you ever seen these before?"

"No, I—yes, I have. No, I haven't." Aunt Lily furrowed her brow. "They're familiar, but . . . I have no idea where I've seen them before."

Jo looked hard at Aunt Lily. "What's wrong?"

"It's like . . . I'm almost remembering something. But I can't . . ." Aunt Lily squeezed her eyes shut. "Maybe it's something I'd rather leave forgotten."

Jo slid the ring on, admiring the twisty silver curves and wriggling fish. She didn't know what the rings meant, either. But something about them felt like a promise.

"Ahem." Colonel Korsakov coughed. "Now, as I mentioned . . . that black box is the property of Ken Kiang, a supremely wicked man. He has been chasing us ever since we stole it. If he finds us here, I shall protect you; and if we must escape, my plane is hidden in the foothills."

Jo looked up. "You have a plane?"

"Oh, yes," said Korsakov. He had devoured everything on his tray and now peered around with mild disappointment. "Er . . . I don't wish to trouble you, but you wouldn't happen to have three or four more eggs, would you? A half-dozen more sausages? Ham off the bone, if you could manage it? My digestion is a precision instrument, you see, and it requires proper maintenance."

"Well . . . I'm a waitress down in town," said Jo. "I was just about to go to work. You could come to the café, or—"

"Capital," said Korsakov, rising from bed. "The day hasn't truly started until its second breakfast. Well, Sefino?"

Sefino glanced up impatiently from a pile of papers on which he had been busily writing. "I doubt Dust Creek is noted for culinary achievement," he snorted. "I shall remain here and work on my twelve-thousand-line epic poem on how Chatterbox is a contemptible hack and a disgrace to modern journalism."

"Of course, of course," sighed Korsakov. "You always do."

THREE

Jo backed out of the ruby palace's garage, yanked the gearshift, and rolled Aunt Lily's gold Mustang out onto the bumpy road. She didn't have a driver's license, but after Aunt Lily crashed their car through the supermarket's front window, Jo had taken over driving between the ruby palace and Dust Creek.

Aunt Lily and Colonel Korsakov were bickering and flirting in the back. Korsakov was so huge that he took up the entire seat; Aunt Lily, to her delight, had to sit on his lap.

"Did you know, Colonel," said Aunt Lily, snuggling up to him, "I used to be a movie star?"

"I did not," said Korsakov, shifting uncomfortably.

"I was, I was. . . . Before that, a bit of burlesque. And magic shows, vaudeville. Maybe that's where I recognize this box from?" Aunt Lily turned the black box over. "You want to see a magic show today, Colonel?"

Jo smiled at the rearview mirror, glad that Aunt Lily had recovered her spirits. She pressed the gas harder, enjoying the dusty wind in her hair. She glanced at her new silver ring, with its strange swirling fish and their jeweled eyes. For the first time in years, she felt like things were changing.

The Dust Creek Café was packed.

It was a grubby room crowded with metal folding chairs and simulated-wood tables, dimly lit and almost intolerably hot, swimming in the thick stink of burnt coffee, fried dough, and maple syrup. The only decoration sat next to the cash register, a plastic armadillo so dented and abused that Jo almost pitied it.

Mrs. Beezy grabbed Jo as she walked in. "Jo! You're over an hour late!"

"Sorry, Mrs. Beezy!" Jo rushed to the kitchen, punched in, and tied on her apron. Then she took a deep breath and started her workday.

Soon Jo was so busy that she almost had no time to think of that morning's events. She had to be everywhere at once, washing dishes, taking orders, settling fights—and Jo had to do everything herself, since the only other waitress, Ms. Quince, was one hundred and seven years old and seldom moved from her wobbly stool.

"Jo! Jo!" shrieked a dried-up, insect-like woman with huge ears and tiny yellow teeth. "Jo!"

"Yes, Mrs. Cavendish!" Jo finished drying a dish and rushed over.

"Where's Mr. Cavendish's birthday hat?" demanded Mrs. Cavendish, and poked her husband violently. "On my husband's ninety-ninth birthday, he's entitled to a birthday hat! I mean, he hasn't got much longer to live! Do you, Mr. Cavendish?"

"Don't bury me yet," said Mr. Cavendish slowly.

"Not *quite* yet! But soon, eh?" said Mrs. Cavendish with relish. "Every minute's a roll of the dice, eh, Mr. Cavendish?"

"I'll get the birthday hat," said Jo.

"And more waffles!" cried Mrs. Horpness.

Jo ran to find the birthday hat for Mr. Cavendish. The senior citizens loved wearing the cardboard crown on their birthdays; Jo could never understand why. The withered Mr. Cavendish sat at the "birthday table," immobile and glassy-eyed, with Mrs. Cavendish, the plump, flowery Mrs. Horpness, the stern-faced Mr. Tibbets, and the undertaker, Mr. Pooter. Colonel Korsakov sat with them, but he was ignored, for he was only seventy-five years old—a child by Dust Creek standards.

"Here's your hat, Mr. Cavendish!" said Jo, placing the yellow crown on his head. Mr. Cavendish's jaw trembled, as if his head couldn't support the weight.

"Adorable! It looks so precious on Mr. Cavendish!" said Mrs. Cavendish. "Why, he should wear it at his funeral!"

"Don't bury me yet!" said Mr. Cavendish desperately.

Jo trotted over to another table to take an order. The café hummed with the familiar din of old people, mostly complaining: about the wretched food, about their painful and embarrassing illness, about their good-for-nothing grandchildren . . .

And about Aunt Lily. As usual, Aunt Lily was bullying the other old people, snatching waffles off plates, "accidentally" spilling people's orange juice, and gobbling everyone's medication. The old people squawked in dismay, and some feebly tried to stab Aunt Lily with their plastic forks.

"Aunt Lily, behave yourself!" said Jo, pouring out some coffee. "I'm busy enough as it is."

"But they won't let me do my magic show!" pouted Aunt Lily. "You said I could, Jo!"

"We want to watch the Belgian Prankster!" said Mr. Pooter.

Jo heard someone else say her name, but the room was loud and the TV was turned up. The Belgian Prankster's theme music jangled, his giant face filling the screen. Jo caught a glimpse and shivered. She turned away from the TV, looking out the window, and was startled to see storm clouds rapidly darkening the desert. The Belgian Prankster's face was reflected in the window, grinning back at her. Jo spun away and stared at the wall.

"Hey! The Belgian Prankster's on!" said Mr. Tibbets. "Turn it up!"

"I can't see! Move the television!" said Mrs. Horpness.

Jo stood still, her eyes closed, trying to block out the noise of the Belgian Prankster. *The Belgian Prankster Hour* was everyone's favorite TV show. Even Aunt Lily was addicted to it.

But Jo simply couldn't watch the Belgian Prankster—a blubbery old man who wore nothing but dirty fur pelts and a rawhide diaper, with gray hair that frazzled in all directions and oversized green ski goggles. It was the goggles that creeped Jo out most. Every time she looked at the TV, she felt the Belgian Prankster staring right back at her.

Nobody knew exactly who the Belgian Prankster was. Some said he had been an anonymous executive in an Antwerp fishstick company, where he had quietly embezzled billions for his pranks. Others maintained the persona was a hobby of Prince Poodoo, a wealthy and mysterious Sri Lankan playboy. And a few swore that the Belgian Prankster was nothing less than the Devil himself, come to unleash a new era of chaos upon the world.

The Belgian Prankster's pranks vexed scientists the world over. Nobody knew how the Belgian Prankster caused Vladimir Lenin to rise from his grave and stroll the streets of Moscow, offering free makeovers to startled ladies—makeovers the embalmed dictator performed with expert skill. Nor could anyone fathom how (as the Belgian Prankster had threatened) everyone in New York woke up to find the entire city covered with hideous orange carpet. And it was the Belgian Prankster who, in the work of a single night, had flooded the Houston Astrodome with piping hot clam chowder.

The Belgian Prankster's pranks could be as playful as releasing ten thousand bichon frise puppies onto the streets of Osaka, or as deadly as turning the Eiffel Tower upside down. The Belgian Prankster was as admired as he was feared, especially by children—parents around the world could discipline their sons and daughters just by saying, "Do you want me to call the Belgian Prankster?"

"Jo! *Jo!*" shouted Mrs. Beezy. "Are you okay?"

Jo shook herself awake. "I'm fine, I'm fine," she mumbled, and looked around the restaurant uneasily. "Wait, does anyone know where Aunt Lily went?"

The women's restroom door banged open, and Aunt Lily danced out in her "magic show" costume (gold top hat, red bustier, glittering miniskirt), waving a wand around, shouting, "Magic tricks! Magic tricks!"

"No! No!" said Mrs. Beezy, hastening from behind the counter. "I told you I don't want you to do your shows here anymore!"

"Magic tricks!" Aunt Lily pranced to the center of the room. "Magic tricks for Christmas! For Mr. Cavendish's birthday! Everybody likes magic tricks!"

"I don't!" said Mrs. Cavendish testily. "And Mr. Cavendish certainly doesn't—how could he?—why, he's half dead!"

"Don't bury me yet!"

Jo steeled herself for trouble. Everyone in Dust Creek had seen Aunt Lily's magic show a million times, and everyone hated it. Last year, Aunt Lily had put on her show at the café almost every day, until Jo had forbidden her to do it anymore. Aunt Lily had sulked for weeks, but Jo was firm. For as frail as the senior citizens were, Jo had seen murder in their eyes.

Aunt Lily was already doing a card trick. "Now, where's that ace of spades?"

"It's in your hat!" shouted everyone.

Aunt Lily raised her eyebrows. "Clever audience today!"

"We've all seen your tricks a hundred times!" snapped Mr. Tibbets.

Jo would've felt embarrassed, but Aunt Lily seemed to enjoy this kind of abuse; she winked at Korsakov and said, "Now, for my next trick, I'll need a volunteer! Who's up for it?"

There was a soft cough.

Everyone turned.

Mr. Cavendish had raised a quivering hand.

"Out of the question, Mr. Cavendish!" said Mrs. Cavendish. "Why, at your age! And your fragile health!"

"Don't bury me yet," said Mr. Cavendish with determination.

"Marvelous! First, let's stick Mr. Cavendish's head in this box!" said Aunt Lily, and in a flash crammed the black box onto Mr. Cavendish's head.

"Stop! Mr. Cavendish will suffocate!" said Mrs. Cavendish.

"Aunt Lily, what are you doing?" said Jo. "Didn't Korsakov say—"

Aunt Lily waved her silent. "Don't worry, Jo. I think I remember what this box is for!"

Korsakov's eyebrows twitched like two panicking caterpillars. "But you won't touch that crank, yes?"

"Ladies and gentlemen!" announced Aunt Lily. "You will now witness an illusion beyond the human imagination! If you have weak health or heart problems, I advise you, do not watch!"

"We all have weak health!" yelled Mr. Tibbets.

"We've all had heart attacks!" groaned Mr. Pooter.

"For this final trick," said Aunt Lily as a waffle flew past her, "I will CUT OFF MR. CAVENDISH'S HEAD! But silence, please—I need absolute silence for this difficult illusion."

The chattering in the room died down. The senior citizens decided to buckle down and sit quietly through it. And then might Lily Larouche go away? It was a wild and desperate hope, but it was all they had. For a moment the café was so quiet that the only sound was a rumble of thunder outside and the first spatterings of rain on the window.

Jo suddenly guessed what Aunt Lily was going to do. "Aunt Lily—"

Colonel Korsakov struggled to his feet. "Ms. Larouche! I implore you, do not touch—"

But it was too late. Aunt Lily grasped the black box on Mr. Cavendish's head—and with a devilish grin, she turned the silver crank.

At first nothing happened. Then a faint click—and Aunt Lily gasped, staggering backward, and collapsed as though she had been punched in the stomach.

"Aunt Lily!" Jo rushed to her. "*Aunt Lily!* Are you okay?"

Aunt Lily was breathing fast. "It's nothing, Jo. I . . . I . . ."

The senior citizens muttered in confusion.

Jo turned to the audience and forced a smile. "Aha . . . No need for alarm! Our magician is just a bit overwhelmed by the magic. . . . Hey! Let's all have a big hand for Miss Lily Larouche!"

Scattered and hesitant applause. Something had gone wrong, and everyone knew it. Jo stared at the black box on Mr. Cavendish's head—jostling, as if something was bouncing around inside.

"Aunt Lily," whispered Jo anxiously, "Aunt Lily, I—"

But she never finished, for the black box's side door burst open and something utterly astonishing flew out.

"FREE! I'M FREE!" Mr. Cavendish's head shot out of the box, flying around the room. "OH, SWEET FREEDOM! OH, GLORIOUS RAPTURE! I'M A FLYING HEAD! LOOK AT ME! NO ONE CAN STOP ME! I'M ALIVE, ALIVE, ALIVE!"

Jo was floored. The café erupted into pandemonium. Those who could, leaped up and bolted for the door; tables overturned, plates smashed, the Belgian Prankster laughed deafeningly; Mrs. Cavendish sat gaping, Mr. Pooter dived under the table, and Mrs. Horpness was rapturously throwing waffles everywhere. Of all the things that could've happened by turning the crank, Jo least expected this—that Aunt Lily's magic trick would actually work.

"WOO HOO!" shouted Mr. Cavendish's head, bobbing like a

balloon. "Goodbye, Mrs. Cavendish—goodbye, Dust Creek! I'm livin' in the sky like the mighty eagle!"

"Great galloping Gorbachevs!" Colonel Korsakov doubled over in agony. "Oh, my delicate enzymes . . . Jo! Do something!"

"What can I possibly do?" shouted Jo, watching Mr. Cavendish's head zigzag through the air.

"Mr. Cavendish, you come back down here this instant!" squealed Mrs. Cavendish.

"Not a chance, Mrs. Cavendish! Where's the window? I'm long gone! RELEASE! SWEET RELEASE!"

Jo stared, the coffeepot hanging limply from her fingers. The seniors were shrieking, throwing their silverware, on the verge of a riot. Somebody was going to get hurt. Jo grabbed a table-cloth and shakily climbed onto a table.

"Catch me? Oho, Jo, you'll never catch me!" taunted Mr. Cavendish's head. "I'm going to live in outer space! I've decided! With the moon men, and the . . . the *hydrogen*!"

Jo hopped to another table, half slipped on a pancake, and nearly caught Mr. Cavendish's head in the tablecloth, but he rocketed away just in time, whooping.

"Good girl, Jo! Almost got him," cheered Mrs. Horpness, waving a waffle.

"Go, go, Mr. Cavendish! She'll sneak up from behind! Look out!" yelled Mr. Tibbets.

Jo jumped from table to chair to countertop, lunging with the tablecloth, as Mr. Cavendish's head streaked around the café. Then she saw her chance and leaped, the tablecloth spread before her, tackling the flying head in midair. The floor rushed up much too quickly, Jo broke through a flimsy plastic chair, and she hit the tiles with a painful smack. But she had Mr. Cavendish's head, squirming in the tablecloth.

The empty box was still on Mr. Cavendish's shoulders. Jo stuffed the struggling head into it, even as he pleaded, "No, not my body again! Please, no, I'll be *good*!"——then slammed shut the box's door. The box sprang off Mr. Cavendish, hit the ceiling, and clattered to the floor.

Mr. Cavendish's head was somehow stuck back on his body, blinking in surprise.

"Oooh! Again!" said Mr. Cavendish happily. "Jo, do it *again*."

Jo had already dashed over to Aunt Lily. "Don't worry, I'm fine," groaned Aunt Lily, waving away Jo's support. "Man! Did you see that sucker fly?"

Jo helped her up anyway. "Did you build the box to do *that*?"

"I don't know!" Aunt Lily grinned. "Still, Jo . . . what a morning, huh?"

Just then, the front door of the café swung open, and a fellow in rumpled overalls walked in—a big, shambling pudding of a man, with a shaggy mustache and a genial, slightly stupid expression. It was Jo and Aunt Lily's handyman, Hoagland Shanks.

"Heck! What's all the hoot and holler? Hey, Miss Jo, whaddya say! Any good pie today?" Hoagland Shanks mussed Jo's hair and tipped his hat to Aunt Lily. "Afternoon, Miss Lily. Just finished spraying your place."

Aunt Lily looked as if she'd swallowed a grasshopper. "Spraying? Spraying . . . my house?"

"What are you talking about?" said Jo.

"Industrial-strength insecticide," said Hoagland Shanks. "You shouldn't go back for eight hours or so, but I'm sure you won't have any more problems with those cockroaches."

"What!" said Jo. "We never asked you to spray for cockroaches!"

Hoagland Shanks chewed his lip. "But I got a phone call . . ."

"Who called?" said Jo.

"Some fella . . . Ken Kiang, I think it was?"

Korsakov let loose a strangled cry: *"Ken Kiang?"*

Shanks shrugged. "Old friend of Miss Lily's, he said. Anyhoo, this Ken Kiang fella told me to go and exterminate all the insects at your house, and—"

Colonel Korsakov leaped up—for a man of his size, quite a feat—and choked out, "Sefino!"

"No, I don't remember any Sefino," said Hoagland Shanks. "So, Jo, any good pie today?"

But Colonel Korsakov had already dashed out the door. Jo stumbled after him, with Aunt Lily hobbling behind. Outside rain was pattering down, faster and faster—lightning cut the sky open, thunder blasted through, and all at once the rain was furiously pouring everywhere. Jo threw open the Mustang's door and jabbed her key into the ignition as Korsakov and Aunt Lily squeezed in the back. The engine roared to life and they took off into the storm, speeding back home.

FOUR

THE gold Mustang tore up the winding desert highway, crashing through the storm. Jo hadn't had time to put up the convertible's top, and rain spattered everywhere, soaking through her clothes, blinding her. Jo still had the black box, squeezed between her knees, but it frightened her now. Even the silver ring on her finger seemed threateningly tight. A stab of lightning, the world lit up, Jo looked for the ruby palace—

It wasn't there.

The palace was gone, replaced by a furious mass of green smoke. A bolt of shock went straight down to Jo's toes. Her home was gone. No—she saw pink parapets, or a crimson arch or turret, poking out of the mist—but they looked out of place, as if all the architecture was scrambled, floating crazily in the fog.

Too late, she hit the brakes and the Mustang slid into the rippling, roiling, blinding cloud of green.

Jo choked, coughed, her eyes stung. She couldn't see a thing—and the Mustang crashed into the palace. Jo was thrown forward, and then all was still.

Jo sat in the slashing rain, buried in the emerald smoke, in a daze. Aunt Lily and Colonel Korsakov were gabbling in the backseat, but Jo just stared ahead dully, her insides tightening into a hard lump of fear.

One thought kept banging through her brain: her life was finally becoming dangerous.

Jo, Aunt Lily, and Korsakov found their way to the kitchen. It still hadn't been tidied up: crepe paper hung from the ceiling, dirty and damp, and half-filled glasses and stale desserts scattered the tabletops.

Jo opened all the windows to clear the air. She was too shaken to think straight. A package falling from the sky, a talking cockroach, Mr. Cavendish's head flying around, and now this . . . Aunt Lily stood at the window, looking shell-shocked, and Colonel Korsakov openly wept, overflowing his chair, panting and wheezing.

"Why did Sefino have to die!" Korsakov moaned, holding Jo's arm. "Gladly I would have laid down my life for him! My digestion would've found a way to carry on—I can just see my intestines crawling out of my mouth and slithering off into the horizon—perhaps to join Sefino in some grand new adventure?— *But no, why Sefino, to die?* Why not me—a worthless old man—an unworthy dwelling of a noble digestion!"

Jo patted Korsakov's head awkwardly. "He could still be alive . . . we could look for him. . . ."

There was a shuffle of footsteps in the hall. Korsakov looked up hopefully—"Sefino?" he said, craning his neck—and in sauntered Hoagland Shanks.

"Howdy!" The handyman beamed around the room. "Heck, what's with all the long faces?"

Her mouth dry, Jo managed to stammer, "Mr. Shanks . . . what—what are you doing here?"

"Y'all lit out of the café so quick! So I thought I'd fly the old crop duster over and be neighborly. Who's the Russian fella?" Hoagland Shanks stuck out his hand. "Name's Hoagland Shanks. Pleased to meet ya!"

"You are the man responsible for this?" Korsakov's mustache quivered. "You have killed my best friend, sir."

"Come again? Must be the old trick ear, can't hear a danged thing." Hoagland Shanks winked at Aunt Lily. "Big job of exterminatin', makes a fella hungry. Got any eats?"

"Mr. Shanks," said Jo, her anger rising, "why did you spray our house without *asking us?*"

"Just following orders," said Hoagland Shanks. "That Ken Kiang fella, he called me up, said he was an old friend of Miss Lily's. Well, any friend of Miss Lily's a friend of mine."

"We don't even know who Ken Kiang is!"

Hoagland Shanks scratched his head. "Well, I can't tell you much about that, Miss Jo. But what I *can* tell you is I see an apple pie on that table."

"What?"

"Is that an apple pie there on that table?"

"Yes, but—"

"Why, I'd *love* a piece of pie!" Hoagland Shanks went over to the table and cut himself a generous piece. "And what's an apple pie without a scoop of delicious ice cream?"

"Put that back!" said Jo. "I didn't say you could have any pie!"

"Tell you what, I'll have some pie and we'll call it even." Hoagland Shanks scooped out half a box of ice cream and plopped it next to his pie. "Pie, pie, pie! Darned if I don't like anything, after a hard day's work, better than a nice apple pie! Don't you?"

Colonel Korsakov sprang to his feet. "Sir, you are a scoundrel!"

Hoagland Shanks blinked at Korsakov. "Beg pardon?"

"I will use plainer terms, if you wish. You are a knave."

"Huh?"

"A rapscallion, sir. A rogue."

"Come again?"

"A cur, a reprobate! A blackguard, a villain, a rascal! No, silence! There is nothing more between us, sir, but honor and the sword. As for now—I must find my partner."

Hoagland Shanks chewed his pie thoughtfully, staring at Korsakov; finally he leaned over to Aunt Lily and whispered, "Is it me, or is he not really talking American?"

Luckily, Jo had already pulled Korsakov away.

Jo and Colonel Korsakov raced down the foggy, twisty passages, searching for Sefino. The deeper they plunged into the palace, the thicker the clammy clouds of insecticide became, until they had to hold handkerchiefs to their noses to breathe.

"Sefino!" shouted Jo. "Where are you, Sefino!"

"Sefino!" bellowed Korsakov, and shook his head. "Jo, the worst has happened. Doubtless Ken Kiang himself will soon appear. We must escape—"

Jo was going to answer when, behind the poisonous mist, she heard the clear ring of silver, the patter of voices and laughter, the sound of tea pouring . . . she opened a door, and stepped into the fresh air of the greenhouse.

And Jo stopped—for the greenhouse had also filled up with residents of Dust Creek.

They had followed Jo back to the palace out of curiosity. Now Mr. and Mrs. Cavendish were crowded around the Victrola bickering over what record to put on, Mrs. Horpness and Mrs. Beezy were devouring the leftover sweetmeats, and Mr. Tibbets and Mr. Pooter were energetically trampling the begonias. More old people from the café streamed in through the greenhouse's back door.

Sefino sat in a red velvet chair, surrounded by senior citizens prodding him with their canes and asking where in tarnation he came from. Sefino looked well pleased with himself; in fact, a little too pleased; in fact, drunk.

"Come in, come in!" Sefino slurred, his cravat dangling limply around his neck. "How lovely of you to drop in on our little, ahem, party. Why you felt the need to multiply, I have no idea . . . I thought one Jo was quite enough . . . and three Korsakovs is something else entirely . . . hello?"

"He's a funny-looking little bugger," said Mr. Tibbets.

"Where you from, son?" said Mrs. Beezy.

"Canada, obviously," said Mrs. Cavendish. "They've got all kinds of funny-looking folks up there. Barely human, Canadians."

Jo whispered, "Sefino, are you okay?"

"Oh, they're from all the best families, I assure you," said Sefino with sudden earnestness; he clung to Jo's arm to keep from falling. "Only the very cream of the . . . crust of the . . . upper crop of the . . . you know, who's who of all's worth . . ."

"What's got into him?" said Korsakov.

"The insecticide just made him drunk," said Jo.

"He's wasted!" shouted Mrs. Beezy triumphantly.

Mrs. Cavendish nodded. "From Vancouver to Ottawa, a race of ignorant savages."

Mr. Tibbets approached Colonel Korsakov. "I'd like to know just what the heck you think you're doing, cutting off heads and bringing drunk Canadians into a decent town like Dust Creek."

"Canadian? Drunk?" roared Sefino. "I invite you to my tea party, and all you do is hurl abuse?"

"Well, as far as I'm concerned, it still adds up to the worst Christmas ever," said Mr. Tibbets.

"Ooh! You've ruined Christmas!" said Mrs. Horpness excitedly.

Sefino climbed onto a table. "Ladies and gentlemen!" he declared. "At times like this, the soaring oratory of a gentleman may be the only way to assuage the fears and anxieties that the modern world engenders! I may not be a Canadian——"

"Lies!" hissed Mrs. Cavendish.

"——but it is true, I am not of your fair city, and as a guest here, I apologize for any irregularities I may have committed——"

"*Canadian* irregularities," said Mrs. Cavendish.

"——in the diligent discharge of the duties that I have undertaken for the general benefit of my fellow citizens, and yes"—— Sefino brushed away a tear——"my friends."

"He always makes speeches when he's drunk," muttered Korsakov.

"But is it not the true spirit of Christmas," continued Sefino, spreading four of his arms wide, "to accept into your community, and yes, your hearts, the outcast, the stranger—even, dare I say, the Canadian?"

"No!" yelled Mrs. Cavendish.

"Yes!" shouted Mrs. Horpness happily.

"Can we not put our differences behind us, to feast together in brotherhood? In short, good citizens of Dust Creek"——Sefino swayed, and weakly put a claw on a tree branch——"can you find it in your hearts, the tender recesses of your souls, to accept us as we are, and forgive us for the inconveniences and the——ah, er, what? decapitations?——that we have caused this morning?"

There was a long silence.

"I'll be jiggered," said Mr. Tibbets. "But dang it, that little Canadian has touched my heart."

And at this the crowd roared with approval, and Sefino passed out, tumbling into the welcoming arms of Dust Creek.

Colonel Korsakov watched this all with anxious impatience, wincing and massaging his belly. Finally, he took Jo aside, whispering, "Jo, my digestion warns me Ken Kiang is quite near. We have no choice—we must escape, *now*—go to your room, pack what you need, and meet Sefino and me in the garden. I will get your aunt."

It was all too fast for Jo. "What are you——"

"Go!" barked Colonel Korsakov. But Jo saw the worry in his eyes, so she obeyed and ran as fast as she could to her bedroom.

Jo knew the twisting maze of the ruby palace by heart. Coming out of the greenhouse, go to the end of the arched hallway, turn right, up the spiral stairs, turn right again into the gallery, take the second left into the library, up more stairs—she could find her way around blindfolded.

But as soon as she stumbled into the foggy hallways, everything went wrong. The green fog had scrambled the ruby palace into someplace she didn't know. She ran into walls where there should have been doors, stumbled into huge rooms where she expected stairways. The green smoke swirled thicker, blinding her, her eyes prickled with needles, her throat tightened, and her ears flooded with—*organ music*?

Someone was playing her organ. No, torturing it, forcing out clashing chords, blasting up and down caterwauling scales—Jo had inhaled too much of the gas, and everything spun around, zigzagging violently—she stumbled through the green smoke, hotter and darker and heavier now, and suddenly realized the palace was on fire.

Flames licked out of the steaming green shadows, leaped up to the ceiling, flew across the papery walls. Far above, something crumpled, collapsed, and all at once an entire room was tumbling onto her head.

Jo threw herself against a brass door, stumbled through the threshold, and fell. She heard the hall fill with debris behind her. She couldn't move—but she was out of the green smoke. Her eyes stung too hard to see, and her ears were pounded by the squall of the organ, discordant and scrambled and too loud to endure.

She was in the ballroom, her face on the dance floor, just a few yards away from the organ and whoever was playing it.

The organ stopped in mid-tune.

Jo opened her eyes.

A man was sitting at the organ—a small, slouching Chinese man with a delicate face. He wore a dandyish white suit and a white wide-brimmed hat, so elegant he seemed to have drifted in from another planet. He studied Jo carefully.

"So this is the 'dangerous' girl," said Ken Kiang softly. "But where is my black box?"

Jo couldn't answer; her throat was swollen and tied up in knots, her head swimming with a hundred half-thoughts desperately trying to connect into some kind of sense. She faintly heard the crackle of the ruby palace burning down, splintering and collapsing. But in this room, there was still a kind of menacing quiet, as the last of the organ's notes echoed in the corners.

"You have tangled with the wrong man," said Ken Kiang. "You should have considered more carefully, Jo Larouche, before crossing me."

Jo managed to say, "I don't . . . I have no idea who you are!"

"Where is my black box?"

"I don't know!"

Ken Kiang stood up. Jo wanted to crawl away but she couldn't move. Very slowly Ken Kiang approached her, his shiny white shoes clicking precisely across the floor. "I don't care how evil, how *dangerous* you think you are, Miss Larouche—"

"But I—I *don't* think I'm—"

"Whoa! Am I interruptin' somethin'?" said Hoagland Shanks, zipping his pants. He noticed Ken Kiang and said, "Well, I'll be diggly-danged! Who's this fella, Jo?"

The ballroom was periously silent. Hoagland Shanks gave a little "oh!", dug into his pocket, and took out a crushed glob of pie.

"Knew I'd left that somewhere!" he said happily, and took a bite. Only then did he seem to notice Ken Kiang staring at him. "Oh, don't mind me, just eatin' my pie. Heck! What's your story, champ? Some kinda Chinaman?"

"You know me. My name is Ken Kiang. I called you earlier, to—"

Hoagland Shanks grabbed Ken Kiang's hand, shaking it vigorously. "I . . . AM . . . HOAGLAND . . . SHANKS! VERY . . . HAPPY . . . TO . . . MEET . . . YOU! WELCOME . . . TO . . . AMERICA!"

"I have lived in America for over twenty years," said Ken Kiang.

Hoagland Shanks pointed to his handful of pie. "THIS . . . IS . . . PIE!"

"I don't have time for this—"

"SAY *PIE.*"

Ken Kiang closed his eyes. "Pie."

Hoagland Shanks winked at Jo. "See, they get it quick enough, if you give 'em half a chance." He turned back to the Chinese millionaire. "YOU . . . GOOD . . . ENGLISH . . . TODAY!"

"*As I was saying,*" said Ken Kiang, turning back to Jo, "I intend to have my box back—"

"That's real, real interestin'," said Hoagland Shanks. "Now, the way I see it, Kenny, there's pie and then there's pie. Right? I like your good old-fashioned American pies as much as the next guy—heck, maybe even a little more—but I'll be darned if I ain't curious about pies they got in other countries!"

Ken Kiang whirled on Hoagland Shanks. "I will kill you!"

"Now, a *Chinese* pie . . ." Shanks smacked his lips. "I hear y'all eat dogs. You got such a thing as dog pie? Woof!"

Ken Kiang snarled, and was just about to leap upon Hoagland Shanks—and tear out the handyman's larynx with his bare hands—when Jo staggered dizzily to her feet.

"Mr. Kiang!" she said, fighting to keep her voice even. "I . . . I don't know anything about this box, or why anyone wanted me to have it. But I don't want anyone to get hurt—"

She stopped.

Ken Kiang had drawn out a long, wicked-looking gun.

"*You* want?" he said quietly. "No. Listen to what *I* want. I want my black box back. And I want to kill you. And that is just what I am going to do."

Jo stumbled backward in baffled terror. Everything was tilting—the smoke and heat of the fire rushed in, loud and suffocating—the world was spinning, flying apart—the gun clicked—

"Get away from her."

Jo almost didn't recognize the voice. Someone familiar was standing at the open double doors across the room, sparks and cinders raining down around her. Jo stared in woozy wonder. It was Aunt Lily. But different—taller, her voice clearer. Aunt Lily strode toward Ken Kiang, her lips trembling in a manic half grin, her eyes glowing wild and astonished, as if her body were moving on its own and she were only enjoying the ride.

Ken Kiang pointed the gun at Aunt Lily. "Watch it, old lady! Not a step closer, or I'll— Hey! I'm going to— Okay, not one more step, or I'll—"

Aunt Lily walked up to Ken Kiang. Then she yanked his gun away, and slapped him.

"Get out of my house," she said.

Jo was flabbergasted. For a moment even Ken Kiang was too stunned to react.

Then the doors flew open, and in charged thirty-seven senior citizens, led by Korsakov and Sefino, all setting upon Ken Kiang at once, baying and coughing and hobbling. The Chinese millionaire turned, shouting and swinging wildly as he was thrashed, clobbered, and overwhelmed by the citizens of Dust Creek.

The old people of Dust Creek were rejuvenated in the glory of battle. Whether their enthusiasm came from the thrill of fighting, or the prospect of finally getting rid of Lily Larouche, it was difficult to say. Jo reeled through a violent, smoky blur, thrown from Mrs. Cavendish to Mr. Tibbets, who ran interference over to Mrs. Horpness, who slung Jo over her shoulder and carried her down the stairs; another mob led by Mr. Cavendish and Mrs. Beezy charged at Ken Kiang from every side, whacking him with canes, walkers, and wheelchairs.

Jo never got a chance to thank them. Before she knew it Korsakov was hustling her up the gangway of his plane, its engines already keening in a rising wail. Seconds later the gangway swung shut and the plane rocketed down the highway, lifting into the air. Jo watched out the window as the ruby palace fell away, and then Dust Creek, and then the desert. Soon there was nothing but clouds.

"Blast!" screamed Ken Kiang, limping out of the burning palace.

Hoagland Shanks ambled out with his pie, chewing it happily.

"Quick, lend me your plane," said Kiang, waving at the handyman's crop duster.

Shanks seemed not to hear. He took another bite of pie.

Ken Kiang barked, "Listen up! I'm a rich man. I'll pay you double what that plane is worth, on the spot! Cash! Just let me use it, now!"

Hoagland Shanks swallowed the last of his pie and looked at Ken Kiang blankly.

"Come on!" shouted Ken Kiang. "They're getting away! Fine—I'll pay *three times* what your plane is worth. Well? Do *you* speak English?"

Hoagland Shanks considered this for a moment. Then he said:

"I only speak the language of delicious pies."

FIVE

But who is Ken Kiang?

Let us rewind to several years ago. Imagine a room—a large room, the size of a theater or cathedral. The room is almost empty, the walls bare, the floor nearly deserted.

In the center of the room there is a small desk.

Sitting at the desk is a small man.

He is Ken Kiang.

He is a Chinese millionaire.

And he is watching a donkey.

It is a small, wind-up brass donkey. Ken Kiang watches it trudge across his desk. The donkey is a medieval Arabic automaton he unearthed at a recent archaeological dig in Syria. He wants to be impressed by its unique workmanship. He longs to glory in its exquisite detail. He aches to be fascinated by its stunning ingenuity.

It bores him.

Ken Kiang bites his lip. He plucks the mechanical donkey off the desk and turns it around. Then he gives a long, weary sigh.

Ken Kiang was a collector. He collected objects, the most rare and beautiful; he also collected experiences, the most exhilarating and sophisticated.

But there was something disquieting. Every time he would complete a certain collection—whether it be medieval surgical instruments, or elephant skeletons, or even mysterious black boxes—he would lose interest, and fall into depression. And there he would languish until some new passion grabbed him.

But nothing grabbed him anymore.

Still, Ken Kiang was a dynamic man. He would not stand by and let the world go on without him.

So he threw himself into doing good deeds. He built hospitals; he funded schools; he fought for the downtrodden, for education, for feeding the hungry . . . for . . . for . . .

It was no use. His connoisseur's instinct would not let him rest. There was, in the end, something trite about yet another homeless shelter; something shopworn about one more literacy program. Where was the originality? Where was the style, the verve—the *showmanship*? Ken Kiang soon lost interest in conventional charities, and became the benefactor of ever more obscure crusades.

Ken Kiang started an ambitious program to ensure that all underprivileged schoolchildren had "postmodern yet easy-to-manage" hairstyles. Never content to merely watch, Ken Kiang became a crackerjack hairstylist himself, and led his own squad of elite barbers from school to school, meticulously styling the hair of the baffled needy. The program was a resounding success, and Ken Kiang followed up quickly: instead of the soup kitchens, he established a nationwide network of "mint kitchens," where a fellow down on his luck could freshen his breath for free, using a pioneering mouthwash Ken Kiang had chemically engineered himself. Ken Kiang graciously accepted the dozens of humanitarian awards heaped upon him, but he did not rest on his laurels—and within a month he had toddler-proofed the entire city of Baltimore. This project was more controversial, but Ken Kiang held firm. "Baltimore is nice and safe now—no hard surfaces or angles to hurt baby," he pointed out, and everybody had to agree.

But even this became tedious. And as suddenly as he had started his charity programs, Ken Kiang stopped them all. He closed up his hospitals, shelters, and kitchens; little by little, the hair of American schoolchildren became less postmodern; the poor were no longer minty; soon it was not even safe to leave one's baby unattended in Baltimore.

And thus Ken Kiang entered the deepest depression of his life.

At the age of thirty-nine, Ken Kiang had done it all. There was nothing worth owning that he hadn't collected, nothing worth doing he hadn't done. He had drunk life to the full, but discovered to his dismay that no one was going to refill his cup. What could he do next? In what bold new endeavor could Ken Kiang set the standard for excellence?

Then, in the third week of his depression, it hit him. Ken Kiang had been huddled under the blankets in his darkened bedroom all day, rereading back issues of *Sassy* magazine and scarfing down candy corn (his secret vice), when inspiration struck.

He sat upright in bed, his heart pounding.

He would become evil.

Why hadn't he thought of it before? Any idiot could be good—he had proven that. And every day, many a fool bumbled his way into being merely bad. But it would take a special kind of genius—Ken Kiang's kind of genius—to be thoroughly, intentionally EVIL.

Evil! Who was evil anymore? The world was full of clods who were convinced they were doing the right thing. And even if they happened to sin interestingly, there was always their tiresome guilt—their ludicrous repentances—their pathetic attempts to lead a "better life"—

But pure, methodical evil—who did *that* anymore?

Ken Kiang got down to work, and for the first time in years he found himself absorbed in a project. He devoured books about evil; he interviewed terrorists, serial murderers, and dictators; he dabbled in strange and wild diabolisms, slit the throats of shrieking beasts on stone altars in far-off lands, drank kitten blood, and sold his soul no fewer than twenty-three times to any supernatural being who cared to bid on it. No price was too low: the fifteenth time he sold his soul it was for a bag of barbecue-flavored potato chips. Ken Kiang had eaten the chips with indecent glee as the demon looked away in embarrassment.

Then, one day, his studies were complete. He was evil! Theoretically, at least. Ken Kiang hadn't exactly done anything villainous yet, but he was certain he would have a brilliant career. He danced around his house, exulting in his damnation.

"I'm a bad man! A bad, bad, *bad* man! Ooh, I'm damned . . . damned to hell for all eternity . . . hmmm. What's that like?"

He looked up *hell* in the encyclopedia.

An abode of demons and lost souls, filled with fire and smoke. "I expected something more imaginative than that," he muttered, and read on. *The bodies are heaped upon each other, crushed and packed tight, without even a glimpse of air.* Ken Kiang put the book down, exasperated. "Why, it's all cuddling!" He gave hell one last chance. *The devils are so horrible that one witness wrote that, rather than look again on such a frightful monster, she would prefer to walk until the end of her life along a track of red-hot coals.* "Oh, please." Ken Kiang rolled his eyes. "Overreacting, surely. More likely the devil was just as afraid of her as she was of it."

No, books had nothing more to teach him. Ken Kiang itched for practical application; he was ready for his first evil project. But what? How could he, Ken Kiang, prove to the world that he was the most stylishly evil man who ever lived?

Ken Kiang laughed diabolically! Then he stopped, disappointed: no, his laugh wasn't quite diabolical. He made a mental note to practice his diabolical laughter for fifteen minutes a day. The devil, he knew, was in the details.

And a few years later, Ken Kiang would have a fine opportunity to use his diabolical laugh, and use it to great effect, as he pursued Jo, Sefino, Aunt Lily, and Colonel Korsakov, a thousand feet over the Pacific Ocean—holding his finger on the button that would destroy them all.

SIX

COLONEL Korsakov's plane, the *Indignant,* resembled a flying box cobbled out of bits of a dozen other planes, lashed together with chains, frayed rope, and duct tape. It seemed ready to collapse at any moment, but somehow kept sputtering through the sky, coughing and wobbling, plowing through the thunder and rain.

Jo was curled up under mothbally blankets, gazing out at the dark storm. She still couldn't believe the ruby palace had burned down—but what shocked her most was how Aunt Lily had walked up to Ken Kiang, taken his gun away, and slapped him. Jo had seen Aunt Lily do crazy things, but she had never seen her do anything courageous.

Aunt Lily was just as startled. "I don't know what came over me. It was like I was fifty years younger! And stronger . . . and braver, and . . ." Her gaze lost focus, but her smile lingered.

Jo had explored the plane, bracing herself against the steel walls as it jolted through the storm. The *Indignant* was Korsakov's and Sefino's home, and every inch was packed with domestic clutter: the cockroach's smoking jacket dangled next to the engine crawl space, the colonel's oboe hung in the bomb bay, and throughout the hull she found a dusty blunderbuss, a shoebox of cufflinks, the jawbone of some underwater animal, a plastic bust of Yuri Andropov . . .

Sefino strolled up, looking around the plane in distaste. "Of course, should Chatterbox find out I was flying around in this untidy bag of bolts, I'd be the laughingstock of society."

"Who is this Chatterbox you keep talking about?" said Jo.

"You tell me! I don't even know anything about his newspaper," Sefino said, waving his copy of the *Eldritch Snitch*. "I've never even heard of Eldritch City."

"Neither have I."

"Nobody has. I've checked. And yet every morning I am somehow delivered a fresh copy of this nonexistent city's newspaper. It is maddening."

"Why don't you just stop reading it?"

"That wouldn't do," said Sefino. "Must keep up on fashionable society, mustn't I?"

"What fashionable society?"

"I have no idea. But I am definitely a part of it. Why else would they write about me so much?" Sefino trembled, his antennae standing on end; suddenly he exploded, "Jo! The eyes of the world are upon me! I must lead a life of daring exploits and breathtaking glamor, to satisfy my hordes of admirers!"

Something out the window caught Jo's eye. "Um, Sefino . . ."

"What's the point of life without spectacular, death-defying thrills? Where are all the beautiful ladies who might want to double-cross me?" Sefino twitched with excitement. "I wouldn't mind being double-crossed a little!"

"Sefino, look outside——"

"Even if I met a femme fatale, though, I very well couldn't bring her back *here*." Sefino's voice dropped low. "Korsakov doesn't exactly keep a clean house."

"Sefino! Look out the window!"

Sefino looked——and stopped in midsentence. His beady black eyes grew large.

Black zeppelins drifted toward the *Indignant* from all sides, floating in ominous battle formation. Then, roaring out of nowhere, squadrons of black fighter planes screeched past, buffeting the *Indignant* in their wake.

A phone call from Ken Kiang had summoned his "Fleet of Fury." Ken Kiang had engineered the planes himself——sleek, terrifying machines, bristling with spikes and weaponry, the kind of planes that left no doubt about how *evil* their commander was.

With a precise ballet of maneuvers, the largest zeppelin opened its cabin bay doors and Hoagland Shanks's crop duster flew inside. As giddy as a schoolboy, Ken Kiang leaped out of Shanks's plane, leaving the baffled handyman behind, and scampered to the control room, hooting for joy.

Minutes later Colonel Korsakov plunged the *Indignant* into a steep dive, dodging a flock of screaming missiles that spun off in corkscrews of smoke.

"I can't hold them off forever!" shouted Korsakov over the noise.

"It's unjust! It's *not fair!*" cried Sefino. "Struck down, in the flower of my youth! For what? The absurd whims of an errant digestion! Oh, pity me, world! Years of puttering around in this stinky plane! Oh, wasted youth! *A wasted life!*"

"I thought you *wanted* spectacular, death-defying thrills!" yelled Jo.

"I want to go home!" shrieked Sefino.

Aunt Lily exclaimed: "The box, Jo! Look at it!"

From her seat, Jo saw the black box rattling in the corner, drawers shooting open and snapping shut, spraying confetti and ticker tape, knobs and buttons popping out all over—the box was squirming, writhing, coming alive.

Colonel Korsakov banked upward, the old engines whining, but he was brought up short by a wall of zeppelins; the *Indignant* screeched in a tight arc, but the planes swung around behind, gaining fast.

"I *can't* die!" wailed Sefino. "I'm not properly dressed! Everyone in heaven will snicker and make catty remarks about my shoes!"

"You're not helping!" grunted Korsakov. Then: "Arghh! Get that infernal cube away from me!"—for the black box had sprouted wings and was now flying around, screeching and wailing, swooping at Korsakov's head.

Jo unbuckled her belt and leaped after the box, swatting it away from Korsakov. The box tumbled across the cabin, shrieking and bouncing off the walls—and suddenly the plane's radio turned itself on in an explosion of static.

"Good afternoon!" said Ken Kiang over the radio. "Just thought I'd call up. A friendly chat, you know, before I kill you."

"Because of this box?" shouted Jo. "You're going to kill us over *that*?"

"Uh . . . yes," said Ken Kiang. "It's not much of an excuse, but it'll do."

"You can have it back!"

"Oh, I don't *want* it back," said Ken Kiang happily. "To tell the truth, I just want to be evil. And rest assured, I've got some elaborate evil planned for today! Why, I almost envy you—the exquisite sensation of being crushed by my genius!"

The radio crackled off and four new missiles tore across the sky, streaming fire. The black box ricocheted around the cabin, beeping and squealing, banging into the controls. Jo leaped after it, shouting, "Sefino! Help me!"

"No, no, we're all doomed," moaned Sefino. "It's all over! We *deserve* to die! The only thing left for us to do is degrade ourselves. Yes, yes! Grovel before our conqueror!"

"I can't avoid these missiles!" shouted Colonel Korsakov.

"Don't avoid them! Fly *into* them!" shrieked Sefino in a kind of ecstasy.

The radio popped on again. "Ken Kiang here! It just occurred to me—you're about to die. Rather makes you wish you'd spent more time cherishing life's little pleasures, doesn't it? Well, too late for that. And you're probably too panicked to remember those pleasures at all. But don't worry, I've drawn up a list! Let's remember them together." He cleared his throat. "Ah, warm summer days . . . your favorite song coming on the radio . . . a hot dog at the ballpark, extra mustard and relish . . ."

"I can't take it anymore!" said Sefino. "When will it all end!"

"In one minute ten seconds," crackled the radio cheerfully. "The smell of freshly mown grass . . . peppermints . . . shiny pennies . . ."

"For the love of Lenin, shut up, Kiang!" yelled Colonel Korsakov.

"Chamomile tea," droned Ken Kiang. "Funny puppies—oh, the silly things they do! . . . the smell of freshly baked bread . . . dandelions . . ."

The black box swerved past Jo's head. She grabbed on to it but it kept flying, dragging her across the plane, banging her fingers against the walls, burping in her face.

"Babies! Beautiful, bouncing babies!" shrieked Ken Kiang.

There was a huge, gut-shredding noise. Jo was thrown across the cabin, and the *Indignant* shook as a missile exploded, just out of range; but the plane somehow still held together.

The radio buzzed again. "Oh, hello. Still there? Ah well, don't you worry, you'll be a ball of exploding flame soon enough. Speaking of which . . . did you know that I wrote a song all about dying in an exploding ball of flame? Shall I sing it for you?"

"NO!" said everyone.

"I've hired the London Symphony Orchestra." A string section welled up in the background, and Ken Kiang crooned: "Oh, that crazy getting-blown-up feeling, it's like falling in love . . ."

A familiar voice came over the radio: "GOT ANY PIE ON THIS PLANE? WHERE'S THAT PIE YOU PROMISED?"

"Ain't it a shame, hoo-hah . . . being blown up in looooove . . ."

"PIE, YOU HAVE, ON PLANE?" shouted Hoagland Shanks. "Criminy, how can I make you understand? FOR ME A PIE, HOW? DO NOW!"

"That's it," snapped Ken Kiang. "Stop, everyone."

The orchestra stopped, and fussy British musicians muttered complaints in the background.

"Enough," said Ken Kiang. "Although there is a rich tradition in villainy of pointlessly toying with people before killing them, I'm finding it tiresome. Well, nobody can say I'm halfhearted at being evil, for I *have* done all the required toying. You will die in thirty seconds."

Jo had finally wrestled down the black box—she could barely hold it as it shuddered and gurgled—and suddenly it spat out a pipe, a furry hat, and a moth-eaten scarf.

Then the box became still, except for the silver crank, which quivered expectantly.

"Hello, that's my pipe!" said Sefino. "And that—that's your hat, Korsakov!"

"So it is," said Korsakov.

"Fifteen seconds," said Ken Kiang.

"Well, what a coincidence." Sefino tamped some tobacco into the pipe and lit it. "At least I can have a pleasant smoke before I die."

"But wait!" said Jo eagerly. "What if I turn this crank?"

She turned it. The box exploded, covering her with soot and leaving a ringing in her ears. Nothing else happened. The box lay scattered on the floor in pieces.

Jo stared at the pieces hopelessly.

"Time's up," said Ken Kiang.

Ken Kiang insisted, as a matter of principle, that all his missiles be works of art, each hand-painted with scenes of famous historical battles. The first missile to hit the *Indignant* was lavishly illustrated with the Battle of Agincourt (1415), with thousands of men-at-arms and longbowmen clashing in the muddy fields of northern France; the next missile had a detailed mural of the entire Crimean War (1853–1856), from the destruction of the Ottoman fleet at Sinop to the final signing of the Treaty of Paris, and . . .

Anyway, they blew up. The *Indignant* plummeted into the Pacific Ocean.

Notably, before the plane reached the ocean floor, it was eaten by a large fish.

SEVEN

"HERE'S to villainy!" cried Ken Kiang, lifting his glass. "Here's to wicked work well wrought! Here's to outrage, injustice! Violence and venom! Marvelous murderers and cutthroat criminals! I embrace you all, brothers! *I'm one of you now!*"

Hoagland Shanks sat with his arms crossed. "Where's my pie? I don't see any pie yet."

"Just you wait!" said Ken Kiang cheerfully.

Ken Kiang and Hoagland Shanks were seated in a small, cluttered Paris bistro, a members-only club, extremely discreet, hidden behind an unmarked door in an unfashionable neighborhood; and open only to men as wealthy and perverse as Ken Kiang.

"Shanks, I can't tell you how lovely it feels," exulted Ken Kiang. "The sticky, clammy, *damning* feeling of blood on my hands. My first murder! It's only a matter of time before I tackle the other major sins." He consulted his checklist. "Let's see, there's torture, sacrilege, treason . . . Shanks, why do I have a whole chapter on mouse abuse? Goodness knows *but I do!*"

"Hey, it's none of my business," interrupted Hoagland Shanks. "But I woulda thought you'd killed plenty of folks. I heard you were supposed to be a really evil guy or somethin'."

"Confession time, Shanks," said Ken Kiang. "I'm really no more than an amateur evildoer. Until tonight, I was all hat and no cattle! It's only now, with this magnificent quadruple murder, that I've married my malevolent mistress of malefaction and started sliding down the slippery slope to sweet sin!"

"Heck if I know what you're jawin' 'bout, Ken," growled Hoagland Shanks. "But I still don't have my pie—and you promised me pie! Now talk sense, talk pie!"

"Oh, I *shall*," said Ken Kiang, refilling his glass. "For that is just what you shall receive. Hoagland Shanks, welcome to one of the most exclusive establishments of Paris, La Société des Friandises Etranges—the Club of Weird Desserts, to you—and your passport to the exhilarating world of gourmet pie!"

Hoagland Shanks scanned the menu with distaste. "Fancy talk, Ken, but I don't see pie on this menu. No *real* pie, anyway. Where's apple pie? Where's cherry pie? I don't like it, Ken; don't like it one bit."

Ken Kiang drew close. "Oh, but only yield your mouth to me, Shanks—lend me your stomach! I shall open new worlds before you. Pies beyond your wildest dreams. Pies you dared not even hope exist!"

"Apple pie," said Hoagland Shanks firmly. "They got that?"

"They have a pie here," said Ken Kiang dreamily. "The Calibrated Cataclysm. Juicy quinces and persimmons and coconut milk, soaked in a hundred different liqueurs precisely measured out in single-angstrom drops to achieve a perfect harmony on the tongue, served flaming in a dish of richest creams and ices; what say you, man—will you try it?"

"Apple pie," said Shanks.

"But just a taste—a taste can't hurt, can it?"

"Apple pie."

"Perhaps you are more sophisticated than I gave you credit for," said Ken Kiang. "Perhaps you prefer the avant-garde. Then would you consider the Phosphorescent Fascination, a shimmering goo of edible plastic mixed with liquid neptunium—a radioactive substance that, if you dim the lights, will shine out of your throat! Oh, you'll quickly become a Class Four biohazard, Shanks; but the exquisite flavor is worth every click of the Geiger counter. How about it, Shanks—like to live dangerously?"

"Apple pie."

"Very well. Never let it be said that Hoagland Shanks doesn't know what he likes. An apple pie it is. But first . . . why not have a spoonful of this?" And Ken Kiang held up a tiny gold spoon, which held the tiniest bit of yellow filling, scooped from a tiny pie on the table.

Hoagland Shanks shrugged, took the spoon, and tasted. His eyes immediately popped wide, his mouth hung open, and he whispered, "Whoa! Ooh . . . I mean . . . wow! What is *that,* Ken?"

"A personal favorite," Ken Kiang said. "Made of a substance that activates dormant taste buds on the *insides of your veins*—and thus you taste the pie *with your entire body* as it pulses throughout your internal organs! Come on, Shanks! Can you bear to pass *that* up?"

Hoagland Shanks shuddered with pleasure as the extraordinary dessert worked through him. He reached for another bite.

"All in good time, my man," said Ken Kiang gently, moving the pie out of Shanks's reach. "You shall have all the pie you like, in good time."

Hoagland Shanks licked his lips. "If they're all as good as that pie, lemme at 'em!"

"You shall have them all," promised Ken Kiang. "But before

we begin, won't you join me in a little pie of my own—a recipe I've concocted myself—won't you do me that favor, Shanks?"

"You bet! Whatcha got?"

Ken Kiang said a few words in French to the waiter, who brought out a pie with a black, lumpy crust. The waiter threw the pie down and stole away as quickly as he politely could, standing far from the table, muttering darkly.

"Jeez, Ken," said Hoagland Shanks. "What kinda pie you got here?"

"I doubt you have tasted it before," said Ken Kiang. "It is the Pie of Innocence Slain. In it, Shanks, you will taste crushed dreams, and defeat; youthful enthusiasm curdled into despair; desperate loneliness; and at the center, Shanks, that rarest, most dainty of delicacies—the heart, Shanks; the pure and uncorrupted human heart. Tonight, Hoagland Shanks, you consume your own soul."

"You talk like a darned fool, Ken," said Hoagland Shanks. "Tastes like peaches."

Fifty-five pies later, Hoagland Shanks trembled with joy.

"I thought I knew about pies," he whispered. "I thought I knew what pies were all about."

"I told you they were good pies," said Ken Kiang.

It was four in the morning. They had been at La Société des Friandises Etranges for eight hours. Ken Kiang sat up straight, fresh as a flower, and drank coffee. The waiter slumped in a booth, watching the Belgian Prankster on a black-and-white TV.

"You must know an awful lot about pies, to know about this place," said Hoagland Shanks.

"Oh, I've picked up a little knowledge here and there," said Ken Kiang carelessly.

"Reckon you know . . . about any other pie places? Like this?"

"Of course!" said Ken Kiang. "But, unfortunately for you, a

deal's a deal. I promised you the most delicious pies you have ever tasted. You have received said pies. End of transaction."

Hoagland Shanks looked hurt. "But telling me about just one—that wouldn't put you out, would it?"

"That's just it," said Ken Kiang. "It *would* 'put me out.' I'm evil, remember? I refuse to tell you where more delicious pies may be found, Shanks, simply because it is a mean thing to do."

Hoagland Shanks started to cry. "But, but . . . all I want is more pies."

"I confess I find your tears strangely satisfying."

"Isn't there a way for me to get pies that still lets you be a mean guy?"

"Hmmm." Ken Kiang cocked his head. "Perhaps there is, Shanks. Perhaps there is . . ."

Ken Kiang was ruminating, considering the problem from several angles, when his eyes happened to fall upon the TV in the corner; the Belgian Prankster was still on; Ken Kiang watched for a few moments—his eyes grew wide; and all at once he let forth a mighty yawp and leaped to his feet, pointing at the TV in horror.

"The Belgian Prankster?" he howled. *"The Belgian Prankster?"*

EIGHT

It was completely dark. Jo couldn't feel anything, couldn't see anything. Only after a moment did she remember how the *Indignant* had been shot down, and she had been screaming, and then everything had ended.

She heard herself say, "So this is the afterlife."

"Do you think we're really dead?" said Sefino somewhere.

"I'm certainly dead," came Colonel Korsakov's voice.

"*I'm* not dead," said Aunt Lily.

There was a long silence.

"Pretty dark, though," said Jo slowly.

"There's no way *I* survived," said Sefino. "Crashing into the ocean, sinking, explosions everywhere, water flooding through the cracks and holes and—"

"That's strange," said Jo. "Are you wet, too?"

"A bit soggy, yes."

There was a pause.

"I thought the afterlife would be drier than this," said Jo.

"Or better lit," said Sefino.

"We're not dead!" insisted Aunt Lily.

No one spoke for a while. Jo fidgeted uncomfortably in the wet darkness. Her body was coming back, and it ached all over.

"Pretty dull afterlife," said Sefino. "I must have been more of a sinner than I thought."

"I expect it picks up later," said Colonel Korsakov.

"Listen to yourselves!" said Aunt Lily. "I don't see how we could've survived, either—but isn't it obvious we're alive?"

Jo coughed up some salt water. "Does anyone have a light?"

"In the compartment above your head," said Colonel Korsakov.

Jo opened the compartment, found the flashlight, and clicked it on. The plane was destroyed, its hull torn and flooded with black, swirling seawater. Jo's beam of light swung over the oily murk, in which floated waterlogged books, lamps, boxes—all of Sefino's and Korsakov's possessions, soaked and ruined.

"Where are we?" said Jo.

"I have high expectations of heaven," said Korsakov. "My grandmother said that if I lived a good life, all my wishes would come true in the next world."

"You must have exceptionally weird tastes," said Sefino.

"C'mon, let's get out of this plane before it totally falls apart," said Aunt Lily. "Jo, you've got the light. Lead the way!"

They got out of the plane, squeezing through the gash on the side. Jo carefully lowered herself down into the darkness, and into more water, which came up to her waist, warmer and slimier than she expected.

Jo didn't think she was dead, either. In fact, she buzzed with strange exhilaration. She felt as though she was on the verge of something big, that she was coming close to a destination that had been pulling at her ever since the package fell from the sky.

Soon they were all wading in the slimy water. The ground was squishy and uneven, and the dark, humid air seethed with living smells. Jo's flashlight swept around the damp cave, in which everything pulsed and squished about in the most sickening way.

Colonel Korsakov was fiddling with the plane. "I've fixed the lights . . . Mind your eyes. . . ."

The plane's lights switched on and a great length of the cavern was lit up—a dim tunnel of glistening pink walls, soft and quivering, with dozens of tubes leading in and out, spilling juices; a red, ribbed, dripping passage, leading off into forbidding darkness.

With a whoop of delight Colonel Korsakov slogged ahead, wading excitedly into the treacherous goo; he looked around with awe, with astonishment, and finally with an unrestrained boyish glee. He turned around, and smiling, held his arms out wide.

"Grandmother was right! My wishes have come true!" he exulted. "It cannot be denied—the miracle of it all! *We are inside my digestion!*"

"I have been sent to hell," said Sefino.

"The organs! The entrails! The enzymes and juices!" rhapsodized Korsakov. "At long last, reward! An eternity to spend *in my own stomach!*"

"Hey!" Jo was looking down the tunnel in the other direction. "Come look at this!"

Jo pointed her flashlight down the dripping tunnel. It dropped into an enormous mucilaginous gorge, thick with running juices, the walls writhing rhythmically.

At the bottom there stood a building.

It was a solid, respectable five-story brick building. In a city, one might pass it a hundred times without noticing it. Inside a giant throbbing stomach, however, it was noticed.

"Wonders upon wonders!" said Colonel Korsakov. "I don't recall eating a small law firm."

Jo squinted down at the building. Carved above the door were these words:

LODGE

ORDER OF ODD-FISH

"Order of Odd-Fish—that's what is said on the package!" said Jo. "Aunt Lily! . . . Aunt Lily?"

Aunt Lily was gazing at the lodge with frozen eyes. Her hands clutched vaguely at her chest, and she turned away with a shiver. "Okay," she said faintly.

Jo, Aunt Lily, Korsakov, and Sefino half climbed, half slid down the gorge, grabbing hold of fleshy knobs and pulsing protrusions, and finally dropped to the bottom.

The lodge loomed before them, dead and silent. Every window was dark. Its crumbling bricks were crabbed with gray, sickly ivy, and cold thin mist twisted around. The whole building looked as if it was sunk into a dreary hibernation.

Jo walked up the porch steps. She raised her hand to knock on the door—and she felt something familiar.

Back at the ruby palace, Jo would often go down to the small movie theater in the basement where Aunt Lily kept all her old black-and-white films. Jo would watch those movies alone, far into the night, trying to figure her aunt out. She felt that somewhere within all those old movies, there had to be some clue that would tell her where Aunt Lily had disappeared to for forty years, and where she had come from; and some hint as to why that note had said she was "dangerous."

Jo fell asleep while watching the movies, but a story would take shape in her dreams, patched together from clips of the dozens of movies she watched—and for a moment she *would* know who she was. Jo always forgot the dream in the morning, no matter how she tried to remember it. But she did remember that feeling of knowing.

She felt it now. The feeling of knowing was in that lodge. It was so real that she almost imagined it as an actual physical thing, a black dot lurking somewhere in there. Maybe the black dot was hidden on top of a bookshelf, or tucked inside a drawer, or sitting under a dish; wherever it was, she would find it. She would tear the lodge apart to find that dot. It was the period at the end of her old life.

Jo knocked. There was no answer. But the heavy oak doors, laced with iron and copper, gave way when she pushed, and swung open into a musty darkness.

The foyer was a gloomy cave of high ceilings and ponderous decor. Smooth, dusty hardwood floors, overlaid with ratty rugs, spread down two corridors and up a gently swooping stairway. The walls housed rows of bookcases crammed with yellowed books and crumbling maps. A shattered chandelier lay crashed in the center of the room, glistening in frozen splashes of light.

"Hello?" called Colonel Korsakov. But nobody answered.

They made their way through the abandoned lodge. There were signs that the inhabitants had intended to return soon, long ago: wineglasses stained red with evaporated wine; a dusty half-finished card game lying on a table; a book cracked open and left on the ottoman; a pipe on a chair. All was veiled with dust.

"I remember this place," said Aunt Lily.

Korsakov stopped. "Exceedingly strange. I, too, remember something about this place."

"I used to live here," said Sefino suddenly.

"So did I!" said Aunt Lily.

"I lived here, too!" said Korsakov, astonished.

"I didn't!" said Jo, starting to feel left out. "I don't remember this place at all!"

Korsakov opened a door, and they stepped into a large

kitchen. A couple of pots bubbled on the stove. Some chopped vegetables sat on the counter, as well as a gentleman.

He was an elderly black gentleman, very tall, thin, and gangly. He wore a tattered three-piece suit and no shoes or socks. His face was freckled and lined, his hair gray, his eyes bright and clear. He hopped off the counter, adjusted his spectacles, squinted at his visitors, and smiled with mild surprise.

"An unusual place for a reunion," he said.

"Reunion?" said Sefino. "What on earth do you mean?"

"Really? You've *completely* forgotten me?" The old man looked hurt. "Your old comrade in arms?"

"Oh, come now—*this is too much!*" said Sefino, waving his antennae. "Sir, I am a gentleman. Ordinarily at this hour you would find me enjoying an expertly mixed cocktail, or cataloguing my award-winning collection of Turkish cufflinks. Instead, my companions and I have spent the last twenty-four hours being shot at, insulted, blown up, tied up, tossed about, threatened, eaten, and forced into social contact with dubious persons. I, for one, shall have no patience for whatever whimsical tomfoolery you may have in store for us."

Jo murmured, "You are a three-foot-tall talking cockroach."

"Not terribly whimsical, once you get used to it," said Sefino. "But all this—it's too much!"

"Sefino, you haven't changed a bit," said the old man.

"What? No!" Sefino pounded the table. "How do you know my name before I've told you? More nonsense! This *entire day* has become too fantastical for my taste."

The old man turned to Jo. "And you must be Jo Hazelwood."

Jo looked up, startled. "What? Oh . . . but my name isn't Hazelwood."

"Ah, yes, I suppose you'd think that." He held out a bony hand, and Jo, bewildered, shook it. "I'm Mulcahy."

Aunt Lily said, "*Oliver* Mulcahy?"

Colonel Korsakov started. "*Sir* Oliver Mulcahy! I remember—"

Sefino stood up angrily. "No explanation, sir, can justify such ludicrousness!"

"What are you doing here?" said Colonel Korsakov.

"Napping in this fish's duodenum," said Sir Oliver. "Very snug. Ah! I was wondering where my scarf had gone. Thank you."

Korsakov was carrying the scarf that had been coughed out of the box along with his furry cap and Sefino's pipe. Sir Oliver took the scarf and nonchalantly wrapped it around his neck.

Aunt Lily looked at the man with mounting puzzlement. "I know you—I know this place—but I can't quite remember who you are—why can't I *remember*?"

"That's easy," said Sir Oliver. "You've all lost your minds. Fortunately, I have them right here, in jars." He rummaged in the icebox and took out three glass jars. Each contained brainy clumps floating in yellow fluid. "Your memories were confiscated when you were exiled from Eldritch City. I held on to them for sentimental reasons. Never thought it would come to this. . . . You first, Korsakov."

Sir Oliver sprang up and seized Colonel Korsakov's nose. Jo was stunned—violence was the last thing she expected from the kind-looking old man. The colossal Russian bellowed in outrage, but the lanky gentleman held fast, even as Korsakov staggered around the kitchen, crashing over tables and breaking chairs, waving his arms and trying to pry the man from his nose. Sir Oliver, still firmly grasping Korsakov's nose, clambered onto his back and opened a jar with his teeth, grabbing a twitching bit of brain; with the other hand he pulled Korsakov's nostrils apart and stuffed the brain up his nose. Halfway in, the wormlike strand of brain took on a life of its own and squirmed with furious energy up into Korsakov's nostrils until it had disappeared.

This was all very shocking for the spectators.

Korsakov, dazed, stood still for a few seconds. Then he grinned at Sir Oliver as though he was an old friend and not a stranger who had just pushed something questionable up his nose.

"Why all the trouble, old chap?" said Korsakov. "I would have consented to do that myself."

"Perhaps," said Sir Oliver. "But it wouldn't have been nearly as fun."

"Er, quite," said Sefino.

With much less fuss, Sir Oliver handed the other two jars to Sefino and Aunt Lily. Sefino distastefully eyed the contents of his jar but opened it with a sigh, poking at the swirling clumps. Aunt Lily wrenched the lid off and grabbed at the brains, stuffing them up her nose with gusto.

"Has everyone gone nuts?" said Jo.

"Just the opposite," said Aunt Lily, brains dangling from her nostril. "I've been waiting for this for years! Do you know how frustrating it is, not to remember half of your life? For the past thirteen years I've wondered about those missing forty years. Now, if it had been anyone other than Sir Oliver who suggested I put this crap up my nose, I would've hesitated. But if there's anyone I trust, it's Sir Oliver. Although I still don't quite remember who he is . . ."

"Perfectly normal. It'll take a few minutes for all the old memories to kick in," said Sir Oliver. He turned to Jo. "I'm sorry I don't have any for you, Miss Hazelwood, but you were too young to remember anything."

"That's quite all right," said Jo. "And my name isn't Hazelwood. I have her ring, though."

"Ah! But you see—"

The entire building lurched.

"Whoa!" said Colonel Korsakov, grabbing on to the counter. "What was that?"

Sir Oliver said something, but Jo couldn't hear—the lodge shook again and everyone yelled as tables and chairs slid across the room and plates crashed to the floor. For a moment, Sir Oliver stood motionless; then he ran out the door, calling over his shoulder.

"What did he say?" shouted Jo.

"It was something about a good view!" said Sefino, ducking a flying chair.

They all dashed after Sir Oliver as he bounded barefoot down the twisting, tilting hallways. The building tipped on its side, and then it turned upside down, and then it righted itself again, and yet Sir Oliver managed to sprint down the walls or ceilings as if they were the floors, his scarf billowing behind. The others struggled after him through the tumbling rooms, where bookshelves poured out rivers of books, couches slid around as though possessed, and chairs bounced off the walls at frightening velocities.

"Marvelous!" said Sir Oliver. "Just up these stairs! Watch your step! Come on now!"

Jo glanced out a window. The lodge was surging forward through a fleshy tunnel, swerving, bucking, and jolting. A yellow-orange foaming liquid had engulfed the bottom of the lodge, sweeping the entire building along—to where?

"No time!" called Sir Oliver. "Up the stairs! Come on, let's go!"

He leaped, sprinted, tore up the stairs, and burst out the trapdoor on top.

"Grab on to something! There you go! Wooo!"

Aunt Lily pointed ahead: "Look!"

At the end of the tunnel a hole was opening up, getting wider every second—and outside were pale stars, the twilit sky, a plump white moon—

The lodge burst out of the mouth of the fish and crashed onto a sandy beach. Jo was astonished to see hundreds of torches, a crowd of people; a great cheer went up; fireworks exploded, and a chant started all around them. Through it all, Jo heard two words in the din, again and again, though she could hardly believe it:

"LILY LAROUCHE! LILY LAROUCHE!" they shouted.

People swarmed the bottom of the building. Jo looked back, flabbergasted; the giant fish was still on the shore, its wide mouth gasping.

"All together now! LIFT!"

The building lurched again. Jo looked down: the people below had lifted the lodge.

"FORWARD!"

Grunting, sweating, shouting, the people heaved the great building forward.

"MARCH!"

Jo looked out onto the mad scene. They had landed on a sandy beach, thick with mossy trees twisted in weird shapes; she glanced back and saw the fish wriggle backward into the water and disappear; looked forward again, at the campfires on the beach amid the jumbled rocks, and in the distance, beyond the forest, a city—a mountain that climbed straight into the sky, covered with a maze of glittering buildings and crowned by a great golden tree. Terraced streets spiraled down the mountain, with little lights and fires and flickering torches and crowds of people looking out from windows and bridges, waving, pointing, and shouting.

The sun was dipping below the lavender ocean, tinting the clouds purple in a sky like a wall of dark gold. Even in the desert, Jo had never seen anything like this sunset; it looked like the sky at the end of the world.

Singing songs and waving torches, the crowd carried the lodge up the beach, through a jungle of crooked trees, over a foaming river, and through the city gates. A whoop went up from all sides as the crowd carried the lodge up the mountain, pitching and tilting through the streets.

Aunt Lily smiled. "I'm finally home. *We're* home."

"You make quite an entrance," said Jo.

Aunt Lily flinched and turned to Jo with panicked eyes.

"What . . . what's wrong?" said Jo.

Korsakov and Sefino gasped and backed away from her.

Sir Oliver said sharply, "I would've expected more from you, Korsakov. After all you've been through, that's how you're going to treat her?"

Colonel Korsakov seemed to be looking at Jo for the first time. "I'm sorry, Oliver." He averted his eyes. "It's that I just *now* remembered."

"Should we hide her?" said Aunt Lily.

"LILY LAROUCHE! LILY LAROUCHE!" shouted the crowd.

"No. Follow me," said Sir Oliver.

Jo ran after them. "What are you talking about, hide me?"

Reeling and tilting from side to side, the lodge staggered forward, aloft on a parade of torches, chants, and songs. More fireworks exploded overhead, and a marching band led the building through the winding boulevards, booming and trumpeting. The crowd carried the lodge up the circling streets, scraping buildings on either side; sometimes the lodge almost tilted too far, nearly tumbling off the mountain entirely; but the crowd held on.

Jo, Sefino, Korsakov, and Aunt Lily followed Sir Oliver downstairs to a small library. The lodge bucked and jounced all around them as the city jerkily passed outside the window.

"I'm glad to have you back in Eldritch City," said Sir Oliver. "It's been rather dull since you left."

"It's awkward, though, isn't it?" said Aunt Lily. "We were exiled, after all."

"Why are you exiled?" said Jo.

"Uh, it's a long story," said Aunt Lily. "It has to do with you."

Jo stared. "You were exiled because of me?"

"No time to explain. Oliver, we have to think of something, quick."

"Are we going to tell everyone who Jo is?" said Colonel Korsakov.

"Absolutely not," said Sir Oliver. "We would be run out of town."

"Are you going to tell *me* who I am?" said Jo.

"She can be my squire," said Aunt Lily.

"Capital idea. That should divert attention from her."

"What's that supposed to mean?" said Jo. She was starting to feel less like a person and more like an unspeakable medical condition.

Aunt Lily turned to Jo. "Give me your ring. Quick now!"

"Why?" said Jo—but Aunt Lily grabbed her hand and wrenched the ring off her finger. Seconds later, a man's face appeared at the window.

"Hey! Hey! Hey!" puffed the man, running alongside the lodge. He had a handlebar mustache and a crooked smile and wore a suit of armor of mismatched brass and silver plates. "Fantastic, *wonderful* to have you back in town!"

"Sir Festus!" Aunt Lily pocketed Jo's ring and stood up. "Is it really you?"

"We're all here!" panted the man. He was having a hard time keeping up. "Isabel said Oliver wouldn't be back in time for the feast, but I just said, you wait and see! But we didn't expect this! And—good gravy, is that old Korsakov? And Sefino? Korsakov, old boy!"

Korsakov grinned. "You seem in fine fettle, Festus!"

"My fettle has never been finer!" puffed Sir Festus; then he ran out of breath and fell behind.

"Who was that?" said Jo, clutching her finger; it rather hurt.

"Sir Festus Bartleby," said Sefino. "One of the knights of the Order of Odd-Fish. Lily, Korsakov, and Sir Oliver—they're all knights, too. Just like your parents were."

Jo shouted, "You knew my *parents*?"

"Shush! You'll give us all away!" said Aunt Lily.

"What's the big secret?" said Jo.

"We're almost there. We don't have any time," said Aunt Lily.

Sir Oliver said, "If those people knew that we were bringing the Hazelwood child back into Eldritch City, this parade would turn into a riot."

The lodge careened around the final corner, and with a loud shout and a final heave the crowd dropped it down between two other buildings. The applause outside was tremendous.

"A riot over *me*?" said Jo.

CRASH! CRASH! CRASH! Jo heard a hammering at the front door, and people streamed into the lodge, whooping and hollering.

"Yes," said Aunt Lily. "You're the reason we were in exile."

"Wait!" said Jo. "Does this have something to do with that note? That said I was . . ."

"Dangerous? Yes," said Sir Oliver. "Actually, I wrote that note."

Jo gaped at Sir Oliver.

"But for now, the less you know, the better," said Aunt Lily quickly. "Don't worry—it's not as bad as it sounds."

Silence fell. It became clear to Jo that it *was* as bad as it sounded; maybe worse than she could guess.

"What . . . what happens now?" she said.

There was a mounting tumult in the lodge: the clomp of boots, the screech of grinding metal, laughter and carousing, coming closer. Aunt Lily, Sir Oliver, and Sefino brightened, and a deep, pleased rumble came from Korsakov's digestion.

"The Grand Feast of the Odd-Fish," said Aunt Lily. "And I, for one, intend to stuff myself until I can't move."

NINE

BEFORE Jo knew what was happening, Aunt Lily, Korsakov, and Sir Oliver all disappeared upstairs to dress for the feast, and Sefino hustled her off to the lodge's banquet hall.

The hall was empty when they arrived, and homelier than Jo expected: a cramped, narrow gallery filled up by a long oak table and twenty-four chairs. An arched brass ceiling housed pots overflowing with vines, and dirty mirrors and old photographs in cracked frames crammed the walls. The table was crowded with candles, bowls of sauce, and plates of unidentifiable fruit, but none of the cups, bowls, or silverware matched; it was as if they had all been stolen from different places.

Sefino led Jo to a small side closet full of filthy black robes.

"Dining gowns," he said, and gave her one.

"I'm supposed to wear this?" said Jo. Like all the other gowns, it was covered in stains, and bits of dried food clung to the sleeves.

"They're never washed," said Sefino. "Squires aren't allowed to wash their dining gowns."

"Why?"

"It's a very honorable and pointless tradition," said Sefino. "Just put it on."

Sefino had changed into a smart waiter's uniform, with a six-button black vest, precisely knotted bow tie, and crisp apron. Jo saw other cockroaches, too, rushing back and forth with teetering trays stacked with plates and saucers and cups. Sefino stood on tiptoe to catch a glimpse, clicking his mandibles eagerly. Above, feet clumped down the stairs.

"Probably the other squires," said Sefino.

Jo didn't know where to start. "Sefino, what *is* a squire?"

"A knight's assistant," said Sefino. "Each knight has a squire and a butler to help them. That's where we cockroaches come in. You're Dame Lily's squire. I, of course, am Korsakov's butler."

"Sefino," said Jo cautiously, "what *is* this place?"

"Ah, that's a bit of a metaphysical question, isn't it? You'd be better off asking Sir Oort."

"What?"

"Sir Oort Helmfozz. You'll meet him. He's the house expert on discredited metaphysics."

"What's—"

"Jo, I *do* have my own duties to attend to," said Sefino. "And asking too many questions is a vulgar habit."

Jo sat down on a bench. "It's too much. I don't know why I'm supposed to be dangerous, and I don't know anything about squires, or knights, or . . . or 'discredited metaphysics,' or anything."

"So?"

"So I don't think I'll fit in here."

"You certainly won't fit in if you keep hiding in this closet," said Sefino. "Though you may become a beloved eccentric. They might even point you out on guided tours. 'And here's Jo Larouche,' they'd announce. 'Went into this closet years ago. Never left. Don't worry, we do feed her from time to time. No flash photography, please.' "

"Thanks, Sefino, you're a real help."

"It could be a relaxing life."

"I just need to catch my breath."

"Suit yourself," said Sefino, and scuttled off.

Jo sat on a wooden stool and tried to get her bearings. The lodge clamored with people, but Jo was in no state to meet anyone. She was exhausted, grungy, her nerves shot. Her pink waitress uniform (which she had always hated anyway) was a crumpled rag now, soaked in the stomach juices of the giant fish. Then she heard voices and footsteps in the hall. Jo remembered the dining gown and threw it on.

Three boys (one tall, one pudgy, and one weirdly birdlike) and a girl came into the closet. They all halted, staring at Jo in surprise.

"Who are you?" said the girl finally. She had red, curly hair and an unfortunate nose.

"Um . . . ah . . . Jo Larouche?" said Jo.

"Oh, so *you're* Dame Lily's squire." The girl seemed unimpressed. "I'm Daphne Brockbank. Dame Delia's squire."

"Maurice Farrar. I'm Sir Festus's." Maurice was a burly, sleepy-looking boy who seemed to be in the middle of a growth spurt in which parts of his body were developing at different speeds, such that his legs were too short, his arms were too long, and his back was curled into a perpetual stoop. He barely glanced at Jo as he fiddled with his dining gown.

"Albert Blatch-Budgins. Sir Alasdair's," grunted the pudgy boy. Albert's hair was neatly parted in the middle, and he wore big squarish glasses. He squinted at Jo with cold, fishy eyes.

"Phil Snurr. Sir Oort," said the birdlike boy. He didn't even look at Jo, but immediately snatched his dining gown and left the closet.

Jo still didn't know what to say. There was another uncomfortable silence.

Daphne exhaled and turned to Jo again. "I heard you had a rough time coming in. You must be used to danger, though, squiring for Dame Lily."

Jo almost laughed. "Danger? Aunt Lily? What's so dangerous about *her*?"

Daphne, Maurice, and Albert looked at Jo with startled disbelief.

"Whoa," said Maurice.

Before Jo could ask what this meant, another boy and girl crowded into the closet. The girl, a tiny, frantic creature with wild black hair and huge eyes, was babbling: "I'm telling you it all fits together. If you'd seen last week's episode you'd *see* it all fits together. Dame Lily actually came back. It's the beginning of the end!"

"I paid you, stop going on about it," groaned the boy.

"Thirteen years, just like the show, *exactly*. It's like living the show, isn't it just like *living* it?"

"For God's sake shut up."

"It's all the work of the Silent Sisters."

"Nora, you think your bad skin is the work of the Silent Sisters."

"Hey, Nora, Ian," said Daphne. "This is Dame Lily's squire."

Nora's eyes bulged even wider. *"Really?"*

There were many introductions, but the names went by so quickly that Jo couldn't keep track. The excitable girl was Nora McGunn, and she became quiet when introduced, staring at Jo with cautious fascination. The boy was Ian Barrows. He had sandy blond hair and wore a tattered tan corduroy jacket, and he had the wispy beginnings of a mustache, which did not suit him.

After a minute of jostling in the crowded closet, the rest of the squires had changed and hurried out. Only Jo and Ian were left behind.

"So you're the new girl, huh?" said Ian, wriggling into his gown. "In case nobody else has said it, welcome to Eldritch City."

"Actually, nobody has."

"Oh, the other squires?" Ian shrugged. "Don't mind them. They just want to show they're not impressed by you. It's not every day that—"

But Ian was cut short by an elderly cockroach, who marched into the closet and hit them with his walking stick until they left for the banquet hall.

Another cockroach dressed in tails directed Jo to her seat, pulling it out for her and scooting it back in as she sat down. Jo looked around for Ian, but yet another cockroach was seating him all the way at the other end of the table.

Then someone whispered in her ear, high-pitched, breathy, and intense:

"This has all been foretold, you know."

Jo turned and was startled to find Nora right behind her. Up close, Nora's face seemed much too small, half hidden under streams of unkempt black hair. Somewhere under all the hair Jo could just glimpse a tiny nose, tiny mouth, and alarmingly tiny teeth.

"Foretold?" said Jo.

"Everything." Nora looked around significantly. "With Dame Lily back, the wheels will only move faster. Eye of the storm, Jo."

"Eye of . . . what are you talking about?"

Nora sucked air through her teeth, leaned in, and said, "All of this. We're all running down a path of doom laid down by the Silent Sisters."

"Who?"

Nora looked shocked. "Don't you know? About the—"

But Nora was drowned out by a blare of trumpets, a great

shout went up—Jo turned to see what was going on—the knights were marching in.

All the knights, including Aunt Lily and Colonel Korsakov, had changed into ceremonial feast robes of gold, scarlet, and blazing purple, festooned with epaulettes, sashes, shining spurs, an ornamental sword, a bejeweled bib, and a trailing cape that looked like a doily gone berserk for seven feet. Crowning all was a towering turban clasped with a ruby in the shape of a fish. The turbans swayed wildly as the knights came tramping in, their weapons and jewelry and medals clinking and jangling, all of them singing and shouting at each other. Every knight and squire wore a ring on his or her left little finger, just like the rings Aunt Lily had found in the black box. Jo still didn't understand—why had she had to give hers up?

The trumpets died down, the knights settled into their seats, and Jo felt a tug on her sleeve—Nora again. "Did you hear what I said?"

"I'm sorry, what?"

"It's—" said Nora, but again she was drowned out by a blare of trumpets. Everyone stood up.

"What?" said Jo, scrambling to her feet.

"I *said*—" started Nora, but then a cockroach steered her off to a different part of the table, even as she frantically mouthed something at Jo; then everybody yelled "HUZZAH!" and something extraordinary rolled into the banquet hall.

It was Sir Oliver.

Sir Oliver's costume was so massive and ornate that he literally could not move. Three wheezing cockroaches had to push him in on a cart. Sir Oliver's face just barely poked out of the monumental cavalcade of frippery, a multitiered mountain of buttons and bows and collars and jewelry and bustles and seven different hats, one on top of the other and each one more outlandish than the last, piled upon a billowing, flapping, teetering mass of crepe and silk and velvet. He looked like he had been imprisoned in a gigantic, nightmarish wedding cake.

"The Grand Bebisoy of the Order of Odd-Fish, Sir Oliver Mulcahy!" bellowed a cockroach.

Prolonged applause. Sir Oliver smiled and nodded, everyone sat down, and he began, "Welcome home, Odd-Fish! It's a relief to have almost everyone back at the lodge——"

"Hear, hear!" shouted the knights and squires.

"It's been a difficult year," said Sir Oliver. "Money's been tight, as usual. I won't dwell on the woes of the past months— including, of course, that this lodge was stolen——"

"Boo! For shame!"

"And for three months we've had nowhere to live. Now, before we start the feast, I will tell you this: in my search for the lodge, I *did* discover who had stolen it——"

A general gasp around the table—

"But I won't tell you who until after dessert," said Sir Oliver.

"No!" came the protests. "Tell us now!"

"You will need a full stomach," said Sir Oliver firmly. "I will say no more. On to happier matters. We also have back in Eldritch City, after a thirteen-year exile, Dame Lily Larouche, Colonel Anatoly Korsakov, and Sefino—as well as a new addition to the Order of Odd-Fish, Dame Lily's niece and squire, Jo Larouche."

Jo flinched as all eyes turned to her, and she looked down, embarrassed. Nobody was staring at her the horrified way Korsakov and Sefino had; still, she was relieved when Sir Oliver spoke again and attention shifted away from her.

"You squires never knew Dame Lily, Colonel Korsakov, or Sefino personally, of course—a bit before your time—but I trust everyone shall make both our new and returning Odd-Fish welcome. I see our soup is becoming tepid. Let the feast begin!"

The cockroaches descended from all sides, bearing soup. Jo was starving, and luckily, the chunky, purple soup was delicious, with a mild pork-plum flavor. Glimpsing to the side, Jo noticed that Sir Oliver's costume prevented him from moving his arms, and a cockroach had to feed him, spoonful by spoonful, as though he were a baby.

Aunt Lily sat on Jo's right. She seemed like an entirely different woman now; or no, Aunt Lily was somehow more *herself* than she had ever been in Dust Creek. Her voice was clear, her body shimmered with renewed health, and even a few wrinkles seemed to have disappeared. It was as though Aunt Lily had grown up.

"So . . . what do knights do?" Jo asked.

"Ooh, tons," said Aunt Lily over the noise. "There are quite a few orders of knights in Eldritch City, each with their own traditions and missions. The Order of Odd-Fish's mission is to research an encyclopedia."

"An encyclopedia?"

"The appendix to an encyclopedia, actually," said Sir Oliver as a cockroach held a spoonful of soup near his mouth. "The project of writing an encyclopedia of *all* knowledge was abandoned centuries ago, but we're still writing its appendix. It is a pleasantly futile task. Our archives take up the entire fifth floor—we're adding new information all the time. For instance, Dame Lily might be amused to know that there's now an entry on *her* in the Appendix."

"Really!" said Aunt Lily. "What's it say?"

"It says you're dead."

"What!"

"Probably should change that in the next edition," said Sir Oliver.

"It doesn't sound like much of an appendix," said Jo.

"Oh, it's usually wrong," admitted Sir Oliver.

"But the Appendix isn't known for its accuracy," said Aunt Lily. "Accuracy isn't the point."

" 'It is an Appendix of dubious facts, rumors, and myths,' " recited Colonel Korsakov. " 'A repository of questionable knowledge, and an opportunity to dither about.' That's from our charter," he said to Jo. "The bit about dithering is the most important. We are a society of ditherers."

"Dithering?" said Jo.

"You know—fiddling about, puttering, loafing. The Order of Odd-Fish has a long and distinguished history of dithering. Sir Oliver is the world's foremost authority."

"Oh, I wouldn't say that!" protested Sir Oliver.

"He wrote a six-hundred-thousand-page dissertation on dithering," said Aunt Lily. "*Puttering, Muddling, and Mucking About: An Inquiry into Idleness.* Quite well known in the field."

"I make no claims," said Sir Oliver.

"Don't be so modest! Your work was years ahead of its time."

"Is it worth reading?" said Jo.

"Nobody's ever read it," whispered Aunt Lily.

"Please!" Sir Oliver smiled.

"Honestly, he can't take a compliment," said Aunt Lily.

The cockroaches swooped in, snatched away the soup bowls, and served plates heaping with a gooey stew. It was spicy and slimy, and after a few cautious bites, Jo decided she liked it.

"Sir Oliver edits the Appendix," said Aunt Lily. "He makes sure that everything in it is properly dubious."

"I don't understand," said Jo. "Your Appendix is *supposed* to be unreliable?"

"Or useless," said Sir Oliver happily. "Unreliable *or* useless. We also print information that is out of date or contradictory. Though, I must stress, we never publish anything misleading."

"Deliberately misleading," said Aunt Lily.

"Good point, yes. All the information in the Appendix is true, as far as we know. Which, er, isn't too far, actually, sometimes."

Jo said, "Isn't it stupid to have an unreliable reference book?"

All conversation stopped at once.

Every single knight put down his or her fork and knife, and glared at Jo.

Jo's stomach dropped. "Sorry . . . I didn't mean . . ."

A general harrumphing, and the knights went back to their dinners.

"Actually, Jo, there *is* a point to it," explained Aunt Lily gently. "There are many things in this world that we know a little bit about, but not enough to say we *really* know. Things that are vague, or only half understood. Or known once and then forgotten, or once thought to be true, and now thought to be false, but maybe they're really true, who knows? This stuff doesn't fit into the encyclopedia. It's too dubious. So we put it in our Appendix instead. Rumors, leads, myths, things that are maybe true, maybe not."

A tiny man almost entirely covered in white whiskers peered over at Jo. "For instance," he said, in a voice that sounded like a rapid series of hiccups, "my research is particularly dubious. Not to mention entirely useless. I study discredited metaphysics."

Jo remembered. "Oh! Sir Oort Helmfozz, right? Sefino said you—"

The furry man was thunderstruck.

"She knows me," he whispered. "She knows my work! She knows my *name*! Somebody cares! At long last . . . *somebody cares*!"

"Well—"

"It has never happened before," said Sir Oort with astonished awe. "Nobody has ever said they cared about my research. Do you know how boring my research is?"

"I didn't actually say—"

"How *tedious* metaphysics is?"

"But—"

"It is *spectacularly* tiresome," crowed Sir Oort. "Some of my metaphysics positively *sparkles* with dullness. Oh yes! You have no idea. My life, year upon year of arcane drudgery—*aha!* I see that you, too, thirst for knowledge!"

"Not—"

"You want to learn more about my work. Don't be shy, girl! I can tell!" Sir Oort tapped his glass with his fork, announcing to the table, "I shall tutor her every week!"

Aunt Lily said, "We wouldn't dream of imposing——"

"Not at all, not at all! No, no, I won't hear of it!" exclaimed Sir Oort. "It is obvious to me that this girl thirsts for knowledge of discredited metaphysics. I will not permit you, Dame Lily— oh no!—to stand in her way. Oh ho ho, oh no, oh no! I daresay it's a dream come true for her. Yes—a dream come true," he said, and went back to muttering into his yams.

"All due respect to Sir Oort, but discredited metaphysics isn't all we study," said Aunt Lily quickly. "Dame Isabel, for instance, studies unusual smells."

"How do you do," said a prim lady down the table.

Jo couldn't help but smile. "Smells?"

Dame Isabel regarded Jo with supreme distaste. "Rest assured," she said crushingly, "*you* have never smelled what I have smelled; and even if you had, you would scarcely understand what you were smelling."

Jo gritted her teeth—she'd made another faux pas. But Aunt Lily briskly moved on. "We also have Sir Alasdair Coveney, who studies unlikely musical instruments."

Sir Alasdair looked like a boiled sausage disguised as a person. His face was bulging but pinched, his pink skin flushed and wet with sweat. He had removed his turban because of the heat, and his head was completely hairless.

"What kind of instruments do you study?" said Jo politely. "I play the organ, actually."

Sir Alasdair seemed not to hear her. He continued to eat his pork chop.

"So . . . do you play anything?"

No answer.

"Do you, um, like music?"

Nothing.

"Can you even hear me?"

Sir Alasdair nodded, tearing off another bite of pork chop.

"Then why don't you answer me?" said Jo, exasperated. Then, under her breath: "You're even ruder than that smells lady."

Sir Alasdair's eyes lit up. He paused over his pork chop. "Ah yes, the . . . *smells lady,*" he said slowly. "Or, as I prefer to call her, *my wife.*"

Jo reddened as Sir Alasdair dissolved into snuffling laughter.

Dame Isabel said stiffly, "Your squire will learn how to properly address a knight."

"She will," said Aunt Lily. "Though you've given her little reason to be polite."

"I wasn't aware I had to grovel to the great Dame Lily's squire," said Dame Isabel. "Apparently the laws don't apply to Dame Lily's squire. That's no surprise. The laws don't seem to apply to anything about Dame Lily."

"Enough, Isabel," said Sir Oliver, with as much authority as he could muster from within his absurd costume. "Don't ruin the feast."

The woman sitting on Jo's left said, "Don't mind the Coveneys, they're insufferable. I was Lily's squire once, too, and Alasdair and Isabel gave me just as hard a time. I'm Delia. Delia Delahanty."

Dame Delia was a middle-aged black woman, angular and elegant, with short hair and rectangular glasses. She looked at Jo with amused kindness, and just when Jo had regained enough confidence to ask, "What do you study?" she interrupted herself with an "Oh!" as a brilliant gold-and-emerald feathered snake with dozens of wings slithered out of Dame Delia's sleeve and stared at Jo.

"Absurd animals," said Dame Delia, petting her snake absently. "Any living thing that's extremely rare, extinct, mythical, or horribly deformed is of great interest to me. Don't worry about Snoodles, he's just curious. Back you go," she said, waving her fingers, and the snake slithered back up into the folds of Dame Delia's gown.

A meek voice from the other end of the table said, "Nobody's asked me what *I* do."

Jo didn't feel at all comfortable about "Snoodles," but asked anyway (even as she darted a glance back at Dame Delia's sleeve), "Oh? What do you study?"

"I'm Dame Myra Uldermulder," said the unseen knight. "I study improbable botany. That is, strange plants. But don't mind me," she said sadly. "Don't mind me at all."

"That actually sounds interesting," said Jo. "What kinds of plants?"

"*I* study ludicrous weaponry," interrupted Sir Festus.

"But Dame Myra—"

"I shall tell you about a certain sort of sword," continued Sir Festus. "Commonly used three thousand seven hundred years ago, in the Fidbiglian Empire. *A sword made out of biscuits!*"

"Dame Myra was talking."

"Never mind Dame Myra. These biscuit-swords were the only weapons allowed in the Fidbiglian Imperial Army. A bizarre palace intrigue had resulted in the coronation of the Imperial Chef!"

"But—"

"The swords were absolutely useless. The entire Fidbiglian army was defeated in the next war. Against the Glovians, no less!"

"Ah—"

"*The Glovians!* Can you believe it? And then the Glovian army ate the swords."

"I see."

"Very humiliating for the Fidbiglians."

"Was it."

"*Biscuit*-swords. Swords made out of *biscuits*. I don't know what the chef was thinking," said Sir Festus. "The Fidbiglians later drowned him in a kettle of his own custard."

"Go ahead, ignore me," sighed Dame Myra. "I'm used to it."

Dinner was finished, and the cockroaches served everyone coffee and bowls of jelly-like cubes floating in blue cream. The cubes were cold, slippery, and tasted like sour apple; after eating a few, Jo felt unexpectedly light-headed. Some of the knights produced pipes and began to smoke.

"Now that we're all snug with our coffees and pipes," said Sir Festus, "could Dame Lily tell us just how she found her way back from exile? Didn't you have all your memories removed?"

"Yes, that was part of the mayor's sentence," said Aunt Lily. "So we'd never find our way back to Eldritch City."

"And then you were dumped back in your old home in . . . California, was it?"

"That's right."

"Never heard of the place. Thoroughly ridiculous name, it sounds made up. But, moving on. How did you get back to Eldritch City?"

Aunt Lily raised her eyebrows to Sir Oliver. He nodded. Then she stood up, and from a carton, dumped onto the table the remains of the black box.

A long silence broke into confused arguing and exclamations of dismay.

Dame Isabel said, "If this is your idea of a joke—"

"It is not a joke," said Sir Oliver gravely.

"I don't believe it," gasped Sir Oort.

"Where—*where* did you get that?" said Dame Isabel.

"It fell out of the sky into my backyard," said Aunt Lily.

"That's your explanation?"

"Isabel, I don't know how it happened. I don't know who is responsible," said Aunt Lily. "But I do know that, yes, it is what you think it is."

"What's going on?" said Daphne. "Everyone seems to know what that thing is but me."

"Hear, hear!" said Albert Blatch-Budgins.

"What is it?" said Nora, whipping out a notebook and pencil.

Sir Festus stood up and spread his arms. "Perhaps it would be best if *I* explained the history of this unique mechanism, which has, by strange chance, found a path back into our hands."

Nobody objected, but Jo did notice some squires roll their eyes.

"Twenty years ago, an experimental project was undertaken by the Order of Odd-Fish," intoned Sir Festus. "A formidable enterprise, its commencement fraught with controversy, its progress beset by hazards, its final outcome potentially catastrophic."

"Okay, okay," said Daphne.

"Our story begins, as many good stories do, with *me*," said Sir Festus. "While pursuing other research, I happened across some curious documents. Ancient documents, from shadowy sources. Documents of a disturbing nature. Terrifying documents. Shaken, I put the documents away and attempted to return to my research. But those documents . . . those documents! They would not let me rest!"

"In the end, did you bravely face the documents?" said Phil.

"I did," said Sir Festus. "For the documents contained blueprints for a device too intriguing for the Odd-Fish to ignore. After much debate, we voted to build the device. But the vote was close. Some among us felt we were toying with forces beyond our control. They argued the principles underlying this device were too bizarre to be accepted. They claimed——"

"I just said it was a silly idea," said Sir Alasdair.

"Same here," said Dame Delia. "I just thought it wouldn't work."

"What wouldn't work?" said Jo. "What was a silly idea?"

"Dame Lily supervised the construction of the device," said Sir Festus. "But everyone's assistance was required for this complex project, a project that had to be undertaken in strictest secrecy. For if any outsiders found out about what we were building—the deep and terrible forces we were wrestling with, the ancient energies we were unleashing, unbeknownst to the city, in our unassuming lodge on its quiet street—the same street where children would run about and play—the children! what about the children!—the mayor would have disbanded the Order of Odd-Fish without trial." Sir Festus quaked with the drama of it all. "The children, the children," he said again. It had a nice ring. He decided to run with it. "The children of Eldritch City. What manner of world were we passing on to them? Would it be a world in which the mechanical marvel we were constructing would exist not as a dark, fevered fantasy—*but as a grim reality?*"

"The grim reality is that we still don't know what you're talking about," said Phil Snurr.

"I will tell you," said Sir Festus. "We built . . . *an Inconvenience.*"

There was a long silence.

"An, um, what?" said Jo.

"It is a device that causes inconveniences," said Sir Festus.

"I told you it was a silly idea," said Sir Alasdair.

"I don't understand," said Jo.

"Nobody truly understands," said Sir Festus. "Not even those of us who built it. Nevertheless, let me try to explain what we do know. Suppose I wanted to annoy someone."

"Surely you don't need a machine for that?" said Jo.

"I mean seriously annoy them. Listen. First you steal a small item that belongs to the person. Then you lock it inside the Inconvenience. Then you get rid of the Inconvenience—toss it out the window, throw it in the garbage, feed it to a walrus, it doesn't matter how. For only if the Inconvenience is properly *lost* can it start operating—that is, the Inconvenience causes a sequence of coincidences and unlikely events to occur to that person, making their life terribly inconvenient."

Ian said, "Like they fall and break their neck?"

"No, that's too much. The Inconvenience only causes moderately irritating things to happen."

Jo felt she was starting to understand. "So when the package fell from the sky and hit that boy on the head—"

Sir Festus smiled. "Annoying, no?"

"And Korsakov and Sefino showed up, and Korsakov was shot, and Sefino was tied up—"

Sir Festus nodded. "A nuisance for both of them, no doubt."

"And the package said something about the Odd-Fish, and then Aunt Lily's magic show went haywire, Mr. Cavendish's head flew all around the restaurant—"

"How marvelously irksome. The Inconvenience must have been working at peak performance."

"Our house was fumigated, Sefino got drunk, senior citizens rioted, a Chinese millionaire tried to kill us, our plane was shot down, and then we were eaten by a fish and brought *here*—"

"What an exquisitely obnoxious twenty-four hours you've had. The device has performed beyond our wildest hopes. Ah, did you, by chance"—Sir Festus's eyes twinkled—"did you happen to turn its silver crank?"

"Yes!" said Jo. "Twice! What's it for?"

Sir Festus settled back, grinning. "That was my little addition. Whenever you turn the silver crank, whatever irritating situation you're in immediately becomes even *more* irritating."

Jo groaned. "But *why*? Why did it make all those insane things happen? Couldn't it just make us, I don't know, lose our keys or something? Don't you think it's all a bit over the top?"

"The Inconvenience has an extravagant sense of style," said Sir Festus. "That's part of its design. It annoys with panache."

"But who wanted to annoy us?" said Jo. "With panache?"

"Nobody wanted to annoy *you*," said Sir Festus. "Nothing of yours was found inside the Inconvenience. But the Inconvenience did contain Sefino's pipe, Korsakov's hat, Sir Oliver's scarf, and Dame Lily's ring. Someone wanted to annoy all of *them*."

Aunt Lily gave Jo an almost imperceptible nod of warning. Jo took the hint. *I should probably shut up,* Jo thought. *But why isn't anyone supposed to know my ring was in there?*

Maurice said, "Why were you all surprised to see the Inconvenience?"

"Nobody expected to see it again," said Sir Oliver. "Thirteen years ago—the very night we finished constructing it—the Inconvenience disappeared from the lodge. At first we thought it went missing because, well, that would be an inconvenient thing for it to do. But it soon became clear someone had *stolen* the Inconvenience. Apparently to make life inconvenient for Lily, Korsakov, Sefino, and me."

"Inconvenient? On the contrary," said Dame Isabel.

"I assure you, we have been *very* inconvenienced," said Sefino.

"I think not," said Dame Isabel.

"What do you mean?" said Aunt Lily.

"Oh, come now," said Dame Isabel. "This whole affair has been *quite* convenient for you. Thirteen years ago you, Colonel Korsakov, and Sefino were exiled from Eldritch City. All your memories of Eldritch City were removed so that you'd never find your way back here to stir up more trouble. And what happens? By some bizarre sequence of circumstances, caused by a device *you* supervised constructing, you are brought back to Eldritch City and your memories are restored. Not only that, but for reasons that completely elude me, an idle nostalgia for your era has set in, and you are now a folk hero in Eldritch City. So you're given a hero's welcome. It's beyond convenient. It's beyond coincidence. It's downright suspicious."

"What are you implying, Isabel?" said Aunt Lily.

"I *imply* nothing," said Dame Isabel coldly. "I merely state facts."

"But that's the least of our problems," said Sir Alasdair. "Ever since the lodge was stolen, the mayor has wanted to revoke our charter. He says we put the city in danger. Well, make no mistake: tonight will send him over the edge. Lily, Korsakov, and Sefino *are* in exile, after all. For them to return to Eldritch City—for them to stay at this lodge—is simply illegal."

Sir Festus spluttered, "Are you saying we should kick Lily, Korsakov, and Sefino out?"

"Excuse me, but is there another definition of *exile*?" said Sir Alasdair.

The table broke into a din of angry protests, but Sir Alasdair raised his hand.

"Quiet down! Listen to sense!" he said. "The mayor will let you stay for a few days. Maybe a week. And perhaps he'll allow Korsakov and Sefino to stay in town—with proper restrictions. But Dame Lily's crime is serious. Her presence is a challenge to the mayor's authority."

"I'll take care of my own problems with the mayor," said Aunt Lily.

Dame Isabel said, "You don't get it, do you, Lily? It's not just you, but *all* of us, who are endangered if you stay here. We are harboring you in this lodge illegally. That's just the excuse the mayor needs to shut down the Order of Odd-Fish. But hey, that doesn't matter to you. As usual, you are above the law, and the rest of us are unimportant."

"Sir Alasdair, Dame Isabel," said Sir Oliver. "When you joined the Order of Odd-Fish, you took an oath to defend and support your fellow knights to the death."

Sir Alasdair said, "If Dame Lily stays, the Order of Odd-Fish will no longer exist."

"No," said Sir Oliver. "If we refuse to let Dame Lily stay, *then* the Order of Odd-Fish will no longer exist. That is, it will no longer exist in any way that makes sense to me. And that is the last I will hear on the subject."

Dessert was over. The cockroaches had silently cleared the table during the debate. Some other cockroaches were gathered in the corner, and Jo noticed they had trombones, drums, violins, and a couple of instruments she couldn't identify. They were arguing over some greasy sheet music, which was being hastily passed around, torn and crumpled in the handling, leading to renewed outbursts of whispered quibbling.

Sir Oort cleared his throat. "Sir Oliver, you said that after dessert you would tell us who had stolen this lodge."

"That's right. I will," said Sir Oliver. "It was someone we all know."

In silence—except for the rustling of sheet music by the cockroaches in the corner—the Odd-Fish waited for Sir Oliver to speak.

Finally he said: "Sir Nils."

This meant nothing to Jo. But all around her, the table erupted: "Sir *Nils*?"—"It can't be!"—"He's dead!"—and Sir Festus shouted over them all: "Dame Lily *killed* Sir Nils! Everyone saw it—By crumb, that's why they exiled her!"

"Did you *see* Sir Nils?" said Dame Delia.

"I did," said Sir Oliver quietly. "Fortunately, he never saw me."

"Why did he steal the lodge?" said Sir Alasdair.

"I don't know."

"You didn't fight him?" said Sir Festus, his hand twitching. "You didn't even *yell* at him?"

"Sir Nils is now a servant of the Silent Sisters," said Sir Oliver. "Nothing can hurt him, or help him, anymore."

With a roar, Sir Festus leaped on the table.

"He's lucky! He got off *lightly*!" shouted Sir Festus. "Why, if I'd got my hands on him, I'd've snapped him in two and stirred my coffee with him! I'd've tied his arms and legs in a knot and used him as a tuffet! I'd've ground him up into a paste and made a hundred tasty snack-packs out of him! I'd've hollowed out his guts, inflated him with hot air, and gone ballooning! I'd've swung him around by his hair until I took off like a helicopter, and then I'd fly to a bakery on the moon, and buy myself a moon cake with my own moon name on it, and then I'd—"

A dignified cockroach coughed. "Sir Festus—if you would kindly not stand *on* the table—"

"Hell's monkeys, Cicero! Sir Nils is back from the dead, Sir Nils is working for the Silent Sisters, and all you can do is tell me to get off the table?"

"Sir!" said the cockroach sharply. "You *will* descend from the table. *Immediately,* sir."

Sir Festus seemed to deflate. Mumbling "Sorry, Cicero, a bit out of hand," he climbed down from the table. Cicero, the cockroach, eyed him with disdain.

"Just because the lodge was stolen," said Cicero, "does not mean that the staff will stand for breaches of propriety. Standing atop a table and blithering like a madman, *indeed*. Where has gone the dignity of the Odd-Fish?"

Sir Festus looked down in his lap.

"It's all very well for you to rave on to all hours of the night, but we butlers are run off our feet," said Cicero. "Benvenuto is already asleep."

"No, I'm not," said a cockroach curled up in the corner.

"Tradition demands that the Honorable Dance of the Odd-Fish commence after dessert," said Cicero. "I will not have tradition trifled with."

All protests from the weary knights and squires were drowned in the din of the small orchestra of cockroaches in the corner: an explosion of trombones, drums, and violins, sounding not so much like a band playing as a band falling down the stairs. The cockroaches that weren't in the band busied themselves pushing and tugging the squires and knights off their seats—even the venerable Sir Oort, who, not rising quickly enough for the cockroaches' taste, was unceremoniously dumped on the floor.

Jo had been looking forward to a pleasant after-dinner doze. She had not expected to be assaulted by an elderly cockroach who feebly hit her feet with his walking stick, muttering "Dance! Dance, will you, dance!"

Soon all of the knights and squires of the Odd-Fish were dancing, making the cramped room a chaos of flailing limbs. Jo managed to shout to Aunt Lily, "What am I supposed to do?"

"The Order of Odd-Fish ceremonial dance!" Aunt Lily yelled back. "We're required by the charter to do it after the feast!"

Jo tried to ask how, but Aunt Lily was whirled away in the shouting, stomping throng. Faces impassive, ceremonial robes hitched up to reveal purple-stockinged legs, their feet thrashing around furiously, the knights somehow looked both ridiculous and majestic.

The squires had a different dance. With a grin, Ian grabbed Jo and flung her across the room to Daphne; Daphne spun her around and sent her reeling over to Maurice; Maurice whisked Jo between his legs and sent her staggering over to Nora, who clutched Jo and yelled, "Throw *me*! Throw *me*!" Jo threw her over to Phil, starting to get the hang of it, and spun back to Ian, who, laughing, took her again and sent her flying over to Albert.

The cockroaches made it a point of honor never to practice their instruments. The rattle and squeak only got louder and more chaotic, a crashing noise barely punctuated by the banging drums. Jo spun through the crowd, clumsy and exhilarated. Glasses and bowls were smashed, and Sir Festus capered unchallenged across the dinner table, soon joined by Dame Myra and Sir Oort; Sir Oliver, still stuck in his costume, rolled all over the room, his eyes lit up and his arms flapping like the wings of a great, ungainly bird trying to fly; and just when it felt as though the dance could get no more frantic and destructive, and they were all about to collapse, the band sputtered to a halt.

"Now go to bed!" said Cicero sternly.

The change that came over the dancing Odd-Fish was instantaneous. From an unruly mob of violently dancing knights and squires, they suddenly became as calm as cows. The Odd-Fish quietly filed out of the banquet hall, and within minutes all had retired to their rooms.

Aunt Lily guided Jo up to a bedroom in one of the upper hallways of the lodge.

"I still don't understand," said Jo blearily. "Who's Sir Nils? What was all that about the Silent Sisters? And I still don't understand why I'm supposed to be dangerous——"

"Don't worry, Jo. I'll explain it tomorrow," said Aunt Lily, patting Jo's head. She looked at Jo wistfully; for a moment, it seemed she was about to say something more, but then she bit her lip, nodded, and repeated, "Tomorrow, okay? For now, just rest."

The door closed. Jo stumbled across the room, and with a sigh flopped onto her bed, the room spinning around her. She fell asleep instantly, bringing to a close the strangest Christmas of her life.

TEN

THIS is all well and good, but what about the Belgian Prankster?

The hottest controversy about the Belgian Prankster concerned the location of his secret base. Some claimed the Belgian Prankster lived in a luxurious complex of subterranean bunkers fifty miles beneath Antwerp; others swore they had witnessed with their own eyes a sprawling system of interlinked airborne platforms, held aloft by dozens of hot-air balloons, hovering malignantly in the ionosphere; and a committed few insisted that the Belgian Prankster did not possess, nor did he require, a secret base, for he transcended mere physical form and was present in all places and at all times as a pure abstraction—as ruthless and indestructible as a principle of mathematics.

Actually, the Belgian Prankster hung out at the Country Kitchen in Muscatine, Iowa.

His entire inner circle was assembled. Each member was a grotesque human being, and yet each a genius in some aspect of prankery: Mr. AAA, a one-eyed Romanian cryptologist; Mr. BBB, a terrifyingly scarred Icelandic assassin; Mr. CCC, an eight-foot-tall Uzbek hacker; Mr. DDD, a steel-toothed Korean toxicologist . . . and so on through the alphabet, up to Mr.YYY, a noseless Nigerian explosives expert, and Mr. ZZZ, a massive-headed Brazilian physicist.

None of the assembled twenty-six spoke. None even moved. For hours the committee sat silent and motionless at the long table, waiting for the Belgian Prankster to speak.

But the Belgian Prankster, too, was waiting. He was waiting for a man whom, he knew, could not help but come to him.

He was waiting for Ken Kiang.

Ken Kiang was sweating in the men's toilet.

"This is it," said Ken Kiang, loading his sixteenth-century Sicilian pistol. "Tonight I kill the Belgian Prankster."

The notion gave him no pleasure. Ken Kiang thought the Belgian Prankster was a splendid villain—in fact, *the* man to beat, were evil a competition. But Ken Kiang preferred not to see it as a mere competition. Surely there was room for plenty of villains in the world! He even admired the Belgian Prankster's evilness—good in its own way, if a bit juvenile for Ken Kiang's tastes—but no, *no,* there are things a self-respecting man will not take lying down.

Ken Kiang had been at La Société des Friandises Etranges, basking in his double triumph of shooting down Korsakov's plane and making Hoagland Shanks cry. But then he had glanced at the TV and saw the Belgian Prankster snickering and waving a sign that read:

ATTENTION KEN KIANG.

LILY, JO, KORSAKOV, AND SEFINO ARE STILL ALIVE.

AND YOU ARE A BOOBLY-BOOBLY-BOO-BOO.

"A boobly-boobly-boo-boo?" raged Ken Kiang. "A . . . *boobly-boobly-boo-boo*? He calls me a . . . a boobly-boobly-boo-boo in my hour of glory?—What *is* a boobly . . . ! No! Too far! *Too far!* Tonight, Belgian Prankster, *you will die!*"

Ken Kiang stormed out of the men's room, ready for action. He crossed the grimy dining area to the corner booth, where the Belgian Prankster and his minions sat around the chipped imitation wood table, brooding over their watery coffees and flaccid french fries.

Ken Kiang knew he was taking an awful risk. The Belgian Prankster was notorious for his unpredictable violence. Ken Kiang had heard of what he had done to the former Mr. HHH, a Cajun judo expert who had been late for a meeting—Mr. HHH had learned the hard way that you can't do judo without arms or legs. Or Mr. EEE, a French avant-garde fungologist who had dared critique the Belgian Prankster's hair. It was said the Belgian Prankster had instantaneously crushed Mr. EEE into a one-centimeter cube and tossed him into Mr. XXX's coffee. Mr. XXX had known better than to complain, and had drunk the coffee as though the gruesomely compressed Mr. EEE were nothing more than an unconventional creamer.

No, Ken Kiang knew he probably would not survive against the Belgian Prankster, or indeed his committee, for every man at the table was rumored to be nearly as evil as the Belgian Prankster himself. Truth be told, early in Ken Kiang's quest to be evil, he had desperately wanted to be on that very committee. He had even sent the Belgian Prankster a resume and a cover letter that explained that he would make an exemplary

Mr. JJJ. But the letter had gone unanswered; and so it was wounded pride, as well as a desire to prove himself more evil than any man at the table, that gave Ken Kiang the extraordinary nerve to approach them. Ken Kiang wondered what he could possibly say, once he reached the table, to prove how evil he truly was. It was oddly like junior high school, when he would approach the popular kids' table, hoping to make some joke, or say something clever, that would admit him to their inner circle.

He came to the table. Ken Kiang stood before the committee—and was at a loss. Nobody in the committee moved or spoke. No one paid any attention to him.

Suddenly it was *too* much like junior high.

"I once drank the blood of a freshly strangled kitten!" he squeaked.

The committee turned as one toward him. This was unprecedented. Nobody had dared interrupt a committee meeting before. Slowly Ken Kiang regained his confidence. He stood before the committee and regarded them coolly—an audacious man, a fearless man—Ken Kiang swallowed—a man about to suffer the Belgian Prankster's grotesque wrath?

"Ken Kiang, you've caught me at my weekly kaffeeklatsch," said the Belgian Prankster genially. "Please, won't you join us? I'm afraid, ah, 'kitten blood' isn't on the menu, but breakfast is served all day."

Ken Kiang sat down—and, with a jolt, realized he'd left his gun in the men's room. He half rose, then sat down again, blushing furiously.

"What's wrong, Mr. Kiang?" murmured the Belgian Prankster. "You look like you've lost something . . . ?"

"It is you who have lost, Belgian Prankster!" retorted Ken Kiang, recovering. If he couldn't shoot the Belgian Prankster, then he'd kill him using something else—he'd have to improvise. His eyes flicked around the room. Ken Kiang could feel the Belgian Prankster's committee staring at him. They were shocked, surely, by his reckless defiance of the Belgian? Let them be shocked! After all, he was *Ken Kiang*—the most evil man on the planet—and nobody, not even the Belgian Prankster, would insult him and live.

"So, welcome to my little social club," leered the Belgian Prankster. "Why don't you treat yourself to one of the Country Kitchen's mouthwatering breakfast specials? I can't vouch for the hash browns, which are indifferent at best, but the three-meat omelet is truly superb."

A waiter sidled up to Ken Kiang and handed him a menu.

In a flash of inspiration Ken Kiang barked "steak and eggs" and shoved the menu back at the waiter. Yes—steak and eggs must come with a steak knife! He could then kill the Belgian Prankster with the knife. It was a beautiful plan. Ken Kiang marveled at his own ingenuity. He was so clever it hurt.

"Actually, Mr. Kiang, it is fortunate you dropped by," said the Belgian Prankster. "There is some business I mean to conduct with you."

"Business!" cried Ken Kiang, standing. "There will be no 'business' between us, you mad Walloon, other than the business of vengeance!"

The Belgian Prankster snuffled merrily. "Still sore from my little joke, Mr. Kiang?"

"No man calls me a boobly-boobly-boo-boo and lives!"

"Oh, but Mr. Kiang, didn't you know?" said the Belgian Prankster slowly. "*I am no man.*"

Ken Kiang stared. The Belgian Prankster's nose, a bloated, purple thing that seemed to have a mind of its own, sniffled and twitched, tilting his goggles. The goggles caught the glare of the restaurant's fluorescent lights and suddenly flashed into a blinding rectangle of eerie green. Ken Kiang gazed at the hypnotic goggles and felt his courage drain away. The Belgian Prankster grinned; his mouth seemed too large to be real; his tongue flopped around like a dying fish.

Ken Kiang fell back into his seat.

"I merely stated facts," said the Belgian Prankster. "Your would-be victims *are* alive. In a place called Eldritch City."

"Never . . . never heard of it."

"Oh, haven't you?"

Ken Kiang wished his steak and eggs would hurry up. The sooner he could stab the Belgian Prankster and get out, the better. The whole situation was giving him the creeps, from the Belgian Prankster's crazy talk and nightmarish goggles to his motionless committee, who seemed to be frozen in place, eyes closed, in perfect silence and stillness—as though waiting for something too horrible to watch.

"Do you like balloon animals, Mr. Kiang?"

Ken Kiang blinked. "What?"

"Balloon animals. I began modestly in my career of prankery," said the Belgian Prankster. "Starting out, I worked as a clown for children's birthday parties. Balloon animals were my specialty. Why, I became so skilled that soon my clients couldn't tell the difference between one of my balloon dogs and a real dog! Balloon animals! Do you like them?"

"I guess . . ."

"I soon tired of inflating balloons and twisting them to look like animals," said the Belgian Prankster. "So I started inflating animals until they resembled balloons. Mr. Kiang, have you ever seen a dozen gerbils, pumped full of helium, float off into the sunset? It is a poignant spectacle. Sometimes they wave their tiny paws."

Ken Kiang frowned. "What's your point?"

"My *point?*" snapped the Belgian Prankster. "My *point* is that any so-called 'villain' can drink kitten blood. But have you ever inflated a little girl's kitten with pressurized hydrogen until it resembled a furry zeppelin? And then lit a match under it—a kind of feline *Hindenburg*, if you will? All this, at the girl's own birthday party? What? No? *No?* Well, I assure you, when the kitten exploded, the little girl's tears were plentiful, and tasted like wine.

But stick with sipping your . . . *kitten blood,* was it? Yes, of course. You must know what you like."

It took all of Ken Kiang's self-restraint not to lunge across the table and throttle the Belgian Prankster right there. This was worse, far worse than "boobly-boobly-boo-boo"—now the Belgian Prankster was mocking Ken Kiang's evilness. *Oh, we'll see about that,* said Ken Kiang to himself. He patiently awaited his steak and eggs, and the knife.

"You said there was some business you want to conduct with me," said Ken Kiang evenly.

"At last we come to the good stuff," said the Belgian Prankster. "You, Mr. Kiang, have enmeshed yourself in a web of inconvenience far larger and more intricate than you can fathom. From the moment you acquired that black box, you were entangled in it; but now, because of your rash actions, you are a doomed man, fate's plaything."

"You like to hear yourself talk," said Ken Kiang.

"You'll soon wish you had listened closer. You have no idea of the dangerousness of the girl on the plane you shot down."

"Jo Larouche?"

"Jo Hazelwood is her name."

Ken Kiang shrugged. "A harmless girl, by any name."

The Belgian Prankster looked at Ken Kiang for a long time.

"Let me tell you a story," he said finally. "It is not long, and you may learn something useful. In particular, you will learn there is more evil in Jo Hazelwood's fingernail than in a dozen of you."

Ken Kiang burst into laughter. He still hadn't perfected his evil laugh: instead of a satanic roar, he invariably dissolved into a braying giggle. He couldn't help it. Such giggling was the kind of fault that made Ken Kiang wonder if, deep down, he might actually be a decent fellow. No; the notion was too abhorrent to consider for long.

Ken Kiang wiped tears from his cheeks. "You're telling me that girl is evil?"

"She is the daughter of chaos," said the Belgian Prankster. "She is the bride of the apocalypse. She is the All-Devouring Mother."

Ken Kiang rolled his eyes. "Well, Belgian Prankster, you *are* a jokester. Unlike you, I have actually met this Jo—Hazelwood, was it?—and she is as threatening as a teaspoon."

"I was at her birth. And she is the teaspoon that will gouge out your eyes."

"You're afraid of a little girl?"

"No, Mr. Kiang. I do not fear Jo Hazelwood. I do not fear, period. Those emotions are no longer available to me." The Belgian Prankster's mouth widened into a display of rotten teeth. "I am Jo's devoted servant. And she—oh, oh—she is my perfect little flower."

"Er, um, ha," said Ken Kiang. The Belgian Prankster was starting to freak him out. "Can a fellow get some steak and eggs around here?" he called; but the kitchen was silent, the cash register deserted. Ken Kiang looked around, startled—at some point all the other customers had left. He was alone with the Belgian Prankster and his inscrutable committee, and the sudden emptiness of the restaurant was more unnerving than any threat.

"As promised, I will tell you a story," said the Belgian Prankster. "A little story I wrote all on my own, about how Jo was born. I cannot guarantee that you'll like it, Mr. Kiang; but at least you'll know something about Eldritch City before you go there."

"Eldritch City? What are you talking about?"

"I am sending you to Eldritch City."

"You're not sending me anywhere."

"You must prepare the way for me, Mr. Kiang."

"I'm not your errand boy, Prankster. You can't make me go anywhere."

"No, I won't *make* you." The Belgian Prankster placed an envelope on the table. "You will eventually go of your own free will."

Never did Ken Kiang want to murder the Belgian Prankster more than at that moment.

And then, as if on cue, the waiter came back and laid a dish in front of Ken Kiang.

He stared. There was no knife. It wasn't even steak and eggs.

"What is this?" he demanded.

"Huevos rancheros," said the waiter.

"I ordered steak and eggs."

The waiter and Ken Kiang looked at each other. Ken Kiang felt himself start to boil. The waiter picked his nose.

"Waiter."

"Yes?"

"I don't want huevos rancheros. I want—will you take your finger out of your nose?"

"Well, la-dee-da." The waiter wiped his finger on his apron. "If I had known we'd have such high-class swells tonight—why, I would've worn my solid gold tuxedo."

Ken Kiang clenched his fists. (It was all the more maddening because he did, actually, own a solid gold tuxedo.) He could hear the Belgian Prankster giggling. He had to take control.

"Listen. I want steak and eggs."

The waiter picked his nose.

"Can you get me steak and eggs?"

The waiter considered his finger.

"STEAK AND EGGS!"

"All right, I heard you," sighed the waiter. "I'll get you your precious steak and eggs, since your little world will obviously fall apart without them. Anything else?"

The Belgian Prankster suddenly said, "Yes. We do need something."

The waiter turned. "What's that, sir?"

"A steak knife," said the Belgian Prankster. "Mr. Kiang wanted a nice, sharp steak knife. To stab me with. Isn't that correct . . . Mr. Kiang?"

Ken Kiang was stunned.

"Perhaps *now* you're in the mood for my story," said the Belgian Prankster.

Ken Kiang looked down and said nothing.

"It's my very own short story I worked so very hard on." The Belgian Prankster extracted a damp wad of loose-leaf paper from his furs, unfolded it, and smoothed it out on the table. He cleared his throat theatrically; then he hunched over, and began to read, in a singsong voice:

"Once upon a time there was a town called Eldritch City. And in Eldritch City there was a young couple, Martin and Evelyn Hazelwood. Sir Martin and Dame Evelyn both belonged to a famous knighthood, the Order of Odd-Fish." The Belgian Prankster looked up. "Like it so far, Mr. Kiang?"

Ken Kiang offered no opinion.

"Wait, it gets better." The Belgian Prankster hunched over again, reading: "Dame Evelyn was pregnant with their first child. But Sir Martin noticed that the more the baby grew inside Dame Evelyn, the stranger she acted. Sometimes Dame Evelyn stared at Sir Martin as if she didn't recognize him. Other times she locked herself in her room and refused to see anyone. Once Sir Martin listened at the door of her room and heard Evelyn whispering to herself, again and again: 'I wish it was dead.' " The Belgian Prankster glanced up, and licked his lips. "See, Mr. Kiang? The plot thickens."

Ken Kiang clenched his teeth.

The Belgian Prankster continued to read. "One day, a dark, boiling cloud was seen far out in the ocean. For weeks it stayed on the horizon, almost out of sight, a huge black-green mass prowling back and forth.

"Then it started approaching the city.

"Every day Dame Evelyn stared out the window at the black-green cloud, whispering to herself. Sir Martin tried to talk to her, but she never gave him a straight answer. Sometimes she would cry. Sometimes she would scream at him. But the worst was when she would just give him a strange smile, and Sir Martin would hardly recognize her.

"Every day the black-green cloud drew closer. Nobody knew what it was or what would happen when it reached the city.

"Then, one day, everyone woke up to find the cloud had arrived.

"It was everywhere. The entire city was swimming in a dirty green soup. You couldn't see your own feet. Many people got sick from it. But the fog would not lift, nor would it blow away.

"Dame Evelyn shut herself up deep within the Hazelwood house. But there was no escaping the fog. No matter how much she sealed the windows or stuffed the cracks under the doors, the black-green fog always found a way to seep in.

"Dame Evelyn went into labor. But according to the doctors, Dame Evelyn was trying to hold the baby inside instead of pushing it out. She kept saying, 'I won't let it out. I won't let it out.'

"Meanwhile, the fog had hatched something. All over the city there was a racket of flapping in the filthy mist. Dogs and cats went missing, snatched up into the air. Then children started to disappear.

"The mayor declared an emergency. Everyone was ordered to stay inside. But that only made things worse. The unseen flying things started attacking each other, and the air was filled day and night with their screeches. The situation was getting desperate. Food was running out. Panic spread throughout the city.

"Then twelve women appeared.

"They stood outside the city gates, dressed in blue dresses and blue veils. Every inch of them was hidden. You couldn't see their faces, their hair, not even their hands. They stood in a circle around a veiled palanquin. They did not speak, nor did they move.

"The hysteria that had gripped the city froze at the sight of the veiled women. Even the howling things that flew about in the fog became still.

"Something was about to happen, but nobody knew what.

"Dame Evelyn was delirious. A week into labor, and she still hadn't given birth. The doctors didn't know what to do. Dame Evelyn was begging them to kill her baby. She wouldn't see Sir Martin, either; she said she didn't know who he was; then she cried that she had done a terrible thing and she could never look him in the eye again.

"The mayor sent out a messenger to the women, whom people had taken to calling 'the Silent Sisters.' Crowds watched the messenger boy approach the twelve women. But the closer he came to them, the slower, heavier, and more awkward his steps seemed.

"Then the messenger fell to the ground and lay still.

"This happened to everyone who approached the Silent Sisters. Nobody could even get close. But the next day, everyone in the city heard a voice in their head. It was an old woman's voice, scratching in the back of everyone's brain, whispering, 'Give us our daughter.'

"The mayor went to the city gates, where the Silent Sisters were standing, and called down to them: 'What daughter?'

" 'The Hazelwood baby,' answered the voice. 'She is ours. Give her to us.'

"All attention turned to the Hazelwoods. But the Hazelwoods had sent away the doctors and midwives and locked themselves in their house, refusing to talk to anyone.

"The mayor asked the Silent Sisters, 'Why do you want the Hazelwoods' baby?'

" 'She is the Ichthala,' came the voice. 'Give her to us, or we will destroy your city.'

"Nobody knew what *Ichthala* meant. The Silent Sisters said no more, nor did they move. But anyone who tried to leave the city became dizzy; if they pressed on, they would collapse. The city was under a strange and unbreakable siege. The black-green cloud did not lift. People were dying from the poisonous air. Still the Silent Sisters did not move. Some people started to say it might be better just to give the baby up. What was one baby compared to an entire city?

"What people once said in private, half ashamed, they now shouted in public. What right? What right did the Hazelwoods have to sacrifice the entire city, so they could keep their wretched baby?

"A mob gathered outside the Hazelwoods' house, throwing rocks through the Hazelwoods' windows, trying to break down the door. Others tried to defend the Hazelwoods. Fights broke out. The mayor assigned constables to guard the Hazelwoods' house. Three knights from the Order of Odd-Fish also volunteered to defend the Hazelwoods: Dame Lily Larouche, Colonel Anatoly Korsakov, and Sir Nils Van der Woort.

"That was when the Hazelwoods' neighborhood began catching on fire. Building after building burst into a strange kind of flames—a fire that was cold and gray and impossible to control. Anyone caught in the fire immediately turned into a statue of ash, and the mob trampled each other trying to escape. But the knights of the Order of Odd-Fish remained at their posts, protecting the Hazelwoods and their dangerous baby.

"The old woman's voice came one last time: 'Give us our daughter.'

"But even with an entire neighborhood on fire, and hundreds of people dead, the mayor still refused. So the city council removed him from office. They appointed a new mayor who promised to give the Silent Sisters what they wanted.

"The new mayor ordered the knights to leave. But Dame Lily, Colonel Korsakov, and Sir Nils refused to abandon the Hazelwoods. The mayor was furious. He said he could do nothing more. He opened the city gates.

"The Silent Sisters entered Eldritch City, heading for the Hazelwoods' house. Dame Lily, Colonel Korsakov, and Sir Nils were waiting for them. But when they finally arrived . . .

"Wait! Did you know, Mr. Kiang, that this has been captured on film? *Lights!*"

* * *

Ken Kiang blinked. He had been absorbed so deeply in the Belgian Prankster's story that he hadn't noticed Mr. XXX and Mr. QQQ were setting up a portable movie screen across the restaurant. Mr. NNN was fiddling with a film projector; Mr. ZZZ turned off the lights, and the projector started rattling away, casting a ghostly image upon the screen.

It was a house—the Hazelwoods' house. It seemed like a modest house, ordinary except that it was floating in a sea of filthy green fog, surrounded by hulks of chalky, smoking ash—the remains of a demolished neighborhood.

There were also three knights, mounted on armored ostriches. Ken Kiang looked closer—was he seeing things? But no, it was undeniable: two of the knights were younger versions of Lily Larouche and Colonel Korsakov. The ostriches flapped fitfully around the Hazelwoods' house, flying in and out of the picture—and something occurred to Ken Kiang.

"Hey, wait a minute. Ostriches can't fly."

The Belgian Prankster gave a tired sigh, heaved himself up, and waddled over to Ken Kiang. The Chinese millionaire shuddered—why had he said anything?—as the Belgian Prankster plopped down and threw his arm, draped in stinking furs, over Ken Kiang's shoulder.

"We could quibble about different species all night, Mr. Kiang, but I think you'll find the movie more entertaining." The Belgian Prankster leaned forward, his breath stinking of sour milk. "*These* ostriches can fly. So whaddaya say we just watch the show, huh?"

The scene had changed. The Silent Sisters were emerging from the fog, carrying their palanquin up the winding streets. Everyone scurried out of their way as they entered the Hazelwoods' neighborhood, where every building—except for the Hazelwoods'—had collapsed into mounds of steaming ash.

The camera drew back. On one side there were the Silent Sisters, trudging through the colorless ruins, advancing toward the

114

Hazelwoods' house. On the other side were the three knights, Dame Lily, Sir Nils, and Colonel Korsakov, standing guard around the house. The knights clicked a latch on their weapons, and both ends of their double-bladed lances ignited with orange flames. Their ostriches clucked nervously as the Silent Sisters separated, surrounding the Hazelwoods' house in a circle.

But the house—

Ken Kiang stared. It was as if some invisible hand were squeezing the house, stretching and twisting it as if it were taffy. The bricks were melting, dripping down the sides in streams; behind the windows red and purple lights flashed, shadows writhed against each other, curling flames jerked and danced—

The Silent Sisters drew their circle tighter.

The house convulsed. It was throbbing, groaning, pulsing in and out, as if any second it would explode into a million bits of brick and wood, flooding with black sludge seeping from cracks between the melting bricks, spurting from the windows, spraying out the chimney into the air. The house strained at the seams, swelling, heaving, gurgling.

The Silent Sisters drew closer.

The doors blew off the house. Every window exploded. The ostriches bucked in panic, the knights barely hanging on, as the house shrieked and stomped and blasted like a living monster.

"What just happened?" whispered Ken Kiang.

"Jo Hazelwood has been born," said the Belgian Prankster.

"That's because of *Jo*?"

"Ah-ah-ah! Watch!"

The Silent Sisters had tightened their circle even closer. The knights were trapped, hemmed in on all sides. Dame Lily, Sir Nils, and Colonel Korsakov brandished their flame-tipped lances, their faces grim.

Then Sir Nils spun and brought his lance crashing on Dame Lily's head.

Ken Kiang gasped.

"My favorite part," snuffled the Belgian Prankster.

"I thought they were on the same side!" said Ken Kiang.

"So did she!" giggled the Belgian Prankster.

Dame Lily sprawled off her ostrich, into the ash. At once Colonel Korsakov roared, charging toward Sir Nils—but Sir Nils yanked his ostrich's reins, flapping up into the sky. Korsakov wheeled his ostrich around and took off. The Silent Sisters quickly drew closer to the house as Sir Nils and Colonel Korsakov tangled in the air, their ostriches swooping, spinning, and clawing each other.

Sir Nils was a whirl of limbs, thrusting and whacking and hurling things at Korsakov, who seemed overwhelmed by his berserk energy. Suddenly Dame Lily was back in the battle, furiously slashing away at Sir Nils. The knights separated in the sky for a moment, Korsakov and Dame Lily on one side, Sir Nils on the other; then they dived back toward each other.

Ken Kiang watched the duel with shocked fascination. He couldn't believe this was the same doddering Colonel Korsakov and Lily Larouche he had met. These knights were terrifyingly fast and fierce. Their weapons were bulky antiques—complex boxes and clumsy double-sided lances spurting fire—and the way they fought baffled Ken Kiang, as they followed an etiquette of combat that made the duel seem like a violent ceremony. Time and again the knights let pass an opportunity to strike their opponent down, but then they would unexpectedly land blows that seemed to ignore laws of physics.

The house bucked and exploded again, blasting out slime and hundreds of snakes and lizards and toads. This was too much for the ostriches—all three panicked, bucked off their knights, and flew away as fast as they could. Sir Nils, Dame Lily, and Colonel Korsakov collapsed in a heap of armor and weapons on the half-destroyed roof of the Hazelwoods' house. The knights rolled away from each other and leaped up, ready to fight again.

Again the Silent Sisters' circle tightened. Colonel Korsakov half glanced, distracted—and Sir Nils spun his lance into a skewering wheel of fire, walloping Korsakov off the roof. Korsakov thudded onto the ground, lying in a heap of armor, his legs twisted unnaturally.

The Silent Sisters stepped over his body and entered the house.

Something in Dame Lily snapped. With a sudden fury that seemed to surprise even Sir Nils, she wildly slashed and lunged and kicked at him—Ken Kiang had never seen such reckless anger—Sir Nils tried to keep up his defenses, but Dame Lily smacked them aside, again and again, and finally, with a yell and a slash of fire, cut him precisely in half.

Sir Nils fell apart, ripped in two like a piece of paper. Dame Lily stood on the roof of the Hazelwoods' house, panting, staring down at Sir Nils's smoking, torn-apart body, her eyes filled with horror and heartbreak.

Then the roof collapsed, the ground collapsed beneath the house, and the whole house, Dame Lily, the Hazelwoods, the Silent Sisters, and what was left of Sir Nils went crashing down into a flaming hole. The green fog was sucked in as well, draining down the hole as if a stopper had been pulled. The scene lingered for a long minute, off-kilter and strangely incomplete. The mist was gone, the Silent Sisters were gone, the streets were empty. Nothing stirred in the wasteland of Eldritch City.

The movie projector spluttered to a halt. Ken Kiang was left in the dark, sitting uncomfortably close to the Belgian Prankster.

"Well, Mr. Kiang, what a night this has been. I think you'll agree that was a first-rate multimedia presentation. And look! Your steak and eggs."

Ken Kiang looked. Sometime during the film the waiter had brought his steak and eggs, and with it, the steak knife he had wanted so badly—what seemed like a lifetime ago.

"Shall I wait while you eat your breakfast?" asked the Belgian Prankster politely. "There's still a bit more to tell."

Ken Kiang did not respond. The Belgian Prankster shrugged, rose, and waddled back to the opposite side of the table.

"Only Dame Lily survived," said the Belgian Prankster, settling in to his chair. "Martin and Evelyn Hazelwood were killed. It seemed the Silent Sisters had taken the Hazelwood baby with them, for they had vanished as mysteriously as they had come.

"In Eldritch City, the punishment for murder is amnesia and exile. The new mayor was furious that the knights had disobeyed him, and many citizens now supported him. His judges declared Lily Larouche, Colonel Korsakov, and Korsakov's butler, Sefino, guilty of murdering Sir Nils Van der Woort. Their memories were confiscated and they were exiled."

"Guilty of murder?" said Ken Kiang slowly. "But Sir Nils attacked *them*!"

"The legal issues don't interest me, Mr. Kiang. Nor did they interest the mayor. He found a reason to exile them, and, flimsy as it was, he got them exiled."

"And that's the end?"

"No," said the Belgian Prankster. "For the Hazelwood baby *was* found. Dame Lily had smuggled the child out of the catastrophe. And with the help of another knight, Sir Oliver Mulcahy, she took the baby with her into exile."

"Why are you telling me this?" said Ken Kiang. "What does this have to do with me?"

The Belgian Prankster began laughing silently, his body wiggling in ghastly merriment.

"Who are you?" shouted Ken Kiang.

"I am Sir Nils Van der Woort," said the Belgian Prankster.

"What? But you said Sir Nils was killed—chopped in half—"

"I *was* killed," guffawed the Belgian Prankster. "I *was* chopped in half. But my friends stitched me back together. I'm not what I used to be, but what of it? I am a servant of the Silent Sisters, and nothing can hurt me, or help me, anymore."

The Belgian Prankster shook like a horrible jelly, snuffling with unholy mirth—Ken Kiang could not bear him a moment longer; with a yell he leaped to his feet and hurled the steak knife.

The knife whistled swiftly through the air and plunged into the Belgian Prankster's laughing face with a sickening THUP.

Ken Kiang stared. The Belgian Prankster continued to laugh, even as the knife stuck between his eyes. But this was not what transfixed Ken Kiang—it was just that he'd never expected the Belgian Prankster's head to *deflate*.

A hissing squeal filled the room. The Belgian Prankster's face shriveled and collapsed, as did the bodies of Mr. XXX, Mr. QQQ, Mr. NNN, Mr. FFF—the entire committee—with a shriek and a howl, their mouths opened, spewing stale air, leaping up to the ceiling and shooting around the room, spluttering into shreds, and the Belgian Prankster's head flew across the table, right up to Ken Kiang, a shriveled empty skin, eyeless and toothless—Ken Kiang screamed—

And the face collapsed onto the table in a rubbery heap.

For this "Belgian Prankster" was not the real Belgian Prankster. He, and his committee, were nothing more than ingeniously complicated balloon animals.

Ken Kiang was deeply humiliated by the prank.

The Belgian Prankster had also stuck him with the bill.

ELEVEN

Jo woke up and for a moment had no idea where she was.

Gone was the vast jeweled egg she'd woken up in every other morning of her life. Her new room was barely large enough for her narrow bed, a wardrobe, and a scruffy wooden desk. Morning sunlight quietly streamed in from a little arched leaded-glass window. There was a tiny bathroom and another door leading out to the hallway. That was all.

Jo suddenly realized she was still wearing her waitress uniform. At once she threw off the sheets and scrambled out of bed—she couldn't get out of the crusty, stinky thing fast enough—hopped, stumbled out of the pink polyester, left it in a heap on the floor, and staggered into the bathroom. She turned on the shower: hot water: glorious.

Jo had never savored a shower so much. She scrubbed every corner of her body in an agony of relief, washed her hair twice, and for a long time just stood under the hot water, breathing the steamy air. She finally came out, wrapped in a fluffy white towel, and opened her window to look out at Eldritch City waking up below: people walking down the sidewalks, market stands being set up, cars and elephants moving in the boulevards. She took a deep breath of the morning air. From up here, it felt as though the city were all hers.

Just then someone knocked on her door. She opened it a little—Sefino.

"Already up and about, I see." The cockroach glanced at Jo and coughed in embarrassment. "Do put some clothes on. Dame Lily would like you to come to her room for breakfast. She has something to tell you."

It was a long breakfast.

The eggs and toast went cold, untouched, as Aunt Lily told Jo about her strange and violent birth. Jo could only stare in appalled shock. The story was the same the Belgian Prankster had told Ken Kiang, except for one detail.

"I was engaged to him," said Aunt Lily.

Jo nearly spit out her coffee. "You were engaged to—you were going to marry the *Belgian Prankster?*"

"No, Jo. I was engaged to *Sir Nils.* I still can't believe what he's turned into." Aunt Lily closed her eyes. "Maybe losing my memory was for the best. It must've been a relief to forget it all and walk away."

Jo stared at her wasted breakfast. She felt so shaken she couldn't think straight. "Then we shouldn't have come here," she said. "We should've stayed in California. We have to go home!"

"We can't." Aunt Lily's voice was strained but calm. "I know this is awful for you, Jo, but it's even more dangerous for you outside the city. The situation is changing fast. Sir Oliver is afraid the Belgian Prankster has something terrible planned."

"Who knows who I really am?"

"You and I. Sir Oliver. Colonel Korsakov and Sefino. That's all."

"Not the other knights?"

"We can't tell them everything right away."

Jo felt more and more helpless. "Why not? If they're our friends, why can't we tell them?"

"Because some people, and not just crazy ones—" Aunt Lily paused, as if what she was saying was painful. "They blame you for nearly destroying Eldritch City."

"Me?" It was as if the ground had reeled under her. "But I was just a baby!"

"That makes them all the more afraid," said Aunt Lily. "Even today, the neighborhood where your parents lived is deserted. All because the Silent Sisters wanted you."

"But I don't even understand who these Silent Sisters are!"

"Nobody does. There's only rumors, old legends . . . Sir Oliver and I are trying to figure it out." Aunt Lily looked carefully at Jo. "All we know is that if anyone found out that you are the Hazelwood baby, your life would be in danger."

Jo felt such a rush of shock she could hardly choke out, "Why?"

"Because some people believe if the Ichthala returns, the city *really will be* destroyed," said Aunt Lily. "All of it. And for good."

Jo shuddered. That word, *Ichthala*—just hearing it made her skin prickle. "Then why did you and Colonel Korsakov fight to protect me?"

"I knew your parents had nothing to do with the Silent Sisters," said Aunt Lily. "They were my friends. They were Odd-Fish."

"But so was Sir Nils!" said Jo. "And you were engaged to him!"

Aunt Lily closed her eyes. "I'll tell you about Nils some other time. For now, I'm going to keep your ring in my jewelry box. If you were caught with it . . ."

Jo shook her head. "Why'd they make me a ring if I was a monster?"

"Jo, you're *not* a monster. Korsakov and Oliver don't think so, either. Most people know the Ichthala stuff is just a crazy old legend, it's—"

"But it's not just a legend!" said Jo. "If those Silent Sisters really did come to Eldritch City, if there really were fires and earthquakes, and if the Belgian Prankster—"

"Jo, don't." Aunt Lily held up her hand. "Just because some cult—some crazy old women—tried to kidnap you, it doesn't mean they were right about who you are."

"But even Sir Oliver wrote that I was dangerous!"

"We weren't sure back then. It was a risk. I suppose it still is." Aunt Lily rubbed her temples. "At my trial, they asked me what happened to you. I said that your mother *had* given birth to a monster. And that the Silent Sisters took it."

"And that's what everyone believes?"

"Well . . . no," said Aunt Lily. "Some people think the Silent Sisters disappeared only because *I* killed the Hazelwood baby."

Jo stared back at Aunt Lily in horror. "Would you have? If I *had* been a monster?"

"Jo, this is hard enough." Aunt Lily looked down. "People were asking questions when we first got here. I told everyone that you're my niece from California. Oliver thinks we can pull it off. Anyway, it's worth it. You don't belong with the Silent Sisters. You belong with us. With me." Aunt Lily took her hand. "You're the only daughter I'll ever have."

Jo's hand sat awkwardly in Aunt Lily's. She stared at her knees and murmured, "What am I supposed to do?"

"Nothing for now. Sir Oliver and I are working on this. Just try to blend in, lead the life of a normal Odd-Fish squire."

Jo pulled her hand away, incredulous. "Try to blend in? Be normal? After everything you've just told me, how could I possibly—"

Someone knocked on the door. Aunt Lily turned and called out, "Yes? Who is it?"

Dame Delia poked her head in. "Everybody's waiting for you, Lily."

Aunt Lily nodded. "We're on our way!"

"Where are we going?" said Jo as Aunt Lily started to gather her things.

Aunt Lily stood up. "Downtown. To Commissioner Olvershaw's. Today we are making you a proper squire."

Downstairs there was much coming and going and jostling in the halls as knights and squires and butlers prepared for the day. Jo descended the stairs slowly, still in a state of numb shock.

The common room was a busy chaos, everyone intent on some project, rushing and fussing and bumping into each other. Dame Isabel and Nora McGunn were repairing a long silver horn stuck into a black vinyl sack studded with chrome spigots—the device, Aunt Lily had explained, that Dame Isabel used to capture her unusual smells. Sir Oliver, Sir Alasdair, and Sir Oort breezed through the room, Sir Oort rapidly hopping around the two larger, slower gentlemen, waving his hands, energetically outlining a metaphysical argument that seemed to leave them unconvinced. And out the front window Dame Delia led a lavishly costumed elephant out of the stables, singing contentedly to herself. Jo watched it all with dazed envy, her head still buzzing. The cheerful uproar of the common room comforted her and almost made Aunt Lily's story of her birth seem safely distant, even unreal. She suddenly wanted something of her own to do, something that would give her a rightful place in the bustle.

"Good morning, Jo!" boomed Colonel Korsakov. "Come down, come down!"

Colonel Korsakov was happily idle in the commotion, sunk side by side with Sir Festus in overstuffed chairs near the fireplace. The gigantic head of a shaggy, viciously fanged, extravagantly horned beast was mounted over the fireplace's mantel, its eyes frozen in bewilderment, its gargantuan bulk making the rest of the room feel cramped.

"The Prancing Gobbler!" said Sir Festus to Jo. "I couldn't help noticing you admiring it."

"It's . . . large," said Jo carefully.

"Now *that* was a beast," said Sir Festus with great satisfaction. "Took ten of us to bring him down. Those were the days, eh, Korsakov?"

"Ah, the glories of youth," said Colonel Korsakov wistfully. "I'm afraid those days are behind us forever."

"Nonsense!" said Sir Festus. "What we lose in vigor, my good man, we only gain in cunning. And Korsakov . . . you *do* have some unfinished business here in Eldritch City . . ."

Colonel Korsakov's eyes widened. "You don't mean . . ."

"I do," said Sir Festus. "The Schwenk."

"The . . . *Schwenk?*" said Korsakov in a strangled roar. "The Schwenk is still loose in Eldritch City? After all these years? The Schwenk still roams our streets unchallenged? I knew it, Festus. My digestion was distinctly disturbed last night, though I could not pin down the cause. Why, the Schwenk must have learned of my arrival and was capering outside my window, giggling Schwenkishly, engaging in rampant Schwenkery, even as I tossed and turned . . . oh, the Schwenk, Festus, the infamous Schwenk, the unholy *Schwenk!*"

"What's the Schwenk?" said Jo.

"A fearsome beast," said Korsakov. "Some say even more fearsome than the Prancing Gobbler."

"*You* say that," said Sir Festus.

"All due respect, my dear Festus, but everybody does," said Korsakov. "Or they would, if the Schwenk could ever be found. You see, Jo, when I was a young squire, not unlike yourself, I was given the quest to slay the Schwenk. So far the clever beast has eluded me."

"Permit me to say it has eluded you for nearly *fifty years*," said Sir Festus.

"Hmmm, well," said Korsakov uncomfortably. "These things take time."

Jo said, "So that's what squires do? Slay Schwenks?"

"*I* get to slay the Schwenk," said Korsakov. "You'll get your own quest at the Municipal Squires Authority. From Commissioner Olv . . . Olver . . ."

Jo remembered the name: "Commissioner Olvershaw?"

Korsakov winced. "Yes . . . well . . . ahem. The commissioner will have to register you first, of course."

"That's what we're doing today," said Aunt Lily, coming around the corner, trailed by a group of curious squires: Ian Barrows, Albert Blatch-Budgins, and Daphne Brockbank.

"Do you mind if we come along?" said Korsakov. "I intend to register Ian myself."

Jo hadn't seen Ian since they were separated at the banquet; she had almost forgotten about him. "So you're not a squire yet, either?" she said.

Before Ian could answer, Nora looked up from Dame Isabel's machine and called out, "Ian just hangs around the lodge and *pretends* to be a squire."

Ian leaned against the wall. "This from a girl who spends every day collecting *smells*?"

"At least I don't have a half-grown mustache."

"You should try it, Nora. It could only help your face."

Nora snorted and turned to Korsakov. "Why on earth are you taking on Ian Barrows as a squire?"

"Sir Oliver recommended Ian, and that is enough for me," said Korsakov, frowning at Nora. "I understand he is a cousin of Sir Oliver's squire, Dugan Barrows."

"Where *is* Dugan?" wondered Sir Festus. "It's disgraceful he missed the feast. How long has he been gone? Two days?"

Albert Blatch-Budgins smiled. "Ah, there's always something up with Dugan."

Nora skirted around the room and popped up at Jo's side. "Hey, Jo! Sefino told me to fetch you. C'mon!"

"Right now? Okay, okay!" said Jo as Nora tugged her sleeve, leading her down the dusty, debris-strewn hallway. Once they were out of earshot, Nora turned to Jo with dancing eyes.

"So you're really getting registered as a squire today? You and Ian?"

"Yes," said Jo. "Why do you give him such a hard time?"

"I give *him* a hard time? That's rich! Don't worry, Ian can handle it. It's about time they made him a squire—I was getting embarrassed for him. Too bad I won't be there to see it."

"Aren't you coming?"

"I've got other business in the city." Nora ducked her head, looked around carefully, and added, "Actually, Jo, I've been meaning to get a minute alone with you."

"What about?"

"I think you know . . . I was trying to tell you last night."

"What?"

"Come on, Jo. The Ichthala."

The word *Ichthala* hit Jo like a bucketful of ice water. At once she tightened all over—was it possible Nora knew?

Nora chattered on, "Now, no disrespect, but I think Dame Lily isn't telling us everything about the Ichthala. That's why I think if we worked together, Jo, we could figure out just what the Ichthala is, *where* it is. Living with Dame Lily for so long, I bet you have tons of clues, don't you? Most people think the Ichthala is dead, you know, or that the Silent Sisters have her locked up somewhere. But I think the Ichthala walks among us. . . . Hey, what's wrong? You look sick."

Jo managed to say, "What do you think this Ichthala looks like?"

"Ooh, anything, don't you think? I imagine the Ichthala is some kind of orange octopus with eyes all over its head, and each of its tentacles is bristling from top to bottom with claws and spikes and goo-shooting tubes. And it can fly, too. But you know,

I don't imagine it having wings? Isn't that funny? Of course, that's nothing what it's like on the show, although it's still a monster, but . . . What do *you* think the Ichthala looks like?"

"Nora, you might not believe this, but I'd never even heard that word before this morning."

Nora gasped. "*Really?* Well, I guess that makes sense, Dame Lily having her memory removed and everything, but . . . well, that settles it. You've got to watch the show."

"The show?"

"That's why I'm going downtown. You remember I said it's all been *foretold,* don't you? Oh look, I'm already late! Here we are, the butler's lounge. Bye!" Nora turned and ran back down the hall, leaving Jo speechless.

Nora had left Jo in a quiet corner of the lodge, next to a closed door that came up to her waist. After a moment, Jo knocked hesitantly, and the door immediately opened, revealing a fat-faced cockroach with an extraordinary mustache.

"Yes? Well? Hmmm?" growled the insect. "What do you need?"

"Is that Jo?" came Sefino's voice. "See her in, Umberto, see her in. Now, as I was saying . . ."

Jo whispered, "What's this all about?"

"This," muttered Umberto, shoving a newspaper into her hand. "Come on."

Jo ducked inside and found herself stooping in a round, low room hung all around with rotten red velvet drapes, stale smoke, and frayed golden tassels. All the cockroaches were here, lounging around a circular table, finishing their breakfasts and listening to Sefino, who was in the middle of a rousing speech:

"Gentlemen, this is the final straw!" roared Sefino.

"Hear, hear!" cried the other cockroaches.

"We cannot laugh this off anymore," said Sefino. "These gossip-mongers have gone too far!"

"Too far! Yes!" shrieked the cockroaches. "Ooo!"

"One newspaperman in particular has repeatedly crossed the line," declared Sefino. "Exhibiting a reckless disregard for our reputations and, indeed, the truth—I hesitate to speak his infamous name—but it must be done—yes, I accuse *Chatterbox*—"

"No! Boo!" howled the cockroaches. "Down with Chatterbox!"

Jo glanced at the newspaper Umberto had given her. It was that morning's *Eldritch Snitch,* and it had a picture of Sefino in a plane, crying and hiding his eyes in terror. The headline read:

SIMPERING SEFINO SUNK IN SKY-HIGH SKIRMISH

KORSAKOV'S COWARDLY COCKROACH CALLOWLY CRINGES, CRIES IN CATASTROPHIC COMBAT

INFAMOUS INSECT INDIGNANTLY IRKED IN INSIPID IMBROGLIO

"How do we respond to these attacks on our honor?" said Sefino. "For our honor has been attacked, gentlemen."

Cicero stirred. "Our honor remains intact, Sefino. No newspaperman can take that from us."

"Our honor is intact, Cicero, but no reputation, however honorable, can withstand the ceaseless slanderous scribblings of these mischievous muckrakers, a ruthless rabble for whom no libel is too licentious, no hearsay too hurtful, to perniciously print in their poppycock periodicals!"

"Hooray!" shouted the other cockroaches. "Hear! Hear!"

"This is what I shall do"—Sefino pointed at Jo—"I shall take Jo Larouche, an eyewitness to the event, to the *Eldritch Snitch* and demand they print *her* version of the story. Gentlemen, we shall combat their scurrilous lies with the light of truth; we shall smash their sneaking slander with the sword of justice!"

"Whoa, what?" said Jo, startled. "I never said I'd write an article!"

"But you must. Oh, Jo, I beseech you, come to our aid in this noble struggle against a tyranny of tattlers, ink-inebriated idlers who hold decent gentlemen up for scorn, atrocities dripping from their pens, calumny erupting from their typewriters, a billion-headed beast of babblement that shall not be silenced until it is *slain!*"

"Hear! Hear! Woo!" shouted the cockroaches. (They all seemed happy to have Sefino back.)

"But why do they write these articles about you?" said Jo.

"Jo, Jo," chuckled Sefino. "As you can tell, we are extremely glamorous."

At this, all the cockroaches fell into fits of grotesque preening.

"Yes, the load we bear is heavy," said Umberto. "Understandably, the public clamors for details of our private lives. This is only to be expected, but *there are limits.*"

"I cannot help it if I am fascinating," declared Sefino.

"Hear, hear!" shouted the cockroaches.

"But my private life *will not* be the entertainment of this city!"

"No!" chorused the cockroaches.

"Though my private life *is* entertaining," admitted Sefino.

"Who could deny it?" roared the cockroaches.

An ugly and withered cockroach laid hold of Jo, causing her to yelp and step back.

"Do not fear! I understand your cries of ecstasy," said the cockroach, leaning forward. "It is not often that I condescend to touch my admirers. I am, of course, the great Benozzo."

Jo's skin winced under the cockroach's slick, hairy claw. "Please take your hands off me."

"Yes, the thrill overwhelms you? Your heart palpitates with passion. You wonder if you can bear the exaltation of my touch for a moment longer. Yet you wish it might linger eternally . . . *I understand.* But listen. I, the great Benozzo, like to take walks."

"Now you're drooling on me."

"Savor it," said Benozzo. "And listen. It is my custom to take long walks through the neighborhood. It is one of the simple pleasures I have in my life. But how, my lady, how, I ask you, how, yes, I say it again, how, *how* can I take my little walks—I like to call them my 'constitutionals'—*how* can I engage in my constitutionals, when I am *stalked,* yes, stalked, I say to you, *hunted,* even, *hounded,* if I may be so bold as to say, *hounded like a common animal,* by these pitiless popinjay paparazzi of the popular press?"

"If I write this article," said Jo, "will all of you stop making speeches at me?"

"We make no promises," said Sefino.

The morning's cool had burned away, and the city was swamped in a sticky tropical heat as the Odd-Fish prepared their caravan to go downtown. The elephants were painted with colorful, swirling designs and cloaked in dazzling mats of gold and purple, brass necklaces, and jewel-studded bracelets. Jo rode on Ian's elephant, her arms locked around his waist, awkwardly squashed up against him to keep from falling off. Jo felt squirmy and tense. Until yesterday, she had never even talked to a boy her own age before.

Ian was in high spirits. "I could hardly sleep last night."

"Are you nervous?" said Jo over his shoulder, glad to find she wasn't alone.

"I just don't want to screw this up," said Ian. "I never dreamed I'd meet *the* Colonel Korsakov—now I'm going to be his squire! You're lucky to be Dame Lily's squire, by the way. She's a legend."

Jo wiped sweat from her brow. "Back home, she's a washed-up actress. The idea of my aunt being a knight seems ridiculous."

"All the knights in the Order of Odd-Fish are a little ridiculous," said Ian proudly. Then his voice dropped to a whisper. "By the way, did Dame Lily tell you what Olvershaw does to you?"

"What? No. Who is Olvershaw, anyway?"

"He's in charge of all the squires in the city. Supposed to be a really tough customer. Dugan told me there's some kind of initiation we have to go through." A cluster of orange-and-red fruits drooped from a passing tree branch. Ian plucked two off and handed one to Jo. "Here, try one of these!"

"Thanks!" said Jo, and kept one hand on Ian's waist as she took a cautious bite. The fruit was juicy, warm, and tart. She took another bite—it was delicious.

For a while Jo and Ian quietly ate their fruit, taking in the chaotic city. The road was jammed with coaches, elephants, bicycles, and puttering cars; everywhere there were people haggling, shouting, chatting, and bellowing prices, news, and advertisements. Jo's elephant stomped down the twisting streets, ducking under low arches hung with curling vines, squeezing between bright minarets and twisting, crooked towers. The city was a lush garden of temple-like ruins swimming in millions of delicate, colorful flowers, mellowing in the shade of huge bulbous trees, side by side with flimsy shacks slapped together from corrugated metal, cracked plastic, and tattered cloth, dark and smoky and swarming with barefoot children, dogs, and shuffling heaps of rags that on second glance were very old people. The seething mix of architectural grandeur and squalor, the sticky heat, the crushing, surging throngs of people, all drowning in tropical vegetation—trees, fruit, vines, moss, flowers tumbling out everywhere—were totally alien to Jo, and every corner overwhelmed her eyes with detail: orange iguanas scampering through the trees, alleys choked with heaps of broken crystal machines, sidewalks whose every inch was carved with tight rows of hieroglyphics.

Where did her parents fit in all this? Jo tried to imagine them haggling in the markets, eating breakfast in the hanging gardens, dodging through the crowds on bicycles—but it was no use. She didn't even know what her mother and father looked like.

Then Jo saw Nora on the other side of the street, arguing with a hunched-up little bundle of wrinkles, curly black hair, and twitching shreds of cloth pushing a metal shopping cart crammed full of film canisters, tied with string and hanging off the sides, clanking and clattering. The man hustled the cart away from Nora, pushing back her money, swatting her hands away from the canisters.

Jo nudged Ian. "Isn't that Nora? What's she doing?"

Ian wiped his mouth and frowned. "So that's why she didn't come . . . I should've known."

"What's she trying to get?"

"The next episode of that show of hers. She's obsessed." Ian's voice had turned strangely bitter. "By the way, have you noticed who's behind us?"

Jo turned and saw that a car was following their elephant: a red, narrow triple-decker automobile, about twenty feet tall, like a rolling tower. A man in a red uniform stood on top, and other red-uniformed men moved behind the windows of the upper and lower decks.

"Police," said Ian. "They've been following us ever since we left the lodge."

"Really? Why?"

"You heard Dame Isabel last night. Lily and Korsakov are exiled. They're here illegally."

"Why haven't the police arrested them already?" said Jo.

"Lily and Korsakov are too popular to arrest right now," said Ian. "The mayor can't do anything right away. So the police are just keeping an eye on them."

"I don't know what I'd do if Aunt Lily went to jail," said Jo. "She's the only person I know in this city. What if she *did* get arrested?"

"The Order would take care of you. Anyway," Ian said earnestly, "you know me, right?"

It was hard to see how this awkward boy with a wispy mustache could help her, but Jo liked him for saying it anyway.

Ian said, "Look over there. That's where we're going, the Municipal Squires Authority."

Jo peered over to where Ian was pointing—a caved-in temple overgrown with gnarled trees. But then Ian steered the elephant in a different direction.

"What are you doing?" said Jo.

"We've got to detour," scowled Ian. "Nobody goes through Hazelwood's Row."

Jo caught a glimpse of the neighborhood—a deserted wasteland of wrecked buildings and gravestones, without even a single tree or flower. It was as if some other ghastly city had been spliced in from elsewhere, so jarring it almost seemed unreal. Jo stared, trying to understand. *That* was all caused by her birth?

"My mother's in there," said Ian quietly. "The Hazelwoods' baby killed her. The Hazelwoods' baby killed a lot of people. I know Dame Lily and Colonel Korsakov fought to save the Hazelwoods, and Sir Oliver said that Ichthala stuff is supposed to be nonsense, but . . ."

Jo looked away from Ian, curling her toes tight, desperately trying not to show her alarm.

"I can't help it," he said. "I hate them. I hate the Hazelwoods."

Jo's heart clenched. If Ian knew who she was, he'd . . . No. She couldn't think about it.

"Dugan had a quest in Hazelwood's Row once," said Ian. "Even though nobody's allowed to go in. He wanted me to come with him, but I—"

Jo couldn't take it anymore; she had to change the subject. "Yeah? So you've gone on quests before?"

"What? Oh . . . well, sure, I've done some quests." Ian relaxed a little, stroking his mustache. "Actually . . . well, more like I've helped out Dugan a couple times."

"Who *is* this Dugan everyone's talking about?"

"My cousin. One of the best squires in town. You'd have to be, if you were Sir Oliver's. But Dugan likes to think of himself as . . ." Ian hesitated. "He's not as clever as he thinks he is. One of these days he'll get in over his head. Maybe he is now."

"Because he's been missing for two days?"

"Dugan's been running with a sketchy crew lately. For instance . . . shhh, I'll tell you later." The caravan stopped, and Ian turned around, smiling. "We're here!"

TWELVE

THE Municipal Squires Authority's offices were housed in the remains of a sumptuous carved temple. The temple had long ago fallen into disrepair, its religion lost, its gods forgotten; now twisty trees grew out of the ruins, breaking open the roof and walls, and roots oozed over tumbled blocks like melted cheese. The temple's halls had been partitioned into dozens of crude wooden stalls, hung with a crazy quilt of tents and cloth-covered galleries—squalid, dimly lit, and crawling with sweaty civil servants in ill-fitting suits.

After stabling their elephants, a clerk ushered Jo, Ian, Aunt Lily, Korsakov, and Dame Delia into a waiting room furnished with plastic chairs, ratty couches, and a card table with a coffee percolator and doughnuts. Some squires were already here: Phil and Maurice lingered at the table, Albert sat reading on a couch, and Daphne circulated around the room, chatting with squires from other orders.

A clerk sidled up to Aunt Lily and whispered in her ear. She turned to Jo. "Olvershaw wants Delia and me to fill out some paperwork upstairs. We'll be back."

"Aunt Lily," Jo said in a low voice, "who is this Olvershaw everyone's talking about?"

"Oh, you'll know Olvershaw when you meet him," said Aunt Lily, and made a low noise that wasn't quite a laugh. She and Dame Delia disappeared chuckling down the hall. It didn't give Jo much confidence.

Maurice punched Ian's arm. "So they're finally going to make you a proper squire, huh? It's about time."

"You've met Jo, right?" said Ian. "She's getting registered, too."

Maurice looked Jo over. "Being a squire can be rough. Think you can handle it?"

Ian said, "Lay off her, Maurice. She's all right."

Maurice was almost twice the size of Ian, and might have flicked him across the room; but he only laughed and said, "All right, huh? Wait till Olvershaw gets through with her."

Who is Olvershaw? The more Jo heard about him, the more anxious she felt. She wished Aunt Lily hadn't left. She did see Colonel Korsakov, but for some reason he was trying to hide behind the refreshments table—and failing, for Phil had turned to him to denounce the pastries. "Olvershaw calls these doughnuts?" said Phil, waving one around. "These are the nastiest, stalest lumps of crud I've ever seen! I wrote my *name* on this doughnut three months ago. In *pen*. Look—it's still here! Does Olvershaw think we don't notice?"

Just then a tent flap jerked aside. Phil froze. The doughnut tumbled from his fingers. A wet cough, the squeak of unoiled machinery, and a crumpled old man in a wheelchair emerged from the darkness, twitching and glowering.

Jo stared at the man—or what was left of a man. He didn't

have any legs. He had no right arm. And his left arm, withered to a string, had no fingers except for a thumb.

Phil swallowed. "C-C-Commissioner . . ."

"I baked those doughnuts myself, you ungrateful wretch," said Commissioner Olvershaw, staring at Phil with one eye (the other was covered by an eyepatch). "Perhaps you've noticed the only part of my body I have left is my thumb. You might wonder how I baked doughnuts using only a *thumb*—but you probably don't. Why should you wonder? You must think it's quite easy. I invite you to try. I'd sarcastically remark that it's a walk in the park, except I can't walk."

Phil stammered, "Er . . . these are the new squires, sir, Ian Barrows and Jo Larouche."

Olvershaw swung his caustic gaze over to Ian and Jo. "Don't bother to shake my hand, because it isn't there. It must feel good to have all your fingers, though, doesn't it? I know what you're thinking. You're thinking, *At least Olvershaw has his thumb.* But what if I told you this thumb is in constant agony? Every day of my life is a living hell. What do you say to that?"

Jo and Ian were left speechless.

"Milquetoasts." Olvershaw swiveled back toward Phil. "One day I'd like to meet squires who aren't utter milquetoasts. I often wish, in fact, that this entire department would be swept away in a great, cleansing fire. . . . This whole week has been a waste."

Phil said, "What have you been doing this week, sir?"

"I would say that I've been twiddling my thumbs, except that *I don't have enough thumbs to twiddle.* Look at this." His thumb moved in a feeble half circle. "That is one thumb, twiddling. It makes me want to cry. It would make you cry, too, if you had a heart. I don't have a heart, of course; did you know? All my internal organs have withered away, except for my pancreas. How I stay alive is anyone's guess."

A plump clerk emerged from the back. "The quests are all written up, sir. Should I—"

"Wait a second, lackey." Olvershaw leaned forward, squinting, and cocked his yellow-fingernailed thumb at Colonel Korsakov. "Well, well, well. I'm surprised you had the nerve to show your face around here, *Colonel* Korsakov."

"What? Er? Ah . . ." Colonel Korsakov was now hiding behind an office plant. "A pleasure to see you again, Commissioner."

"Spare me your pleasantries, Korsakov! Where's that Schwenk?"

"Um . . . I've been occupied, sir. Exiled, you see, and——"

"Excuses!" rasped Olvershaw. "I suppose you want to register this boy as your squire? Boy! What's your name?"

Ian frowned. "It's Ian Barrows. We already told you."

"Already told me! I'm sorry I forgot! It must be so easy to remember everything when you have your arms and legs! Have you noticed that I do not? No, Ian Barrows, you listen to me. This Korsakov, this so-called knight of yours, is a *fraud*."

Korsakov winced, closing his eyes. Jo stared, aghast, and Ian said, "What!"

"When Korsakov was a squire, I gave him the quest to slay the Schwenk. It should've taken no more than two weeks. But here we are—*forty-nine years later*—and this worthless Korsakov of yours still hasn't brought me the head of the Schwenk. *Ignominious!*"

A hush fell over the room. Colonel Korsakov blushed, staring at the floor. Jo ground her teeth, her insides prickling. But what could she do?

"When I was a squire, I completed *all* my quests," coughed Olvershaw. "Without the luxury of arms or legs, mind you, or a left eye—*only this thumb*. Don't ask me how. But I got the job done. I also had headaches. Did I mention that? Would you appreciate it? Could any of you even begin to understand? No, no, no—you couldn't, none of you, you worms, you *insects*! On the other hand, here's Korsakov—two healthy arms, two healthy legs—who *calls* himself a knight—"

"Colonel Korsakov *is* a knight!" said Ian angrily.

"One more word from you, Barrows," said Olvershaw, "and I will veto your squireship."

Ian started to speak, but Korsakov shook his head. Ian seemed to collapse a little, though his mouth hung slightly open, looking at Korsakov in confusion.

"Colonel Korsakov *should not be* a knight," said Olvershaw. "Nor would he be if regulations had been properly followed. Regulations demand squires finish all quests before being knighted. Korsakov did not slay the Schwenk, but Sir Oliver knighted him anyway. An unprecedented, irregular, and unprincipled insult to the entire knightly code."

Jo looked at Korsakov and squirmed. Each word Olvershaw spoke was like a physical blow to the fat old man, visibly withering him. She could hardly contain her anger. Why wasn't anyone other than Ian sticking up for him?

"But I secured one small satisfaction," Olvershaw continued. "Korsakov may be a knight, but he may not be addressed as one. Until he brings me the head of the Schwenk, nobody may call him Sir Anatoly. He is merely Colonel Korsakov."

Korsakov turned away.

"And not only that," said Olvershaw. "As a point of law, Korsakov is still under my authority. As are all you squires. That is, you must follow my orders without hesitation! Now, there's a little game I liked to play with Korsakov back in the old days. . . ."

"Please, Commissioner," said Korsakov quietly. "Not in front of the squires."

"Excuse me, Korsakov? Did I give you permission to speak? One more word and I will order you to strip to your unmentionables, hop around on one of your grotesque legs, and sing the Eldritch Municipal Anthem in its entirety. Is that clear?"

Colonel Korsakov fidgeted miserably. Squires from other orders started to snicker.

"In fact, why not?" said Olvershaw. "Colonel Korsakov! If you would be so kind as to——"

"SHUT UP!"

A gasp went up around the room. As soon as Jo said it, she knew she shouldn't have. Olvershaw swung his head around, fixing her with a fierce glare.

Olvershaw jerked his neck. A clerk pushed Olvershaw's wheelchair over to Jo. Olvershaw's face loomed closer, closer, like a swelling, sickly moon, until it was only a few inches from her own. His single yellow eye, sunken in a face as dry and brittle as a dead leaf, stared angrily. It seemed to go on forever. Jo tried to look back coolly, even though her stomach felt full of bees.

Olvershaw finally rasped, "Watch your mouth, girl. You don't want to cross me."

Jo swallowed and said nothing. More than ever she wished Aunt Lily would come back.

"You're new in town—Jo Larouche, isn't it?" Olvershaw coughed and spat something black and slimy on the floor. "Let me ask you something, Jo Larouche. Do you like to eat fine food?"

"Yes."

"That's great, that's really great. You know what I eat? The only thing that I can eat?"

"What——"

"*Lint*. That's it. I've eaten nothing but lint for the past fifty years."

"You eat lint?"

"I eat *lint*. If I ate anything else, my pancreas would literally explode. But you'd like to see that, wouldn't you? That'd be a big hoot for you and your good-time pals. Mean old Olvershaw's pancreas explodes—should be good for a larf! Well, here's another 'larf.' Do you know what the only thing I can drink is? Don't say water, because I can't even drink that. It makes my ears bleed. No, I have to drink a special kind of water that has all the water taken out of it——*I don't even know what that is!*

"WHY? Why do I do it? Why do I bother to keep on living? Dear God, why? *Because this city would fall apart without me.* Because someone must uphold the knightly code. When someone violates the knightly code, I must lay down the law. Does that make me popular? No. But how popular can I be, when I have no legs, and no arms—just this thumb? I won't leave you wondering: *not very popular.* So go ahead, hate me. But if you cross me, I will bring the power of this thumb crashing down upon you. And you will not be a happy little lady."

Jo kept her mouth shut. But she managed to glimpse at Korsakov, and he gave her a small, bashful smile. That was all Jo wanted; that was enough.

"I am a fair man," said Olvershaw. "I won't ruin your career right at the start, just because of one obnoxious remark. I will overlook your impertinence—this time. Lackey! Take Miss Larouche back and register her. I'm ready to assign this week's quests."

To Jo it sounded like the entire room gave a sigh of relief. Olvershaw turned away from Jo and was at once surrounded by a tense cloud of clerks, who rushed hither and thither in a panic of efficiency, delivering envelopes and taking back stamped documents. One of the clerks glared at Jo and motioned her to follow.

The clerk guided her through a maze of wooden partitions and ragged tents, back to a tiny stall covered by a patched cloth roof, every available surface heaped with stacks of loose papers. The clerk filled out some forms, snatched a ring from a box, ran it through a stamping machine, and then threw it at her, muttering, "Congrats, you're a squire. Next!"

Jo walked past the rows of office-stalls in a daze of anticlimax. She looked at her new ring. Compared with the beautiful silver ring Aunt Lily had found in the Inconvenience, it wasn't much: just a cheap iron band with JO LAROUCHE punched on the inside.

She passed Ian on his way in.

"Well?" he whispered. "What do they do to you?"

"They stick you full of pins to see if you'll scream. Good luck."

The squires were standing in line against the wall when Jo returned. At first she didn't know what to do, until Maurice impatiently motioned her to stand next to him. Olvershaw was being wheeled back and forth in front of the line, scrutinizing the squires, mumbling insults and coughing on them. Every once in a while he nodded, and a clerk would give an envelope to a squire. A minute later Ian returned and slid in next to her, grinning goofily and examining his new ring again and again.

Jo shifted from foot to foot, trying to keep calm. She was vague on what exactly a quest was, but she wanted one anyway. Especially after Maurice's wondering if she could "handle it," and especially after Olvershaw had chewed her out.

But when the final envelope was passed out, there was no quest for her.

"That's all," said Olvershaw. "See you next week. Enjoy your arms and legs. Damn you all."

Jo blurted out, "Wait! Don't I get a quest?"

"None left. Well, I do have a quest for Dugan, but since he's not here . . ."

Jo said, "I'll take it."

Olvershaw closed his eye and sighed, as if calling upon a rapidly dwindling patience. "Pushy little creature, aren't you? No. You couldn't handle this quest. It's from Lady Agnes."

At the mere mention of "Lady Agnes," the other squires began clamoring: "Oooh! Let *me* do it, Commissioner!"—"I don't have a quest, either!"—"I haven't had a quest in weeks, sir!"

Ian shouted over the noise: "Commissioner! What if Jo *and* I take it?"

"Silence, all of you! Absolutely not, it's out of the question! Especially you two—you're rookies, greenhorns, got it? This quest will wait for Dugan."

"But I've helped Dugan on quests before," insisted Ian. "And

Jo, she's been Dame Lily's unofficial squire for years! Doesn't that experience count for anything?"

Jo didn't have the heart to point out that most of her "experience" with Aunt Lily consisted of watching old movies and playing canasta.

"For the last time, the answer is no!" said Olvershaw. "And if my remaining eye is any judge, I believe our man has arrived."

The doors opened, and Dugan Barrows came in—a tall, olive-skinned boy with shaggy black hair and bright green eyes, hauling a squirming burlap sack. A great shout went up as Dugan was surrounded by squires. Dugan hoisted up the kicking, wriggling sack and dumped it onto the refreshments table.

"Finish your quest, Barrows?" growled Olvershaw.

Dugan said, "It nearly finished *me*."

Everybody laughed—a bit louder and longer than really necessary, Jo thought. Over the hubbub, she asked Ian, "What did Dugan do?"

"A squat-snouted nangnang escaped from the zoo. Dugan's quest was to catch it and bring it back. He always gets the good quests."

"Why?"

Ian shrugged. "Because he's Dugan. You'll understand."

Jo watched Dugan; she already kind of understood. With his mussed dark hair and glazed eyes, Dugan seemed more adult than the other squires. He also looked as if he hadn't slept in days, and seemed barely to be listening when Ian said, "Dugan, this is Jo Larouche. Jo—"

"Oh, the new girl," said Dugan. "I heard you got barfed out of a fish last night."

"I travel in style," said Jo.

"Enough introductions!" coughed Olvershaw. "Let's have your report, Dugan. How'd you catch the nangnang?"

Dugan bowed to Olvershaw. "Thank you, sir. As you know, I'd been tracking the nangnang for days. I couldn't go to sleep or

I would've lost its trail, but I was getting more and more exhausted. And I was running out of fingernails."

Jo couldn't help but interrupt. "Wait, fingernails?"

"The nangnang eats fingernails," said Dugan. "That's why it's such a dangerous animal."

"Doesn't sound so bad."

Dugan smiled. "Oh, really? Tell that to someone who's had his fingernails chewed off. Anyway, I was clipping my own fingernails and using them to bait the nangnang. I was in Lower Brondo, and I thought I had the nangnang cornered, but then the—HEY! *Watch out!*"

Dugan's sack had burst open, and a wrinkled, yellow, shrieking seahorse-like creature popped out—its nose curling and uncurling wildly, its bulging eyes as big as grapefruits, squealing so piercingly everyone's hands flew to their ears.

"Catch it! Don't let it get away!" shouted Olvershaw.

The nangnang stretched out its bony arms, coiled its tail, and sprang straight into the crowd of panicking squires. The squires scattered, pushing each other out of the way as the nangnang bolted across the room, crashing through the cloth walls.

"What are you gutless mollycoddles doing?" roared Olvershaw. "Catch that thing!"

The nangnang exploded out of the waiting room, rampaging through the maze of stalls, tearing down the tattered cloth and splintering the wooden partitions. Squires dashed after the nangnang, blundering through a storm of flying papers; Colonel Korsakov lumbered back and forth, blocking off the exits, and Olvershaw howled at his clerks, who ran around in panic, trying to wheel him out of danger.

"Save my thumb!" screeched Olvershaw. "It's all I've got left! My beautiful, beautiful thumb!"

But Olvershaw's thumb had a long, juicy fingernail. And the only thing standing between the nangnang and Olvershaw's fingernail was—

Jo didn't intend to be there. She had no desire to save Olvershaw's fingernail. But before she could move, the nangnang barreled into her chest, and she clutched at it as they rolled across the floor, with clerks shrieking and squires trying to grab them.

"Hold on to it, Jo!" shouted Colonel Korsakov.

The nangnang leaped up and smashed through a bookcase, dragging Jo behind. Jo could hardly keep hold of the panicking thing—and then she had an idea.

She shoved her finger, with its new ring, into the nangnang's mouth.

Her finger exploded. Jo screamed as the nangnang tore through her fingernail, tears sprang to her eyes, stars blinked furiously all around—and then Ian tackled them, wrestled the thrashing animal down, and forced open its jaws.

Jo snatched out her chewed-up finger as the nangnang howled in disappointment, and suddenly Dame Delia and Aunt Lily were there, grabbing the kicking, shrieking thing and thrusting it back into the sack.

Jo lay on the ground, her eyes closed, the world spinning under her. Her fingernail was ragged and crushed, she was bruised all over, she tasted blood—but her heart was pounding so hard and her body felt so electrified that she almost didn't notice the pain.

"Are you okay?" said a dozen voices. There was a confused babble, and then Dugan said, "I don't know whether to tell you that was brave or stupid."

"Tell me later," said Jo. "Where's Ian?"

"Right here." Ian crouched, helping her get up. "Easy . . . there you go. Is your finger okay?"

The squires gathered around Jo and Ian with a new respect. As Maurice, Phil, Daphne, and Dugan congratulated them, Jo could hear squires from the other orders murmuring: "That's her, Dame Lily's squire. I saw her last night, riding on top of that building. . . ."

Clerks started to emerge, blinking and trembling, from the wreckage. Some of them wandered in a shocked daze through the stew of torn-up papers and trampled files; others quietly wept, cradling heaps of documents, singing tenderly to them. A half-dozen clerks fussed over Olvershaw, offering him tea, hot towels, and backrubs, but Olvershaw seemed dryly amused.

"It will take years to repair this damage," he said with a certain relish. "What a marvelous ruckus . . . Larouche! Barrows! Front and center!"

Jo looked up at Olvershaw. Dread settled in her stomach like a block of ice. She and Ian limped up to Olvershaw, who glowered down on them.

"As a rule, I do not approve of ruckuses," he said sternly. "Ruckuses churn up my insides. Of course, I have no insides . . . just dust and cobwebs, and a tiny pancreas rattling around in me like a gray, shriveled pea. And still . . . and still . . . I find myself agreeably invigorated." Olvershaw rocked back and forth, considering. Finally, he said: "Very well. You may take the Lady Agnes quest. You and this Barrows boy. But I hold—"

He had to pause over Ian's whoop of joy.

"But I hold you both to the same standards as an advanced squire! My lackey will give you the details. Lackey! Where's the envelope? Be quick about it! Now get me out of here—I can't stand the sight of these young, healthy children a moment more. It makes my hair ache."

A clerk thrust an envelope into Jo's hand, and then Olvershaw was gone, trundling and coughing deeper into the dark maze of offices. Aunt Lily patted her on the back.

"Well done, Jo. But you do leave a mess, don't you?" Aunt Lily looked around the torn-up offices with amused satisfaction. "Okay, squires, move out! We've got a lodge to clean!"

Jo found her way over to Ian. Olvershaw had given him an envelope, too, and he was already reading aloud its contents, surrounded by a group of curious squires. Ian turned to her, excitedly telling her about the quest they had been assigned. Jo didn't understand what he was saying; she was still scattered and woozy, and she wasn't listening very carefully, anyway. She was too caught up in a strange feeling, something she almost couldn't recognize. For the first time in her life, she felt like she belonged.

THIRTEEN

When Jo and the others came back to the lodge, they found the rest of the Odd-Fish gathered in the common room with brooms, mops, and buckets of soapy water—and Cicero, the head cockroach, already in the middle of a passionate speech:

"It shatters my heart to utter these words," said Cicero, his voice trembling. "But this is without doubt the blackest day in the history of the Order of Odd-Fish. Before our lodge was stolen, I would defy you to find a cleaner, tidier, tighter-run establishment in all of Eldritch City. And yet now . . . now . . ."

"Steady on, Cicero," said Sefino, handing him a handkerchief.

"And *now*," wailed Cicero, swatting the handkerchief away, "after three months of festering in the Belgian Prankster's unsanitary clutches, our lodge has degenerated into a grimy, seething muckpot—a feculent, slime-soaked, filth-dripping crapshack—oozing with the greasiest, scummiest—oh! I dare not say more!"

"Oooh! Say more!" begged the cockroaches.

"Odd-Fish, our mission is clear!" roared Cicero. "With a will, we shall beat back this encroaching wave of putridity, and restore our lodge to its pristine splendor! Who is with me?"

"Hoo-hah!" shouted the cockroaches, exultantly shaking their mops and brooms (the knights and squires shook theirs rather less exultantly) as Cicero went on to announce everyone's chores.

Jo was assigned to clean out the basements with Daphne and Phil. At first she thought Cicero had been exaggerating—the lodge was messy, yes, but certainly no "filth-dripping crapshack"—but that was before she opened the basement doors and was hit by a stink so foul it was like a punch to the head.

The basement was full of rotting fish slime. A swamp's worth had oozed into the foundations when it was in the giant fish's stomach, and now the basement was waist deep in milky, chunky sludge, here and there crusted over with pink mold. The sour air withered Jo's nose and wrenched tears from her eyes.

Daphne took one sniff and said, "I am *not* going down there."

"Oh yes you are," said Phil. "I don't like it, either, but it's no good whining. Let's go."

They pulled on plastic boots and overalls and got down to work. Jo was sure there was no fouler job than this. First they had to wade through the sea of fish goo and shovel it into wheelbarrows; then they had to haul the wheelbarrows outside and dump them into wagons headed for the eelmen's neighborhood (who the "eelmen" were, and why they wanted rotten fish gunk, Jo didn't even want to know).

When they were finally done, Jo was worked to the bone, as wrung out as an old rag. But there was some satisfaction in it. By helping to clean the lodge, Jo felt she was earning her place there. And working with Phil and Daphne broke the ice much better than any awkward conversation could have.

That night the cockroaches served a late dinner out on the roof of the lodge. After cleaning Jo took a long, hot shower, changed into a sweater and jeans, and came up onto the roof. The evening was chilly, with a salty wind blowing off the ocean, and the roof blazed with hundreds of flickering candles. Other knights and squires were already there, eating bowls of steaming beef stew and drinking spicy cider. The cold night air smelled fresh and clean, and everyone's face looked more intense in the warm light. Jo sat with Daphne and Phil, devoured her stew, took second helpings, and sopped up the juices with warm hunks of bread. When she was finished, sitting back and drinking hot cider, she had never felt so satisfyingly exhausted.

"I still can't believe you got a Lady Agnes quest," said Daphne. "Some squires have been trying for months."

Jo held up her bandaged finger. "It did nearly cost me this."

"Totally worth it," said Phil between bites.

"Why?" said Jo. "Have you ever had a quest with Lady Agnes?"

"Yes, just last year," said Phil. "One of her better ones. Lady Agnes made me take off my clothes and put on a pink furry bear suit and a saddle. Then she rode me around town all day, chasing down children, throwing eggs at them. We got arrested!"

"What!" Jo put down her cider in shock. "*That's* a quest?"

"Oh, sure. If you have enough money, you can submit any quest you want to the city, and the squires have to do it."

Jo crinkled her brow. "But isn't that . . ."

Daphne said, "I had a quest with Lady Agnes, too. She ordered me to assassinate the mayor's cat. She swore to me it was broadcasting evil radio signals into her dentures."

"But . . . this woman sounds insane!" said Jo.

"Oh yes," said Daphne. "Mad as mutton."

"But I don't understand—if Lady Agnes's quests are ridiculous—"

"Or pointless."

"Okay—if Lady Agnes's quests are ridiculous or pointless, then—"

"Or impossible."

"Ridiculous, pointless, or impossible—no, wait! let me finish—then why does everybody want one?"

Phil and Daphne looked at each other blankly, as if that kind of question had never occurred to them before. Then Daphne finally replied: "Well—for respect."

"That's right." Phil nodded slowly. "For respect."

Dinner was over, and the knights and squires started to mingle. The cockroaches had dragged out a xylophone, a clarinet, some drums, and a brass contraption that looked like a half-dozen tubas and a pinball machine mashed together, and they were struggling through a chaotic waltz. Soon Sir Alasdair was dancing with Dame Isabel, Phil asked Daphne out onto the floor, and Sir Festus was teaching an awkward Nora how to jitterbug.

Aunt Lily swung over, looking fresher and younger than Jo had ever seen her. "It's all just as I remember it," she said, looking around the roof happily. "I've missed this so much. Even when I didn't remember it. But this is it."

Jo said, "I still don't understand this place, but I think I like it."

"I'm glad to hear that. You'll make a splendid Odd-Fish."

"Aunt Lily, why are *you* an Odd-Fish?" said Jo. "How did you come here in the first place?"

"Ah, that's a long story. Too long for now." Aunt Lily took a deep breath and smiled. "What a day! You did yourself proud this morning, Jo. All the knights are talking about you. They expect big things."

"Do they still expect me to destroy Eldritch City?" chuckled Jo.

She was stunned at how quickly Aunt Lily's face fell. The old woman's smile shrank to a tight grimace, and her eyes hardened.

"Don't do that again, Jo. Don't ever, ever speak in public about that again."

"I . . . was just trying to joke about . . ."

"Not even as a joke."

Aunt Lily was staring so ferociously Jo had to look away. "I'm sorry. I didn't understand."

"This isn't the time." Aunt Lily glanced around the party warily. "I'm warning you—be careful. You see all this? Everyone laughing, dancing, having a good time? If they knew the truth, this would all explode in our faces."

Jo was bewildered into silence. Aunt Lily turned and, as if a switch had been flipped, started laughing and making her way over to Dame Myra and Sir Oort.

Jo moved away, too, and wandered the party, hanging around the edges of conversations. But she didn't know what to say anymore. She still could feel everyone else's happiness all around, but she felt locked out of it now. Aunt Lily had never spoken to her like that before.

Then Jo saw Ian and Dugan, quietly arguing behind Dame Myra's greenhouse. She made her way over to them and overheard Ian saying, "Where were you for the last few days?"

"You heard me," said Dugan. "Tracking the nangnang."

"We both know that's not true."

"A squire for barely a day, and already you're lecturing me? You're not my mother, Ian."

"I meant—"

"I know what you meant. By the way, what's up with that mustache?"

"It'll look better when it's fully grown."

"No, it won't." Dugan noticed Jo. "Hey, Jo! What do you think of Ian's mustache?"

Ian muttered, "You don't have to answer that."

"I'll let you two discuss it. I'm off," said Dugan, seeming relieved to get away.

After Dugan was gone, Jo said, "What were you two fighting about?"

"Nothing." Ian's eyes flicked tensely over to Dugan; then he turned to Jo and whispered, "Hey, this party's almost over. Do you want to go downstairs?"

"What's downstairs?"

Ian smiled strangely. "There's something I want to show you."

Jo hesitated. What, exactly, did he want to show her? But something about his smile sparked her curiosity, and she found herself saying, "Okay, but it had better be good."

"Make sure nobody notices," said Ian, and slipped off into the shadows. Jo double-checked that nobody was watching them and then followed him downstairs into the empty lodge.

With all the other Odd-Fish upstairs, the deserted halls felt lonely. Jo could still hear the cockroaches' music, the thump of dancing, and the buzz of conversation above as they threaded their way down the corridors, turning left and right, and then down some more stairs, and then right and left and right again, and down even more stairs, and the music and conversation became fainter. Soon they were so deep into the lodge that Jo was lost.

Finally they entered a closet with a trapdoor in the ceiling. Ian hoisted himself through the trapdoor, then reached down, gripped Jo's wrists, and pulled her up into a vast dim room.

At first Jo could see very little. But she smelled something raw and alive, like a forest after a hard rain. Ian lit some hanging lanterns, and as the room became brighter, Jo realized she was surrounded by a huge tapestry.

The more she saw, the more she couldn't stop staring. The tapestry was dazzling and full of pictures: fire-scorched, blood-spurting battles; immense jungles full of looping, twisty trees, scowling lizards, and secret golden rivers; a ballroom full of laughing girls dancing with beautiful monsters; an army of glitteringly armored spiders; queer-shaped people with sickly smiles and dead eyes cutting open their stomachs and pouring forth floods of centipedes and beetles and snakes. Jo could hardly take it all in, it was too relentlessly detailed, too hugely beautiful. The tapestry hung on every wall, from ceiling to floor, packed with color and detail, every last corner crammed with a capering tiger, convoluted flower, or snickering face.

Ian wound up a large wooden wheel. And then—with a great creaking, clunking, and squealing—the tapestry began to *move*.

Jo gasped, turning around, as the tapestry flowed past her—a scroll of tapestries, unspooling from one corner of the room, rolling around the walls in a circle, and disappearing back into the corner. A raucous parade of images danced past, with hardly enough time to take in each scene before it was gone, followed by even more scenes.

The tapestry was full of stories about Eldritch City. In one scene, two enormous walrus-like demons wrestled each other, one neon green, the other candy-apple red, stomping up and down the mountain, kicking down buildings and tearing great gashes in the rock while thousands of people scattered away like ants. In another scene, Eldritch City was attacked from the sea by shambling beasts like a lobster crossed with an octopus, riding out of the ocean on jellyfish-like blobs. In yet another scene, the mountain itself split in half and a great chunk of Eldritch City floated off into the stars as tiny people on both halves reached out their arms, crying out, desperately trying to hang on to each other.

Jo and Ian sat on a couch, watching the tapestry. For a long time there was no sound but the steady creaking of the spindles unwinding. It seemed the tapestry went on for miles.

"It's my favorite thing in the lodge," said Ian. "I wanted to show you."

Jo glanced sideways at Ian. That morning, when Ian said he hated the Hazelwoods, she hadn't known how to feel; she had been almost frightened of him. But in the end Ian was so earnest, so eager to show her his world, that she couldn't help warming to him. She tentatively leaned up against him. He shifted closer to her. For a minute they were so close she could hear him breathing, smell his skin, feel his chest rise and fall.

Then Ian became tense. Jo looked up at him, and his face had gone pale. The tapestry rolled on, Ian went very still, and a scene crawled into the room that struck Jo as familiar.

Her bones turned to ice.

It was . . . she swallowed, tried to stay calm. It couldn't be anything else.

The tapestry was a blizzard of demolishing gray fire, wave upon wave spiraling wildly outward, collapsing buildings and evaporating people into swirling ashes. In the eye of the storm there was a little white house, and inside the house . . . Jo tried not to stare, but she couldn't help it. A thousand times she had imagined what her parents might have looked like. But this man, this woman, were nothing like what she'd expected.

Her father was a gaunt, black-skinned man with round glasses and a mass of tangled hair; her mother boyish-looking, with straight red hair and startlingly white skin. Her father had turned away, hiding his eyes in horror, pointing at her mother, who writhed in bed, her face twisted in agony—and a scab-covered slug was bursting out of her.

It was the birth of the Ichthala. She was looking at her own birth. Jo couldn't tear her eyes away.

Ian sat quite still, staring at a different spot on the tapestry—at a woman, far out on the edge. The gray waves of murderous fire were rolling straight at her. The woman had just started to turn around, her surprised face caught in the moment before she, too, was killed.

"They say the entire history of Eldritch City is supposed to be in this tapestry," said Ian. "Some people say you can even find yourself, if you search enough. Or your friends. Or . . ."

Jo swallowed. She didn't need him to tell her who the woman was. She recognized his wistful eyes, his blond hair, his slightly crooked nose. The image of Ian's mother jerked past them, and Jo felt the world shrinking around her, drawing in closer, so tight she couldn't move.

"Dame Myra gave us a lecture once," said Ian. "Said the tapestry's alive, kind of—made out of a special moss that's always growing, so the pictures are always shifting. It's true. Sometimes my mother is smiling. Other times she just looks tired. To-day . . . she just looks far away."

"Ian," said Jo nervously, "why are you showing me this?"

Ian stared at her with sudden intensity. "Jo, what do you think of the Hazelwoods?"

Jo's heart lurched. "Aunt Lily only told me about them this morning." She cautiously added: "It, um . . . it sounded to me like they were just in the wrong place at the wrong time, or . . ."

Ian's lip curled.

"What are you getting at, Ian?"

"I know that Nora wants you to help her find the Ichthala. I think she's crazy. But if this Ichthala nonsense turns out to be true . . . if you do find out who she is, or *what* she is, if you find out where the Ichthala's hiding . . . I want you to tell me."

"Why?"

"Because I'm going to kill her."

Jo's skin felt like cold jelly. Ian looked at her with strangely brutal eyes. She wanted to push him away, get out of the room, out of Eldritch City—the whole town was insane, Aunt Lily was right: they would murder her if they knew who she was. "I'll do what I can," she whispered.

Ian smiled, and his teeth seemed sharper than Jo remembered. "I knew there was something about you I liked."

Jo stood up, tearing herself away.

"Where are you going?" said Ian, startled.

"Back upstairs," said Jo. "They're probably missing us."

"But Jo, don't you—" began Ian. Then he stopped, for a part of the tapestry scrolled into view that stunned them both.

A great hole had been hacked in the tapestry. Shreds of moss dangled from the hole, revealing a gray brick wall behind. Jo and Ian stared as the hole emerged from the corner and began circling the room, strangely menacing. Slashing through the gorgeous fertility of the tapestry, it looked not like a mere hole, but as if reality itself had been torn open.

"That wasn't there before," breathed Ian.

The hole steadily inched along, almost unbearably slowly. Then it passed over a wooden door on the other side of the tapestry—twelve feet off the ground, and closed—and marched on.

"What's that?" said Jo, but Ian had already leaped up and grabbed the wheel. The machinery groaned as he forced the tapestry to a halt; then he cranked the wheel backward, winding the tapestry in reverse, until the hole moved back over the door.

"I never knew there was a door behind there," whispered Ian.

"Let's go in!" said Jo.

"No, Jo. We have to tell the knights."

"But I want to see what's behind that door," said Jo, and she only half heard Ian's reply. She was staring transfixed at the tapestry, at the scene around the hole. The scene was dark and swallowed up in decoration, but once Jo saw it, it burned into her eyes.

It was a circle of twelve women in blue cloaks and blue veils, standing around the hole, pointing toward the door.

The Silent Sisters. Jo knew she should be afraid, but something pulled her toward it. Aunt Lily had told her almost nothing about the Silent Sisters. It almost seemed as though she was holding something back. And now here they were, ringed around a door, inviting her . . . where?

"Let's go tell Sir Oliver," said Ian.

"But Ian," said Jo quickly. "It won't hurt to just peek."

Ian frowned. "How would we even get up there?"

"I don't know, let's see . . . You could stand on the couch, I guess, and then I could get up on your shoulders and—oh, come *on*, Ian! Are you scared or something?"

Ian seemed about to protest, but his eyes hardened. "I'm not scared."

In guilty silence Jo helped Ian push the couch under the door. She knew she shouldn't have said that, but she couldn't help it; now the easy friendliness from before felt strained. Without a word Ian got up on the couch and Jo climbed onto his shoulders. She reached for the doorknob—at first she could just barely brush her fingers over it, but then she got a grip and turned it. The door opened slightly. Jo grabbed the threshold and pulled herself up into darkness.

"What do you see?" said Ian.

The passage was almost entirely dark, twisting upward in an odd way. Jo rose to her feet, every bit of her quickened and trembling. "It goes on a bit. I'm going to see what's up there. . . ."

"Be careful."

Jo edged forward and upward, excited. The passage was cramped and dark and low, but there was something unnerving about the weird angles of the beams, something disorienting about the slope of the floor. Jo could barely see her hands, feeling her way upward almost blindly, until the passage contracted into a little hole, almost too small to get through. She couldn't see anything beyond it.

"Hey, Jo!" said Ian, far away now.

Jo stopped, tingling with danger. If something happened to her up here . . . She suddenly felt very afraid. The darkness pressed in on her on all sides, and her buzzing confidence curdled in her stomach. "Okay, okay, I'm coming back," she said shakily, and began to edge back down. But a last spasm of curiosity made her stop—and in a reckless rush she clambered up, squeezing through the hole.

She was in a dark room full of motionless people. She couldn't see anyone's face. The people were absolutely still and silent, some sitting on chairs and sofas, a few standing or leaning on tables. But even in the darkness, Jo almost started to recognize their faces. She crept up to one of them, so close that her nose was only inches away.

Suddenly she knew who it was—a very familiar face with a wicked yellow grin.

"Aunt Lily?" whispered Jo.

Aunt Lily's head popped off, screeching with laughter. Jo stumbled back in shock, crashing into something like Colonel Korsakov, who grabbed her roughly, bulging and melting out of his uniform like a great hairy pudding. She punched, kicked to get free, but she was crushed between Aunt Lily and Colonel Korsakov, writhing and clutching each other, tearing each other's bodies apart. Jo tried to scream but her throat locked up, she couldn't even breathe.

The knights of the Odd-Fish jerked and jiggled all around her, closing in, their mouths hanging open, their eyes hollow. A leering Sir Oliver grabbed Jo, his bony fingers all over her like spastic tarantulas. She broke free, pushing against Dame Myra, whose body collapsed like cottage cheese, and when Jo squirmed the other way she found an eyeless Dame Delia that seemed about to bite off her face. The knights were falling to pieces all around her, the floor strewn with a mishmash of arms and legs and torsos, and Jo was pulled into a mixed-up pile of Sir Alasdair, Sir Festus, and Sir Oort, their limbs twitching wildly. She squeezed her eyes tight, and finally she found she could scream, and she screamed and screamed.

Jo didn't know how long it was until someone came banging into the room. She opened her eyes and saw *two* Sir Olivers—a ghastly life-size doll, which had already fallen to pieces on the floor, and the real one, who was looking around the room in unsteady shock.

Aunt Lily came running right after him and stopped, with the same look of confused horror; then she dashed over to Jo, gathering her up in her arms. Jo couldn't stop shaking.

"What happened here, Oliver?" whispered Aunt Lily.

Sir Oliver said, as Jo kept trembling, "It seems the Belgian Prankster left us a little surprise."

Jo had a hard time falling asleep that night.

After she found the secret room, all cleaning had stopped. The knights gathered for a closed-door meeting, without the squires, that lasted for hours. The dolls of the Odd-Fish knights were taken into the meeting for examination.

But Jo couldn't get them out of her mind. Every time she

closed her eyes she saw the evil yellow grin on Aunt Lily's face, felt herself trapped and suffocated between her and the grinding, groping Colonel Korsakov. The dolls had been vicious caricatures, made with a merciless accuracy by someone who knew the Odd-Fish not only in physical detail but also with a bitter emotional intimacy.

Jo didn't see the knights again before she went to bed, except for when one or two of them took a break for a smoke. Their faces showed them to be the opposite of the happy, laughing knights they had been only hours ago. She tried to eavesdrop, but they seemed guarded in their words; they obviously did not want to panic the squires. But Jo remembered what Aunt Lily had said that morning:

"The Belgian Prankster may have something terrible planned."

Later that night, Jo woke up—and immediately knew there was someone else in her room.

She froze in her bed. A scratching noise was coming from below the floor. In her bedside mirror, Jo saw a floorboard wriggle loose, and gray hands place it aside.

Then a low, raspy voice: "Jo."

She didn't move. Something crept out of the hole—she couldn't tell what. Something was moving toward her bed. She tensed. A shadow loomed up around her.

Jo spun around, ready to scream—

"Are you awake?" whispered Ian.

"I am now," said Jo, her heart beating wildly. "Why are you in my room, Ian?"

"Shhh. Follow me. Squires' meeting."

Ian lowered himself back under the floorboards. Jo reluctantly sat up, her head fuzzy, still muddled as to whether she was dreaming or awake; finally she rolled out of her sheets and followed Ian under the floor into a narrow crawl space. She reached up and replaced the floorboards. The moon shone weakly on her empty bed.

It was a tight, blind, prickly squeeze through the crawl spaces of the lodge. Exposed nails and splintered beams threatened from all sides, stabbing and scratching her in the dark; in some places the wood sagged, nearly collapsing under her weight. She felt like a tiny germ secretly swimming through the veins of a vast, mysterious body. The only sound was Ian, scraping quietly ahead, whispering "Go left" or "Careful here." Everything smelled of rotting wood, old mothballs, and decades of dust.

At last she followed Ian down a crumbling chimney, wedging her trembling feet and fingers in between bricks—and finally she crawled out of a hearth and into a room.

The room had no doors and no windows: the only exit was back up the chimney. It was black and gloomy, caked with dust, and raggedly furnished with bare mattresses, a low table piled with bric-a-brac, and heaps of mildewed garbage. Dirty dishes lay scattered around, cobwebs clogged the corners, and a silver chandelier hung over all, flickering with black, dripping candles.

Albert and Daphne were huddled together on a mattress, talking in low whispers, Phil was half asleep on some pillows, and Maurice was fiddling with a battered metal movie projector. Nora sat by herself, clutching a film canister; she beckoned Jo and Ian to sit with her in a pile of pillows. Everything was hushed and tense, but Jo hoped that whatever was going to happen would be quick. She ached to be back in bed.

Dugan sat at an ornate desk, looking at everyone solemnly. "Everyone's here," he whispered, and tapped the desk with a gavel. "Let's bring this meeting to order. Albert, drinks."

Albert Blatch-Budgins produced a twisty amber bottle, opened it, and took a gulp. The bottle was passed from squire to squire, each drinking in silence. When Jo's turn came, she nervously sipped, and a smooth scorching juice rushed down her throat, bitter and fruity. It was all she could do not to cough it up. She passed the bottle on, and it finally rounded back to Dugan.

Dugan took a final pull and capped the bottle. "Down to

business. First off—Jo, welcome to the Odd-Fish. I admit some of us had doubts about you, but not anymore. Catching the nang-nang and finding those dolls of the knights . . . not bad for your first day."

"Thank you," murmured Jo. She dimly realized she was being complimented, but the soft pillows and fiery drink only made her want to fall back asleep.

Dugan nodded. "Next point of business. We hear that Sir Nils—"

"We're not supposed to call him Sir Nils anymore," said Maurice. "Sir Oliver said his knighthood has been revoked. Now he's just the Belgian Prankster."

"Thanks, Maurice. The Belgian Prankster . . . well, whatever you call him, it's obvious the knights are keeping something from us. So I asked Albert and Daphne to spy on the knights' meeting tonight."

A dull ache pounded behind Jo's eyes. She didn't want to hear about the Belgian Prankster, she didn't want to know any more—she buried herself in the pillows and felt foggy and thick.

"We only caught a little," said Albert. "Sir Oliver was talking about how he tracked down the lodge. And what the Belgian Prankster was doing in there. In *here*."

"And that's what we don't understand," said Daphne. "In the lodge, he was . . . um . . ."

Ian looked at her oddly. "What?"

Daphne took a breath and said: "He was *playing* with those dolls. The ones Jo found this afternoon. He made them, and then he posed them around the lodge and acted like they were real. He talked to the dolls. He danced with them. He sat them around the table and ate with them, had tea parties with them . . ."

"He would get in fights with the Korsakov doll," said Albert.

"He would *kiss* the Dame Lily doll," said Daphne.

A horrible tingle crawled up Jo's body. She dug her nails into her arms. The idea of the Belgian Prankster turning the lodge into an overgrown dollhouse was creepy enough. But the idea of the Belgian Prankster kissing that evil doll of Aunt Lily made her feel nasty all over.

Then she realized everyone was looking at her.

"What do *you* know about the Belgian Prankster, Jo?" said Dugan. "Sir Oliver said that where you're from, he's famous."

"Well . . . that's right, he is famous," said Jo, trying to put her thoughts in order. "He had a television show . . . he went around the world doing strange things, like he covered everything in New York with orange carpet once, or he turned the Eiffel Tower upside down, or . . . um . . ."

All the squires were looking at her blankly.

"You must come from a very weird place," said Daphne.

"Never mind," said Jo. "I don't really know anything about him, actually."

"I do," said Nora.

Everyone turned. Nora sat on the edge of her pile of pillows, her skin so pale it seemed to glow, her eyes bright and her body trembling. She held up her canister and said in a high, wild whisper, "I got this downtown. *Teenage Ichthala.* Advance copy."

"Nora!" said Dugan. "You've had that all this time and haven't told us?"

"How did you get it?" said Daphne.

"What happens? Have you watched it yet?" said Albert.

Jo was jolted awake. *"Teenage Ichthala?"*

"That's what I was trying to tell you about before, Jo!" said Nora. "The most important show in Eldritch City!"

Ian exhaled loudly and said something under his breath.

"Can you . . . the . . . what's it about?" said Jo.

Nora gave Ian a dirty look and said, "Okay, Jo. You know the Ichthala was kidnapped by the Silent Sisters thirteen years ago, right? Well, *Teenage Ichthala* is all about what the Ichthala is doing *now.* How she's plotting to destroy the city with the Silent Sisters. And not only that—"

"Here we go," muttered Ian.

Nora jerked around to face him. "What's that mean?"

"Oh, nothing, nothing. Please, keep on talking."

Nora glared at Ian and plowed ahead. "Anyway, I've already watched this episode, but I need to watch it again. There's a couple of parts that look like they might have *clues*."

It was all coming too fast for Jo. "Clues?"

"Don't ask her about it, Jo," groaned Ian. "Not unless you want to be here all night, listening to her conspiracy theories."

"So you still won't accept the truth!" said Nora. "Even after last night!"

"I have no idea what anyone is talking about," said Jo.

"Let me ask you something, Jo," said Nora quickly. "Haven't you wondered why last night—on the beach, when you came with the fish—a lot of people were *expecting* Dame Lily? Why they were all shouting her name?"

"Well . . . yeah," said Jo. "How *did* they know she'd be there?"

Nora said, "Because three episodes ago, on *Teenage Ichthala,* your aunt came back to Eldritch City. Barfed out of a giant fish."

Jo looked around the room. Most of the squires were nodding.

Nora continued, "That's why *Teenage Ichthala* is so important. Nobody knows why, but for the past year, a lot of things that happen on *Teenage Ichthala* end up happening in real life."

"Like what?" said Jo.

"For instance, just before our lodge was stolen for real, our lodge got stolen *on the show*."

Ian said, "Just a coincidence."

"Oh, come *on,* Ian! What happened last night was beyond co-incidence. Everybody in Eldritch City thought Dame Lily was dead. Nobody expected her to come back. But then she *did* come back, just like the show predicted." Nora turned back to Jo and whispered: "That's why people are scared. Because in the next episode . . ."

Jo had a dreadful feeling she knew what Nora would say next. "What?"

Nora waited as long as she could; then said, so quietly that Jo could hardly hear: "Because in the next episode, *Ichthala* came back to Eldritch City."

Jo looked around, trying hard to hold on to her calm. She knew she was on dangerous ground now. The mood in the room had changed. The squires had the same expressions that Korsakov and Sefino had when they first remembered who Jo was—a look of queasy terror.

"Sounds like there's a lot your aunt isn't telling you," said Nora. "Do you know what Sir Nils's specialty had been for the Odd-Fish?"

"Not really . . ."

"You know how Sir Festus studies ludicrous weaponry, right? And Dame Isabel studies unusual smells?" said Nora, her words tumbling out more and more quickly. "Well, before he became the Belgian Prankster, Sir Nils researched *bad jokes* for the Odd-Fish. His goal was to discover the worst joke, using scientific methods. So he wrote thousands of stupid riddles, dumb wisecracks, and unfunny scripts for nonexistent sitcoms, all rigorously proven to be incontrovertibly unhilarious by a mathematics that Sir Nils himself invented. Everyone was awed by Sir Nils's grand ambitions. Some whispered that Sir Nils might even, in time, write an article *even more pointless* than Sir Oliver's. Sir Nils was set to become the greatest Odd-Fish ever."

Jo bit her tongue. This was probably not the time, she decided, to ask why Odd-Fish believed pointlessness was akin to greatness.

Nora continued: "The rumor is that while the Silent Sisters were taking over his mind, Sir Nils was writing his last theoretical television show. The director of *Teenage Ichthala* won't admit anything, but a lot of people think the Belgian Prankster wrote all those episodes of *Teenage Ichthala* thirteen years ago. Why he wrote them, nobody knows. Maybe the only way he could deal with the horrible things the Silent Sisters were doing to him was to make a joke out of it. Or maybe he hadn't become totally evil yet and he wrote this show as a coded message, to warn us what would happen when the Ichthala came. Either way, when the show's run is finished, Sir Nils truly *will* have created the worst joke of all time. For its punch line will be the return of the Ichthala—the destruction of Eldritch City—maybe even the end of the world."

The way this all rolled off Nora's tongue, it was clearly something she'd said a thousand times before. But as she spoke, the squires were silent and tense, as though they were being told a ghost story. *But if this is a ghost story, then* I'm *the ghost,* thought Jo. *She's talking about* me!

Daphne said, "So are we going to watch it or not?"

"Yeah, put it on!" said Albert.

Nora didn't need to be asked twice. Jo watched carefully as Nora opened up her canister and threaded the film into the projector. Maurice and Phil hung a white bedsheet on the wall. Every bit of her twisted into frantic little knots. If this show was really about her life, what was she about to see?

A blurry circle of light sprang onto the sheet, jumping and flickering, and the projector's clattering drowned out the burbling sound. Nora slapped the projector and twisted some knobs until the picture snapped into focus and the sound settled down. The other squires found spots on the couch and cushions to watch, all except for Nora, who sat on the floor close to the sheet, notebook and pencil in hand.

Jo watched anxiously as the words TEENAGE ICHTHALA jittered on the sheet. A fanfare of bells, drums, and organ blared as crude black-and-white images jerked across the screen—knights running around papier-mâché caves, women dancing in cheap-looking veils, an obviously fake model of Eldritch City on fire. It reminded Jo of low-budget movies Aunt Lily had done. A monster was running around the city, being chased by knights. Then people stood around making stupid jokes. Then more chasing, this time with women in veils.

The other squires watched with excited interest, but Jo

found herself baffled. On the show, the Ichthala was a powerful monster, causing havoc wherever she went, with the Silent Sisters as her loyal army. Fire streamed from the Ichthala's eyeballs as she flew around the city, demolishing all she touched. Jo couldn't help but giggle, even when she was angrily shushed by the other squires. *Teenage Ichthala* was so wrong, so ludicrously far from her own life, that her dread collapsed into relief. Even the actress who played the Ichthala looked nothing like her: she was hidden under elaborate makeup that made her resemble a diseased lizard. Still, Jo found herself fascinated by the Ichthala's icy, lonely eyes . . . *That* was supposed to be her . . . ?

The day finally caught up with Jo. She let her heavy eyelids close as she listened to the stiff line readings, the explosions, and the tinny music mixed up in the clicking whir of the projector. The candles burned low and she started to doze; Jo curled up deeper into the pillows, warm and drifting, and as the show's closing music played and the squires murmured around her, she finally fell asleep.

FOURTEEN

FOR the next couple of weeks Jo explored Eldritch City. Everything she saw fascinated her. It was all so different from home, even the air was different——the desert had smelled of clean dust and empty miles, but Eldritch City was soaked in dirty tropical stink, the wet breath of plants, the sweat of strangers, peppery smoke, brackish seawater, rotten cheese, melted manure on baking paving stones, the sweet fruity thrill of ten thousand flowers.

The streets thronged not only with people but also giant cockroaches, centipedes, and beetles, swishing about in jeweled capes and shimmering pantaloons, swinging chromium walking sticks and tipping precariously tall hats at each other. Near the swampy bottom of the mountain Jo also glimpsed gray eel-like creatures in shabby cloaks, eating a struggling baby octopus or hustling a jar of twitching worms to some unspeakable location. Some neighborhoods were twisty caves burrowing deep into the mountain, hung with strings of glowing paper lanterns; other neighborhoods were practically airborne, teetering off cliffs, propped up by scaffolding. The sheer size and variety of Eldritch City, its creatures and architecture, its noise and chaos, shook Jo's brain, spurred her senses, made her feel sharp and alive.

Every neighborhood had its own holidays for its own local gods, and sometimes while Jo was exploring she would be swept up into a boisterous parade of Eldritchers who had, say, dyed their skin blue and were all wearing identical white robes, shaking branches of jingling bells at each other in a jerking, bouncing dance; or she would come upon a silent huddle of shrines that had been hastily constructed in the middle of the street, all chugging out clouds of thick, greasy smoke, each of them with a peephole through which Jo could just barely glimpse golden idols of squids, jellyfish, and crabs silently grimacing at each other in the foggy darkness. Some of the festivals seemed almost like games, with priests kicking around hairy, jeweled animal skulls or scampering after each other in some ancient form of hide-and-seek; but other rituals were ponderous and solemn, such as the agonizingly slow all-night procession of a giant balloon in the shape of a local whale-god, a floating mountain covered with candles and sparklers drifting in a billowing ocean of incense. Jo asked about what the festivals meant, but Eldritch City's mythology was such a bewildering mishmash of thousands of gods and contradicting stories that even the people who could answer Jo's questions seemed uncertain.

Jo spent most of her time with Aunt Lily, learning how to be a squire. With Sir Festus's help, Aunt Lily showed Jo how to use the weapons in the Odd-Fish arsenal, including the notoriously clumsy flame-spurting double-sided lance that was the discriminating knight's weapon of choice. Aunt Lily and Dame Delia also taught Jo how to fly an ostrich, swooping and diving hundreds of feet above Eldritch City, so high and fast Jo could hardly breathe for the thrill.

Aunt Lily guided Jo around her old haunts, meeting up with long-lost friends. Aunt Lily was always in a vivacious mood nowadays, joking with Jo, whispering in her ear, pointing out curiosities as they walked down the street. Strangers murmured excitedly when they saw the legendary Dame Lily, and Jo couldn't help but feel proud. The day they visited Eelsbridge, the swamp neighborhood at the bottom of the mountain, a brilliantly vivid, flower-dripping, three-story hut on jointed stilt legs walked up to them—the home of one of the most distinguished eelmen in Eldritch City, and an old friend of Aunt Lily's. Aunt Lily and Jo climbed up a flowered ladder and had tea with the eelman as the walking hut lurched beneath them, its bubbling iron pot swinging wildly over a fire pit, filling the air with sweaty, fishy-smelling smoke. Jo gawked at the eelman, a monstrous heap of greasy rags, wrinkled gray flesh, and throbbing blue eyes, who traded delighted gargles with Aunt Lily (who could speak eel-language fluently) as he delicately held his teacup between thumb and forefinger.

When they were alone, Jo asked Aunt Lily, "Have you seen that show *Teenage Ichthala*?"

"Oh yes! What a load of hooey!" cackled Aunt Lily. "If people believe that applesauce, we've got nothing to worry about."

"But Nora says the Belgian Prankster wrote it," said Jo. "She says it predicts the future."

Aunt Lily's smile became brittle. "You've seen it, Jo. If that show was true, you'd look like a monster, and you could blow things up just by waving your hand."

"But why were so many people *expecting* us when we came out of that fish? Didn't the show predict that?"

"Sir Oliver and I are looking into it." Aunt Lily's face tightened, then relaxed. "Anyway, that fish happened to vomit us up right into the middle of a festival. They weren't gathered there for us, exactly. Please, Jo! It's best if you just leave the worrying to Sir Oliver and me."

Jo did find it easier to leave her problems to Aunt Lily and Sir Oliver. There was so much to learn, so many new things to do, she felt it was impossible to take everything in. Even in the evenings, the knights would gather the squires together to give seminars about their own specialties: Dame Myra would show off some man-eating flowers or metallic, glassy blobs she'd collected in the fens, or Sir Alasdair would give each squire a different strange musical instrument and watch in silent amusement as they unsuccessfully tried to play them, never offering any help— not even when Nora's instrument got angry, sprouted wings, and flew away. And Dame Isabel was notorious for making the squires smell dozens of her favorite odors and write essays about their impressions.

"A properly trained nose is a passport to a world of wonders!" Dame Isabel declared. "Do you know I can find my way through a maze blindfolded, simply by *smelling my way*? Are you aware that no matter where you hide in this city, I am able to track you down—using only my talented nose? I can even predict the weather! Jo! What does a thunderstorm smell like a week before it hits?"

"I honestly couldn't say."

"It smells precisely like *boiled cabbage*. The nose is a muscle!" Dame Isabel flared her nostrils, like a weight lifter flexing. "Most people use less than two percent of their nose! Do you know how much of *my* nose—"

"Thirty-eight percent," said all the squires wearily, for they had all heard it a hundred times.

It was sad but true: the knights were capable of being utterly tedious, such as Sir Oort, who finally made good on his threat to teach Jo about discredited metaphysics. Every Wednesday at 5:00 A.M. Jo was obliged to drag herself out of bed and stumble down the hall—usually still in her pajamas—to Sir Oort's rooms, where he taught his excruciatingly dull lessons.

Sir Oort would babble away happily, covering chalkboards with mathematical symbols, and Jo hardly understood a word of it. But she couldn't bring herself to quit, for Sir Oort seemed to get such pleasure from it. And there *was* one metaphysical question Jo meant to ask Sir Oort, a question that had been nagging her ever since she'd come to Eldritch City.

"Sir Oort, could you clear something up?" said Jo. "Where *is* Eldritch City? I'd never heard of it before I came here, and nobody from Eldritch City knows anything about my home, either."

"Yes, yes, it's an *intriguing* question," said Sir Oort eagerly. "And a coincidence you should mention it! For I have just put the finishing touches on my newest theory of metaphysics, which deals with just such questions! I will explain it now! *Using a visual aid!*" he squeaked vehemently, and took a large, rolled-up map from his satchel.

Jo looked at Sir Oort with silent apprehension, wondering what she'd gotten herself into, as the tiny metaphysician enthusiastically spread the map on the table. "Now, Jo, let me ask you— do you notice anything familiar on this map?"

"Um . . . no."

"No, but you *do,* you *do.* Look over here—and there—and way over there. *Eh?*"

Jo squinted and tilted her head. "Well, it looks like a map of the world—but it's wrong, isn't it?" she said. "I mean, there's Africa, and North America here, and Europe . . . but they're not in the right places. And there's a lot of other continents I've never seen before."

"Precisely," said Sir Oort. "What you recognize, Jo, are just your little corners of the world. The *real* world, the total reality of the world, is a thousand times larger than that. What you had thought of as your world—and what people in Eldritch City think of as their world—are just *small, disconnected bits* of the actual entire world. According to my theory, there are thousands of these regions, all hidden from each other. Most of the world is still unexplored!"

"Wait, I *know* that's not true!" said Jo. "The world has been explored, at least where I'm from. They've taken satellite photos from space, and—"

"No, no, no. How can I explain it?" Sir Oort frowned, lost in thought; then he suddenly leaped up, seized the map in his furry hands, and crumpled it into a wad.

Jo protested, "Sir Oort, what are you—"

Sir Oort waved her silent. "Jo! Let's say, for the sake of argument, that you are a bug! Okay? You're a tiny flea who lives on this crumpled-up map. Naturally, you can't see most of the map, because it's crumpled under you, inside the wad. But you can see *some* of the map—the parts on the surface—right?"

"Okay, but—hey, how'd you do that!" said Jo, for she suddenly realized that, by a miracle of origami, Sir Oort had crumpled the map so that it resembled a globe of the world: folding all the continents she didn't recognize inside the wad, and exposing the parts of the map she did recognize on the surface.

Sir Oort held up his finger. "Up until recently, Jo, you've been like a flea, crawling around on the surface of this wadded-up map. Naturally, you only saw the parts of the map on the *surface*. And thus never realized"—Sir Oort uncrumpled the map—"that there was a hidden world crumpled beneath you. Not physically beneath you—I mean crumpled into another dimension. A world you never knew about. Until now."

Jo's mind wrestled with the concept, and then, as if something had unlocked deep in her brain, she understood.

"And that," breathed Jo, astonished, "*that's* what the world is really like?"

"Well, no." Sir Oort smiled. "But you must admit I had you going for a second."

"*What?*" said Jo. "So all this you've been explaining . . . *It's not true?*"

"Oh, it might be true," said Sir Oort mildly. "But of course my job isn't to find out what's true. My job is to think up as many dubious theories of the universe as I can, and the more dubious, the better. Most of my theories are wrong most of the time, but some are entertaining."

Jo threw up her hands. "This is ridiculous! You're not even *trying* to be right?"

At this rebuke Sir Oort halted, grew grave, and drew himself up; for a moment, he radiated a kind of majesty; then he spoke, in tones both severe and inspiring, and his awkward voice rang out like a bell.

"As an Odd-Fish, it is not my job to be right," said Sir Oort. "It is my job to be wrong in new and exciting ways."

Sometimes the knights cooperated in joint projects that combined their specialties, such as when Sir Alasdair and Dame Delia announced an undertaking bringing together his expertise in odd musical instruments and hers in strange animals. The day of the seminar, the squires were milling about in the common room, wondering what it could possibly be, when there appeared at the top of the stairs—*a gigantic worm;* a great blubbery thing, dark yellow with red streaks, with little wriggling tubes sticking out all over and a single bored-looking red eye. Dame Delia and Daphne came tumbling after the seething beast, pulling at ropes, frantically trying to rein it in as it cascaded down the stairs.

The appearance of a monster in the lodge was shocking enough, but the most shocking thing was when the worm's huge jaws opened and Sir Alasdair's face poked smugly out. The squires shouted in alarm, but Dame Delia calmed them down as Sir Alasdair started to lecture.

"As you know, my specialty is unusual musical instruments," announced Sir Alasdair. "And for all my life, I've dreamed of playing the most unusual instrument of all: a living animal! One day, Dame Delia told me about the anatomy of this beast—the *urk-ack*—and I realized my dream had come true. The urk-ack has forty-one orifices that can emit sounds; not only that, but a full-grown man may fit comfortably in its esophagus! Thus, by climbing inside the urk-ack and squeezing its various internal organs, I will perform the most unusual music ever!"

Jo was delighted. "Can you play anything now?"

"Oh no, not yet. I couldn't possibly——"

"Come on!" clamored the squires. "Play something, at least! Give us a hint!"

"Out of the question," said Sir Alasdair. "I climbed inside the urk-ack for the first time barely an hour ago. In theory, I know which of its organs to squeeze or pinch, but in practice——"

"Oh, give it a go!" said Ian, and everyone started insisting. Sir Alasdair, red-faced from the attention, murmured, "Well, maybe just a little—couldn't hurt."

Jo immediately wished she hadn't asked. There followed a minute of the most horrible noises she'd ever heard—a howling, farting crescendo of gurgling belches and groans. Even the urk-ack looked mortified as Sir Alasdair grunted with effort, poking and squeezing its innards.

When he finished, there was an awkward silence.

Sir Alasdair coughed. "Of course, it needs a little work."

One morning Sefino woke Jo up and said, "I do hope you've finished with that piece I asked you to write, because today we're going to the *Eldritch Snitch*."

"Sefino, do we have to?" yawned Jo. "I'm sure everyone's forgotten Chatterbox's article."

"My dear girl, *I* have not forgotten it," said Sefino severely. "I shall not rest until they print a retraction. And an apology. And your version of the story. Is this it? You mind if I take a look?" Sefino took her papers and began to read.

"It's a first draft," said Jo cautiously. Actually, it was her fifth. She'd tried to be as truthful as possible without embarrassing Sefino, but that was difficult to manage.

The cockroach read: "*Sefino's conduct reminded us time and again that he is a gentleman*. That's a fine sentence. Hmmm. Ah . . . *Sefino passionately threw himself into the moment. We may very well owe our lives to his energetic action.* Ooh, that's good. A little vague, but good."

"I'm glad you like it."

Sefino stroked his chin. "Why not change *We may very well owe our lives to him* to just *We owe our lives to him?*"

"No."

"It flows better."

"No."

"You needn't get snippy," said Sefino. "It's purely a matter of grammar. Hmmm . . . *Sefino passionately threw himself into the moment* . . . there's a touch of bravado in that, isn't there? *Passionately* . . . Yes, I threw caution to the wind, odds be damned . . . I charged into the thick of the fight . . . like a swashbuckler . . . what does *swashbuckler* mean? Who cares? *Swashbuckling Sefino passionately saved our lives.* There, that's perfect. Write that."

"You're pushing it, Sefino."

"Nonsense. I have excellent taste, and I can assure you that *Swashbuckling Sefino passionately saved our lives* would heighten the tone of the piece. It would lift it to a higher plane, to the psychological, to the sublime . . . the mystical, I daresay . . ."

Sefino strolled off happily, rolling the words about in his mouth. "*Swashbuckling Sefino* . . . *Swashbuckling Sefino* . . . why, it's like a little poem."

That afternoon Jo and Sefino visited the *Eldritch Snitch*. The newspaper's offices were a hive of dark wood, a claustrophobic maze of mahogany niches, coves, and cubbyholes, and everywhere there was the soft, steady din of typewriters, hundreds of them, chattering away relentlessly. The newspaper was staffed by centipedes, and Jo watched in wonder as they scuttled through the twisting maze of wood, darting up and down ladders and popping in and out of narrow cracks. It was dark and smoky, which made the centipedes' appearances and disappearances into the gloom, and their silhouettes in the haze, seem almost sinister.

"They're going to hassle us," warned Sefino. "They're going to snub us. They're going to make us wait. They're going to play mind games with us. *I know their kind.* Be careful. Anything we do or say could be snatched up, blown all out of proportion, and blasted across the front page of the evening edition. It's a nest of vipers! Anyway . . . what do you think of my necktie?"

"It's a fine necktie."

"Technically it's an ascot. It's a very forceful ascot. I call it the 'Intimidator.' You're overwhelmed by it, aren't you? The ascot overwhelms you. It's almost *too* bold. When you see an ascot like this, your only choices are submit to it or fight it. And that is a fight you will surely lose."

"How about fleeing?" said Jo. "One could submit, fight, or flee."

"True," said Sefino thoughtfully. "One might flee."

A receptionist said, "Welcome to the *Eldritch Snitch*. May I help you?"

Sefino drew himself up. "I demand to speak to Chatterbox."

"Right away, sir. Follow me."

"That was unexpectedly easy," said Sefino as the receptionist led them down the hall. "Of course, it may very well be a trap. They're playing games with us, Jo, *psychological games*."

"Maybe it was your ascot."

"That's certainly possible. This ascot almost constitutes an unfair advantage. I've even knotted it in an aggressive manner. It *juts*. It springs forth, it is a barely restrained beast, this ascot. It picks you up and shakes you. It says, 'If you want this cockroach, you'll have to come through me first.'"

They entered a waiting room with some comfortable couches and a frosted glass door with the word CHATTERBOX on it.

Sefino whispered, "This is where they're going to start being rude to us. Just you watch."

The receptionist said, "I'll go tell Chatterbox you're here.

For now, why don't you enjoy some of our award-winning appetizers?"

"*Award-winning*? I'll be the judge of that," said Sefino icily, and picked a sausage off a plate with a toothpick, dipping it in a bowl of mustard. The receptionist disappeared behind the door, leaving Jo and Sefino alone.

"Jo, let me do the talking here," said Sefino. "I'm afraid the subtleties of this battle of wits may be beyond your abilities to keep up with, or indeed understand. Just sit back and be dazzled by the vigorous verbal vituperation as Chatterbox and I engage in a battle royale of intricate insult and calamitous calumny. You know, these appetizers really *are* delicious, and I shall have another."

"Do you remember what Chatterbox looks like?" said Jo.

"All centipedes look the same to me. I will recognize him by his sheer ungentlemanliness."

"Good, good."

The receptionist reappeared. "Chatterbox is out at the moment. Would you please wait for five minutes?"

"*Five minutes?*" thundered Sefino. "I shall not wait *five seconds*! I have come to this unholy temple of slander to seek justice, not to lounge about for five minutes and eat award-winning appetizers! Oh, I know your strategy. First you have us wait five minutes—then ten minutes—then an hour—then *ten hours!*—while you and Chatterbox giggle behind a one-way mirror—*such as this one!*" Sefino swung his walking stick, smashing a mirror to pieces.

There was only a wall behind it.

"Please stop breaking our mirrors," said the receptionist.

"Another trick!" shouted Sefino. He grabbed Jo's arm and, before she could protest, brushed past the receptionist, dragging Jo into Chatterbox's office, where a centipede wearing a seersucker suit and a porkpie hat was standing at a desk.

"So! The infamous Chatterbox!" cried Sefino. "We meet again! But this time the advantage is *mine!*"

The centipede looked at Sefino calmly.

Sefino brandished a stack of newspaper clippings and waved them around. "Ooh, I have you now, you ink-stained *wretch,* you scandal-sniffing *hack*—I have it all here, all your salacious slander from the last ten years, libelously lambasting me in my exile!"

The centipede raised his eyebrows.

"Evidence!" roared Sefino. "You ask for evidence! What is this? Evidence! Ha, ha! Of what? Oho! Evidence of you, besmirching the sacred reputation of a gentleman! But it shall not stand! No! Sir! I call you to account!"

The centipede looked at his watch.

"You!" spluttered Sefino. "You . . . you look at your watch! To find out what time it is, no doubt! Well, I will *tell* you what time it is, my good man! It is time for you to apologize in full and retract the lies, once and for all! And print this correction," he added, snatching Jo's story away from her and flinging it onto the desk. "Ah ha, ha! No need to look at your watch now! I, Sefino, have told you what time it is. Now then!"

The centipede sighed softly.

"And still you do not speak!" said Sefino, dancing about in rage. "What do you have to say for yourself? Well, Chatterbox? *What do you have to say?*"

"I say," said an unseen voice, "that your impertinence is matched only by your insufferable taste in neckwear."

Sefino whirled. A huge centipede, twice his height, was looming behind him.

"Chatterbox!" said the centipede at the desk.

"Chatterbox?" said Jo.

"Er," said Sefino.

Chatterbox circled Sefino, his long, snaky body undulating under his exquisitely tailored "fifteen-piece" suit. The centipede curled and stooped, closely inspecting the little cockroach; finally he reared to his full height and turned away.

"As a general rule, I do not speak to people with mustard on their ascots. Good day."

Sefino looked down in horror. Indeed, he had dripped mustard from his award-winning appetizer onto the "Intimidator."

At once every ounce of courage drained away from him. Sefino picked up his hat and, mumbling apologies, went out the door. Jo ran after him, but he waved her away. They left the *Eldritch Snitch,* and she kept trying to comfort him, but Sefino would not respond the whole way back to the lodge.

"Sefino, don't take it so hard. You shouldn't care what they write about you. Come on, Sefino! . . . Sefino? . . . Sefino, why won't you answer me?"

"Please, Jo." He turned away from her. "I know that I'm . . . I'm just a buffoon."

Sefino went to his room, his jaw trembling. Jo did not see him again for days.

FIFTEEN

A couple of weeks later, Colonel Korsakov and Sir Festus gathered the squires on the porch.

"Today we go Schwenk-hunting," said Korsakov. "My digestion feels adventurous this morning. A sprightly zing in my gastric acids . . . but enough! The Schwenk is out there," he rumbled, gesturing at the street with a broad wave, "and we shall find him. Sir Festus?"

"Thank you, old boy." Sir Festus stood beside a big oak chest full of curious devices. "As you all know, my field of study is weaponry. Now, Korsakov and I hit upon an idea—that is, to use the weapons I've collected over the years in today's hunt! Yes, the Schwenk is a dangerous, elusive beast, and you should all be appropriately armed!"

The squires murmured excitedly as Umberto distributed the weapons. As a spiky, powerful-looking gun was pressed into her hands, Jo asked, "How will we know if we see the Schwenk?"

"Don't worry, you'll know," chuckled Sir Festus. "It is five times the size of a full-grown man, although it can curl into a tiny ball. It is covered in purple, yellow, and red feathers. And it has four mighty wings that, when spread, span fully thirty feet."

"So it flies?"

"No."

"But it has wings?"

"Oh, it *can* fly. But it rarely does."

"Why not?"

"Modesty."

Umberto finished distributing the weapons to the squires. Each weapon was unlike the others; some were unlike anything else on earth. Ian was given a tiny, thin, jewel-encrusted tube; Daphne held a damp mass of prickly fur between her thumb and forefinger, looking confused about what to do next; and Dugan was unsuccessfully wrestling with something that resembled a hissing, gurgling clump of old computer parts.

"Of course," said Sir Festus breezily, "it's only fair to warn you that I have little idea how they work, or what they actually do."

"You don't know what these weapons *do*?" said Albert.

"I was hoping you'd help me figure that out. Well, I do know about *some* of them." Sir Festus took the spiky gun from Jo. "This is one of the most impressive weapons in my arsenal, and a personal favorite—a long-range, triple-accuracy Apology Gun."

"That doesn't sound so impressive," said Jo.

"Are you off your head, girl? The Apology Gun is *most* impressive. And quite ancient. This little lovely goes back to the legendary war between the Vondorians and the Snoosnids, known to history as the Very Polite War."

By now, Jo could tell when Sir Festus was about to launch into one of his long, confusing, tedious stories. His mustache perked up, he licked his lips, and he wiggled his fingers with delight, beginning:

"The Vondorians were renowned throughout the ancient world for their etiquette. Their civilization had a proper way to do everything, from opening a door to proposing marriage. Their entire lives were elaborate ceremonies, in which you were required to recite a certain thousand-line poem every time you bumped into someone on the street, or do a traditional dance whenever you took off your hat. Every action of a Vondorian was ritualized and beautiful.

"But then the Vondorians came up against the Snoosnids. The Snoosnids were ruthlessly, dangerously polite. They were masters of the deadly thank-you note, the murderous curtsy, the lethal tea party. It was rumored the Snoosnids had a special way of saying 'excuse me' that could kill you instantly. Snoosnid assassins were so charming and courteous that their victims would literally die of tact.

"So when the Snoosnids declared war on the Vondorians (because of a disagreement over the placement of the soup spoon at a diplomatic dinner), it was one of the strangest wars in history. Luckily, some artifacts of the era still survive, such as the Apology Gun."

"I still don't understand what it does," said Jo.

"There were many great battles in the Very Polite War," said Sir Festus. "But so many improper things happened in those battles that both sides were bound by etiquette to continually apologize for what they were doing. The apologies on either side grew more extravagantly effusive as each side tried to outdo the other, degenerating into chaotic mass apologies, an ugly free-for-all of manners. Imagine the horror! Thousands of soldiers charging toward each other, saying they were sorry, and then running away before they could hear their opponent's apologies. The war was stalemated like this for years—until the Vondorians invented the Apology Gun."

"Why?" said Jo.

"Watch." Sir Festus pointed the gun at Colonel Korsakov. There was a POW, a puff of blue smoke, and a small tube of paper flew out and bounced off Korsakov's chest.

Colonel Korsakov picked up the tube, unscrolled it, and read aloud: " 'Sorry for the rudeness.' Thank you, Sir Festus. Apology accepted."

"You're welcome," said Sir Festus, bowing slightly. "See? Very civilized. And this baby can shoot up to three hundred apologies per second. Pretty devastating stuff."

"But what good did that do in the war?" said Albert.

"Aha," said Sir Festus. "The apologies were extremely sarcastic."

"A brilliant strategy," nodded Korsakov.

Sir Festus showed Jo a small dial. "You can adjust this knob from 'sincere' to 'sarcastic,' depending on what kind of apologies you want to fire. Because of the overwhelming number of apologies the Vondorians made, and the withering irony of each apology, the Vondorians swiftly crushed the Snoosnids and won the war."

Jo said, "But what good will this be against the Schwenk?"

"Against the Schwenk? Oh, none at all."

"What about these other weapons——?"

"Utterly useless."

"Then why are we using them?"

"Style, my girl. Style."

Sir Festus divided the squires into groups and assigned each group a neighborhood to search for the Schwenk. Jo, Ian, and Nora were assigned to East Squeamings, a district of wooden shacks, narrow streets, and a sprawling fish market.

All morning Jo, Ian, and Nora snooped through stinking alleys packed with stalls of outlandish undersea creatures. There were slimy purple sacs hanging in dripping bunches, moist piles of wriggling white blobs with shimmering fins and panting mouths, neatly arranged rows of bulging tubes with staring eyes and dozens of tentacles, and the occasional massive sea beast, twenty times bigger than Jo, trussed up and gored on thick hooks. The market was raucous with the shouts of hawkers, customers, and auctioneers calling out to circles of gesticulating bidders. The slime, stink, and noise were overwhelming; Jo almost forgot about the Schwenk and let herself be swept up in the bustling cacophony.

But even after hours of combing through the markets, they found not a trace of the Schwenk. Ian suggested lunch at one of the neighborhood's famous fish restaurants.

"I don't come down here often enough," said Ian happily as they settled into a booth. "This is one of my favorite restaurants."

"I'm down here *all the time,*" groused Nora. "Dame Isabel can't get enough of the smells. She says that for someone with a trained nose, it's like being at the bottom of the ocean. I say, why settle for second best? She can *go* to the bottom of the ocean, and stay there, for all I care. And take her precious nose with her."

"I thought you liked Dame Isabel," said Jo.

"Are you kidding? She doesn't give me a minute to myself. If I'm not out hunting smells with her, I'm cataloguing her stupid collection. I barely have enough time to work on my *Teenage Ichthala* theories. . . . You know, Jo, Isabel has it in for you, but I can't guess why."

"Maybe because she hates my aunt," said Jo.

"Could be."

The waiter came around. Jo didn't recognize anything on the menu, so Ian and Nora ordered for her.

Ian was tapping his fingers. "I really hope we find the Schwenk."

"I don't," said Jo.

"What, aren't you excited to take on your first monster?"

"Take on? How? By telling it I'm sorry three hundred times per second?"

"At least you know what your weapon does," sighed Nora. Hers was a metal sphere bristling with antennae, buttons, dials, and lights, all equally mysterious. She had lugged it around all day, pressing buttons and trying the dials; occasionally the sphere would light up, vibrate, smoke, and make promising noises; but so far, it had done nothing else.

"I just want to get Commissioner Olvershaw off Korsakov's back," said Ian.

"Olvershaw really let him have it, didn't he?" said Jo. "I thought Korsakov was going to cry."

"He wasn't going to *cry*," said Ian.

"Don't snap," said Nora.

"I'm sorry. I know, I get defensive about him," said Ian. "I mean, everyone admires Dame Lily. She's the one who killed Sir Nils, right? But Korsakov . . . he's just the guy who got knocked down and then was saved by his *butler*. I hear what people say."

Their food arrived, and conversation paused as they passed around the plates, taking a little from each. Jo had never had food like this: it was like sushi from Jupiter. Blubbery cubes floating in black-licorice broth, spheres of flaky crust enfolding morsels of nutty meat, a bowl of warm eyes that burst juicily in her mouth, blue worms wriggling in a pot of cream . . .

Just as they were finishing eating, Nora sat up in surprise, staring at a group of people across the restaurant. "Look, look! Over there!"

"Who is it?" said Jo.

Nora said, in an awed whisper, "That's Audrey Durdle. That's the girl who plays the Ichthala on *Teenage Ichthala*. I think that's the whole cast right there!"

Jo could just barely make out, through the hubbub of diners, a blond girl slouching in her chair, indifferently studying a script and drinking coffee, ignoring the half-dozen chattering men and women at her table.

Ian snorted, "Nora, you are too into that show."

"I'm going to casually walk over there and eavesdrop," said Nora, standing.

Ian said, "Why don't you ask them to do an episode about us

finding the Schwenk? According to your logic, then we're sure to find it."

"A comedian," said Nora, and left.

After Nora was gone, Ian said to Jo, "I saw them setting up to film their show around the corner, but don't tell Nora. She'll just hang around the set all day and forget about hunting the Schwenk."

"What'll you do if we find the Schwenk?"

"I'm not sure. Well, I do have this." Ian took out the jewel-encrusted needle Sir Festus had given him and placed it on the table.

Jo said, "Did Sir Festus tell you what it does?"

"He said he forgot," said Ian. "He does recall it was something devastating."

"Big deal. Mine's 'devastating,' too."

"I'm hoping for the best," said Ian. "Sir Festus advised me to hold my fire until I actually see the Schwenk, though. He said there's only one shot left in it."

"So there's no way of telling what it does," said Jo. "It might shoot flowers and romantic poetry."

"It might. But that's all right."

"Really?"

"Colonel Korsakov says hunting the Schwenk is a gentleman's pursuit. It wouldn't be sporting to use effective weapons."

"There's something in that," said Jo.

Nora was haunting the area around Audrey Durdle's table, drifting back and forth, desperately trying to eavesdrop. But after a few pointed glares, she got embarrassed and slunk back to Jo and Ian.

"Well?" said Jo. "What'd they say?"

"It's so exciting!" said Nora. "They had just gotten the scripts for the latest episode! They're all talking about what will happen—there's a scene in the Silent Sisters' secret cathedral, and—"

"Nora, do you talk about *anything* other than that show?"

murmured Ian as he scanned the bill. He dropped some money on the table and stood up. "Come on, let's go find the Schwenk."

Just outside the restaurant and down the street there were some actors in costumes, surrounded by cameramen. Nora grabbed Jo's arm and said wildly, "I knew it! They're filming *Teenage Ichthala* right here! That's why Audrey Durdle was in the restaurant!"

Ian winced. "I was hoping you wouldn't see that."

Nora stopped short. "You *knew* they were filming in the neighborhood? And you *didn't tell me?*"

"If I'd told you, you wouldn't have helped us look for the Schw—"

"Screw your Schwenk!" said Nora, her eyes blazing. "You know what this means to me!"

"I thought you were going to help us," said Ian.

"Just because Korsakov can't finish his own quest doesn't mean we should do it for him," said Nora.

"That's not fair," said Jo.

"No, it's not fair," said Nora. "Neither is lying to your friends so they'll do what you want. Good luck, Jo. I hope *you* find it." She gave Ian a final glare and stalked off to the *Teenage Ichthala* set, dragging her bulky sphere behind her.

Ian glumly watched her go. "I didn't know she'd get that mad."

"C'mon, let's get out of here," said Jo.

Jo and Ian resumed the search for the Schwenk, but it wasn't the same now. Nora, bouncing along at their side, breathlessly babbling her theories, had seemed exasperating before, but now they missed her. Searching for the Schwenk wasn't fun anymore.

Then Ian saw Dugan about a block away. Jo was about to call out to him, but Ian stopped her.

"What's he doing down here?" said Ian. "He was assigned to Eelsbridge. Look, he doesn't even have the weapon Sir Festus gave him!"

"Let's go ask him," said Jo.

"No, wait. Let's follow him."

"Isn't that sneaky?"

"Dugan himself has been sneaky lately. I think he's up to no good. Come on, he's getting away."

Dugan slipped through the streets easily, slicing through the crowds like a knife. Jo and Ian loped behind, caught in snarls of traffic, baffled by Dugan's twisting route. Sometimes Dugan doubled back, ducking down an alley, as though he suspected someone was following him.

Ian looked around nervously. "I don't know this neighborhood very well. Be careful."

They had followed Dugan into Snoodsbottom, a dark warren of caverns hewn out of the heart of the mountain. Sunlight was replaced by the pale glow of luminous fungus and strings of lanterns flickering dimly over the streets. But any light seemed unnatural here. It was gloomy, hot, and stuffy, and the cramped lanes made Jo claustrophobic, the buildings crowding her on either side; she could almost feel the millions of tons of mountain looming over her head.

Dugan pushed on, faster now, his eyes anxious, glancing around every few seconds, now and then breaking into a hurried trot. Finally, getting a hold of his nerves, he turned a corner and walked calmly toward a storefront, where a long lean man awaited him.

What happened next was quick. The man, dressed in an ugly maroon suit with a three-cornered hat, looked up at Dugan with sleepy eyes. Dugan gave the man a small red bag. The man turned and left without a word, and Dugan walked off in the opposite direction.

And then Dugan might have turned to dust, for Jo and Ian could find no further trace of him, and now they were lost, deep in an unfamiliar neighborhood.

"Um . . . I think there's a subway that goes from here to West Rumple," said Ian. "That's probably our best bet."

"Where's the station?"

"I don't know. I think I can find it."

"Let's ask directions," said Jo.

"No! Don't speak to anyone!" hissed Ian.

Jo blinked at Ian's sudden fierceness but said nothing. Still, they needed directions: the maze of tunnels and caves confused them, and more than once they found themselves at a dead end or forced to hurry through pitch-black alleys toward uncertain lights at the other side. One time they saw the subway station, but from a cliff that overlooked a vast cavern, and there was no direct route down to it, and their efforts to head toward it led to a quagmire of wrong turns and frustrating circles. They never saw the station again.

"What was Dugan doing down here?" murmured Ian. "It doesn't make sense."

"What are *we* doing here?" said Jo. "This is like a bad dream. Can't we just ask someone?"

"Don't talk to anyone!" growled Ian. "I mean it!"

Now Jo was annoyed. Who did he think he was, talking to her like that? She silently fumed, but Ian didn't explain himself, and so they walked on together in angry silence.

Even though Jo's mood had soured, and the labyrinth of caverns only led them in circles, there was a crammed, convoluted beauty to the neighborhood. Creepers dangled down over carved walls, blooming with flowers that half hid stone monsters underneath. The streets twisted, dipped and curved, and there were bubbling little fountains everywhere—silver basins of black water in which lilies floated and strange shapes slithered. There was no escaping the sweaty, dismal heat, and the stale air was spiced with heavy incense, smoking in brass pots hanging from the windows. The stuffy vapors went to Jo's head; she was beginning to feel woozy.

"Watch out!"

"Out of the road!"

Three sleds burst out of the gloom, rocketing past—silver sleds, shimmering in the darkness, carved in patterns as delicate and complex as lace. Each sled was pulled by three lizard-dogs tearing down the tunnels with startling energy, their eyes bugged out, long black tongues flapping out of their mouths. A driver with a whip and reins stood in each sled, but the sleds flew by so quickly it was impossible to see anything about them other than purple cloaks, steel goggles, and long yellow scarves billowing behind.

"Who are *they*?" said Jo.

Ian groaned. "I knew this would happen. We've got to get out of here. They're squires from the Order of Wormbeards."

"So what?"

"This is their territory. Shhh, they're not on to us yet . . . keep your head down."

More sleds came barreling around the corner, crashing and clattering down the cobbled street. The sleds' iron runners scraped, jounced, and threw sparks, skipping off the stones as the lizard-dogs hauled them down the tunnels.

"Looks like fun," said Jo.

"Why don't you ask them for a ride?" said Ian sarcastically. Then: *"Get back!"*

Ian yanked Jo out of the road just as a sled burst out of the alley. They pressed their backs against the wall as the lizard-dogs went bounding past, nearly running them over, barking and howling down the tunnels.

"Hey! Odd-Fish!" shouted the driver.

"Now we're in for it," said Ian. "Stupid, *stupid* coming down here . . . we've got to hide."

Jo frowned. "Hide?"

"There's ten of them and two of us. If you want to get through this alive—" Ian looked around quickly; down the tunnel, whips cracked, the lizard-dogs yapped, and the ferocious shouts of the Wormbeard squires got louder as the sleds turned around toward them. "Get in here," said Ian, pushing her into a small crag behind some vines. "Don't come out until I come for you."

Jo poked her head out of the cave. "Wait, you're going to *leave* me here?"

"There's not enough room for both of us!" said Ian. "I'll be all right. Just stay in there."

He pulled the vines back over her, and then he was gone, his footsteps echoing down the alley. Soon she couldn't even hear the footsteps.

Jo crouched in the little cave and shuddered as the sleds shot past her in shimmering streaks, back and forth, bouncing and skittering over the paving stones. She could barely see through the thick vines, but she heard the Wormbeard squires, shouting, cursing, and mocking:

"Hey! Odd-Fish!"

"Come on out!"

"We know you're here! You can't hide forever!"

So that's why Ian didn't want to talk to anyone, she thought—just as a horrible moistening sound came from behind her and a boneless arm wrapped itself up her leg.

Jo didn't even have time to scream before another tentacle pushed into her mouth. She turned, kicked, and struggled, but she couldn't see what had grabbed hold of her. A huge tongue ran all over her. She was being dragged backward toward—what? She kicked out wildly, and her foot struck something soft and gooey in the darkness.

The groping thing behind her moaned, the tentacles slackened, and she kept kicking, like kicking a bag of jelly, which finally burst with a liquid noise, spilling out in loose gulps. The tentacles went limp, and Jo, gasping, broke free and stumbled from her hiding place out into the open square.

Her skin was pocked with little welts from the suckers. Still, there wasn't enough time to think about injuries, because she was out in the open, with nowhere to hide.

A silver sled hurtled into the square. Before Jo could run, the driver saw her and with a vicious whoop yanked the reins, sending the sled skidding in an arc, plunging toward her.

Jo grabbed her Apology Gun and aimed it at the sled.

At once the driver's eyes went from cruel to panicked. The

lizard-dogs continued to close the distance, but Jo stood still and pointed her gun. The driver pulled at the reins, and the lizard-dogs shrieked as their bits cut into their mouths. They bolted every which way, and the sled tilted, skating along on one runner, throwing a shower of sparks—and then the sled flipped, tumbling with the squealing lizard-dogs into the gutter.

Jo turned to run, but there was nowhere to go. Already more sleds were screeching up the tunnels. And when Jo looked back at the wrecked sled and the limping lizard-dogs, she was startled to see the driver had already got up and was approaching her with quiet menace.

Jo spun and pointed her gun at the driver.

It was a girl with short black hair and fierce eyes. Her skin was sickly and pale, but her face was jarringly beautiful. Her hair was cropped short and bristly, as if to spite her delicate face, but this only made her more hypnotizing, as though she had beauty to throw away. Her lips wavered on the edge of a sneer, and she had merciless eyes, eyes so sharp that a stare hurt. This girl was named Fiona Fuorlini, and the first two words she said to Jo were "You're dead."

Jo replied, "The gun is pointed at *you*."

"I'm not afraid of you," said Fiona.

"You should be," bluffed Jo. "You don't want me to use this."

"You don't have the nerve," said Fiona. "You're an Odd-Fish. You don't have the guts."

Sleds clattered to a stop around them. The Wormbeard squires climbed out, surrounding Jo and Fiona with anticipation.

Where is Ian? Jo thought, looking around, but he was nowhere to be seen.

Fiona sensed the weakness and stepped toward Jo. Jo gripped the useless gun tighter and waggled it at her, saying, "I'm leaving. Get out of my way. I'm leaving."

"You're not leaving."

"I'll shoot you."

"Then shoot me!" said Fiona. "Go ahead, do it!"

"What?"

"I dare you!" snarled Fiona. "I want you to! *I want you to shoot me!* DO IT!"

Jo pulled the trigger. With a puff of blue smoke, an apology shot out and hit Fiona's nose with an almost inaudible *bip*.

The other Wormbeard squires had been holding their breaths; now one whispered, "It's an Apology Gun."

"Oh, an apology!" Fiona relaxed and nodded at Jo. "It's fine, everyone. All she wanted to do was apologize. Let me just read this. . . . Wait—*this apology is sarcastic!*"

The dial had been set to maximum sarcasm.

With an angry bellow, the Wormbeards rushed in. Jo whirled around, looking for a way out, but in every direction she was surrounded by the purple-cloaked, yellow-scarf-wearing, steel-goggled squires.

Then there was a deafening roar, and a powerful force knocked everyone on their backs. The roar went on and on, a mounting chorus of heightening howls, and everyone was picked up and tossed around as if they were caught in a hurricane. Jo blundered through the smoke and noise, staggering over the fallen bodies of the Wormbeards, and into Ian.

He held his little bejeweled tube gingerly, looking embarrassed.

"Sir Festus was right," he said. "This is a pretty devastating bugger."

The temporary tornado whirled faster and faster, throwing the Wormbeards around like paper dolls. Jo and Ian tore themselves out of the miniature storm and took off running.

"Where now?" gasped Jo.

"I found a way out. Come on!"

The lizard-dogs were released from their sleds and bounded after Jo and Ian with great springing leaps, barking and shrieking. The Wormbeards ran behind the lizard-dogs, roaring for blood. Fiona Fuorlini mounted another sled and whipped its lizard-dogs forward.

Jo ran after Ian, twisting and turning through the tunnels of Snoodsbottom, clambering over fences and walls to throw off the lizard-dogs. Then Jo saw sunlight and sprinted toward it with all her might. A lizard-dog's jaw nipped at her thigh, and she artfully kicked it and sent it squealing to the gutter.

They ran out into East Squeamings, throwing it into an uproar, dashing through the fish markets, overturning tables of twitching squids and squishy blobs. The hawkers and merchants scattered as the Wormbeards and their lizard-dogs galloped after them, slipping on the slimy stones and crashing through the stalls with reckless glee.

Jo and Ian blundered around a corner and onto the set of *Teenage Ichthala*. A couple of actors were reciting their lines as the cameras rolled. Nora was there, too, watching intently. Jo and Ian came barreling through, and cameras overturned with sparks and hissing smoke, scripts were flung into the air, and actors scattered as the lizard-dogs and Wormbeards came in pursuit.

The police trundled up in their rolling towers, descending upon the scene with their red uniforms and swinging clubs. The Wormbeards shouted, "Cops!" and tried to scatter, but the policemen had them surrounded. Jo was whirled, yanked, and pushed through the roiling crowd, actors and Wormbeards and police thrown together, blindly bashing each other. Just as the police closed in to control the mob, Jo felt her shoulder grabbed. She turned to see who it was—and gave a little shriek.

It was a hideous gray mask of scabs: the Ichthala.

No—she looked into the monster's eyes—it was the actress who played the Ichthala. Jo stared at Audrey Durdle, and the girl peered back at Jo with surprise and a strange sadness.

"Jo! Over here!"

Ian grabbed Jo away from the actress and pulled her over to Nora, who waved them through a door on the side of the road and slammed it shut behind them. A narrow stairway led up to the next level of the mountain. Jo and Ian ran up after Nora, leaving the roar of lizard-dogs and the angry shouts of policemen and Wormbeards below.

Nora said, "I leave you two alone for one hour and you start a riot!"

"Where are we going?" Ian wheezed behind her.

The stairs led up into an abandoned garage, a quiet cave with a tall archway that looked out onto the cobbled streets. There were a few half-assembled automobiles here, in various states of rust and disrepair, and the garage curved and continued back into darkness.

As soon as Jo and Ian realized they were safe, they broke into relieved laughter.

"That was the most fun I've had in weeks!" said Jo.

"Thanks, Nora," said Ian. "We owe you one."

Nora scrunched her face. "You'll get your chance to have fun again soon, Jo. The Wormbeards have a long memory."

"Oh, whatever, bring it on," said Jo. "Woo!"

"Hey," said Ian. "What's this red, yellow, and purple feather doing here?"

For a dreadful second, Jo, Ian, and Nora stared at the feather on the ground.

And then something burst out of the dark corner of the garage—a gargantuan, flapping, snorting, screeching bird, crashing through the garage toward the exit, bowling them all over and blasting out of the archway with a triumphant screech. When Jo, Ian, and Nora got up, they saw the proud shape of the Schwenk soaring overhead, all four of its wings outstretched, turning slowly in the sky; then it plunged away from the city, toward the forest, with incredible speed, and was seen no more.

A few seconds later, Sir Festus, Colonel Korsakov, and a few squires came jogging up, their wild assortment of unreliable weapons cocked and wielded, but too late—the Schwenk was gone.

"Too late!" sighed Colonel Korsakov. "And we were so close!"

"Next time, Colonel Korsakov," said Ian. "We almost had him."

"Oh, come on, Ian!" said Jo. "That was pure chance."

"Congratulations, nevertheless," said Colonel Korsakov. "My digestion had deduced the Schwenk was in this neighborhood, but all my efforts to pinpoint its precise location were in vain. I blame the nearly indigestible soufflé I had for lunch, which had the effect of decalibrating my large intestine."

"I thought you said the Schwenk didn't fly," said Jo. "I thought you said it was modest."

"A disturbing development," said Colonel Korsakov. "The Schwenk is getting cheeky."

"Does this happen every time you hunt the Schwenk?" said Jo.

"More or less."

"Have you ever even come close to catching it?"

"Not exactly. Not as such. No."

"I've never asked—what's *your* specialty for the Odd-Fish?" said Jo.

"Lost causes," said Korsakov cheerfully.

SIXTEEN

BUT what about Ken Kiang?

Ken Kiang had come up against a wall—and that wall was the Belgian Prankster. Ken Kiang was overwhelmed. He was overpowered. He could not even think about the Belgian Prankster for too long before he would feel his soul dwindle and teeter on the precipice of being blasted to nothing by the sheer demonic grandeur that was the Belgian Prankster.

Ken Kiang had gone to the Belgian Prankster to prove himself; he had come away baffled and reeling. He had hit his limit, and his soul broke upon it. He had staked the meaning of his life on becoming the most evil man in the world, and now he was shattered against something so much more evil, so hugely, senselessly lawless, that he was staggered by the almost infinite gulf between the piddling mischief he was capable of, and the unimaginably gargantuan evil of the Belgian Prankster. He knew, like a slap in the face, that he could never bridge that gulf.

The envelope the Belgian Prankster had given him sat unopened on his desk. Ken Kiang had vowed never to open the envelope. He knew that would only play into the schemes of his incalculable foe. He understood that as soon as he opened it, he would cease to be the protagonist of his own story and would become a mere supporting character in the Belgian Prankster's story, which engulfed all stories and made everyone bit players to his colossal personality.

But late one cold, sleepless night, Ken Kiang's curiosity got the better of him, and he sprang out of bed, ran down the stairs, and threw open the doors to his office, where the envelope sat innocently on the windowsill. He tore it open and started to read.

His fascination only deepened as he read. When he realized he had been standing and reading for an hour, shivering in his thin dressing gown, he retreated to his cozy library, where he built a crackling fire and poured some brandy. He read the mass of papers until the early morning.

They were instructions: instructions on how to get to Eldritch City, and orders detailing what he must do when he arrived there. The Belgian Prankster had drafted him as a foot soldier in some vast, complex plan, and Ken Kiang was told only what he needed to know to fulfill his small part; nevertheless, he could feel the shape of the sublime structure of evil he was invited to join, even if he could understand neither its methods nor its aim. The plan, like the Belgian Prankster, was a bottomless entity that threatened to swallow Ken Kiang if he thought about it too hard. He could, at best, play around the edges of this abyss; he could never defeat it.

But it is the willingness to set oneself against the invincible that makes a hero. Of course, Ken Kiang wasn't a hero in the sense that he would, say, save a child from a fire—the very notion nauseated him—but he was a hero in that he was willing to stake everything on a hopeless gamble. He was overwhelmed by the Belgian Prankster, but nevertheless he vowed to fight him. He might disrupt the inscrutable mechanisms and awesome calculations of the Belgian Prankster's grand design; it might be impossible, for after all he was invited to be only a minor functionary in the great plan, but he would attempt it nonetheless. There was no swagger here, no vainglory. The Belgian Prankster had burned away Ken Kiang's vanity. He resolved to fight the Belgian Prankster with the resignation of one who knows he will fail and die in the attempt.

Sadly, but with a quiet dignity, Ken Kiang put his affairs in order. He knew that wherever he was going, there would be no coming back. He sold his vast collections; he gave away the villainous costumes he had so lovingly and painstakingly sewn himself; and he left the black zeppelins and jet fighters of his "Fleet of Fury" to freeze in the Antarctic.

Ken Kiang felt he was saying goodbye to a kind of childhood. The nostalgia he felt was similar to what he'd experienced when, as a moody teenager, he had half contemptuously packed away his toys into cardboard boxes and stashed them under the stairs, vowing never to open them again. Just as then, when he had paused over a box of action figures, tempted to play with them one last time, Ken Kiang now lingered over a wicked-looking sacrificial knife. Should he perform that unspeakable ritual once more, on that blood-drenched altar deep in the New York subway tunnels, where the chanting of the damned reverberated with unholy magnificence and a crawling chaos was coaxed from the darkness to feed on innocence? Heck, just once more, for old times' sake?

Just as before, Ken Kiang mastered his childish whim and mildly packed the knife away. Ken Kiang was still committed to evil, but now it was evil of a higher sort. He needed no silly props or showy fanfare. Purity of heart is to will one thing, and Ken Kiang's heart was pure with a single wish: to destroy the Belgian Prankster.

But there was one last project from Ken Kiang's former life that he had to attend to before he could wholeheartedly embrace his new cause. It was petty, yes, but Ken Kiang feared that to leave this task unfinished might disturb the peace of mind he needed to pursue his profound quest. Ken Kiang could not bear to leave anything undone; and so he resolved, before he left this world, to secure the damnation of Hoagland Shanks.

For Ken Kiang loathed Hoagland Shanks. No, it went beyond loathing: Shanks repulsed him, filled him with almost unbearable disgust. Ken Kiang didn't understand why, but there was something so smug about Shanks, so stupid and self-satisfied, that Ken Kiang could barely tolerate his existence.

Thus Ken Kiang vowed to send the happy-go-lucky handyman to hell.

Ken Kiang knew how a man could make a hell of his own life. Fortunately, most people are not exposed to the temptations that destroy souls, and so they muddle through their small lives harmlessly, a little frustrated but more or less content, enjoying the humdrum happiness that is the lot of the common man.

Ken Kiang guessed that Hoagland Shanks led the life of the common man. But what if Ken Kiang provided Hoagland Shanks with the money and connections to experience wild pleasures that would inflame his appetites to unnatural heights? That is, what if Ken Kiang gave Hoagland Shanks unlimited access to any kind of *pie* he wanted?

Ken Kiang calculated that five months would be sufficient to get Hoagland Shanks addicted. Then Ken Kiang would suddenly put a stop to his generosity, and Hoagland Shanks would be a changed man. This new Hoagland Shanks would do anything to get his pies back. He would steal; he would do desperate things with desperate people; he would sell everything he had, and what he could of himself; in the end, he would kill, not once but many times, in order to keep coming the pies that, by then, would not even be pleasant, but at best would serve to numb him against his sordid existence.

Ken Kiang smiled. His work would then be complete. A real masterpiece, a last hurrah before he threw himself into the suicidal quest to dethrone the Belgian Prankster. Any idiot can fire a gun and kill someone. It takes real evil to ruin a soul.

Ken Kiang dwelled on these plans at length, patiently fussing over each detail, if only to distract his sickened intellect from the Belgian Prankster, who loomed around every dark corner of his mind and encroached upon every idle moment. Something had happened at that Country Kitchen and implanted in Ken Kiang's heart a horrifying idea, about a man who was not a man but an unquenchable emptiness, a ravenous nothing that grew hungrier each passing moment. Ken Kiang's mind would gingerly approach this Belgian Prankster, but a moment's contact made him jerk back as though burned. It was too unnerving for him to think about it for long, and he would push it away; but invariably, in due time, he would circle around it again, and approach it once more, with mounting terror, and a fascination no punishment could subdue.

Ken Kiang summoned Hoagland Shanks to his Manhattan castle. Workmen had boxed up the last of the intriguing artifacts that had once filled his home. Now the cold hallways and empty rooms made Ken Kiang feel wistful. The next occupants were bound to desecrate his beloved castle, with their obligatory kitchen remodelings, their "rec rooms," their ludicrous collections of what they took to be modern art.

The meeting was brief and businesslike. Ken Kiang had once fantasized about this moment, the beginning of the process that would end in Hoagland Shanks's damnation. And yet now Ken Kiang regarded the handyman with neither pity, nor anticipation, nor hope. Crafting the plan was what had satisfied Ken Kiang; its implementation was a mere formality.

"Well, Mr. Shanks, as you can see, I am about to go on a long journey."

Hoagland Shanks, hat in hand, sat down nervously across the

desk from Ken Kiang. "I gotta admit, Kenny, I don't feel good about being here. That was a weird message you left me. I almost . . ."

His voice died.

"Yes, but you did come, didn't you?" said Ken Kiang softly. "You came."

"Yes," said Hoagland Shanks, staring at the floor in shame.

SEVENTEEN

Jo and Ian sat in a gloomy parlor, waiting for an old woman to speak. Even though it was a sunny afternoon, the room was dim and dreary: ancient lace drapes strangled the sunlight, and all was silent except for a loudly ticking clock. It was the sitting room of Lady Agnes, and the old woman sat far across the room, mumbling in the shadows.

Jo couldn't stop her leg from jiggling. For weeks she and Ian had waited for Lady Agnes to call them about their quest, so long that Jo almost believed Lady Agnes had forgotten. Ian had gone sour on the whole enterprise—"It's insulting to make us wait like this, even if she *is* Lady Agnes!"—and the last of his enthusiasm vanished when other squires told him just how ridiculous Lady Agnes's quests could be. "Maybe we *should've* let Dugan do this," said Ian as they rode the subway to her house.

The butler showed Jo and Ian into the parlor where Lady Agnes waited. She was a withered noodle of a woman, her ancient skin gray and wrinkled, her face hidden by thick dark veils. For a long time she didn't speak. Then she suddenly rasped, in tones of incredulous disdain:

"*You* are Ian Barrows and Jo Larouche? I expected squires to look more impressive!"

"We are squires of the Odd-Fish," snapped Ian, "and that should be enough for you. *We* expected something better than being ignored for two months."

"Do you use a napkin when you eat?" Lady Agnes peered closer at Ian. "It seems you left bits of your breakfast on your lip."

There was an icy silence.

"That," said Ian with tightly controlled rage, "is a mustache."

Lady Agnes lost it. She hooted, gurgled, and shrieked, her bony body shaking as though it might break into bits. "Hoo nelly, that's rich! A mustache! Oh, you can't make this stuff up!" she whooped. "Butler, get in here with some cake! Oh, the poor dear thinks he has a mustache! *Too much!*"

Ian silently seethed as the butler served cold tea and moldy cake. Lady Agnes fumbled with her fork, straining to lift a bite; finally she gave up, panting, "This cake is too heavy."

After a moment Jo said, "Do you need help?"

"Ooo-hoo-hoo! Oh, I wouldn't say no."

Lady Agnes's gray chin poked out from the veil, and her shriveled lips parted with relish. Jo guided a forkful of cake into the ancient mouth, and the lips closed with an effort, disappearing back into the shadows of the veil, smacking dryly.

Ian exhaled. "Lady Agnes, we've been waiting for weeks. What's our——"

"Someone is trying to murder me!" croaked Lady Agnes with sudden energy, and Jo and Ian were startled into silence. Lady Agnes snickered, drawing from her robes a jeweled key on a necklace. "*That* is why I didn't let you in my house for two months. *Nobody* comes in! This is the only key to this house, and I keep it around my neck at all times. Meanwhile, I was researching your backgrounds. Very carefully. Very *thoroughly*. Oh, there's nothing about Ian Barrows and Jo Larouche that I don't know."

A rattling cackle emerged from the veil. Jo fidgeted. *She couldn't possibly know about my secret,* she thought. *Could she?*

Ian said steadily, "Why do you think someone's trying to murder you?"

"I have received dozens of threatening letters," said Lady Agnes. "And all signed with a mysterious name I do not recognize: Duddler Yarue! Have you heard of Duddler Yarue? No? Then that is your first task. *Who* is Duddler Yarue? *How* does—"

"I'm sorry, Lady Agnes," said Ian. "But this isn't a job for squires. If you really think this, um, 'Duddler Yarue' plans to kill you, you should go to the police."

"Impossible! I committed spectacular crimes in my wild youth. If the police knew I was alive, they'd throw me in prison in a split second. You must stop Duddler Yarue on your own!"

"Oh, come on, this isn't a proper quest," said Ian with rising irritation. "It's something out of a bad detective novel! Duddler Yarue—what kind of name is that? You obviously made it up! This is just another of your joke quests—we all know you're just doing it to make idiots out of us!"

Lady Agnes growled, "Are you accusing me of lying?"

"Of course you're lying!" Ian nearly shouted. "Nobody's trying to murder you, there is no Duddler Yarue, you're just a crazy old woman and *you're wasting our time!*"

Just then a rock crashed through the window, flying through the crumbling curtains, sending clouds of dust blooming and swirling. Lady Agnes yanked a blanket over herself, shrieking, "Duddler Yarue! He's come for me at last! I'm doomed, it's all over!" Ian sprang up and flung open the curtains to see who it was, and Jo tried to help Lady Agnes, but she howled back, "Don't touch me! And close the drapes—sunlight makes my skin itch! Oh, Duddler Yarue, make my death swift and merciful, ah, ah!"

Ian picked up the rock, looking at it in surprise. He poked Jo and handed it to her. There was something written on it:

Jo Larouche and Ian Barrows—
    If you want to live, don't try to help the villainous Lady Agnes.
Sincerely, Duddler Yarue

"What does it say?" screeched Lady Agnes from under the blanket.

"Um, nothing," muttered Jo. She and Ian looked at each other in bafflement.

"I have a right to know what's written on rocks thrown through my window!" wailed Lady Agnes, clutching her jeweled key in terror.

The butler ran into the room, out of breath. "What is the matter, milady? I heard a crash. . . ."

"Duddler Yarue, it's Duddler Yarue! Go on, get out, you two useless squires! Catch him! Oooo," groaned the old woman, and fainted.

As the butler fussed over Lady Agnes, waving smelling salts under her nose and massaging her hands, Jo said to Ian, "What do you think?"

"We definitely should've let Dugan take this quest," muttered Ian. "Come on—maybe whoever threw this hasn't gone far."

Jo and Ian ran out the door and onto the street.

The door slammed and locked behind them.

Jo and Ian searched the neighborhood, but they didn't really know what they were looking for. It wasn't clear what "Duddler Yarue" would look like, and anyway, the streets were almost deserted. After a half hour of wandering, Jo despaired of ever making any headway, and was ready to give up when they saw an effeminate boy smoking a cigarette on the corner. He watched Jo and Ian idly.

"Hey!" said Ian. "Did you see who threw a rock through Lady Agnes's window?"

"What's it to you?" said the boy.

"We don't have time to explain," said Ian quickly. "Have you seen anyone suspicious?"

The boy looked away, uninterested.

"Great, thanks," muttered Ian. "Let's go."

"Wait, he might be our only clue," said Jo.

"I have a name, you know," said the boy. "And from the look of things, I have much more of a *clue* than either of you."

Ian seemed ready to boil over, but Jo cut in, "I'm sorry. We've been rude. I'm Jo Larouche, and this is Ian Barrows. What's your name?"

"Nick."

"Nick what?"

"Nick—that's all." The boy shrugged. "Why, I'm just a lad of the streets."

"Fascinating," said Ian impatiently. "What do you say you use some of your 'street wisdom' to tell us where—"

"Where your guy went? He ran off that way." Nick waved down the boulevard. "A half hour ago. You've lost him."

"Really? What did he look like?" said Ian.

"I don't know, he was just some guy." Nick turned away from Ian with distaste; then he seemed to see Jo for the first time. "Say, you look familiar. Don't I know you from somewhere?"

"You don't know her," said Ian.

Nick snapped his fingers. "I remember. The newspaper. Came in with Lily Larouche in the fish, right? The new girl in town?"

Jo was startled and a little pleased. "I didn't know I was famous."

"You can't ride into Eldritch City on a fish and expect people not to notice," said Nick. "Is your Dame Lily as dangerous as they say she is?"

"That, and more," said Ian. "Keep that in mind, lad of the streets."

Nick ignored him. "You know, Jo, there's more to this town than knights and squires. You want to see the sights? I know a couple of secret places. And I don't show just anyone."

Jo was intrigued, but Ian said, "Thanks, but no. We're going."

"Your friend can come, too, of course," said Nick, barely looking at him. "I wouldn't want you to miss it. I'm the only one who knows about it."

"I doubt that," snorted Ian.

Nick started toward the subway station. "Well, come on, if you want."

Jo started following after Nick, but Ian touched her shoulder. "Jo, I don't like this—there's something funny about him."

"I know," said Jo, rather enjoying Ian's jealousy. "I like him."

"You're taking a risk."

"I want to take a risk. Are you coming?" Jo went after Nick a couple of steps, then stopped and looked back. Ian teetered back and forth and finally gave in.

"All right," he grumbled. "But just to keep an eye on him."

When they reached the subway entrance, Nick glanced around to make sure nobody was around, and then nimbly jumped the turnstile. "Don't bother with tokens. Come on!"

Ian looked at Nick with contempt. "You're supposed to pay!"

Jo usually paid for things, but she was sick of Ian's attitude. She jumped the turnstile, too, leaving Ian alone on the other side.

Ian bought three tokens and went through properly.

"What's got into you, Jo?" he said.

They descended to the crowded subway platform and waited for the train. But when the train finally came, Nick just shook his head. The train coughed out a few passengers and took some others on, and then it was gone, hooting down the tunnel. The last straggler climbed up the stairs, and for a moment the platform was deserted.

Nick hopped down onto the tracks. "Hurry! It's this way. No point in paying if you're not riding, right? Don't touch the tracks!"

"This is ridiculous. Let's go, Jo," said Ian, and started walking away.

Jo hesitated, caught between two opposite pulls. Nick's eyes reminded her of something; even if Jo didn't exactly trust him, she wanted to follow him anyway. Almost without thinking, she climbed down.

"*Jo!*" shouted Ian; but finally he, too, jumped down, and went after them.

They followed Nick down into the dark, dripping train tunnel. Soon they had gone so far that there was almost no light to see. Nick cleared away some trash, revealing a hole in the corner, and climbed down, jerking his head to indicate they should follow. And then he was gone.

"I suppose he takes all the ladies here," said Ian.

"Will you stop it?" said Jo. "If you don't want to come with us, then don't."

"*I* should stop it? Do you know how stupid you're being?" Ian shouted. "You met this kid ten minutes ago, and now you're following him down into who knows where! This is *Eldritch City,* Jo, not a game. It's dangerous." He took her arm.

"Let me go!" said Jo, twisting away. "I want to do this. I can tell he won't do anything bad."

"You can, can you? I'm not so sure."

"I'm going." The more Ian resisted, the more she wanted to go. "You don't have to come."

"But if anything happened to you—"

"I can take care of myself," said Jo.

"No, you can't," said Ian. "Nobody can."

Nick's head popped out of the hole. "Hey! Are you two coming or what?"

Jo looked at Ian, and he slowly let go of her arm. Together they followed Nick down the hole.

Down, down, down. Nick led them deeper into the cramped and filthy passageways, and the farther they went, the less manmade the passages seemed, becoming darker, slimier, and rougher. Nick had a lantern, but it provided only the weakest dribble of gray light as they crept down ladders and stairways and corridors into the forgotten depths of Eldritch City.

After a half hour, they stopped in a small round room. There was a wet hole in the floor, coated with slick, spongy moss that gave it a disturbingly fleshy look.

Nick handed Jo the lantern. "I'll go first. Wait for one minute and then follow me."

"What is it?" said Jo, bewildered.

"That would be telling. See you." Nick crawled headfirst into the hole, which suddenly contracted and slurped, and then he was gone.

"What is *that*?" Jo moved closer to Ian. "Where is he taking us?"

Ian looked around warily. "It could be anything. Eldritch City is thousands of years old, built on ruins built on ruins, going back to who knows when. We might very *well* see something only Nick knows about."

Jo felt a creeping panic building inside her. She wanted out of these filthy, cramped tunnels. The lantern cast weird shadows, strange noises echoed through the darkness, and the hole was almost unbearably disgusting to look at—almost like a sloppy, drooling mouth.

"Ian . . . I'm sorry I dragged you into this," said Jo.

"We might be able to find our way back . . . ," said Ian doubtfully; then he shook his head. "Never mind. I'll go first. Just to make sure."

Ian climbed down the hole—and with a sickening slurp, he was gone, too.

Jo felt her stomach curl. Now she was alone. *Why* did *I come down here?* she thought. She liked Nick and had enjoyed making Ian jealous, but now she was so nervous she could hardly see, she couldn't swallow, and the walls seemed to be growing thicker, drawing closer . . . She turned around. Maybe she could find her way out.

But no. She couldn't leave Ian.

Jo turned back to the hole. She took a breath and gingerly climbed down into it, little by little, trying to keep her hold. Suddenly there was a huge gulping noise all around her, she lost her grip, and a flood of water swept her away, tumbling and sliding into the twisting darkness. Then the tunnel unexpectedly opened into empty space, and Jo fell far, far down and splashed into a deep pool of water.

Jo floundered to the surface, coughing and spluttering. Nick and Ian grabbed her arms, dragging her up some slimy steps. They both had torches, and their faces looked strange and red in the flickering fire.

"Fun ride?" whispered Nick.

Jo coughed up dirty water. "You're crazy—I almost got killed in there—"

Nick looked offended. "Killed? Oh, no, it's perfectly safe. I ride it all the time." He spread his arms wide. "For this, my friends, is home!"

"Home!" said Ian in awe.

Jo wiped her eyes and looked around. They were in a flooded stone rotunda encrusted with twinkling jewels. Elaborate arched passages led out on either side into watery darkness, and the ceiling of the dome was pierced in the center by a dripping hole.

It was a cathedral from the early days of Eldritch City, buried by centuries, its stone halls left to rot and ruin under the busy metropolis. It was thousands of years old, and even though it was wrecked and flooded and humbled by age, it was astonishing to see. The dome over their heads was coated with thousands of tiny jewels, blue, green, red, purple, and yellow, arranged in glimmering mosaics of half-human shapes and strange animals, cavorting and twisting all around the ceiling and walls.

Ian's contempt of Nick had turned into respect. "How did you find this?"

"Poking around," said Nick. "I was looking for a place to live. Yeah, I live down here! And it's not such a bad life—if you're careful."

"Does anything *else* live down here?" said Jo.

"Sure. Lots of things. Watch."

Nick clapped his hands and whistled. Watery howls answered down the dark tunnel, then splashes and snorts, coming closer. The dark water became a seething broth, churned into a writhing foam, and out of the depths of the flooded cathedral rose three gigantic squids. Jo gasped, and Ian stepped back a few paces, but Nick seemed unconcerned.

"Don't worry," he said. "They're tame, mostly."

The squids were each the size of a large car, with rough orange skin, dangling tentacles, and eyes as big as plates. They rolled over, gurgling with pleasure as Nick scratched them. Then Nick waded down the steps and mounted the largest squid.

"C'mon, get on a squid," he said. "We'll go for a ride."

Jo and Ian exchanged incredulous looks. But Nick insisted, and eventually Jo cautiously crawled up onto a squid, while Ian got on his. Nick held their torches patiently and, to his credit, did not laugh as Jo and Ian kept falling off, trying to figure out how to sit on them properly.

"Hold on to their head with one hand, and squeeze them with your legs. That's it," said Nick. He handed back their torches. "Let's go!"

Nick dug his heels into the squid's side, and it began swimming toward one of the dark passages leading out of the rotunda. Jo and Ian's squids followed, pulsing and gliding.

Jo gazed around in astonishment as they rode the grunting

beasts down the glittering tunnels. The cathedral was cracked and stained but encrusted everywhere with thousands of gems, glinting red, green, orange, and blue. The torchlight licked the jewels to glittering life, bringing them glowing out of the darkness like colored stars. Water oozed from the walls, roots dangled from the ceiling, and everywhere gems dripped from grooves and hidden holes, seeming to grow out of the rocky wall, itself shot through with veins of icy sapphire. These jeweled tunnels felt like the roots of the city, laid down when the world was young, holding secrets as old as the world. Jo almost imagined she could hear the secrets, whispered in the darkness.

She started. It wasn't her imagination—something *was* whispering. Little voices all around her chattered softly in the darkness.

A rock struck the back of her head.

Even before Jo could cry out, Nick whipped out a slingshot and fired a stone into the darkness. There was a squish and a shriek, something tumbled from far above; a hushed gibbering echoed in the gloom all around them, and then there was silence.

"What was *that*?" said Jo.

"What? What?" said Ian wildly.

"Shhh! Calm down!" said Nick, bringing his squid around. A creature was floating dead in the water—a gray, furry, monkey-like beast with a cruel little face and clawed hands and feet.

"The groglings are out," muttered Nick.

"Groglings!" said Ian. "I've never actually seen one before."

"You'll see plenty of them down here," said Nick.

The whispers returned, all around them now, louder and angrier. Nick held up his hand and listened to the hushed voices. Jo and Ian looked around into the darkness but saw nothing.

"It's not safe here anymore," said Nick.

"Where—"

"Shhh! Follow me!"

Nick spurred his squid onward, and Jo and Ian followed, surging through the thick water. The voices got louder and bolder, and stones whizzed through the air, struck off the walls, and made little splashes explode around them. Jo could just barely see gray little shapes climbing the ceilings and popping in and out of holes, every moment fiercer and more numerous. What had been an excited whispering and then an agitated chattering was now the roar of a hundred tiny throats, echoing up and down the caverns, filling their ears with a raucous gibber.

"Go!" shouted Nick. "Don't stop! Faster!"

The groglings leaped out, flying from everywhere at once, as though the darkness had congealed into a hundred snarling shapes, dropping from the ceiling, springing from the walls, bursting out of the water. Nick tore them off and flung them away, Ian flailed uselessly at them, and Jo screamed as they climbed all over her, nipping her with slimy teeth.

Nick flung away his torch. "Hold your breath!"

"What?" yelled Ian.

Nick's squid reared and then plunged underwater with a tremendous splash. Jo grabbed her squid with both hands as it too bucked and dived. The slimy water gurgled all around her as the squid twisted wildly through underwater tunnels, and Jo could barely hold on. Then she broke the surface again, into darkness. She heard Nick's voice somewhere, and a moment later Ian's. Jo clutched her squid nervously. It was so dark she might as well have been blind.

"Jo? Ian? Everybody here?" came Nick's voice, just as jaunty as before. "That was close. The groglings have been getting peevish lately."

"Peevish, you say!" said Ian with heavy irony. "A touch out of sorts, were they, old chap? Perhaps a spot of tea would set them to rights, what?"

"I'm sorry if that was too interesting for you," said Nick coolly. "Perhaps you'd prefer something less stressful. I understand that knitting is very soothing."

"Knitting? I'll knit *you*!" said Ian.

There was an awkward pause.

"Okay, that was kind of stupid," said Ian.

"Enough," said Jo. "Where are we?"

"Um . . . I've never been in this part of the cathedral before, actually," said Nick, and Jo's confidence sank. "But don't worry. The squids know their way. I think."

The squids snorted quietly as they nosed their way down the pitch-black tunnel. Jo didn't like being unable to see—her imagination created claws reaching out in the darkness, or a rotting face smiling inches from her own. When Nick's squid brushed against hers, she gave a little shriek.

"I think we're coming to the center of the cathedral," whispered Nick.

"There aren't any groglings here," said Jo. "Why not?"

Nobody answered. And the farther the squids swam down the flooded passageway, the nearer they drew to the cathedral's center, the weirder Jo felt. She felt they were approaching a huge, slowly beating heart, murmuring just beneath human hearing. The water seemed warmer here, the darkness thicker, as though it was a substance of its own.

They were suddenly dazzled by a flood of light and heat.

A gigantic golden mouth opened before them. The huge, strange mouth was set in a carved brass wall swirling with olive and apple jewels and silver glyphs cut in curling grooves. The light blazed from the mouth itself, although the throat beyond was dark. Jo screamed and the squids panicked. It seemed the ruby-lipped, black-throated mouth was rushing forward to devour them, with all the noise and fury of an oncoming train, and Jo saw, or thought she saw, crouching in the darkness deep in the throat, a horrible shape.

Jo barely got a breath and dug her fingernails hard into her squid's hide before the squids howled and dived underwater. Her ears felt crushed with pressure, the water rushed by so fast she almost lost her grip, her lungs were tight and empty, she needed to breathe—soon she couldn't wait another second—her grip was loosening, sharp lights were stabbing behind her eyes—and then the squid burst above water. Jo gasped for air as the squid plunged away, and was gone.

Jo was left treading water. She couldn't see anything. She couldn't touch bottom. All was silent except for the occasional drip.

"Ian!" rasped Jo.

Nothing.

"Nick . . . ?"

There was no answer. She swam a few strokes, but she couldn't see where she was going. She tried not to think that she might be trapped or hopelessly lost—that nobody would ever find her down here, not even her body. For a dreadful minute she treaded water, her legs tiring, breathing deeply, trying not to panic. Then, echoing somewhere in the darkness, she heard a faint coughing. She swam toward it and saw a dim light ahead, and two figures on a concrete shelf near a sewer pipe where— thank God, thought Jo—daylight trickled through.

Too tired to speak, Jo paddled the last few strokes and grabbed the shelf. Ian helped her crawl onto the concrete, where Nick lay sprawled out as if dead. Ian kicked open the sewer grate, and Jo smelled the fresh air. They were out.

Jo and Ian stood outside the pipe awkwardly. It was a hot, cloudless day, and not a breeze stirred in the humming city.

"Are you okay?" she said at last.

"I don't know . . . yeah, I think so," said Ian weakly. "But Nick got knocked on the head pretty hard. Luckily I had a chance to grab him, before that . . . I don't know. It was all too fast."

There was a nasty cut across Nick's brow, and his scalp looked sickeningly askew. Jo gingerly smoothed his hair.

She was astonished when it all came off at once.

Jo was left holding Nick's wig in shock—staring at his real hair, which was long, wavy, and blond. Nick's face seemed even more effeminate than before. Even—

Ian shouted, "I knew there was something strange about this guy!"

"Nick's a . . . girl?" said Jo, unable to believe what she was seeing. "Then what—"

"Go through her pockets," said Ian. "Maybe she has a wallet, or identification, or something."

Jo awkwardly searched through Nick's clothes and found a familiar jeweled key. She held it awkwardly for a second before she realized what it was.

Ian said slowly, "What . . . *what* is Nick doing with Lady Agnes's key?"

Jo stammered, "M-maybe we should go back to Lady Agnes's house, or . . ."

"If she's still alive!" said Ian. "I think there's more to this 'lad of the streets' than we thought! Jo, what if *Nick* is 'Duddler Yarue'? This is a fiasco—I bet if we go to Lady Agnes's house, we'll find her dead! How else could he have gotten the key? This Duddler Yarue probably just took us underground to finish us off!"

"Impossible," said Jo weakly—but it all hung together. Lady Agnes's house wasn't far away. They took off, half running, half walking, dragging "Nick" roughly between them. They were all drenched, their bones ached, and they smelled like the sewers; people in the street watched them suspiciously. Just when Jo was afraid the police were going to stop them and ask why they were dragging around an unconscious girl, they finally arrived at Lady Agnes's. Jo slipped Nick's jeweled key into the lock and opened the door.

There was nobody home. Jo and Ian carefully called out "Hello?" and "Lady Agnes?" but no one answered. Ian searched the house, looking in all the rooms, while Jo heaved "Nick" onto Lady Agnes's chair in the front parlor, examining the cut on her forehead.

"It doesn't make any sense," said Ian, coming in with some bandages he'd found. "Where's Lady Agnes's butler? Didn't Lady Agnes say she never left the house? And why was this girl acting like a boy?"

Jo suddenly realized what must have happened.

"That's it!" she said. "I knew I recognized Nick somehow!"

"You recognize Nick?" said Ian slowly. "Then why didn't you tell—"

"No, Ian, there *is* no Nick! And no Duddler Yarue—no Lady Agnes, either. This girl—she just *made it all up!*"

Ian looked at Jo as if she had told him Lady Agnes was an ape.

"Listen, it all fits!" said Jo. "Why would Nick have Lady Agnes's key? And why isn't Lady Agnes here now? Because Nick *is* Lady Agnes! This girl dressed up as an old woman, gave us a quest, and then dressed up as a 'lad of the streets' and met us outside! Lady Agnes, Duddler Yarue, Nick—they're all the same person—they're all *characters,* played by this girl!"

"Wait, wait—"

"You said it first," said Jo. "You told Lady Agnes this wasn't a proper quest, but something out of a bad detective novel. You were right—we *were* in a bad detective novel! It was all a game! This girl—Nick, Lady Agnes, whatever—she's been playing with us!"

"But how could she fool us into thinking she's two different people?" said Ian.

"Because she's an actress! She even practically told us her name! It's the oldest cliché in the book. Unscramble the letters of Duddler Yarue. This is the girl from *Teenage Ichthala!*"

Ian gasped. *"Audrey Durdle?"*

"Right, you've got me. I knew I'd get caught sooner or later."

Jo and Ian turned, confounded. Audrey Durdle—for it was she—opened her eyes, nursing the lump on her head. "Nick" was gone, and so was "Lady Agnes"; Audrey's real voice was husky and low, as if she had a slight cold, without a trace of Nick's boyish drawl or Lady Agnes's deathly croak. Even her eyes were different—not feeble like Lady Agnes's, or bright and hard like Nick's, but sleepily mischievous.

"I'm actually glad you found me out. I don't know how many more fake quests I had in me, you know?" Audrey smiled uncertainly at Jo and Ian, as if hoping that they'd appreciate the joke, and a little nervous that they wouldn't.

Jo said, "I've seen you on *Teenage Ichthala,* but seeing you here—"

"Oh, *please* don't talk about that show," said Audrey, wincing. "I am *so sick* of it. I wish I'd never taken that role. All anyone wants to talk about are those idiotic Ichthala myths. The show bores me to death. The only way I have any fun or meet people is by making up these fake quests."

Ian snapped out of his astonishment.

"You wanted to . . . to *have fun?*" he said angrily. "You wanted to *meet people?* We are squires of the Odd-Fish, not your toys to play with! We could've been doing other quests! Real ones!"

Audrey had looked shyly hopeful, but all at once she froze in embarrassment.

"Ian, don't be petty," said Jo quickly.

"No, he's right. I guess I was wasting your time." Audrey looked away. "I didn't call you at first because I was tired of doing this Lady Agnes thing. But then one day I was shooting in East Squeamings when you two ran through the set, chased by all those Wormbeards and the police, and I thought, *Here are two people I want to meet.*"

Ian said, "That was not exactly our finest hour."

"I don't care," said Audrey. "I just want to see your lodge. I want to meet the other squires."

Jo whistled. "If we took you to the lodge, Nora's head would explode."

"Who's Nora?" said Audrey. "What's wrong with her head?"

"She's a *Teenage Ichthala* fanatic," said Ian. "If she met you, she'd tie you down and slap you until you'd told her every last thing about that show."

Audrey hesitated, then finally said, "But . . . can I really come?"

"Of course," said Jo. She looked over at Ian.

"I'd be glad to have you," said Ian.

For the first time, Audrey smiled. "Thank you," she said.

Audrey walked with Jo and Ian back to the Odd-Fish lodge. It was a beautiful night, and the city felt young and new; all of Eldritch City glimmered around them as they walked and talked. Jo felt something fragile, as if she was on the verge of something that was all the better because she didn't know exactly what it was. The streets were invitingly dark and the lights seemed fresh and bold: glaring lights over the boulevards, lonely lights in apartment windows, garish lights in the shops, the red flash of a lit match, the buttery glow of the moon. Jo looked from Ian to Audrey and back again as they talked and walked, their faces passing in and out of the light. They took the long way home.

EIGHTEEN

Jo and Audrey became fast friends. Audrey dropped by the lodge often, usually in some new disguise: one day she was a stuttering deliveryman, the next a hapless tourist, and once she fooled everyone into thinking she was Sir Festus. Audrey had a seemingly inexhaustible collection of false whiskers, men's clothes from thirty years ago, and fat suits.

At first the other squires didn't believe Audrey was really *the* Audrey Durdle; only after she reluctantly acted the Ichthala part, with its peculiar voice and mannerisms, did everyone shout with recognition and crowd around her in wonder. Audrey also admitted she was the "Lady Agnes" who had sent them on so many ridiculous quests. Some of the squires were furious at first, but Audrey was too charming for anyone to be angry with her for long.

Then there was Nora. When they'd first met, Nora had said, trying to stay calm, "So, is it really true that the Belgian Prankster wrote *Teenage Ichthala*?"

"Oh, he's the one who wrote that crap?" said Audrey. "I just read whatever they give me."

Nora flinched, slightly daunted, but pressed on. "Still, you can't deny that the nefarious plans of the Silent Sisters are foretold in your show! Doesn't that scare you?"

"You don't seriously *believe* that Silent Sisters nonsense?" said Audrey, surprised. "That's just fantasy, you know."

The expression that came over Nora was like watching two speeding trains collide. Her face went from incomprehension to shock, pity, and then barely restrained contempt in a matter of seconds. "Well, of all the—-whatever," said Nora, and for a few days treated Audrey coolly.

Audrey hadn't meant to be rude; to make up for it, she gave Nora the scripts for all the episodes of *Teenage Ichthala* that hadn't been released yet. "We finished filming the series last week," said Audrey. "So I don't need them anymore, anyway."

At first Nora was elated and threw her arms around Audrey, but then she suddenly pulled away, gasping, "Wait—did you say *Teenage Ichthala* is ending?"

"Yeah, we wrapped it all up last week," said Audrey. "Those are the last eight episodes."

Nora looked as though she had been stabbed. Clutching the piles of scripts to her chest, she whispered, "Excuse me . . . I've got . . . a lot of work to do. . . ."

After that day, Nora was rarely seen anywhere but at the café around the corner from the lodge, where she pored over the scripts obsessively, scrawling notes in the margins, constructing bewildering charts of arrows and boxes and labels. Sometimes Jo would ask her what she was doing, but Nora would only answer, "No time. I'll tell you later. It's all here, Jo—*everything,*" and then go back to her notes, trembling with excitement.

* * *

Jo's life became more interesting with Audrey around. Audrey breezed through the lodge as though she owned the place, opening doors and exploring places that Jo hadn't even guessed existed. Sometimes they were caught straying into forbidden rooms, but if a knight scolded them, Audrey's face would go blank, as though the knight were speaking a foreign language. When the knight was gone, Audrey would go back to doing whatever she pleased.

One forbidden room was Dame Myra's greenhouse, a glass fortress on the roof of the lodge full of freakish plants either nearly extinct or the unhappy results of Dame Myra's cross-breeding experiments. The squires stayed away from the greenhouse. Rumor was that a couple of years ago, Dame Myra's squire had carelessly brushed against a shrub, and a few days later, leaves grew all over his body; a month later, his skin became bark-like; finally, his feet sprouted roots. There was nothing to be done. He was discreetly planted outside the city and not spoken of much anymore. Dame Myra hadn't had a squire since.

So when Jo and Audrey sneaked into the greenhouse, they crept very cautiously down the aisles of plants, careful not to touch the bizarre flowers and weeds. A clump of chartreuse moss muttered scathing insults as they passed; a writhing, hanging lump reached out oily vines, desperate for affection; deliriously colored butterflies as big as Jo's head fluttered all around, and the air felt warm and heavy with moist smells.

Audrey prodded a large, fleshy mass. "Jo, what's this plant?"

"That's not a plant. That's Dame Myra."

Audrey frowned. "Well, how odd."

Dame Myra sighed, got up, and trudged away to water some beeping crystal-like flowers on the other side of the greenhouse. Audrey followed, chattering casually at her. Dame Myra seemed alarmed that anyone would talk to her and kept casting confused glances back at Jo. Amazingly, Jo and Audrey never got in trouble for this or anything else they did; there was an air of innocent privilege about Audrey that somehow excused her.

One afternoon Audrey and Jo picked the lock to Dame Delia's secret dissection lab, and they spent hours examining dozens of Dame Delia's dead monsters. A huge spider was still spread on the dissection table, its underbelly opened up to expose its colorful guts; other creatures floated in barrels, hung from the ceiling, or were squashed away in drawers; still others were sliced into sheets and bound like books. Audrey stole what looked like a furry starfish and hid it in Ian's bed, and that night Ian's roar of shock woke up the entire lodge, and Audrey and Jo had to bite their pillows to muffle their hysterical giggling. (This was part of Audrey and Jo's campaign to torture Ian until he got rid of his mustache. When he finally shaved it off, Audrey organized a small funeral for it.)

Sir Oliver's astronomical observatory wasn't off-limits, but the squires and even the knights stayed away lest they disturb the great man at his work. But when Jo and Audrey knocked on his door, Sir Oliver opened it with relief and invited them in for a tour.

"You came just in time," said Sir Oliver. "My dithering isn't what it used to be. It's become harder and harder to fritter away the entire day."

Sir Oliver showed them around his observatory, packed with telescopes, star charts, and whirring machines. "I don't know the first thing about astronomy!" Sir Oliver admitted cheerfully. "As a result, I've done some first-rate dithering in here. You see, I keep all the equipment broken, so I can fiddle with it for hours."

Jo asked, "If all you do is dither, how do you manage to do anything useful?"

"Useful . . . ?" said Sir Oliver, as if this was a new word to him.

"Like when you found the lodge and brought it back?"

"Oh, I don't know," said Sir Oliver brightly. "But I do know that when I was young, I noticed that the more I wanted something, the less likely it was that I'd get it. Therefore, it stood to reason that the *less* I wanted something, the *more* likely it was that

I'd get it. The lesson is clear: if I have a problem, I ignore it—but I ignore it in an advanced, sophisticated way. Sooner or later the problem usually solves itself. Such is dithering."

"How did you learn how to dither?" said Audrey.

"Practice," said Sir Oliver gravely. "For twenty years I lived in my mother's basement and did nothing at all. It is not a training to be undertaken lightly."

Jo loved exploring with Audrey, but it was on her own that she found her favorite thing in the lodge. One evening, while creeping through the crawl spaces, she discovered a peephole to Sir Alasdair's and Dame Isabel's bedroom. It was only nine o'clock, but the Coveneys were already in their matching pajamas, reading in separate beds.

Jo saw Sir Alasdair had a sly look; he said something to Dame Isabel that Jo couldn't hear, and they both excitedly kicked off their sheets and ran over to something that looked like a home-made organ, an ungainly engine connected by hundreds of wires and rubber tubes to an oak cabinet of labeled bottles. Another tube connected the cabinet to a gas mask.

Sir Alasdair sat at the keyboard, Dame Isabel strapped on the gas mask, and after adjusting some switches and dials, Sir Alasdair started to play the organ. Jo didn't hear any music, but Dame Isabel began dancing in a wild, looping jig, one hand waving around frantically, the other clutching her gas mask, huffing and snorting with gusto.

The next day Jo and Audrey sneaked into the Coveneys' room to investigate. They discovered the machine was a *smells organ*—each key on the keyboard, when pressed, caused a different smell to spray into the gas mask. They also found handwritten sheet music, Sir Alasdair's attempts to write the very first "Symphony for the Nose."

Jo and Audrey spent a happy afternoon abusing the smells organ. One of Jo's smell-songs started with a trill of leather, seaweed, and popcorn, then climbed scales of soap, hot sand, and burning hair, and finally burst in a flourish of rose, blood, and wet dog. Audrey played arpeggios of steak, cigar, boy sweat, hair spray, and horses, and then noodled with nutmeg, ozone, and lemon. Jo discovered a sublime chord of autumn leaves, banana pie, morning breath, and cilantro.

Then they heard Sir Alasdair clumping up the stairs. They escaped just in time. But the next day the Coveneys' door had a new lock, and this time it was too hard to pick.

But sometimes, late at night, Jo would sneak in the crawl space and peek again into the Coveneys' room. And occasionally she would see Sir Alasdair grunting as he played the organ, and Dame Isabel pressing the gas mask to her face, waving her free arm in the air, staggering in jerky ecstasy. Jo didn't know why she liked to watch this. It was embarrassing and strange. But it was also the picture of happiness. She watched it hungrily.

On Tuesdays the squires met at a café near the lodge. It was a dingy, nameless place, its walls yellowed with decades of smoke and stains; an ornery dog skulked under the tables, biting ankles, and the food was godawful, but Jo felt at home here. It reminded her of her old café back in Dust Creek. It even had a similar smell, of cigarettes, burnt coffee, and grease.

The squires held weekly meetings at the café to help each other figure out what their specialties would be. To become an Odd-Fish knight, a squire had to invent a new specialty for the Appendix and write an original article about it. This caused some worry among the squires, for after a thousand years of Odd-Fish history, almost all the good ideas had already been done. All the squires were here, as well as Audrey, who was curious to see what an Odd-Fish squires' meeting was like.

Today was Nora's turn to present her theories about *Teenage Ichthala*. Her corner booth was dripping with loose papers, convoluted diagrams, and scrawled-upon napkins; she was standing on her chair, her swirly, snaky black hair even more hyperactive than usual and her lip trembling, as she got ready to speak.

Jo sipped her coffee apprehensively. After their first morning in Eldritch City, Aunt Lily had explained little about the Ichthala. Her answers to Jo's questions were so vague it almost seemed as if she was holding something back. But almost everyone in Eldritch City was like this. It was as if even to mention the Hazelwoods or the Ichthala were in bad taste. This left Nora, as fanatical and paranoid as she was, as one of Jo's few sources of information.

"I've finally got it," said Nora, waving Audrey's scripts around. "I've got it—the truth, the secret, everything. It had been there all along, all in these scripts! It just needed to be dug up, brushed off, translated, *solved*. What I've found may be invisible to the layman—"

"Or sane people," said Ian.

"—but I've discovered a subtle code running through all these *Teenage Ichthala* episodes. As you all remember—and Ian conveniently ignores—lots of stuff that happens on the show ends up happening in real life. But there are *other* prophecies, too horrible to be explicitly described, hinted at in these coded messages."

At this Jo pricked up her ears. She hadn't heard this one before. She put down her coffee.

"From these scripts, I can predict what the Ichthala will do in the next couple of months." Nora paused. "And what the Belgian Prankster will do *to her*."

Jo bit her lip. For weeks she had managed, if not completely to put the Ichthala out of her mind, at least to distract herself out of thinking about it too much. The more time that passed, the more she was convinced it all had to be a mistake—that her birth was simply misunderstood.

But today something was different about Nora. Her squeaky whisper, her freakish mop of wild black hair, and her frantic energy were all screwed up to an unprecedented intensity, and her speech was jitteringly tentative, as though she couldn't bring herself to say what she wanted.

Nora continued, "A couple of months after the Ichthala

returns to Eldritch City, the Belgian Prankster will also return to Eldritch City. The Ichthala will go to him and meet him secretly. And then they will . . . er . . . they have to . . ."

Jo was staring at Nora, silently urging her to finish the sentence; if she could, she would've gone up to Nora and physically yanked the words out of her mouth. But Nora seemed to pull up short and lamely concluded, "Er . . . and then the world will end. Remember, Sir Nils's specialty was bad jokes. The goal of his studies was to create the worst joke possible. And he just might have done it, because—"

Daphne cut in, in a singsong voice: "Because when the show's run is finished, Sir Nils will indeed have created the worst joke of all time, for its punch line will be the destruction of Eldritch City, maybe the end of the world."

Nora frowned. "It's not funny."

"It *is* funny," said Phil, "because you say it fifty times a day."

"You . . . you aren't taking this seriously!" quavered Nora. "You *never* take me seriously—none of you! But—but you're just afraid to face the truth! The Ichthala is somewhere in Eldritch City, okay? Right now! And soon the Belgian Prankster will come, too, then the Silent Sisters—and Eldritch City will be destroyed, or worse. *That's* why the show is coming to an end—because the end of history is at hand!"

There was an embarrassed silence. The squires tried not to look at each other. Nobody knew what to say; Nora had gone too far.

Suddenly there came shouts from outside. Everyone turned around, confused, as a loud tramping of shoes came closer. It was a mob, chanting something—Jo suddenly realized the mob was chanting *her name*.

The doors flew open and the butlers burst in. Sefino, Umberto, Cicero, Benozzo, Benvenuto, Barrachio, Lorenzo, Belpo, and Petrucchio—all the cockroaches swarmed into the café, roaring jubilantly, waving that afternoon's *Eldritch Snitch,* crowding around Jo, lifting her into the air, shouting "Hip, hip, hooray!"—"She's done it!"—"A full retraction!"—"We are vindicated!"—"Honor is satisfied!"

It wasn't until the cockroaches had carried Jo around the café a couple of times, knocking over chairs and making the dog bark irritably, that she saw the headline of the *Eldritch Snitch*:

LILY LAROUCHE'S LACKEY LETS LOOSE LIVID LETTER LAMBASTING LURID LIBEL

SNITCH SAYS "SORRY, SEFINO"; SEEKS SOFTER STYLE

CHATTERBOX CHASTENED

It took a second for Jo to figure it out: the *Eldritch Snitch* had printed her letter. She had never seriously believed the *Snitch* would publish it. Now that they had, she was embarrassed.

"Jo Larouche, girl reporter?" said Daphne.

"Since when are you a writer?" said Ian.

"I'm not, it's just something Sefino—"

Jo was drowned out by a loud chanting from the cockroaches: "Hat! Hat! Hat! Haaaat!"

"Ladies and gentlemen," Sefino announced. "Jo Larouche has done the butlers of the Odd-Fish a chivalrous service of superlative distinction! We therefore present her with . . ."

"Hat! Hat! Hat!" shrieked the cockroaches. "Hattity-hat-hat-hoo-hat!"

"The HAT OF HONOR!" roared Sefino. Before Jo could react, she was yanked toward Cicero, who held aloft a five-foot-tall, black, cobwebby monstrosity of a hat. The hat was dropped on her with hardly any warning and she nearly collapsed under its weight. "Hat! Hat! Hat!" sang the cockroaches. "See her in the glorious hat!"—but Jo couldn't see a thing, her body swallowed up by the dusty mass of black velvet, jingling bells, and swaying tassels.

"For all of her life, Jo has longed to wear the Hat of Honor!" declared Sefino.

"I have?"

"When we were in exile and Jo was still a wee tot, many a bedtime she would tug my waistcoat and beg me to tell her once more about the Hat of Honor. 'Tell me again, Uncle Sefino,' she would lisp. 'I *do* love the Hat of Honor so. Tell me again how it looms majestically!'"

"*Uncle* Sefino?"

"Her heart bursting with innocent wonder, Jo would plead, 'Tell me again about the heroes who risked their lives so that they might wear the hat. And tell me about the noble cockroaches who zealously guard the Hat of Honor, and bestow it only upon the worthiest citizens of Eldritch City!' Indeed, in the darkest days of our exile, the *only* thing that kept Jo going was her hope that one day she might lay her tender eyes upon the Hat of Honor!"

"Sefino, *what*—"

"And now, on this splendid day, not only has Jo Larouche seen the Hat of Honor, *she is actually wearing it!* This is beyond her wildest dreams. This is the happiest day of Jo's life!"

"Hat! Hat! Hat!" shouted the cockroaches. "Hat! Hat! Hat!"

Ian and Audrey lifted up the massive hat, and Jo managed to gasp through the ancient velvet, "How often do they do this?"

"I'm afraid they do it all the time," whispered Ian.

"Hat! Hat! Hat!" shouted the cockroaches with delirious joy. "Hat! Hat! Hat!"

Jo was forced to parade through Eldritch City all afternoon wearing the Hat of Honor, in the center of a prancing throng of cockroaches. The parade halted outside Chatterbox's apartment.

"Come forth, Chatterbox!" bellowed Sefino. "Show yourself, if you dare!"

Chatterbox opened his window and looked out languidly. "Yes?"

"Behold this girl, Chatterbox!" roared Sefino. "Who has vanquished your empire of lies! Who has slain your dragon of deceit! Who has brought your kingdom of calumny crashing down around your head! Chatterbox, face your conqueror!"

"My conqueror is wearing a silly hat."

"It is the Hat of Honor!" shouted Sefino.

Chatterbox sipped his coffee. He seemed unimpressed.

Sefino said, "I assure you, Chatterbox, that *you* will never wear the Hat of Honor!"

"Heavens, what an empty life I must lead."

Jo said to Sefino, "I think he's had enough. We don't want to rub his nose in it."

"You're right, of course, Jo; we must be gracious in our victory," said Sefino. He turned back to Chatterbox. "Chatterbox, we now leave you to writhe in your own shame."

"Yes, thanks awfully. I've got a lot of writhing to do."

"Godspeed!" said Sefino. The parade did an about-face and started back to the lodge. Jo took off the hat, and some cockroaches helped her drag it behind her.

"Jo, I have to thank you," said Sefino. "Your article has single-handedly restored the honor of the butlers of the Order of Odd-Fish."

"I'm just glad to see you happy again," said Jo.

"Wear the hat as often as you like!" said Sefino. "That is, until we find a new hero to honor."

"You wouldn't mind," said Jo tentatively, "if I didn't wear it . . . *all* the time, would you?"

"I suppose you needn't wear it *all* the time," said Sefino, puzzled. "But why not?"

"Modesty?"

"Nonsense," said Sefino. "No doubt you'll want to wear it all day. Put it back on!"

"But—"

"I said put it back on."

* * *

Later that evening, after the parade, Jo went to help Aunt Lily in the basement of the lodge. Aunt Lily's research specialty was irregular contraptions, and her workroom was ankle deep with experimental mechanisms, dissected machines, and the tangled guts of a hundred scavenged appliances. Crowded shelves loomed on every wall, loaded down with gears, spindles, home-made batteries, and bottles stuffed with nails and bolts and wires.

It was just before dinner. Sir Alasdair was practicing his urk-ack upstairs, and every so often, whenever Jo and Aunt Lily stopped hammering, drilling, and sawing, they could hear the mellow tones of the urk-ack linger in the early evening air as squires' feet pounded up and down the stairs and distant shouts and laughs erupted in different parts of the lodge.

Jo was helping Aunt Lily tinker with the Inconvenience. It was complicated work, and for long stretches they didn't talk, but it was a comfortable silence. Jo enjoyed working with Aunt Lily. Back at the ruby palace, Aunt Lily had been mildly content but often distracted, as though there was something she felt she should've been doing but didn't quite know what. Now she knew, and threw herself into it with a vengeance, sometimes working in the workroom all day and night, having her meals sent down to her, even sleeping on the cot. From what Jo could tell, it seemed Aunt Lily was using the broken pieces of the Inconve-nience, along with some new parts, to build a completely differ-ent contraption—the purpose of which Jo couldn't guess.

After a while Aunt Lily said, "I read your article in the *Snitch*. It was well written."

"Thanks," said Jo. "It was nothing much, really. . . ."

"I agree," said Aunt Lily. "You shouldn't spend too much time on that kind of thing. You should be out raising hell. I was happier to hear about your exploits in Snoodsbottom . . . the Worm-beards were splendidly humiliated."

Jo put her tools down. "You know about that?"

Aunt Lily smiled. "Please, Jo, I'm not stupid! Just because

you and Ian escaped doesn't mean you weren't seen. But there's nothing the police can do now. It was embarrassing for the Wormbeards, and that's the important thing . . . oh, they're hopping mad!"

"So you're not angry about it?"

"I'm delighted! You're in training to be a knight, not a Girl Scout. I'd be disappointed if you didn't make some good enemies. It keeps you sharp."

"You're telling me I *should* get in trouble?" said Jo.

"I should hope you're clever enough to stay *out* of trouble, but there's more to being a knight of the Odd-Fish than researching the Appendix. The first duty of a knight is to defend the city if it's attacked. If you don't know how to fight, you won't be much use."

"So you want me to go out and brawl with the Wormbeards?"

"*Brawl* is not the word," said Aunt Lily. "Having an enemy is a delicate art. It demands dedication and a certain style. If you handle it right, it can even be good for you. I've learned just as much from our rivalry with the Wormbeards as I have from making friends with the Odd-Fish. You learn how to fight back."

Jo said, "That all sounds grand, but I still don't want an enemy."

"The Odd-Fish and the Wormbeards have been official enemies for over eight hundred years," said Aunt Lily. "They'd be disappointed if you didn't play along. Don't worry—as long as you behave honorably, bravely, and with due respect to your foe, you'll be fine. There's an etiquette to having an enemy, just like anything else. Just don't let it get out of hand and get the police involved, okay?"

"This, from you?" Jo smiled. "The illegal exile, whom the police might arrest any moment?"

Aunt Lily raised an eyebrow. "Oh, haven't you heard?" She gave Jo the evening edition of the *Eldritch Snitch*. The front page was dominated by a picture of Aunt Lily and Colonel Korsakov with the mayor in front of city hall, and the headline read:

ELDERLY ELDRITCH EXILES EXONERATED!
EXUBERANT EX-EXPATRIATES EXULT!

MAGNANIMOUS MAYOR MAKES MERCIFUL MOTION
MANDATING MURDER MATTER MENDED

STRIKE FORCE STEADFASTLY SCORNED SURRENDER TO
SILENT SISTERS, SUBSEQUENTLY SUFFERED SEVERE SANCTION;
SENTENCE SINCE SUSPENDED

"Hold on, wait," said Jo. "This means you're not exiled anymore?"

"Yes, the mayor's dropped the case," said Aunt Lily. "For now, at least."

"Sefino didn't tell me!"

"He doesn't know yet. We'll tell him after his nap."

"So the pressure is off for *you*," said Jo. "*You* can relax!"

"What's wrong?" said Aunt Lily. "You sound upset."

"Well . . . I *am* upset!" said Jo. "I'm sick of lying! I'm tired of always being afraid that someone's going to guess who I really am! You're no longer a criminal—why should I be?"

Aunt Lily seemed about to reply, but she just shook her head and said nothing.

Jo kept going. "What am I supposed to do? If Nora ever figured out who I was, she'd be terrified. And Ian—he thinks I killed his mother! He'd hate me if he knew! I have all these friends, but it's all lies! Why can't we just admit who I am? *I am the Ichthala!*"

Aunt Lily slammed the door shut so hard the machine parts jumped on the shelves. "Are you crazy?" she whispered fiercely. "If anyone heard you . . . Sir Oliver and I have our reasons for keeping this secret! Do you think you're out of danger? You think Nils—the Belgian Prankster has been idle? That the Silent Sisters have gone away? They are all on the move. You don't know the half of what we've been doing to protect you."

"But I'm living a lie!" said Jo.

"At least you're living. If you told the truth, I doubt you could get out of this city alive."

"Then why did we come here? The one place where I'm hated?"

"We weren't safe in California. We never were. At least we're among friends in Eldritch City." Aunt Lily paused. "Even though it is, in fact, Nils who caused us to come here."

"*What?*" said Jo, aghast. "The Belgian Prankster *wants* us to be here?"

Aunt Lily closed her eyes, as if she'd said too much. "A couple weeks ago we figured out that it was Nils who had stolen the Inconvenience. When he became the Belgian Prankster, he turned it against us. It's the Inconvenience that brought us all back to Eldritch City. And it's not done with us yet. That's why I'm trying to repair it—maybe I can construct a mechanism that can reverse the workings of the Inconvenience, turn it back against the Belgian Prankster."

Jo frowned. "But if the Inconvenience was programmed by the Belgian Prankster and the Inconvenience brought us to Eldritch City . . . doesn't that mean we're playing right into his plan?"

"Maybe you have a better idea," snapped Aunt Lily. "Maybe you know better than the people who've been sticking their necks out for you since before you were born."

"Maybe I do!" said Jo. "I'm living in a city where everyone would try to kill me if they knew who I was—and for what? I'm doing exactly what the Belgian Prankster wants! It's a *stupid* plan. It's the *worst possible* plan!"

Aunt Lily fixed her eyes on Jo, but Jo stared back angrily. For a moment she almost didn't recognize Aunt Lily. She didn't seem like a mother to her anymore, or even an aunt. She was a stranger.

"Why did the Silent Sisters choose my parents?" said Jo.

Aunt Lily's gaze wavered. She went back to her work, prying at a mishmash of intertwined mechanisms.

Jo kept pushing. "Why don't you ever talk about my parents?"

Aunt Lily wrenched a fragment of the machine away. "Don't be too curious about them."

"Why?"

Aunt Lily looked irritated. Usually Jo backed off when Aunt Lily didn't want to talk, but she couldn't help it anymore. Months of silence, of awkward pauses, of avoiding the topic broke down. Jo was starving for something, anything.

"Actually, Sir Oliver and I found out something that changes everything," said Aunt Lily. "Your mother really *did* have suspicious dealings with the Silent Sisters. The Silent Sisters might truly have a claim on you."

Jo felt as though she had been slapped. "You don't really believe that!"

"I . . . I don't know, Jo."

"You *do too* know!" said Jo. "Either I belong with the Silent Sisters or I don't! Why can't you ever tell me the least thing about me? Or my parents? Maybe it would've been better if the Silent Sisters *had* taken me! At least I would've belonged with them!"

Aunt Lily murmured, "You don't know what you're talking about."

"Then *tell* me! What is it about my parents you can't say? Or the Belgian Prankster—or no, *Nils,*" she spat. "You can't keep yourself from calling him Nils—why? That's it, isn't it? You're still soft on him—you still love him—and you hate me, you hate my parents, because they stuck you with *me* and ruined your life!"

Aunt Lily looked at Jo in a way she had never seen before. Her face had warped and sagged; Jo couldn't tell whether Aunt Lily looked betrayed, heartbroken, or furious. Then she understood.

For the first time, Aunt Lily was looking at Jo with disappointment.

Someone knocked on the door, and the doorknob rattled. A

second later the door opened, and Sir Alasdair and Dame Isabel came in. Jo stepped back and looked around for an escape—had the Coveneys heard them?

But apparently they hadn't heard anything. They both looked awkward, almost sheepish. Sir Alasdair shuffled back and forth, unable to look Aunt Lily in the eye. Dame Isabel's manner was stiff but grimly enduring, as if she were about to take a foul-tasting medicine.

Aunt Lily turned away from Jo with something like relief. "Yes, Isabel?" she said, her voice cracking. "Alasdair?"

Sir Alasdair harrumphed shyly. "We're just coming by to . . . well, now that everything's squared with the city . . . thought we'd . . . well . . ."

"We heard the mayor called off your exile," said Dame Isabel. "So . . . we're just glad to have you back at the Order, Lily. *Legally* back—you understand."

"No hard feelings?" coughed Sir Alasdair, and stuck out his hand.

Aunt Lily shook it. "I'm happy we can be friends again."

"Minor difference of interpretation of city ordinances," mumbled Sir Alasdair.

Jo watched, revolted, as Aunt Lily made nice with Sir Alasdair and Dame Isabel. If her secret was revealed, she knew, no easy reconciliation like this would be possible with *her* friends.

"I'm going," said Jo.

"Oh no—please stay," said Dame Isabel. "Now that this nonsense with the Ichthala is behind us, Sir Alasdair and I thought we'd celebrate with a little drink. We wanted you to join us."

"No, you three have fun," said Jo.

"Jo—" began Aunt Lily.

Jo left the room as quickly as possible and didn't look back.

After dinner Nora whispered to Jo, "We need to talk." Jo was in no mood for it, but Nora insisted, and she made Jo promise to meet her later in the squires' secret room.

At midnight Jo slipped under her floorboards and crept through the crawl spaces to the secret room. As she emerged from the chimney, she saw that Ian and Nora were already there, quietly conferring over candlelight. Jo joined them. She was exhausted, her nerves frayed.

"Okay, what's this all about, Nora?" said Jo.

"The underground cathedral you visited with Audrey Durdle," said Nora. "I didn't want to mention it this afternoon in the café, in public . . . just in case."

"Well?" yawned Jo.

"It's a cathedral of the Silent Sisters."

Jo's eyes widened. She froze in mid-yawn.

Ian snorted. "I didn't see any Silent Sisters there."

"They must've been hiding," said Nora.

"Oh, come on. The place was flooded, falling apart, full of groglings—"

Fear dripped slowly into Jo's heart. "Why . . . why do you think that cathedral belongs to the Silent Sisters?"

"The idol," said Nora. "According to Audrey's scripts, only a cathedral of the Silent Sisters would have an idol of the All-Devouring Mother."

"We didn't see any idol," said Ian.

"Yes, you did," said Nora. "You told me. *The mouth.*"

Jo kept quiet. The golden mouth shining in the darkness, rushing at them as if to gobble them—Jo had glimpsed it for only a moment, but she remembered it vividly. Nevertheless, she, Ian, and Audrey rarely talked about it. It was as if it was too strange, too disturbing to mention.

"Legend says the All-Devouring Mother nests in the throat of that mouth," whispered Nora. "In the darkness she broods, lurking deep beneath the city, waiting for her time to STRIKE!" Nora leaped up and waved her hands around.

Ian groaned. "Can you, for once, not be overdramatic?"

"I can't be dramatic enough!" said Nora. "You've stumbled

upon the lost cathedral of the most mysterious cult of all time, and you act like it's, what, a trip to the grocery store?"

"The Ichthala isn't something to joke about," said Ian quietly. "It killed a lot of people. It killed my mother. It's not just a character on your stupid show."

"But Ian, *I'm not joking,*" insisted Nora. "Sometimes I think I'm the only one who takes it seriously! And if you would only listen . . . don't you know *anything* about the Silent Sisters?"

Ian said, "Nobody does, Nora. Oh, I suppose *you* do?"

"I know what *Teenage Ichthala* says," said Nora.

Jo could tell Ian was biting his tongue. "Okay, Nora. What's it say on your show?"

"It says," said Nora darkly, "that the Silent Sisters are midwives to the rebirth of the All-Devouring Mother."

Ian humored her. "Oh? And why does the All-Devouring Mother need help being reborn?"

"Well, since you asked," said Nora, excited to be talking about her favorite topic, "the story goes that at the beginning of time, the All-Devouring Mother was a wild goddess who nearly destroyed the world. The other gods had to stop her if the world was going to survive. They couldn't kill the All-Devouring Mother, since she was a goddess—but they were able to destroy her body. Without a body, the All-Devouring Mother's soul burned with rage, but she couldn't *do* anything. Until the Silent Sisters came along."

Jo fought down the quiver in her voice. "Who *are* the Silent Sisters?"

"They want the All-Devouring Mother to wreak havoc again," said Nora. "So they searched all over the world, looking for the shreds of the Ichthala's body—her bones, her blood, her brains, everything—in order to rebuild the goddess, to stitch her back together. And now, according to *Teenage Ichthala*, the Silent Sisters are almost finished. The All-Devouring Mother is complete, it is alive—but it doesn't yet have its soul. The Silent

Sisters now have to perform the final and most difficult ritual and reunite the Ichthala's soul with its body."

"This is ridiculous," said Ian. "How could they—"

Nora bristled. "Do you want to hear this or not?"

"Fine, whatever." Ian shrugged. "Go ahead."

Nora looked back and forth at Jo and Ian. "The Silent Sisters chose one of their own women to bear a baby girl," she whispered. "But this baby has the soul of Ichthala, the All-Devouring Mother. When the girl comes of age, the Silent Sisters awaken the Ichthala within her and feed her to the monster they rebuilt. The monster eats the girl, the girl dies, and her soul is released into the monster. Then the devouring begins."

"Hold on," said Jo. "What do you mean, they 'awaken the Ichthala' in the girl?"

"Exactly, Jo. *That's* my discovery," said Nora. "The legends talk about how the Silent Sisters will 'awaken the Ichthala,' but none of them say how it's to be done. Well, now I know. It's described in the secret messages I've decoded from the show. That's why I didn't want to blab about it at the café. It's too disturbing to tell just anyone."

"Well? Out with it!" said Ian. "What is it?"

Nora said, "Do you really want to hear this?"

"Yes!" said Jo.

Nora paused. "Really?"

"C'mon, Nora, *tell us!*" said Ian.

Nora smiled. She had them now, and she knew it. "The Silent Sisters first have to give the girl some of the powers of the All-Devouring Mother. They do this by putting a little bit of the All-Devouring Mother's blood in her. This awakens her evil Ichthala soul and makes her ready to fuse with the body they reconstructed."

Jo was trying hard to understand. "*Put* the blood in her?"

"Yes. And here's how," whispered Nora. "Thirteen years ago, the Silent Sisters lured a man to their cathedral. They sucked out all his blood and filled him with the All-Devouring Mother's blood. That blood turned him into a half monster. The man was . . ."

Jo gripped her knees tightly. "The Belgian Prankster?"

Nora nodded. "That's right. Sir Nils is cursed to carry the Ichthala blood until the girl comes of age. But to have that demonic blood gives you unpredictable powers, powers a human shouldn't have. The Ichthala's blood chews away at your soul, drives you mad."

"And that's why the Belgian Prankster did all those weird pranks," said Jo tensely.

Ian looked at Jo. "What do you mean?"

"The Belgian Prankster . . . he was always pulling some stunt or another," said Jo. "One time he filled the Grand Canyon with pistachio pudding. Another time he rearranged all the stars over Mexico City to make a picture of his face. And you know how he stole the lodge. Strange things like that."

"It was the Ichthala blood, boiling over inside him," said Nora. "The power was too strong for him. It drove him crazy. He wants nothing more than to get rid of it. And the only way he can get rid of it . . . is . . ."

Jo and Ian looked at each other. "What?"

Nora closed her eyes, forcing the next words out of her mouth with difficulty. "His . . . *stinger,*" she said. "I know it doesn't make sense, but the show says he grows a stinger, or beak, or some kind of second nose somewhere inside him. When the Belgian Prankster comes back to Eldritch City, the Ichthala will go to him, and he will somehow use that to give her the Ichthala blood. Then the Silent Sisters take her to their cathedral and feed her to the All-Devouring Mother. Then the All-Devouring Mother eats up all of Eldritch City. And then the world."

For a second it seemed the world was about to end right then—Nora's high, breathy voice describing the rituals of the Silent Sisters hypnotized Jo with its intense rhythm. She nearly expected the Silent Sisters to step out of the shadows and take her to the cathedral that very moment.

But only for a moment. Ian laughed, a bit too loudly, and said, "You almost had me, Nora. But come on. A stinger? A *beak*? That's even stupider than your usual."

Jo kept quiet, withdrawing into the darkness so Ian and Nora couldn't see her panicking eyes. *Is that what the Silent Sisters have planned for me?* she thought, nauseous dread building up inside her. Her fear hardened into anger. *I can't take this waiting anymore. I wish the Silent Sisters would just get it over with. Just come and get me, or leave me alone!*

"Jo?" Ian was looking at her strangely. "Are you okay?"

"I'm fine. Give me a second." Jo dug her nails into her thighs as Ian and Nora continued to whisper.

"So where do the Silent Sisters come from?" said Ian.

"Nobody really knows," said Nora. "On the show, the Silent Sisters are ordinary people who had horrible lives. They hate the world. Suicide isn't enough for them—they want revenge. They want the whole universe to die."

"So who are they?" said Ian.

"Some of them walk among us," said Nora. "But they say when you reach a certain level in their cult, you must gouge out your eyes, cut off your tongue, slice off your ears, lock yourself in a coffin deep underground, and never move again. It's their way of seceding from the universe. Some Silent Sisters have been lying still for centuries. That's how they get their powers—if you stay still for long enough, the universe whispers its secrets to you."

Ian's voice was edged with revulsion. "And you're saying that cathedral we saw—"

"It's where the Silent Sisters are hiding. Yes." Nora turned to Jo. "How *did* Audrey know about the cathedral? Do you think she might be connected with the Silent—"

Something inside Jo broke.

"No!" she snapped. "Why do you have to drag Audrey into it? Not everything has to be connected to your stupid Silent Sisters! Honestly, do you think about anything else?"

Nora's glow faded sharply. She had been excited, animated, her hair flung back, eyes shining; now she shrank behind her tangle of hair and mumbled something apologetic.

Ian shot Jo a puzzled look. "I'm sure Jo didn't mean . . ."

"I'm sorry, Nora," said Jo. "I'm just exhausted." But she just couldn't take another word about the Silent Sisters. Worst of all was dragging Audrey into it. Audrey didn't believe in the myths, and Jo clung to Audrey's skepticism with something like faith.

Yet even Aunt Lily believed it now. And it couldn't have been coincidence that Audrey had led her to the cathedral of the Silent Sisters. Jo had the helpless feeling of being manipulated, that the Belgian Prankster was pulling the strings of her life. Jo suspected her choices counted for nothing—that no matter what she did, the Belgian Prankster would get her.

Jo ground her teeth and quietly panicked as Nora and Ian argued over *Teenage Ichthala*. Nora scurried to the cabinet where she kept all the old episodes of the show and put one of the reels into the projector, to show how a certain episode supported her case. It was an old episode Jo had seen many times before; the show played on, Nora and Ian continued to quarrel, but Jo just felt exhausted, and let her eyelids droop.

Jo opened her eyes.

It was completely dark.

The show was over. Jo must have fallen asleep, and Nora and Ian left her in the secret room. Or perhaps Ian and Nora were asleep, too. But she couldn't hear them. There was an electricity in the air, a faint buzzing in the darkness. Her skin felt prickly and cold.

"Ian?" whispered Jo. "Nora?"

No answer. She couldn't see anything. But then she heard something in the darkness—a moist sucking sound. Nora or Ian snoring, or . . . Jo groped around. She couldn't find them.

Something *else* in the room? Jo couldn't find the light. She got up, held her hands out, and crept forward, eyes wide open in the blackness, looking for a wall to orient herself. The snuffling got louder. It was to the left—no, to the right—she couldn't tell—in back of her—closer—

The projector switched itself on.

Jo turned around.

The Belgian Prankster glowed in the darkness.

An invisible fist gripped Jo. She couldn't move, couldn't speak, couldn't scream. Her eyes were fixed on the Belgian Prankster's image, projected on the sheet. His gigantic purple nose was runny and engorged, a shapeless mass of skin and fat and veins.

"I'm coming," whispered the Belgian Prankster.

Jo couldn't close her eyes. The Belgian Prankster was slowly reaching up to his nose. Jo winced as she heard the flesh rip. The detached nose twitched in the Belgian Prankster's hand. Where the Belgian Prankster's nose should have been, there was now a black hole. Jo couldn't see the Belgian Prankster's eyes behind his ski goggles, but she felt them creep up her body.

Jo shuddered.

The Belgian Prankster reached up to the hole in his face and started pulling something long, pale, and scabby out. He grunted and strained as the thing inched out, further and further; finally his hands dropped to his side and he grinned.

A writhing stinger pointed straight at Jo.

Jo screamed, broke free, stumbled, crashed to the floor. The lights were on. The projector was still running, film flipping and flipping. The sheet had nothing on it, just a blank white glow.

Shakily Jo stood up and turned off the projector. It had been a nightmare. Still, she felt as though someone had sent electric shocks all through her. Her heart thudded. She tried to think about something, anything, other than the Belgian Prankster.

But it wasn't the Belgian Prankster that scared her. It was that when she saw him, a hidden part of her had quickened. Something strange inside her had recognized him, and responded.

NINETEEN

THE next month it was Jo and Ian's turn to groom the ostriches. About two dozen ostriches nested on the roof of the lodge, but they were semi-wild, and came and went as they pleased. Occasionally all the ostriches took off at once and flew out over the sea, banking and swooping raucously over the water, their armor glittering in the sun.

Grooming was nasty, smelly work, but it had to be done, or the ostriches would get embarrassed about their dirty plumage and refuse to fly. So every night that month Jo and Ian had to pluck out the ostriches' ragged feathers, prune their talons, and rub oil into their leathery necks.

Jo loved the ostriches. She loved their proud, stupid eyes, their powerful wings, their ornate armor and colorful regalia.

Now that she and Ian had finished their first quest, they were allowed to have ostriches of their own. Her ostrich was a fledgling named Ethelred, a little excitable and awkward, but just the right size for her. Jo loved clutching him as he sprinted off the roof and hurtled into the air, dipping and weaving between the buildings, flapping up into the sky and leaving the city far below.

She loved Ethelred all the more for his cranky personality. He always looked slightly offended, as if someone had just told a joke he didn't understand but suspected was about him. If she didn't ride Ethelred for a few of days, the next time he saw her, he would try to bite her. And he was reckless: Jo felt barely in control as Ethelred took her faster and faster over dangerous territory, flying over the sparkling, foamy sea, zigzagging through the maze of buildings of Eldritch City, or racing wild pterodactyls in the fens outside of town.

Flying Ethelred, Jo discovered little surprises scattered throughout the countryside. She flew far above rambling farmhouses and tidy fields of crops, and spied the occasional hermit's hut or a half-collapsed castle. Once in the swampy forest, she thought she saw the Schwenk lurking in the trees, but by the time they wheeled back it was gone.

When it got too hot in the city, Jo, Ian, and Nora would climb on their ostriches, Audrey would hold on to Ian's back, and they would fly out to a deserted beach where a river streamed out into the ocean, near a decaying mansion overgrown with weeds. They would spend all day swimming in the ocean, picnicking in the cool forest, and exploring the abandoned mansion. The ostriches ran around on the beach, chasing the crabs. Those days were close to perfect.

It also helped put out of Jo's mind the specter of the Belgian Prankster.

Jo tried to think of the Belgian Prankster as somehow safely distant, as something she could keep at bay just by immersing herself in everyday life. But sometimes she caught herself daydreaming about him. She couldn't understand why. She would see someone on the subway who for a split second looked like the Belgian Prankster. Or she would suddenly hear his name whispered in a crowd, and when she turned around she couldn't figure out who had said it. Sometimes even certain smells overwhelmingly reminded her of the Belgian Prankster. She tried to ignore it, but she couldn't help it. The more time passed, the more the ordinary world almost seemed like the thinnest piece of tissue, and the shadow of the Belgian Prankster was moving behind it.

The rainy season had started. It was a dim, drizzling morning, and a big thunderstorm was rapidly moving in. Jo was just returning to the lodge after riding Ethelred. These days she liked to wake up before dawn and fly with Ethelred before everyone else woke up, breathing the fresh morning air and watching the sun rise over the city.

Jo was soaked with sweat and rain, happily exhausted, when she landed on the roof of the lodge. She unfastened Ethelred's armor, dried it, and put it away. Then she put fresh sand in Ethelred's stall, toweled him off, and gave him some lizards to eat. Finally, ready to face the day, she started downstairs.

There was an emergency. Footsteps pounded up the staircase. Jo barely had time to step aside as Aunt Lily, Colonel Korsakov, and Sir Oliver rushed past, all carrying strange contraptions. Aunt Lily didn't even notice her until Jo said, "Hey! What's going on?"

Aunt Lily turned, startled. "Jo! I was looking all over the lodge for you!"

"I was flying Ethelred——"

Aunt Lily signaled the others to go ahead. Jo heard the peevish croak of ostriches waking up, their armor clanking as Korsakov and Sir Oliver got them ready.

"I'm leaving," said Aunt Lily. "I have to leave right now."

"But a storm's coming. You can't ride today."

"It doesn't matter," said Aunt Lily. "The Belgian Prankster has made his move."

Jo stumbled backward. *"What?"*

"The Belgian Prankster is coming back to Eldritch City," said Aunt Lily. "We have to stop him—me, Sir Oliver, Korsakov. Every minute counts."

A gunshot went off in Jo's stomach. "But . . . but you said I was safe from him here!"

"I was wrong," said Aunt Lily. "We received new information just an hour ago. Nils—I mean, the Belgian Prankster—it's much worse than we'd thought."

"What are you going to do?" said Jo with rising panic.

"We're going to try this." Aunt Lily held up her contraption. Jo recognized it as the Inconvenience, but transformed by Aunt Lily's tinkering, its components twisted and attached to new parts so that it was now a zigzagging pole stuck all over with prongs, wheels, and corkscrews, wrapped up in fur and blinking lights. It looked like a mess. "Theoretically, we can use this to turn the Inconvenience against the Belgian Prankster, maybe block him from getting to Eldritch City, or—"

"Theoretically?" Jo looked at the jury-rigged thing with zero confidence. "But . . . when will you be back?"

Aunt Lily crouched down and took Jo's hands. "I'll be back in a couple of weeks. Maybe a few months. I don't know. Maybe . . ."

The sentence hung unfinished in the air. Jo was startled to see that for the first time since they'd come to Eldritch City, Aunt Lily looked close to panic.

Jo said, "But why do *you* have to go? I need you here! Why isn't anyone else helping?"

Aunt Lily seemed about to crack. "Nobody else knows, Jo. They know we're going to stop the Belgian Prankster, but—"

"But what if the Belgian Prankster comes and . . . you're not here?" said Jo wildly. "Nobody else knows except Sefino, and he's useless! What can I do?"

Aunt Lily went very still. "Listen, Jo. If the Belgian Prankster somehow does manage to come back, whatever you do, *do not* go to him."

Jo stared at Aunt Lily. "Go *to* him?"

"I'm serious. Don't go to him, no matter what!"

"Why on earth do you think I would?" shouted Jo.

Sir Oliver and Colonel Korsakov were calling for Aunt Lily to hurry up. Aunt Lily looked like she wanted to say more. "I'm sorry, Jo. I wish I had time, but . . ."

Jo grabbed Aunt Lily's arm. "Don't leave me here! Let Sir Oliver and Korsakov go! I don't know what I'll do without you. What if people find out who I am? What if you—if—"

Aunt Lily took Jo in her arms and held her tight. But it was too quick; Jo tried to hold on to her, but before she knew it Aunt Lily had let her go and was running up the stairs. Jo stumbled after her, but by the time she made it up Aunt Lily had already mounted her ostrich and it was sprinting forward, off the roof and up into the air, joining Sir Oliver and Colonel Korsakov in the clouds. Jo watched helplessly as the three knights hurtled off into the dark morning, into the thick fog and spattering storm.

The rain pelted Jo. She was soaked and terrified and she didn't know what to do. The only people she trusted to protect her were gone.

The sudden exit of Aunt Lily, Colonel Korsakov, and Sir Oliver was the talk of the lodge. Nobody knew why they had gone, other than that it had something to do with the Belgian Prankster. Jo was sick of thinking about it. She took a long shower, put on dry clothes, and went to find Ian. He brought up the subject, but when Jo didn't reply, he knew enough to talk about something else.

The butlers weren't around for some reason, so Jo and Ian rummaged through the kitchen to make breakfast for themselves. It was her first breakfast in Eldritch City without Aunt Lily; it didn't feel right. They sat in the chairs by the fireplace, eating dry toast and drinking coffee, as the other knights and squires bustled around, getting ready for the day.

"Where are the butlers?" said Jo dully. "Shouldn't Sefino be around somewhere?"

Ian took another bite of toast. "Daphne said the cockroaches went out on another bender last night. I doubt they'll be back anytime soon."

At that moment the front doors burst open and the cockroaches came roaring in. Their evening suits were wrinkled and sweaty, their ties stained or missing, and Petrucchio and Cicero were carrying a snoring, drooling Benvenuto. They were singing, but the words were slurred, and it mostly came out as nonsense.

"Give us a *Snitch*! Where's a *Snitch*?" said Sefino, snatching a copy away from Jo and ripping it open to the society column. "Nothing . . . nothing . . . *nothing*!" he cried, throwing the paper back at her. "Not a *word*!"

"What's wrong?" said Jo.

"Listen, Jo!" said Sefino fiercely. "Last night I broke *three* windows, fell down the *stairs,* got in a fight with a *beetle,* danced on *eight* separate tables, and drank things most people don't even know *exist*! I threw Cicero out the window, ate enough caviar to kill a man, and, as a grand finale, set some curtains on fire! And still, NOTHING in the *Eldritch Snitch*!"

"You can't be serious," said Jo. "You're upset because Chatterbox *isn't* writing about you?"

"It's all your fault, Jo," said Sefino. "You and your meddling article!"

"You begged me to write it!"

"I *highly* doubt that," snapped Sefino. "What are we going to be outraged about now? What about my notoriety? What if people stop talking about me? I'll stop existing!"

Barrachio said, "Chatterbox said he won't write about us again unless we do something newsworthy."

"*Everything* I do is newsworthy!" shouted Sefino. "If I pick my nose, it should be on the front page! As it is, I'm knocking myself out here! I don't know how many more nights like this I've got left in me! *What if he never writes about us again?*"

"I'm not vomiting onto any more debutantes until Chatterbox comes to his senses," declared Belpo. "I mean, what does he want from us, blood?"

"I'll give blood!" said Sefino. "I'll open a vein and let it run until we're back on the society page, where we belong!"

Jo said, "Why don't you start your own newspaper? Then you could write about yourselves all you want."

"Please, Jo," said Sefino, rolling his eyes. "We're trying to be serious here."

The front door creaked open and Dugan peeked in. It looked as if he'd intended to make a discreet entrance, but with the butlers making a spectacle in the front room, Dugan became the unexpected center of attention.

Cicero rounded on Dugan unsteadily. "You! Where've you been the last three days?"

Dugan cringed at the questionable smells coming off Cicero and tried to shuffle past. "Nowhere," he mumbled.

Cicero blocked him. "I demand to know where you scurry off to, squire!"

"None of your business!" said Dugan. "Sir Oliver doesn't care where I go, so I don't see why I have to answer to his butler!"

"Insolence! Insolence and impropriety!" slurred Cicero. "Sir Oliver will hear of this!"

Dame Isabel, Sir Alasdair, and Dame Delia had been watching this with amusement. Finally, Dame Isabel broke in, "But Sir Oliver just left on expedition. And doesn't the Odd-Fish charter say that when a knight is on expedition, authority over the squire falls to his butler?"

"Sir Oliver's . . . *gone?*" Cicero's mouth hung open in a

drooling grin. "You're right, Dame Isabel! Ah, Dugan, I have you now! You are *grounded,* sir, for a week—no exceptions!"

Dugan looked like someone had hit him with a brick. He started to speak, but nothing came out except a strangled cough. His eyebrows squeezed together, his lips quivered, and he hurried from the room, mumbling about having to make some calls.

Jo and Ian were playing pool in the games room when Dugan came in and closed the door.

"Ian, you have to help me," he said shakily.

"So you're back," said Ian. "Where *do* you go for days and days, Dugan? I'm curious, too."

"Ian, please, listen to me," said Dugan.

Ian returned to his shot. "I'm surprised you haven't been kicked out of the Order yet."

Dugan said sharply, "If it weren't for me, you wouldn't even be in the Order. So could you stop being a prig and listen?"

Ian started to shoot, wavered, and put the cue aside. "Okay. What's going on?"

"There's someplace I have to go tonight," said Dugan. "I need you to go for me. Please."

Ian looked irked. "Why should I?"

"Hear him out, Ian," said Jo.

"I know you've been up to *something* shady," said Ian. "I don't want to be sucked into it."

"Ian, just once," said Dugan. "I'll never ask you for anything again. I don't want to get you involved, either, but considering who I'm working for, I don't have a choice."

Ian approached Dugan, his arms crossed. "Working for? Who are you working for?"

Dugan said, "Oona Looch."

Jo had never heard the name *Oona Looch* before, but the words seemed to freeze the room with a dreadful electricity. Dugan kept his eyes on the ground, looking more bashful than Jo had ever seen him. Ian stood frozen in horrified surprise.

"Oh no, oh no," Ian said finally, holding his hands up and backing away. "Dugan, what were you thinking? How could you be so *stupid*? Oona *Looch*? You're working for *Oona Looch*?"

"Ian, don't be so judgmental. We don't have much time, listen to me!"

"*You* get in trouble because you think you're invincible, *you* get in some mess and I have to clean it up for you, and *I'm* a prig, *I'm* judgmental, there's something wrong with *me*?"

"So you'll do it?" said Dugan hopefully.

Ian had been energized by his anger, but now he faltered and stuttered. Finally he said, "Yes. Okay. I'll do it. God, Dugan . . ."

"Who's Oona Looch?" said Jo.

Dugan said, "Oona Looch is a . . . well, you could say she's a businesswoman . . ."

Ian cut in. "She's a mafia boss. She's the queen of the Eldritch City crime world!"

Dugan looked uncomfortable. "That's a limited way of looking at it, Ian. Oona Looch has done some sketchy things, yeah, but the alternative's worse. Somebody has to take control, or—"

"You've been hanging around them too long, Dugan. You sound like one of them."

Dugan bristled. "You're naive."

"You don't know right from wrong anymore," said Ian.

"Shut up!" said Jo. "I'm sick of your arguing, both of you!"

Dugan slumped into a chair. Ian started pacing. "Okay, Dugan. What do I have to do?"

"Oona Looch will be at the Dome of Doom tonight," said Dugan. "Some of her bet boys have been roughed up, and Oona Looch has decided to show some muscle. I'm Oona's bet boy tonight, so—"

Ian groaned. "What? You're kidding!"

"Don't worry, it's simple. You'll just be taking bets and paying out for Oona Looch."

"I know what it *means,* Dugan," said Ian. "But you said the bet boys have been getting hurt!"

"Well, that's my job, and now I can't do it! And if I don't at least send a substitute, I'm dead."

Ian looked shaken. "Dugan, I could get killed!"

Dugan threw up his hands. "I wouldn't ask you if I had the choice!"

Jo said, "Can I come?"

Dugan frowned. "I don't think so, Jo. Oona Looch prefers to have as few outsiders as possible, and it's pretty dangerous down there. And even if——"

"Whatever. I'm going," said Jo.

Later that night Jo and Ian took the subway to Lower Brondo, an out-of-the-way neighborhood of warehouses and old factories, desolate by day and mostly abandoned by night. The rain bucketed down, churning the puddles into mist as Jo and Ian splashed down the unlit streets, past boarded-up buildings and heaps of scrap metal, down an alley to an unmarked door.

After a hurried knock and a whispered password, the door opened to reveal a monstrous beetle. The beetle led Jo and Ian into a dark factory. Their soaked shoes squished noisily down the quiet assembly line, and there were swift movements and hisses in the darkness around them—other, unseen beetles following their every move. Jo took a deep breath and tried to calm herself. She looked at Ian. He gave a thin smile, trying to put on a brave face. He looked sick.

They entered a grubby elevator. The beetle gave them a hard stare and slammed the door. Jo felt for Ian's hand and took it. The elevator started its rapid descent, and two minutes later the doors opened. They were at the Dome of Doom.

The Dome of Doom was a cavern buried deep in the mountain—three levels connected by stairs, surrounding a great spherical arena enclosed by a cage of iron grillework. The gaps in the cage were large enough to see into the arena, and a pool of black water glittered at the bottom. The three levels were crowded with tables, bars, couches, and tunnels leading off to private rooms. These areas were dim and seedy, but the arena was brilliantly lit.

Jo and Ian made their way through the spectacle of disreputable-looking characters and bizarre creatures who stared suspiciously as they hurried by: cockroaches, centipedes, beetles, eelmen, and some creatures that Jo had never seen before, weird organisms that seemed dredged from the depths of the swamps, yet dressed in the height of fashion.

They descended to the lowest level, which was not as crowded. Ian went to the bar and said, "Two black milks." They were served, and they sat down.

Jo was still nervous. Everything seemed menacing in the dim, flickering noise, and the people looked rougher, more brutal than people she saw every day in Eldritch City. Jo wished they were back at the lodge. She had the queasy feeling that if she got in trouble down here, nobody could help her.

She sipped her black milk—and nearly spat it out. The drink tasted peppery and rancid. Jo saw that Ian's mouth was puckered with disgust, and she started to laugh.

Ian grimaced. "First time I've ever had this stuff."

"It's my last," said Jo. "What is it?"

"Fermented centipede milk."

"You might've warned me! Ian, I'm going to throw up!"

Ian tried another sip. "I'm told it's an acquired taste."

Jo sighed and looked around the room. "What's this place all about?"

"It's where knights fight duels," said Ian. "Squires fight here, too, but technically only knights are allowed to fight duels. Actually, all dueling is illegal, but it still goes on. The mob runs it."

"Have you ever been here before?"

"No way! If we got caught here, we'd be kicked out of the Order of Odd-Fish so fast . . . Everyone here is incognito." Ian drained the rest of his black milk. "God, that's really awful. Why did I drink that?"

"I don't know. Listen, shouldn't you be looking for Oona Looch?"

"We're early. I need to steel my nerves first." Ian looked around, exhaling and nodding. "Say, can I have your milk, too?"

"Knock yourself out."

Just then a gloved fist slammed on the table. Jo and Ian looked up to see a ferocious man with blue skin and a face bristling with grotesque moles, decked out in an ornate military uniform from an army that existed only in his overheated imagination, with a helmet of equal parts chrome and crocodile skin. He leered over them, growling, "That's *my* drink."

Jo said, "Hi, Audrey."

Audrey seemed disappointed. "Oh . . . was it that obvious?"

"No, we just know you," said Ian.

Audrey slumped into a chair. "Still, I would've liked to have scared you a *little*."

"How'd you know we'd be here?" said Jo. She was relieved to see Audrey; their situation didn't seem so menacing now.

Audrey started pulling the fake moles off her face. "I called the lodge, but you were already gone. I talked to Dugan and he said you'd be here. I wish you'd told me."

"Why?"

Audrey grinned. "I love watching the fights!"

Ian was astonished. "You've been here before?"

"Oh, all the time. I've lost tons of money betting on duels. But they're exciting," said Audrey, her eyes blazing. "There's nothing like it!"

"Did Dugan tell you why we're here?" said Jo.

"Yes. He thinks he's quite a little gangster!" Audrey snickered. "He can't have it both ways, squiring for Sir Oliver *and* running odd jobs for Oona Looch. What kind of gangster gets *grounded*? He's absurd."

"I just want to get this done with." Ian finished Jo's milk. "And then I want to get out of here."

"Ian, I'm starting to think you have no appreciation of the finer things in life," said Audrey. Then, to Jo: "One time, I saw a guy get his arm torn off!"

"Ah, a connoisseur," said Jo.

A beetle sidled up to Ian and whispered something in his ear. Ian quickly stood up, looking around nervously. "I've gotta go. Wish me luck."

"Break a leg," said Jo.

"Don't let them break yours," said Audrey.

"If it came to that, your boyfriend wouldn't have much of a choice," said the beetle, and led Ian away into the crowd.

Jo was worried. "Should we help him?"

"Aw, he'll do fine," said Audrey. "It'll put hair on his chest. Let him sweat—*we're* going to make a proper night of it. Ugh, did Ian really have you drinking black milk? Let me buy you the real stuff."

Audrey went to the bar. Jo stayed at the table and took in the scene. It was very crowded now, and every table was occupied. The tension in the room, the expectation of blood, was intoxicating. Everything seemed both sleazy and glamorous. Even the candles on the tables flared with hellish energy. Jo noticed that only the highest and lowest classes of Eldritch City society were here: the criminals, spongers, and addicts, but also celebrities and politicians, smoking hookahs, spewing clouds of pink smoke, sipping gruesome, bubbling cocktails.

Audrey returned. "This is jinxjuice. Drink up! Here's to the Dome of Doom!"

"Cheers!" said Jo, and drank. Audrey was right, jinxjuice was much better: it tasted of caramel and marigolds, and it made her lips tingle. When Jo finished it, a drenched moth flew out of the bottom of the cup. Audrey's moth joined Jo's, and they both fluttered away.

"Does anyone eat the moth, too?" said Jo.

"You're gross," said Audrey. "Hey, look—there's Ian."

Ian was standing in a little booth. A line had formed, and he was rapidly taking money from people and making notes on a pad of paper.

"What's he doing?" said Jo.

"Taking bets," said Audrey. "The mafia uses people from outside the mob families to take the bets and pay out the winnings, just in case there's a disagreement."

"Why?"

"Most of those disagreements end in someone getting murdered," said Audrey. "And somebody from outside the mob world can be killed without causing a gang war to break out."

Jo gasped. "You don't really think Ian might get killed!"

Audrey shrugged. "It's a possibility."

Just then a great rhythmic booming started. Somewhere drums slowly thumped, accompanied by a crash of cymbals and gongs. The drums throbbed faster and the cymbals banged more frantically, so thunderingly loud Jo soon had to put her hands over her ears, and just when it became sheer deafening noise, it suddenly stopped, and a voice rang out:

"Welcome, ladies and gentlemen, to the DOME OF DOOM!"

Raucous cheers and wild applause. Audrey stood on her chair and hooted. Jo clapped tentatively and looked over at Ian. He was taking final bets from some stragglers. He then closed up his cash box and looked at her. Jo smiled back.

The announcer continued: "Tonight! Fumo, the Sleeping Bee, versus Zam-Zam, the Dancing Ant of Sadness! Duelists— present yourselves and make your boasts!"

Audrey tugged Jo away from the table, leading her up to the metal cage that fenced off the arena. Jo saw two duelists on opposite sides of the arena, each astride an armored ostrich. Both duelists wore costumes, but Jo couldn't quite tell what they were supposed to be.

"Why are they dressed like that?" said Jo.

"Part of the dueling ritual," said Audrey. "You have to dress up as one of the gods of Eldritch City. That way, the duel isn't really between you and your enemy, it's between the two gods, and the violence becomes more abstract. And it looks cooler."

"How many gods do you have in Eldritch City?"

"One hundred forty-four thousand, four hundred forty-four. The duelist on the right, he's dressed as Fumo, the Sleeping Bee. The one on the left is Zam-Zam, the Dancing Ant of Sadness. Now wait, listen, before they actually fight they have to exchange ritualized threats and insults in the old classical style."

Fumo and Zam-Zam had struck stylized poses for the exchange of insults. Fumo wore an elaborate costume of black and yellow, with jiggling antennae and a long stinger; when she spoke, her voice was distorted by an electric box that made it sound as though she were buzzing. Zam-Zam wore sleek sheaths of segmented steel that made him look like a baleful robotic ant.

"You are named Sleeping Bee," bellowed Zam-Zam, "but I shall wake you from your slumber and turn your own sting upon you, to pierce you with your own foolishness! Rivers shall run red with *your* blood, *your* name shall be cursed by generations, and *your* children shall be three feet tall, totally hairless, and perpetually drenched in their own stinking sweat! When I am finished with you, your body shall be torn asunder by five wild boars and buried in five ignominious places, each one more shameful than the last! I have spoken!"

"So, Dancing Ant of Sadness! Bold words!" buzzed Fumo. "But your ant-dance shall be to the music of *your own* sadness! For I, Sleeping Bee, shall buzz and bewilder you; verily shall I construct honeycombs of your carcass; verily shall I feast upon your shame! I have spoken!"

"Your words are as empty as your sting, Sleeping Bee!" retorted Zam-Zam. "Your feast shall be of the ashes of defeat, and on those, you shall feast heartily! Your corpse shall be torn to bits by my thousand children, who shall raise each morsel to their mouths, chew your disgraced innards with contemptuous joy, and excrete them with a smirk! I have spoken!"

"Vile boaster! Just as I, Fumo, the Sleeping Bee, have defeated both Quafmaf, the Pigeon of the Moon, and Nixilpilfi, the Gerbil Who Does Not Know Mercy, so I shall dispatch you, Zam-Zam, to the realm of obloquy, and force to your lips the flagon of infamy! I have spoken!"

"Idle threats, Fumo! They hold no terror for me, Zam-Zam, the Dancing Ant of Sadness! I, who have vanquished not only Mizbiliades, the Bleeding Butterfly, and Paznarfalasath, the Rhinoceros Whose Laughter Destroys Worlds, but also Zookoofoomoot, the Maggot of Dismay, and Pft the Mouse! In a similar fashion shall I tuck you, Sleeping Bee, into a bed of disgrace, and sing you the lullaby of destruction! I have spoken!"

As the insults went on, Jo whispered to Audrey, "Why do knights duel?"

"Usually they have a grudge that can only be settled by fighting," said Audrey. "But knights like to duel. Sometimes they'll make up a grudge just so they can fight."

"Why don't they just fight by themselves somewhere?" said Jo.

"That's unheard-of," said Audrey. "For a knight to disobey the traditions of dueling would lead to complete disgrace. And there are a lot of traditions to obey."

"Like what?"

Audrey counted off the traditions on her fingers. "First, when you challenge someone to a duel, each side has to get two seconds—those are fellow squires or knights who help you in the duel. Then, before the duel, you have to sleep at your opponent's house for one night, and your opponent has to sleep at your house for one night. Also, before the duel you both have to write a hundred-line poem insulting your enemy, and read your poems to each other at a tea ceremony in the Grudge Hut in Snerdsmallow. *And* you have to pick what god you're going to be in the duel, and make the costume, and work out what you're going to say in the opening round of insults . . ."

"It sounds like a lot of trouble."

"Originally that was the idea—that if there were a lot of difficult rituals surrounding the duel, knights wouldn't bother, and they'd solve their problems peacefully. But everybody enjoys the rituals, and so that kind of backfired."

"How do you challenge someone to a duel?"

"Oh, that's easy. You just take off your left shoe, throw it at their nose, and say, 'Consider yourself challenged!' Then they take off their right shoe, throw it at your nose, and say, 'Challenge accepted!' After that, you are both bound by all the rules and traditions of dueling."

"And if you break the rules?"

"Great dishonor," said Audrey. "You wouldn't be able to show your face in Eldritch City again. The lowliest cockroach would spit on you. Actually, the cockroaches would be the first to spit, they're sticklers for ceremony. . . . Oh, look, it's starting!"

Both duelists had mounted their ostriches. The duelists' seconds bustled about, buckling on the ostriches' armor and securing the duelists in their saddles; then the ostriches ran forward, leaping off the platforms and into the arena. The crowd roared. The ostriches hurtled toward each other, clawing and flapping and shrieking as the duelists ignited their double-bladed lances, blossoming on either side with flame. The duel had begun.

"What are they trying to do?" shouted Jo over the noise.

"Whoever gets knocked into the water first loses!" yelled Audrey. "Watch!"

The ostriches scrabbled at each other in midair. The duelists spun and twirled their lances with blazing speed, clashing, sparking, lunging and blocking faster than Jo's eyes could follow—a blur of smoky arcs of fire. Her heart surged with excitement and her eyes went wide as the ostriches circled, snarled, and snapped at each other's throats. A gong crashed and the ostriches disentangled from each other, swooping back up to opposite corners of the arena; their armor heaved as they panted, and the duelists slumped slightly, catching their breaths; their seconds squirted water in their mouths and rebuckled or replaced loose and smashed armor. The ostriches stamped and growled, ready for another go. The seconds scattered, the ostriches took off again, and the fight began anew.

"Watch Fumo," said Audrey. "She looks like a dirty fighter. Ooh—ouch!"

Fumo had whooshed past Zam-Zam but gave her lance a wicked backward thrust, smacking the back of Zam-Zam's head. He went off into a loopy twirl. The crowd broke into a roar.

"Like I said," sighed Audrey. "Dirty tricks."

"The crowd likes her," said Jo.

"The crowd likes her because she fights nasty. That's what they came to watch. But for a true aficionado of the sport . . ." Audrey sniffed. "It's bad form, you know?"

Fumo circled back and suddenly dropped right on top of Zam-Zam's head, crushing him with her ostrich. The crowd went wild as Zam-Zam struggled to recover.

"Ugh, now she's *toying* with him," said Audrey. "Very, *very* bad form. Let him go out with some dignity."

Fumo whipped around and headed full speed at Zam-Zam. At the last second, Fumo jerked her ostrich upward, making it crash into Zam-Zam—and Zam-Zam's lance went flying.

"Disarmed!" said Audrey. "Not bad, I have to admit."

Jo frowned. "She's really mistreating her ostrich."

"Huh? What do you mean?"

"I don't pretend to be an expert, I've only been flying Ethelred for a few weeks—but look at her!" Jo winced. "There! She's using her ostrich as a *weapon*! She dropped her ostrich on the other guy's head, and now she's ramming her ostrich into him—it's horrible for the bird."

"Never thought of it that way."

"I wouldn't have, either, if I didn't have Ethelred," said Jo. "But this Fumo should know better. It's like she doesn't even care if she hurts her ostrich."

Regardless of Jo's opinion, the crowd loved Fumo's style. Zam-Zam started to panic and make mistakes; Fumo was ferocious and didn't give an inch. She kept coming and coming, overwhelming Zam-Zam, driving him from one side of the arena to the other. Finally Fumo swooped down from above, plucking Zam-Zam right off his ostrich.

The crowd howled with delight. Zam-Zam flailed as his ostrich chased behind, nipping at Fumo's ostrich's tail, trying to reclaim his dangling master.

"So humiliating," said Audrey. "There's no call for that."

Fumo's ostrich's claws released Zam-Zam, who hung in the air for a second, scrabbling at emptiness——then he fell, plunging into the water far below. Zam-Zam's ostrich hid itself in a corner of the arena, gurgling with embarrassment. Fumo's ostrich hobbled as Fumo spread her arms wide, basking in the applause.

"Obnoxious," said Audrey. "No grace at all."

"I'd like to know who's Fumo," said Jo. "I'd like to take her down a notch."

"Victory!" shouted Fumo as her bloodied ostrich limped miserably under her.

Jo couldn't watch any more; it made her too angry. "How's Ian doing?"

"He seems to be on top of things," said Audrey. "Let's go over there and get a better look."

Ian was back at his booth. A small crowd had formed around him, and he was quickly paying out the money for the bets, too absorbed in his task to glance at Jo and Audrey.

Audrey whispered in Jo's ear, "Look, look——Oona Looch."

Oona Looch had arrived during the duel, carried on a gaudy throne. She was a mannish, square-jawed woman, about sixty years old, mammoth but not fat, a stout giant of muscle and bone. Her bald skull was gouged with scars, her nose and ears seemed nailed on, and her smile revealed she had no teeth at all. Her voice was a low rumble and her laugh sounded like a dozen old men clearing their throats at once. Four big, bald, tough-looking women carried her throne.

Jo said, "Who are they?"

"Oona Looch's daughters," whispered Audrey. "Almost everyone in the mafia is related to the Looch family. She has fifty-two daughters, and they all look exactly like her. She's always pregnant. . . . She barely notices when she gives birth. The babies just pop out and beat up the first guy they see."

"Who's the father?" said Jo.

"Whoever Oona wants," said Audrey. "There's her current husband, Fipnit. Poor sap." Jo noticed a skinny little man trailing behind the throne, continually wringing his hands and looking about nervously.

"Nothing like a night at the fights!" thundered Oona Looch. "The smell of sweat! The smell of blood! The smell of ostrich poop! It's all good! Give us a kiss, Fipnit!" She grabbed Fipnit, whipped him around like a rag doll, and covered his face with her huge lips; then she spat him out. "God, you taste terrible! Why am I married to you?"

Fipnit could only answer with a series of soft meeps and whimpers.

"You disgust me, Fipnit!" shouted Oona Looch. "You don't do anything for me *as a woman*. You don't know how to treat *a lady*! One of these days, Fipnit, I'm gonna sit on you! And then I'll forget about you. . . . Maybe a few weeks later I'll pick you out of my behind and say, 'Well! There's Fipnit! So that's where he went!' Then I'll throw you away. What a tragic end to a beautiful romance!"

"Meep," said Fipnit.

Meanwhile, there was a disturbance at Ian's booth. A gangly man in a yellow waistcoat was gripping the table with shaking fists, pleading with Ian, "You've *got* to give my money back. It's all I've got, *please*."

"Then you shouldn't have bet it," said Ian.

"Give it back, kid. C'mon—it can be like the bet never happened."

"Beat it," said Ian.

"I'm a close personal friend of Oona Looch—she lets it slide from time to time for me—it's no big deal, you can ask her. Just help me out this once. This is my last chance!"

"Next!"

The man seemed about to walk off—then lunged for the cash box, snatching it away. Ian immediately jumped over the table, tackling the man, and they rolled on the floor, wrestling. The man pinned Ian down, but just as Oona Looch's daughters were about to jump in, the man pulled out a black tube.

"Nobody move!" shouted the man. He was crying, his hands were shaking, but the tube was aimed straight at Oona Looch. "If that's the end of my life, it's the end of yours, Oona Looch! *You ruined my life!* I have *nothing*! NOTHING!"

A screech, a flash like a thousand flashbulbs popping, and the air filled with flying dust; an earth-shaking jolt, as though the entire mountain were about to collapse; nobody could see; Jo felt as though she had been kicked in the stomach—the dust-choked air was filled with stumbling bodies bumping into each other, screams, yelps, shouts of panic: "What's going on?"—"Get him!"—"Protect the Looch!"

When the dust settled, Ian was on top of the man. He had jerked the gun away and it had gone off harmlessly, tearing a gash in the rock ceiling. The man whimpered as Ian pried his fingers from the gun. It dropped to the floor with a thunk, and four bald, burly Looch daughters immediately pounced on the man.

Oona Looch laughed as though she was having the time of her life. "Get me over there! Take me to that kid!" Her daughters carried her throne over to Ian.

"Look at this kid!" said Oona Looch. "What a kid! We got a hero right here! Who knew!"

Ian stood baffled and blinking.

"This kid saved my life!" said Oona Looch. "Whaddaya know! First night on the job! Kid, I doubt Dugan could've done any better! Eh?"

"I couldn't say," said Ian, terrified.

"Listen to that! Cool as you please! This kid doesn't waste

words." Oona Looch nodded with approval. "I like this kid! This kid's got moxie! C'mere, Barrows, ever been in a headlock? There you go! How's that feel, kid, you like that?"

His face shoved into Oona Looch's huge breasts, Ian could only make a muffled reply.

"Get outta here!" said Oona Looch affectionately, shoving Ian away. Then she yanked him back. "Naw, come back, ya big lug! I can see great things for this kid. I owe this kid a favor! You don't save Oona Looch's life and not get a favor! Whaddaya say, Barrows, what do you want? The world's your oyster, you name it!"

Ian trembled. "Don't worry about it, Mrs. Looch."

"*Mrs.* Looch!" chortled Oona Looch. "*Mrs.* Looch! What a gentleman! What manners! Some of you bozos should take a page outta this kid's book! Mrs. Looch, he says! Come on, kid, whatever you want, you say it, it's yours! One good turn deserves another, eh!"

"Please, I'm fine."

"I won't hear of it!" roared Oona Looch. "Everybody wants something! C'mon, kid, you name it, don't leave me hanging here—I can do great things for a li'l scamp like you!"

Ian said, "Maybe later."

"*Maybe later!* Maybe later, he says! Why do I like this kid so much? This kid, he cracks me up! This kid, I wouldn't mind keeping him around! Whaddaya say, Barrows? You and me, we can be pals—I'll take you hunting on the moors, shoot us some mofflehoppers!"

Ian stammered, "I don't—I'd rather not get involved—"

"*Not get involved!* Too late, Barrows, I owe you one now, you're *involved!* Look at this guy! A noble fella like this, I could use! I can make you a big man in the family, Barrows! Hell, you can be my new husband—*Shut up,* Fipnit! I blow my nose on guys like you! What the hey, I'll do it right now!" Oona Looch picked up her husband, pressed him up to her face, and blew her nose all over him.

Fipnit wriggled in her hand like an earthworm. "Meep," he said.

"Well, Barrows?" Oona Looch grinned and flung Fipnit aside. "This is a once-in-a-lifetime proposition! You say the word, this chump gets the boot, and you and I are on our way to married bliss!" She fingered Ian's chin fondly.

"I'm very honored, Mrs. Looch," said Ian carefully. "But—"

"I know, I know, you're not ready for marriage, well, heck, I can understand that! When you're older, Ian, when you're older, I'll make you the happiest man alive. Till then, come on, what can I do you for?"

"Can I . . . have a while to figure it out?"

"Sure! Yeah! Why am I so pushy? You take your time, kiddo! Come by *chez* Looch when you're ready, and we can *talk* about rewards. Until then, here's something to remember me by."

Oona Looch seized Ian and kissed him. It looked like she was eating him; when she was done, Ian staggered back, gasping, as though she had sucked all the air from his lungs.

"Back to business," said Oona Looch. "Pleasure before business, I always say. Business can wait, but I gotta kiss my beautiful boys. Now, who tried to kill me? Ah, yes . . . Snicky!"

Oona Looch's daughters hauled the man in the yellow waistcoat—"Snicky," apparently—up to the throne. Oona Looch palmed his head like a basketball and picked him up.

"You've disappointed me, Snicky," said Oona Looch.

"I didn't mean it," cried Snicky, his legs kicking and dangling. "I'm just out of money, Oona, it's all I had, I need to—you see, Oona, don't you remember the good times, Oona?"

"Ah, Snicky, Snicky." Oona Looch sighed. "You let me down, Snicky. But what's worse, you let yourself down. What happened to you, Snicky? I remember when you were young, God you were handsome, you were going to set the world on fire, weren't you, Snicky? I looked up to you, Snicky, I was just a little girl then! Why did it have to come to this? . . . Oh well."

Snicky's skull popped like a grape.

"Yep, life's funny," said Oona Looch, wiping Snicky's brains off her hand. "Now take me home, girls, I think I've had enough excitement for tonight. And I think I can trust the rest of you to behave yourselves?"

Jo looked around the room. The gangsters mumbled, "Yes, Oona Looch. Sorry," like shy schoolchildren.

"Good then. God bless ya, I know you're all good kids, deep down. Well, I've gotta go home and do my needlepoint, maybe get some loving from Fipnit. Come along, Fipnit!" Oona Looch's daughters picked up her throne and carried her out; Fipnit scampered alongside like a dog. But just before she left the Dome of Doom, Oona Looch turned to Ian and said, "Remember, Barrows! I owe you one!" It almost sounded like a threat.

As soon as Oona Looch was gone, Jo and Audrey flew to Ian's side. He was still wiping Oona Looch's slobber off his face, looking winded.

"Are you all right?" said Jo.

"Yes. No. I think so," said Ian. "I never thought . . ."

"What?"

"I thought my first kiss would be different from that."

"She's taken a shine to you, Ian," said Audrey. "I'd be careful."

Jo said, "Unless you want Oona Looch to be your girlfriend."

"She's *not my girlfriend*!" protested Ian.

The all-night party at the Dome of Doom was just beginning, but Jo, Ian, and Audrey were ready to go home. Jo noticed, though, that they were treated with more respect now that Oona Looch had favored Ian.

But when they went to the elevator, a hostile voice came out of the darkness.

"I heard you disapproved of my fighting style."

Jo turned and saw Fumo, the Sleeping Bee, still in full costume, flanked by her seconds. Jo couldn't see Fumo's face, but she was no longer speaking through the buzzing voice box. The voice was familiar.

"Yes I did, *Fiona,*" said Jo. "If I was your ostrich, I'd turn around and bite your head off."

Fiona Fuorlini's face poked out of her Fumo costume. "What do you know about dueling, Odd-Fish?"

"At least I know how to take care of my ostrich. You didn't deserve to win."

Fiona said, "If you dueled me, I'd smear you all over the arena."

"What are you saying?" said Jo hotly.

"What do you *think* I'm saying?" said Fiona.

"What, you don't have the guts to come out and say it?" said Jo, hopping around on one foot as she wrenched off her shoe.

"Jo, don't!" exclaimed Audrey.

It was too late. Jo hurled her shoe at Fiona. The shoe struck Fiona in the face.

"Consider yourself challenged!" said Jo.

Everyone in the area stopped talking. All eyes turned to the little space where Jo and Fiona stood across from each other.

Jo glanced over to Audrey. "Isn't that how it's done?"

"I was kidding about the shoe," said Audrey.

TWENTY

KEN Kiang was quite pleased with himself.

He had been in Eldritch City for only two months, but his project—to outwit the Belgian Prankster, to disrupt his plans, to overthrow his infernal machinations—was unexpectedly succeeding.

It had not always been so. At first his situation had been desperate. Ken Kiang had followed the Belgian Prankster's lengthy, seemingly senseless instructions on how to find Eldritch City, and after weeks of exhaustion and frustration, he finally arrived—but he had nothing. No money. No friends. Nowhere to live.

All he had was the Belgian Prankster's packet, and a strategy. Ken Kiang's first goal was to find a job, to support himself while he schemed against the Belgian Prankster. He answered an ad in the *Eldritch Snitch* and got a position as a clerk at the Municipal Squires Authority, working for Commissioner Olvershaw.

It was a tedious job. It took a small army of clerks to manage the paperwork for receiving quest submissions, approving quests, and assigning quests to squires. Ken Kiang settled into the drudgery of his new career, filing documents nobody would look for, making copies nobody wanted, and writing reports nobody would read.

He was disgusted by the other clerks, who shamelessly groveled to Commissioner Olvershaw at every opportunity. The sound of Olvershaw's wheelchair creaking down the hall made all the clerks work ever more furiously, panicked that Olvershaw would catch them in a moment of idleness. But after Olvershaw passed, the clerks nearly swooned with joy, and then quarreled over who was Olvershaw's favorite, for they idolized the commissioner as much as they feared him.

Ken Kiang scorned the clerks' craven ways and made it a point to slack off, even yawn ostentatiously, whenever Olvershaw rolled by his office. He had hoped his devil-may-care attitude might broaden the other clerks' worldview, but the clerks just shook their heads at Ken Kiang, wringing their hands and murmuring, "Olvershaw . . . but Olvershaw . . . oh, oh, Olvershaw!"

Ken Kiang's meager salary obliged him to live in one of the subsidized boardinghouses set aside for city clerks, a dingy dormitory in the unfashionable neighborhood of Bimblebridge run by Eleanor Olvershaw, the commissioner's spinster sister. The dormitory was already full of boarders, but Ms. Olvershaw let Ken Kiang sleep in the kitchen, behind a partition, in the corner where a garbage can used to sit.

And yet the tiny space suited him. "Some might say I've 'come down' in the world," he reflected. "But actually I've simplified my life. I've stripped away all distractions. Now I can really concentrate on defeating the Belgian Prankster. I'm on top of the world!" Ken Kiang huddled in his moth-eaten blanket and quietly giggled.

"No giggling after ten o'clock," snapped Ms. Olvershaw.

All the lodgers at Ms. Olvershaw's boardinghouse also worked at the Municipal Squires Authority. Ken Kiang loathed them all. The worst time was Friday nights, when the other clerks came shouting boisterously into the kitchen, dressed in their "good" suits, the smell of pomade and cheap cologne wafting offensively from them. They pounded on Ken Kiang's partition, trying to get him to join them for a "big night on the town."

"Come on, Ken! We know you're in there!" The flimsy partition rattled under their knocking. "We're going to paint the town red. What do you say?"

No! Ken Kiang's mind was on loftier matters! Every night he opened the Belgian Prankster's packet and laid the hundreds of papers out on his mattress. The papers specified his role in the Belgian Prankster's grand plan to destroy Eldritch City. He was directed to perform countless small acts of sabotage, all around the city: a bolt loosened, a wire cut, a key stolen, a file destroyed. Each action was nothing in itself, but taken together, they would make the seemingly solid metropolis into a house of cards, which one push in the right spot would send into collapse.

Ken Kiang admired the Belgian Prankster's elegant plan. It was genius, and it would work. But he had no wish to destroy Eldritch City—and he had every desire to defy the Belgian Prankster.

So Ken Kiang subverted the plan at every opportunity. He tightened the bolts, replaced the wires, duplicated the keys, backed up the files. But the Belgian Prankster was not so easily beaten. Later Ken Kiang would find his own countermoves themselves inexplicably countered. Ken Kiang knew he was but one cog in an unthinkably complex scheme; perhaps the Belgian Prankster's agents were monitoring him; perhaps the plan was so perfectly conceived that the sheer force of circumstance frustrated his attempts to disrupt it. Ken Kiang countered the countermove of his countermove, and the battle was joined.

Eldritch City became for Ken Kiang a vast, complex chessboard, the stage for an exhilaratingly complex game between him and the Belgian Prankster. He analyzed the Belgian Prankster's master plan, and for each of its objectives he devised a strategy to thwart it. But soon Ken Kiang found he was both cat and mouse in a bewildering showdown with the Belgian Prankster, in which strategies of ever greater sophistication were deployed, canceled, reversed, appropriated, adapted, and foiled; pawns sacrificed, attacks repulsed, fortresses stormed and captured, treaties signed and betrayed, retreats faked and traps sprung, territory gained, lost, besieged, divided, despoiled, and exchanged—it was a shadow world, of infinite levels of deceit and disguise, of decoys that were Trojan horses full of more decoys that were red herrings in non-mysteries that had neither a solution nor a problem, concerning people that didn't exist in a place that was nowhere in a situation that was impossible! It was a five-dimensional smorgasbord of invisible meals, and he was both chef and guest at a dinner party for which the guest list was both infinite and zero! Ken Kiang's mind reeled. The battleground was the ordinary streets and buildings of Eldritch City, and yet the battle itself was undetectable to the untrained eye, for the smallest detail—a broken lightbulb, a misplaced book, an intercepted letter—made all the difference in a war no less savage for its almost excruciating subtlety.

Many of Ken Kiang's plans were executed at night, so he usually slept at work. And sometimes, as he dozed at his desk, he wondered how Hoagland Shanks was getting on. Just before he left for Eldritch City, Ken Kiang had given Shanks a credit card with an unlimited account—a credit card valid only for buying pies or traveling to the pie capitals of the world.

Ken Kiang hadn't told Hoagland Shanks that the credit card would be automatically canceled in five months. But by then it would be too late for Hoagland Shanks! Yes, he would already be addicted, already well down the road to pie damnation . . . Ken Kiang nodded at his desk, his mind becoming fuzzier, fantasizing about Hoagland Shanks's desperate plight.

By now, Hoagland Shanks would have become jaded in his tastes. Apple, cherry, blueberry—Shanks would scorn such pies now. Now Shanks would prefer only the most sophisticated pies: toad pie, pickled squid pie, pies made of the sweet dung of a rare African bat—pies filled with certain Arabian beetles that keep their sumptuous tang only when eaten *alive*!

But those days are no more, Hoagland Shanks! Ken Kiang imagined Hoagland Shanks after the credit card was canceled. . . . Yes! Hoagland Shanks penniless on the streets of Ankara; spiritually broken in Tokyo; floundering in a ditch near Berlin; selling his blood in London; tearfully trying to make a pie out of things he found in the gutter in New York . . . Did the man who once ate twenty avant-garde pies a day now scavenge in an alley, trying to make a "pie" out of cigarette butts and government cheese? Yes! Ken Kiang chuckled in his dream as Hoagland Shanks shook his fist at the sky, sobbing, "Why? How? Oh, woe! How did I become such a man? Ken Kiang! You master of evil, you have destroyed my soul! Ken Kiang! Ken Kiang . . . !"

Ken Kiang woke up. A cringing clerk stood at his office door, sweating and fiddling with his hat. "Ken Kiang? Commissioner Olvershaw wants to see you. He . . . I don't know, Ken! He seems . . . Oh! . . . Trouble . . . Olvershaw . . . ahhh . . . you better get to his office on the double, Kenny!"

Ken Kiang glanced leisurely at the clock. "I might get around to it," he yawned.

An hour later, Ken Kiang slouched into Olvershaw's office, quite as if he had wandered in by accident. Ignoring Olvershaw, he slumped into a chair and started picking his teeth.

He barely listened as Commissioner Olvershaw sternly lectured him. Ken Kiang's shoddy work, his sleeping on the job, his coming in late—and sometimes not at all!—he knew all the accusations in advance. He sighed loudly, infuriating Olvershaw even more, causing the old man to vibrate with rage. Ken Kiang saw the clerks cowering in the hall, wringing their hands and sucking their breaths nervously. When Olvershaw finally fired him, Ken Kiang barely noticed, for he was staring out the window with a distant smile on his lips.

He had the most wonderful idea.

It was this. Ken Kiang felt he was winning the war against the Belgian Prankster. Ken Kiang believed that the Belgian Prankster had several times actually attempted to return to Eldritch City—only to be blocked by his brilliant strategies. He knew the advantage was his; but how to press it? He felt he was on the verge of striking the blow that would finally crush the Belgian Prankster's grand plan, perhaps even destroy the Belgian Prankster himself.

But—the eternal problem—how to do it with style? For Ken Kiang, it was never enough to win. It was the verve, the showmanship, above all the *arrogant stunt* that mattered—the crucial cherry on top that said, "Not only have I won, but I won with enough leisure to toss in this final, outrageous flourish."

But *what*?

A musical!

The inspiration had come to him while Olvershaw was firing him. It occurred to Ken Kiang that nobody in Eldritch City properly appreciated him. Here he was, Ken Kiang, saving the city from the Belgian Prankster on practically a daily basis, and nobody knew! So why not write, direct, and star in a *musical* about his adventures in Eldritch City, and his audacious victory over the Belgian Prankster? He imagined a grand spectacle, a cast of hundreds, glittering costumes, gorgeous scenery . . . was this too ambitious? No, Ken Kiang scorned the thought! He had once thought it was too ambitious to take on the Belgian Prankster—and now the Belgian Prankster was wriggling in the palm of his hand! He calculated he need only toy with the Belgian Prankster a few weeks more, while he wrote and rehearsed his musical.

Then he could both premiere his musical and crush the Belgian Prankster in one fell swoop—and thus the demands of both duty and style would be satisfied!

Upon returning to the boardinghouse, Ken Kiang learned that he was evicted.

"These rooms are for city clerks only, Kiang," said Ms. Olvershaw. "I expect you out by supper."

Dazed but strangely unruffled, Ken Kiang gathered his belongings. Clutching them to his chest, he stumbled down the hallway of the boardinghouse as the other clerks peered fearfully out of their rooms. Ken Kiang heard them sigh with relief as he passed. He couldn't hold on to all his stuff at once; crusty socks and scribbled-on paper fell from his bundle; he didn't bother to pick them up.

The clerks gathered on the front porch as Ken Kiang trudged into the street. Ms. Olvershaw's face glared from an upstairs window, but the clerks seemed genuinely sad to see him go. He heard their farewells: "Hey, Kenny! Hope it works out for yuh!" "Keep pluggin' away!" "Just remember the good times we had at the old boardinghouse!"

Ken Kiang turned around, incredulous. Were they mocking him? Were they sincere? He honestly couldn't tell. Rainy season was starting; droplets of water splattered around him, faster and faster. But it didn't matter what happened to him, he didn't care, *he knew* he had the Belgian Prankster on the ropes; and once he finished his musical, *everyone* would know his true worth!

"Endgame, Belgian Prankster!" roared Ken Kiang triumphantly. "You played well, but the advantage is mine! Endgame! Check *and* mate, old fellow. *Endgame!*"

Ken Kiang jumped up and down on the street corner, squawking and waving his arms. People discreetly crossed the street to avoid him.

TWENTY-ONE

RAINY season struck hard. It was as if a flying ocean had hit the city. Thunder banged and growled at all hours, fog wrapped the mountain in an unbreakable cloud, and water crept in everywhere, flooding basements, soaking through clothes and shoes, making the streets into muddy rivers. The rain droned endlessly, thudding on the roof, spattering on the windows, trickling down from the leaky ceilings.

The damp grayness of the season drained Jo. She wanted to do nothing but stay inside the lodge, drink hot chocolate, and lie on the couch in front of a fire—but she had to prepare for her duel. Jo trained with Dame Delia every day, although she didn't tell her why. It was wet, grueling work, but as much as Jo wanted to stay in the cozy lodge, she couldn't bear the thought of Fiona

Fuorlini beating her. Still, Fiona was undefeated in seven duels. Jo hadn't fought once.

One night Dame Delia said, "I did some asking around, Jo. I know you have a duel coming."

Jo tensed up. "Sorry, Dame Delia. I should've told you."

"Ah, don't worry about that," said Dame Delia, taking out her pipe. "I fought illegal duels when I was a squire, too. Lily knew. She wouldn't mind if you got your hands a little dirty." As she lit her pipe, she added, "Actually, Lily would be pleased. Between you and me, she was waiting for you to do something like this. She was worried you didn't have enough fight in you."

Jo shivered and pulled her jacket closer. "I think I had a bit too much fight."

Dame Delia paused over her pipe. "What do you mean?"

"We had an argument right before she left. Aunt Lily and me. We never made up. And now I don't know if she's even coming back, or . . ."

"Ah, she'll be home soon. If anyone can stop the Belgian Prankster, it's Lily. Did it before, didn't she?" Dame Delia puffed on her pipe. "Then we won't have to worry about the Belgian Prankster, the Silent Sisters, or the Ichthala again. That'll be a relief, eh?"

Jo couldn't even look Dame Delia in the eye. "Yeah. That'll be a relief."

The archives of the Order of Odd-Fish had just recently reopened to the public. Here the Odd-Fish kept the Appendix, the very reason for the Order's existence—not an actual book, but a disorderly library that took up the entire fifth floor of the lodge, where one could find articles written by generations of knights on the dubious, the improbable, and the bizarre. Sir Festus's blueprints of ludicrous weaponry, Dame Myra's sketchbooks of strange plants, Dame Isabel's periodic table of smells, Sir Oliver's infamous dissertation on dithering . . . it was all here, the accumulated research of the Order's thousand-year history.

Like the other squires, Jo worked at the library one day a week. This meant not only learning the complicated filing system and keeping the unwieldy collection in some kind of order but also answering questions from the public. Jo had the Monday shift with Daphne, but Daphne was sick and so today Jo had to work alone. She found it hard to concentrate—Fiona was coming over tonight to fulfill the dueling tradition that required each side to sleep at the other's lodge before the duel. Jo wasn't looking forward to it.

As usual, there was nobody in the reading room but Mr. Enderby, a portly little man who, for some reason, had made it his life's goal to read the entire Appendix in alphabetical order. Mr. Enderby had just arrived, drenched from the rain, and was taking off his coat.

In a way Jo was glad she was working alone. It meant she could do what she'd been itching to do ever since the archives had reopened: read her parents' files. Jo glanced out into the reading room, where Mr. Enderby was just getting settled in his chair, pouring himself a mug of coffee and sharpening his pencils. Pale, watery morning light filtered through the windows, and rain hammered down on the roof so loudly that Jo had to raise her voice when she said, "Everything okay there, Mr. Enderby?"

"Oh, yes, yes. Just reviewing my notes. I may need your assistance in a few minutes, though, young lady."

"Just ring the bell," said Jo. Then she turned and entered the archives.

The archives! Jo stepped into the silent library with cautious curiosity. File cabinets spilling over with papers, folders, and note cards; teetering stacks of composition books; envelopes stuffed with crumpled documents; great rolled-up maps; boxes and shelves packed with countless notebooks, pamphlets, and reports—Jo was overwhelmed. The corridors of the archives twisted and turned unpredictably, and Jo wondered how anyone could find anything in this hopeless mess, which was catalogued by a wildly arbitrary system even the knights didn't seem to fully understand. The aisles were flooded knee deep with piles of loose paper, such that you had to wade through, or even climb over, great heaps of documents to get anywhere. All the articles of the Appendix were stored here, as well as notes, reference works, rough drafts, bibliographies, and commentaries; everything, from the most authoritative encyclopedia to the most random idea scribbled on a scrap of toilet paper.

After a half hour of searching, Jo found what she was looking for: two cardboard boxes labeled SIR MARTIN HAZELWOOD and DAME EVELYN HAZELWOOD. Aunt Lily had told Jo that her father's specialty was imaginary languages and that her mother had studied obscure cults. Jo guessed that her mother had probably researched the Silent Sisters, so she opened her box first.

For the next hour Jo browsed her mother's articles. Dame Evelyn had written about dozens of cults, from the Azoobs (who believed not only that God was dead, but that He had a notarized will in which He thoughtfully bequeathed everything to the Azoobs) to the Yipniblians (for whom every day was a holy day of rest, and who thus considered it a sin to get out of bed). But oddly enough, Jo couldn't find a word about the Silent Sisters.

Jo opened her father's box next. Here she found mostly dictionaries, all written by Sir Martin, for the various imaginary languages he'd invented. One of his languages was based on tasting patterns of spices, so that books were read by eating them, page by page; there was another language entirely of sneezes; he also invented a language for plants (though his attempts to teach it to a petunia met with only "mixed success").

The bell rang in front. Jo went back out to the counter, where Mr. Enderby was waiting.

"Can I help you?" she said.

"Oh yes, I believe you can; I believe you most certainly can," said Mr. Enderby. He looked at Jo closely. "You're new here, aren't you?"

"Yes. Dame Lily's squire. Jo Larouche."

"So you are, so you are. Well, you might not know this, but I have set myself the task of reading the entire Appendix. I'm on a schedule," he said proudly. "The lodge getting stolen threw me off a bit, but now I'm right back on track. Let's see . . . this week is . . . Sir Humphrey Mundlebottom. The complete works of Sir Humphrey Mundlebottom, if you please, young lady. Oh, and could you make some more coffee?"

"Right away, Mr. Enderby!" Jo trotted back to the archives and searched through the card catalogue for Sir Humphrey Mundlebottom. As usual, the card catalogue contradicted itself, listing Sir Humphrey's files in nine different locations. After an hour, she finally found Sir Humphrey's file, in a dusty corner that looked as though it hadn't been disturbed in decades. Sir Humphrey was a relatively minor figure in Odd-Fish history. He had lived over seven hundred years ago and specialized in the philosophy of napkins.

Sir Humphrey's files were kept in an old wooden chest wedged high up in a bookcase. Jo had to climb up a ladder to reach it. She found it difficult to dislodge the chest, even as she pulled and tugged at it, harder and harder—suddenly it tumbled off the shelf, almost taking Jo with it, and fell fifteen feet, thumping down in the swamp of papers.

A manuscript stuffed next to the chest also fluttered to the floor. Jo climbed down the ladder, picked it up—and her eyes went wide.

It was by her father.

Misfiled? Hidden? Forgotten? Jo couldn't guess—then she heard Mr. Enderby faintly baying, "Miss Larouche! Have you found Sir Humphrey's files yet?"

"Just a minute, Mr. Enderby!" Jo stuffed the manuscript in her pocket and hauled Sir Humphrey's chest down to the reading room.

"Hard to find?" said Mr. Enderby.

"Yes," said Jo, sweating a little. "Is that all you'll be needing?"

"And the coffee?"

"Oh right—the coffee—" Jo was burning to read the

manuscript, and now she had to make some ridiculous coffee . . . she threw the ground beans in the filter, stuffed it in the machine, and turned it on. "Okay, everything all right now?"

"Ooh, Miss Larouche, this chest is pretty heavy . . . do you think you could . . ."

"Yes, Mr. Enderby!" Jo helped the pudgy scholar drag the chest over to his desk. "Everything okay now?"

"Oh yes, I think this will do nicely."

Jo hurried back to her desk and started in on the manuscript. Nothing she had read yet by her parents had told her anything about her situation. Maybe, by sheer luck—or was it fate?—she had found something. She opened it to a picture of a dozen fish, entwined in each other in a circular chain, tiny letters in their eyes—and stopped cold at these words:

FOR MY DAUGHTER

Her heart bolted. It was crazy, impossible. Jo flipped through the manuscript. But it was only page after page of slashing, swirling rows of colors—gold, purple, green, silver, red, orange, yellow—quickly scrawled, burning and blooming like a fiery garden. She couldn't understand any of it. She quickly went back to Sir Martin's dictionaries, searching for something about a language of colors, but found nothing.

Jo kept struggling with the manuscript. She could feel a hidden logic in the patterns of color, even though she still couldn't make sense of it. Whatever the message was, Jo felt it had to be important. Maybe her father had calculated how long it would take for Mr. Enderby to work his way alphabetically up to Sir Humphrey and hidden this book there so that it would be discovered only now? But that was so unlikely. Maybe he'd written it in a code that only Jo could break. But what if she couldn't? What if . . .

An hour later Jo threw down her pencil, exasperated. It wasn't happening. She had to do something else. With glum resolution, she decided to start reading *everything* in her parents' files. True, it was a lot to read; but maybe there was some hint buried in the pages and pages of articles. Jo got down to it.

Hours passed. The reading room was silent except for the percolating coffeepot and the rain steadily drumming on the roof. Occasionally Mr. Enderby would turn a page or write in his notebooks. Nobody else visited.

Jo found it easy to lose herself in the wild religions her mother studied and the strange languages her father invented. Still, Jo had the feeling she was missing something. From time to time she would go back to the swirlingly colorful manuscript, but it was just as incomprehensible as before. And as closing time approached, Jo's attention strayed from her parents' files and she started to worry about Fiona, who was due to arrive any minute.

"Five minutes to closing, Mr. Enderby."

"My, how time flies, Miss Larouche," sighed Mr. Enderby fondly. "I never knew napkins could be so philosophical."

Jo came over to help Mr. Enderby put Sir Humphrey's files back in order. As she absentmindedly sifted through sheafs of paper, a little metal thing plopped out and bounced on the table. She looked down—Sir Humphrey's Odd-Fish ring.

Mr. Enderby cooed with pleasure. "Oh, such a charming tradition! I always thought it was touching that you Odd-Fish entombed knights' rings with their files. A fitting memorial to their life's work, you know, or—"

"I'm sorry, Mr. Enderby, I've got to go!"

Jo took off running, leaving a baffled Mr. Enderby behind. How could she have been so dense? It was obvious now—Jo tore downstairs, skidded around the corner, dashed down the hall to Aunt Lily's room, fumblingly unlocked the door, threw it open, and went for Aunt Lily's jewelry box. She yanked out every drawer until she found it—Jo's own original silver ring, with its jewel-eyed fish twisting all around, each eye a different colored gem.

Mr. Enderby was already gone when she got back. Jo darted back into the archives, turned to the first page of her father's manuscript—the illustration of the ring of entwined fish. Yes! Each fish had a tiny letter in each eye. Jo looked at the first color in the manuscript—red. She scrutinized her ring, looking for a fish with a red eye—and found a tiny ruby. She checked the position of the ruby eye on the illustration and found a tiny *J* in the eye. The next color was blue. Jo found the sapphire on her ring, checked it against the illustration—an *O*. Jo's pencil trembled as she wrote her translation in the margin of the manuscript:

JO THIS IS YOUR FATHER

Jo felt a triumphant panic. She started to sweat. She darted a couple of lines ahead:

CAN'T RISK TELLING LILY

Jo almost stopped, tingling all over; then she plunged back in, translating rapidly and wildly.

MOTHER UNDERCOVER IN THE SILENT SISTERS
SHE COULDN'T HAVE KNOWN THAT

"Jo!" called out Ian's voice. "Fiona's here!"

Jo snapped out of her translating. Not Fiona, not now—hosting her would take up the entire evening. She skipped ahead, furiously decoding:

TWO YEARS OF RESEARCH
SHE WAS ACTING STRANGELY

Ian and Nora were running up the stairs, shouting her name. Jo gasped, her heart hammering. She knew if she was caught rummaging through the Hazelwoods' files, translating secret messages, it would be impossible to explain—but she couldn't stop.

"Jo!" Ian barged into the reading room, breathless. "Jo, Fiona's waiting at the doorstep!"

Nora came right behind. "You have to go down and let her in!"

"You let her in," said Jo. "I'll be down in a minute—"

"No, no," said Nora. "We have to do it according to dueling tradition, or the dishonor—"

"Okay, okay, I'll be down!" said Jo. "Just let me clean up."

"We'll help," said Ian quickly. "What files need to be put away?"

"No!" said Jo with a sudden fierceness that surprised Ian and Nora. "I mean, only I know where this stuff goes. Don't worry, I'll come with you. Just wait a minute."

Jo closed the cardboard boxes and hauled them back where she found them, hiding them under some loose papers. But she couldn't help herself—and while Ian and Nora waited in the reading room, she translated something from the middle of the book:

WILL SEEM INVINCIBLE BUT IF YOU CUT OFF HIS STINGER
AND TURN IT ON HIM

"Jo!" called out Ian, outside the archives. "What's taking you so long?"

Jo furiously flipped the pages, decoding one last bit:

FOLLOW THE GOLD THREAD

Ian and Nora burst into the archives. "Jo! What are you *doing* back here?"

Jo jumped. "Just putting this away! Out in a second! Hold

on!" She stuffed the manuscript and ring in her bag, stood up, and smiled. Nora looked confused, but Ian looked positively angry.

"Okay, let's go!" she said.

Fiona Fuorlini and her seconds were waiting at the doorstep. Jo met them at the door with Ian and Nora. Dueling convention required Jo and Fiona to exchange traditional insults at the door.

Fiona said, "I enter this house, even as I spit on it. For this is the house of my enemy, and when I leave, may a thousand wild pigs overrun it and defile it with enthusiastic snorts."

Jo had learned the recommended response. "No defilement by any number of wild pigs equals the defilement you bring upon my house by your mere presence. Enter my house, but when you leave, may you be overrun by a thousand wild pigs and trampled into gruel, to be gobbled by those thousand wild pigs with hearty slurps."

Fiona said, "So be it."

"So be it," said Jo.

Fiona entered the lodge. Her seconds bowed and withdrew into the night. Ian and Nora closed the doors and stepped away. Fiona acted as though Jo wasn't there, and looked around the lodge coolly. It was clear she wasn't impressed.

"So what are we going to do?" she said.

"Dinner is in five minutes," said Jo.

Dinner at the lodge was loud and rowdy, as usual. The seats of Sir Oliver, Colonel Korsakov, and Aunt Lily were empty, but the remaining knights and squires made up for their absence, all talking at once. Jo stewed impatiently. She wanted nothing more than to go to bed early, lock the door, and get back to translating her father's manuscript.

Her mother, "undercover in the Silent Sisters"? "Cut off the stinger"? And "follow the gold thread"? Jo burned to excuse herself, to get back to the manuscript—but Fiona was wide awake, and surprisingly polite and sociable with the knights. And a few hard glances from Ian and Nora made it clear to Jo that she had to entertain Fiona all evening, if only to cover up that Fiona was there as part of an illicit dueling ritual.

As the butlers cleared away the plates Jo asked, "What would you like to do now?"

Surprisingly, Fiona had a ready answer: "I want to see the tapestry."

"Capital idea, Miss Fuorlini!" said Sir Festus. "I think it would be grand if we all went to the tapestry room and you enlightened us on its history and meaning."

"I'd be only too glad," said Fiona.

"History and meaning?" said Daphne. "What would Fiona know about that?"

"Oh, didn't you know?" Fiona's eyes were cold, but her words were mild. "That tapestry was originally woven by the Wormbeards. One of my grandfathers many times over, the Grand Bebisoy of the Wormbeards at the time, designed it. Pity it ended up here." Fiona smiled, even as the knights shifted uneasily in their seats. "But everyone knows life's not fair, right?"

The awkward silence was broken by Cicero clearing his throat. "Dessert will be served in the tapestry room in ten minutes," he said.

Jo hadn't visited the tapestry room since the night she and Ian had found the secret door there. Some of the creepiness of that evening still lingered, and even now Jo felt weird sitting on the couch, watching the tapestry roll by. She clutched her bag, impatient to get back to reading her father's message. But first she had to get through this evening. All the other knights and squires were there, listening to Fiona explain the stories on the tapestry.

"The tapestry is supposed to tell the history of the world from many different perspectives," said Fiona. "The Wormbeard artists crammed all the available legends of Eldritch City into it. Most of these legends contradict each other, but the artists thought it best to put them all in, instead of settling on just one. That's why the tapestry is so many miles long."

Nora raised her hand. "But doesn't the tapestry have the birth of the Ichthala on it? That happened only thirteen years ago."

"That's what makes the tapestry special," said Fiona. "It's woven out of a rare moss that grows to make pictures of whatever you say to it. The original artists spent years telling the moss the legends of Eldritch City in great detail, and let the moss grow to describe those scenes."

Dame Myra piped up. "And I read the newspaper to the tapestry every morning, to keep its pictures up to date."

"Thank you, Dame Myra," said Fiona, bowing. "I'm relieved to find our tapestry is under responsible stewardship. So the tapestry has dozens of interwoven stories of how the world began, and how it might end, and all the things that happen in between. Let's see . . . what we're looking at right now is the beginning of the universe."

"Looks weird." Maurice pointed up at the tapestry. "What's that supposed to be? Over there."

"That?" Fiona gazed up. "That's the origin story of the All-Devouring Mother."

As always when the All-Devouring Mother was mentioned, the atmosphere in the room became awkward—as if they were talking about something best left unspoken. Jo felt her heart lock up in panic. She tightened her grip on her bag and glanced at Nora. Behind her tangled hair, Nora's huge eyes had lit up, and she had already taken out her notebook.

Finally, Sir Festus coughed. "Ah . . . not all the squires know this particular legend of the All-Devouring Mother. Could you explain it to them, Miss Fuorlini?"

Fiona nodded. "Certainly, Sir Festus. Although this is just *one* legend about the All-Devouring Mother—there are many others, and nobody knows which is true. It starts over here, to the right, before time even exists. Nothing exists but one goddess, the All-Loving Mother."

Albert broke in. "I thought it was called the All-Devouring Mother."

"I'm getting to that," said Fiona smoothly. "Now, the All-Loving Mother's substance is nothingness, but she contains all *possible* things within her—a god for every potential thing in the universe. All one hundred forty-four thousand four hundred forty-three of these gods live inside the All-Loving Mother's stomach, unborn but fully conscious. See them? There, there, and there—they're very tiny."

Jo watched Fiona point out the tiny gods inside the All-Loving Mother. Despite herself, Jo was impressed by Fiona. She patiently put up with Sir Festus's constant questioning, and it seemed she actually knew what she was talking about. Jo hoped she was as poised for her visit to the Wormbeards' lodge.

Fiona continued: "The problem was, these gods are bored living inside the All-Loving Mother. They want to escape and fully grow into themselves. But the All-Loving Mother won't let them out. So for a long time, the universe is nothing but void as the gods stew restlessly, cramped and packed inside the All-Loving Mother's stomach."

Fiona paused as the tapestry rolled past. A new scene appeared, and Fiona waved her hands around the scene, explaining it: "In this scene, the gods ask the All-Loving Mother to open her mouth and let them out. But the All-Loving Mother refuses. She loves them so much that she wants to keep them forever safe, perfectly quiet, and eternally at home in her belly.

"So the gods decide to trick her. The cleverest of all the gods, Aznath, the Silver Kitten of Deceit, tells the All-Loving Mother some of the gods have *already* escaped from her and that they want to return, and that she has to open her mouth to let them back in. But as soon as the All-Loving Mother opens her mouth—this illustration here—Aznath squeezes the All-Loving Mother's stomach and makes her vomit out all the other gods. I think this part is particularly well done. Look there, in the center."

The All-Loving Mother was spewing thousands of gods into the black nothingness of space. A silver kitten sat alongside, grinning maliciously.

Phil snickered. "So in your legend, the universe began because a god barfed?"

Fiona just stared at him. The room was silent except for the drumming of rain on the roof.

"It's not a dignified way for a universe to begin, but that's the legend," said Fiona finally. "Now, in this next scene, all the gods are fleeing from the All-Loving Mother. As you can see, she's furious at being tricked, and has changed from a loving goddess to a vengeful monster. Now she is the All-Devouring Mother, and she will not rest until she gobbles up all the gods and brings them safely home again, inside her belly."

The All-Devouring Mother was indeed a terrifying vision. All of the maternal features of the All-Loving Mother had twisted in on themselves, into a ravenous beast that flew in a thousand directions at once, straining to swallow up the other gods. Jo stared at the All-Devouring Mother. It didn't make sense—how could she have anything in common with *that*?

Fiona said, "Here's the conclusion of the legend. The other one hundred forty-four thousand four hundred forty-three gods know they can't run away from their hungry mother forever. So they all surround the All-Devouring Mother and cut her into one hundred forty-four thousand four hundred forty-three pieces— a piece for every god. Each god hides their piece of the All-Devouring Mother in a different secret place, so that the All-Devouring Mother can never be reassembled. And thus the soul of the All-Devouring Mother wanders the universe in torment, searching for the pieces of herself so she can put herself back together. But this must never happen, for if she does, she will devour the gods again, and gobble up our universe. And then everything will again be nothingness."

The artists had illustrated what it would look like if the All-Devouring Mother regained her body. It was a grisly scene of the skies being torn open like paper, of galaxies crashing into each other and melting into the All-Devouring Mother's hands, of entire worlds being sucked into the All-Devouring Mother's laughing, bloody mouth.

"If I remember correctly, the tapestry continues into another story," said Fiona. "In a minute, it'll unwind to the scene where the Silent Sisters first appear. It was thousands of years ago, so the history is cloudy. But the theology of the Silent Sisters is simple. They believe that all the conflict and pain in the universe comes from having left the All-Loving Mother's care. They want to bring back the All-Devouring Mother, let her eat up the universe, and bring everything back home inside her again. According to the Silent Sisters, the All-Devouring Mother will then again be the All-Loving Mother, with everything safely, quietly, and harmoniously contained within her once more."

Nora was perched on the edge of her seat, listening closely, pencil in hand, her breath held lest she miss a single word. "And how," she said, "how do the Silent Sisters plan to help her?"

Fiona said, "The Silent Sisters believe that if they reassemble the All-Devouring Mother's body, the All-Devouring Mother will reincarnate herself in human form. The Silent Sisters choose a woman from their own ranks to give birth to the reincarnated All-Devouring Mother and transfer the soul to the monster they rebuilt. Unfortunately for Evelyn Hazelwood, the Silent Sisters chose—Hey! *What's that?*"

Jo cringed. The hole in the tapestry had rolled into view.

Fiona watched it with mounting rage. "*Who* put a hole in the tapestry? Do you know what used to be here? It's the oldest image of the Silent Sisters! Who tore it out?"

Sir Festus coughed with some embarrassment. "I assure you, we did not. It was only after Sir Oliver got the lodge back that we found this tear."

Fiona had maintained a cool composure all night, but now she lost it. "Nobody can trust you Odd-Fish," she said. "In good faith the Wormbeards made you a gift of the most tremendous work of art we'd ever done, and this is how you Odd-Fish treat it?"

"We didn't do it!" said Ian. "The Belgian Prankster must have!"

"May I remind you that the Belgian Prankster's original name was Sir Nils Van der Woort?" said Fiona. "And Sir Nils *was* a knight of the Odd-Fish."

"But why would the Belgian Prankster tear out a picture of the Silent Sisters?" said Daphne.

"Why does the Belgian Prankster do anything?" said Dame Delia. "He's in league with the Silent Sisters and is trying to destroy the universe. He is committed to madness. Hardly anything he, or they, do could make much sense to us."

"By cracky, I can't take it anymore," said Sir Festus suddenly. "All these secrets and plots and skullduggery . . . we are knights! The Silent Sisters lurk among us in Eldritch City, the Belgian Prankster is looming abroad, and there's nothing we can do? Look at me—I'm not young anymore. I've waited all my life for a proper war. I'm getting fat, I'm getting slow—it's not befitting a knight! I'm not meant to die of old age, but in the glory of battle! Still, year after year goes by, and no fight! Why can't the Silent Sisters show themselves for an honorable combat? Why must the Belgian Prankster always skulk and strike from afar? These invisible enemies are driving me mad. Give me something I can see—give me something I can do!"

"I think you've all done quite enough," said Fiona loudly.

Everyone's attention turned to her.

"What do you mean?" said Jo.

Fiona said, "I *mean,* Jo, that most of the trouble in Eldritch City actually comes from the Order of Odd-Fish. Sir Nils used to be an Odd-Fish; now he's the Belgian Prankster, working for the Silent Sisters. He stole the Odd-Fish lodge last year, and now it's back—but who knows what infections the Belgian Prankster hid in this building that are now spreading around the city as we speak? Not to mention that the Odd-Fish built the

Inconvenience, a very dangerous device, and then blundered into letting the Belgian Prankster gain control of it. Last but not least, there's Martin and Evelyn Hazelwood, the most irresponsible of all—bringing into the world a baby that should have been strangled in the womb. I can come to only one conclusion: the Order of Odd-Fish, whether by treachery or by stupidity, is the Silent Sisters' greatest ally in Eldritch City. That's all I have to say. Now. Where do I sleep?"

All the Odd-Fish erupted in loud outrage, but no matter how loudly they blustered, accused, and protested, Fiona sat with her arms crossed and ignored them.

Jo was furious. But she was all the more furious because there was no retort she could make. Everything Fiona had said was perfectly true.

The Odd-Fish dispersed to bed. The butlers helped the knights and squires of the Odd-Fish to their rooms, and Fiona was curtly shown to the guest quarters. Jo stalked out of the tapestry room before anyone, not bothering to say good night to Fiona, or to Ian or Nora, for that matter. She went back to her room and slammed the door.

And remembered the message from her father.

In her bag.

She had left her bag in the tapestry room!

Jo threw open her door and ran downstairs in a panic. How could she have been so stupid? She sprinted down the dark passageways, popped open the trapdoor, clambered up—and went weak with relief. Her bag was sitting where she had left it.

She grabbed her bag, opened it—

Her father's manuscript was gone.

TWENTY-TWO

THE rain kept coming. Two months into the rainy season, Jo found it hard to remember life without rain. A dull weariness crept into her bones. All of Eldritch City felt colorless, drenched, and dead.

In the middle of the night, when the rain pattered gently on her windowpane, Jo could almost believe that the rainy season wasn't so bad. But then there would come a bang of thunder so loud it sounded like an exploding bomb, and Jo would sit up in a panic, certain it meant the return of the Belgian Prankster. After a breathless minute, she would calm down, and drift back to uneasy dreams as the rain pelted down like bullets.

Jo couldn't stop thinking about her missing manuscript. The only explanation was that Fiona had taken it. Of course, Fiona couldn't translate it without the ring, but Jo had scribbled her own translations in its margins. If Fiona read them, she would know everything. But *did* she have it?

Jo tried to shove it into the back of her mind, but that didn't work; that part was already full of the Belgian Prankster. Anxiety simmered as background noise to everything now, like the rain endlessly drumming on the roof. But the constant worry about the Belgian Prankster didn't dull its edge. Every time she thought of him directly, a fresh stab of dread twisted her guts.

And a dark corner of her was waiting for him. The grayer the season became, the more washed-out the world seemed, the more Jo caught herself almost wishing for him to come. Sometimes it seemed as if everything around her was silently saying his name.

She needed distractions. She took on extra work in the lodge, studied up on all the knights' specialties, and trained harder than ever with Dame Delia. There were also more dueling traditions to keep. Just as Fiona had slept over at the Odd-Fish lodge, Jo was required to sleep over at the Wormbeards' lodge. But if Fiona really *did* have her father's manuscript . . . but no, it was too nerve-wracking to think about. The closer the day came, the more Jo dreaded it. Especially when she learned that it fell the night before Desolation Day.

Jo had never known when her birthday was. Now she knew: Desolation Day was the most hated day on the Eldritch City calendar, the anti-holiday that marked the birth of the Ichthala and the destruction of half the city. Jo knew some special festival was going to happen, but she had no idea what. Nobody talked about it. It was bad luck even to mention Desolation Day. Jo couldn't help feeling as if the whole city were keeping a secret from her.

The night before Desolation Day, Jo, Ian, and Nora huddled from the rain under an awning in East Squeamings, waiting to be picked up by the Wormbeards. Where there once had been a bustling fish market, now there was just a sodden, empty field of bricks. The stalls had been dismantled and put away, and the fish market was closed until the rainy season was over.

Ian said, "It wasn't so long ago we were running around here, looking for the Schwenk. Remember?"

"And we first met the Wormbeards," said Jo.

"And I saved you both," added Nora. "You two don't know how close you came to being torn apart by those lizard-dogs. . . . Jo, I *still* can't believe you're going to duel Fiona! Awful things happen at the Dome of Doom. Are you still sure you want to do it?"

"I've seen Jo practice," said Ian. "She's really good. She'll beat Fiona, don't worry."

Jo looked out onto the gray city and remembered the first time she'd met Fiona. It seemed like so long ago. Back then, the city had seemed fresh, with a surprise waiting around every corner. Now Jo walked the streets and felt a quiet satisfaction in *not* being surprised. She liked knowing her way around, nodding at the stores and apartments, seeing everything right where it should be.

"Where *are* they?" said Jo. "They were supposed to pick us up twenty minutes ago."

Ian said, "It's a calculated insult. They'll be just late enough to irritate us, but not late enough to break etiquette."

"There they are," said Nora.

Fiona's seconds emerged from the fog in purple cloaks, steel goggles, and long yellow scarves, hidden under yellow umbrellas. "Let's go," they said.

The Wormbeard squires led Jo, Ian, and Nora out of the rain and down into the subterranean neighborhood. Snoodsbottom was just as Jo remembered it: the glowing fungi on the cave ceilings, the stale, spicy air, the cramped tunnels, the unwholesome heat. As before, the walls were covered in minutely detailed carvings, so unsettlingly convoluted that they seemed like not art but an intricate geological disease chewing away at the insides of the mountain.

Finally, the Wormbeard seconds stopped. "We're here."

"We are?" said Jo. All she saw was a pit.

"Look down."

Jo approached the pit's edge and peered in. The lodge of the Wormbeards was not a building; it was almost the opposite of a building. It was a pit two hundred yards deep and fifty feet square, dotted with windows on every side, and filled by a great glistening tree. The tree's bark had the hard sheen of steel and copper, and its branches gleamed with thousands of purple and yellow bulbs—organic gems, or a kind of glassy fruit. The tree filled up the pit with glittering branches, supporting a staircase descending to the bottom. Lizard-dogs slept within its metallic leaves, their tails tightly wrapped around the branches.

The seconds led Jo, Ian, and Nora down the staircase. Through the branches, Jo could see lighted windows all around the pit, and Wormbeards going about their business.

Fiona Fuorlini was waiting at the bottom, reading a book by the light of the glowing tree. She stood up, her seconds crossed over to her, and at last the six squires faced each other.

Jo was ready with the traditional insult: "So! I have found you, simmering in this cauldron of dishonor—"

Fiona interrupted. "Please, Jo. Can we dispense with the etiquette for tonight?"

Jo was startled into silence. Fiona smiled and looked at her kindly. "I know, I know," said Fiona. "According to the rules, we have to insult each other, and everything has to be tense, but do either of us really want that? I'll take the dishonor for disregarding the proper dueling formalities. I'd rather just have you here as a regular guest. How about it?"

Jo looked at Nora and Ian. Nora seemed at a loss; Ian reluctantly shrugged.

Jo turned back to Fiona. "Um . . . thank you. That sounds refreshing."

"I'm glad you think so," said Fiona. Jo tried to detect trickery in Fiona's tone, but there was none; Jo was mystified. Before she could change her mind, Nora and Ian bowed and withdrew, followed by Fiona's seconds.

Now Jo and Fiona were alone. Jo watched Fiona closely, searching for a sign—*had* she stolen the manuscript? But Fiona only smiled again at Jo, turned, and entered the gate of the Wormbeards' lodge. Jo took a deep breath and followed.

They came into a dim cavern of rough rock and moss. Unseen waterfalls trickled from the ceiling, and little pathways twisted away into a jumble of stunted trees and chunky boulders. The gnarled, dwarfish trees grew in well-tended little groves, disappearing into the darkness. All around, dozens of bubbling little pools gurgled and steamed.

A porch was poised over the underground garden, like a pale, ghostly ship sailing just above the boulders and trees. Jo and Fiona climbed the stairs to the porch. It was bright and spacious, constructed of smooth timber and white, paper-like walls, giving a view of the dark garden. White globes glowed with mellow light from the high ceiling, and the straw-mat floor yielded pleasantly under Jo's feet. A table had a vase of cut flowers, artfully arranged.

Jo had never felt ashamed of the messiness of the Odd-Fish lodge before, but in the elegant lodge of the Wormbeards, she felt awkward. She understood now why Fiona had regarded the Odd-Fish lodge with distaste. Compared with this, the Odd-Fish lodge was a slum.

Jo said, "So . . . I like your lodge."

"Thanks."

"I have a question," said Jo. "The mission of the Odd-Fish is to research our Appendix. What's the Wormbeards' mission?"

"We're artists," said Fiona. "We have all sorts here—painters, composers, musicians, architects, whatever. I'm a sculptor. In fact, I'm working on something for the Desolation Day festival tomorrow. You can come to my studio after dinner, if you want."

Jo and Fiona had a private dinner in a little room overlooking the courtyard, where a few branches from the shimmering tree poked in through the window. The food was bland, and there wasn't much of it, but Fiona apologized: "Everyone here is fasting before Desolation Day. I suppose they're doing the same at your lodge."

It was true, Jo thought; everyone *was* fasting at the Order of Odd-Fish. But why? Jo didn't know what to expect from tomorrow's Desolation Day ceremonies. She knew that almost everyone in the city was expected to attend. But whenever Jo asked anyone about the festival, she only received vague replies.

"So . . . how long have you been in the Wormbeards?" said Jo.

"All my life," said Fiona. "My parents are both knights. They're on expedition right now, but the lodge takes care of me. Fuorlinis have always been knights, going back hundreds of years."

Why was she being so nice? Fiona made pleasant dinner conversation with Jo, without a trace of the nasty tone she had taken at the Odd-Fish lodge. Jo almost thought that it might be possible to have Fiona as a friend. After dinner, Fiona invited Jo up to her studio, and by that time Jo was entirely at ease.

Fiona's studio was a large concrete bunker smelling of plaster and clay and paint. The studio housed tons of bulky equipment, including kilns, throwing wheels, and bins of found objects. Fiona's bedroom adjoined the studio, and there was a large furnace in which some pots bubbled over with goo. Reinforced glass doors insulated the studio from the heat and flames.

As soon as Jo entered, her attention was struck by a giant sculpture in the center of the room. She felt her throat shrink. She hoped it wasn't what she thought it was.

"It's for the Desolation Day parade tomorrow," said Fiona. "Guess what it is."

"It's . . . the Ichthala," said Jo.

Fiona smiled. "What do you think?"

It was horrifying. The sculpture was a monstrous idol, twenty feet tall, a lumpy, bulging, grotesque tower ridged with fins and scales, a mishmash of teeth, claws, horns, tentacles, arms, bones, and legs, blazing with viciously clashing colors, and all somehow wrong: swollen to disturbing size, shrunken to meaninglessness, discolored, grafted on or torn off. But Fiona was a skilled artist: Jo could see the difference between the lean muscle, the protruding bone, the rough hide, and the blisters and boils that erupted all over. Tangled hair, hardened with dried blood, bristled from between cracks in its reptilian armor and dangled down its scabby back. Its mouth seemed ready to snap up and devour her. The idol looked *alive,* a shambling, snarling, unclean beast, built out of all the rejected parts of the world.

"The city commissioned me to make the Ichthala this year," said Fiona. "Why don't you have a seat? We can talk while I finish this up."

Jo sat down. Fiona climbed a stepladder next to the idol and started painting on the opposite side. For a while they didn't speak.

"The All-Devouring Mother fascinates me," said Fiona.

Jo had noticed. All around the studio, there were paintings, sketches, and sculptures of the All-Devouring Mother. Photographs from *Teenage Ichthala* were scattered on a workbench.

"So you watch *Teenage Ichthala?*" said Jo.

"A lot of my work follows the show and the traditional myths about what the Ichthala looks like," said Fiona. "But this is more of my own vision. You're friends with Audrey Durdle, aren't you? She does a pretty good job, considering."

"Considering?" said Jo.

"Well, the show *is* a fantasy, isn't it?" Fiona smiled. "Although the Ichthala is real. I don't necessarily agree with how they make the Ichthala look, or how Audrey Durdle plays her. I mean, the All-Devouring Mother could look like anything, couldn't she? She could even look like me. Or you."

Fiona's hand was gripping a knife. Jo stiffened—but then she saw Fiona was just using it to carve the face of the idol. She slowly relaxed.

"Maybe the Ichthala doesn't even know that she *is* the Ichthala," said Fiona, almost as though she was talking to herself. "Maybe the Ichthala is just a normal girl and doesn't know what she is or the terrible things she's done. Or . . . maybe she does know?"

"That could be," said Jo carefully.

Fiona gazed at her sculpture. "When I was a kid, I used to fantasize that *I* was the Ichthala. I guess every girl does at one time or another. Who knows? Maybe I am. It would be something to have that kind of power, wouldn't it?"

"It sounds tempting," said Jo.

"I can tell we're both interested in the Ichthala," said Fiona.

"It's an interesting topic," said Jo. She had tried to sound non-committal, but she feared she had sounded dismissive. For a while Fiona didn't reply, and Jo wondered if she had offended her. But then Jo realized that Fiona was simply absorbed in her work. For about fifteen minutes Fiona worked, and Jo sat quietly, wondering if Fiona had forgotten she was in the room.

"There." Fiona leaned back and nodded. Then she came down the ladder. "I'm finished. It's my best so far. . . . Want to see what I've done?"

Jo came around and looked.

She couldn't help it—she gasped. Fiona smiled with silent triumph.

It had Jo's eyes.

"I think it's a good addition, don't you?" said Fiona. She came over to Jo and looked at the sculpture with her. "Kind of brings it all together, doesn't it? Makes it make sense?"

The eyes were definitely her own. And the head—Fiona had resculpted the monster's face in such a way that it now bore a resemblance to Jo's own. It was hideous to see, like a mirror of herself in hell.

Fiona grabbed Jo's arm. Jo struggled to get away, but Fiona forced her into the corner, pushing herself against her. Jo tried to scream, but Fiona roughly covered her mouth, murmuring:

"Don't worry. I won't tell anyone until after I've killed you. At the Dome of Doom. I'm going to kill you, Ichthala."

"I'm not—"

Fiona bit Jo's earlobe, hard.

"Oww! What's wrong with you?" Jo touched her fingers to her ears. They came away bloody.

Fiona smiled, blood on her teeth. "Now I know it's true."

"I don't know what you're talking about," shouted Jo, backing away.

"I saw the way you looked at those eyes!" said Fiona. "*I know it's you!* And I'm the one who's going to destroy you!"

"Fiona, stop, I—"

"No! Shut up! Stop lying!" Fiona opened a drawer and took out Jo's manuscript; Jo gave an involuntary shriek. "I know *everything!*"

"That's mine!" shouted Jo, running at Fiona. "You stole it! *That's mine!*"

Fiona opened the furnace doors, and before Jo could stop her, she tossed the manuscript into the furnace. It burned up instantaneously, and the room filled with a powerful exhalation of heat.

Jo stopped in her tracks.

"Now get out of here," said Fiona.

Jo couldn't move. Fiona shouted and lunged, and only then did Jo snap out of her shock, scrambling toward the door. Fiona was still walking toward her, her eyes filled with hatred. Jo ran out of the studio, stumbling down the hallway. She heard nothing but the blasting moan of the furnace. She backed away blindly down the dark hallway, pain stabbing through her ear, not knowing where she was going.

A butler showed her to her room.

Jo couldn't sleep. At any moment she expected Fiona to slip into her room and do something terrible to her. Her head was spinning, too many frantic thoughts bubbling and boiling to even come close to sleep, but she needed sleep badly, and morning was fast approaching. She finally fell into a thin and dream-wracked doze; it felt as if she had only been asleep for a minute when someone banged on her door.

"Everyone up. It's Desolation Day."

Jo couldn't tell what time it was. There was no day or night outside her window, just the underground courtyard and its glittering tree. It could have been morning or afternoon—she didn't know. She was exhausted and disoriented, and everything seemed painfully vivid and yet unreal.

A cockroach butler entered the room and laid out some clothes for her to wear.

"What time is it?" said Jo.

"Four in the morning."

"Go away. I need to sleep."

"No sleeping in today," said the butler sternly. "Get up and put these on."

Jo looked at the unfamiliar clothes the butler had laid out. "Get me my own clothes. I don't want these."

"You have to wear these."

"I want my own clothes. That's an order, butler!"

The cockroach withdrew without another word. Jo was astonished. A butler had never disobeyed her before. She had nothing else to wear, so she reluctantly put the clothes on: a long gray dress with a gray veil. She was so bleary and muddled that only after a minute did she realize it was the costume of a Silent Sister.

Butlers swept through all the rooms, forcing everyone out of the lodge and into the courtyard. There were about two dozen people under the metallic tree, all dressed as Silent Sisters. Jo couldn't tell who was who. Nobody spoke. A lit candle was handed to her. Soon everyone had candles. A line formed and began to climb the staircase through the tree.

Where was Fiona? Jo ached to see a familiar face, or any face. But there were nothing but blank veils everywhere. She stumbled to the back of the procession. Wax dripped from her candle onto her dress. She could hardly see what was happening through her gauzy veil.

The procession trudged through the tunnels of Snoodsbottom. Everywhere Jo looked, everyone was dressed as a Silent Sister and holding a candle. There was no sound but the shuffling echo of footsteps and the rustle of skirts.

The procession exited the gate of Snoodsbottom into a gray, drizzly morning. Jo looked up and down the streets in astonished fright—*everyone* in Eldritch City was dressed as a Silent Sister. Dozens of lines of Silent Sisters shuffled around the mountain, all headed to the same place. Jo nearly dropped her candle when she realized that everyone was going to Hazelwood's Row.

Jo didn't know why they were going there, she didn't want to know—she wanted more than anything to turn back, but she couldn't fight the crowd, and she too was swept up and pushed into the abandoned neighborhood. She staggered in a daze through the forbidden streets, blasted of all buildings—nothing but grave after grave in a field of colorless ash.

Up until now everyone had been silent. But now Jo heard crying everywhere. The processions broke up, and the ghostly mourners drifted from grave to grave, setting down their candles, falling to their knees, and softly weeping. It felt like the entire city was in tears.

Then Jo saw the pit where her parents' house used to be. Nobody else had come near it. She walked to it, queasily and unsteadily, and looked down.

Far at the bottom, she could see the smashed remains of a house.

She stared at it numbly. She didn't know what she was feeling—a mix of confusion and horror and guilt and underneath it all, wrapping her up and clutching her from every side, panic that any second she would be found out, and then . . .

Jo now heard a different kind of wailing—not a human sobbing, but a tuneless hooting of wind, the noise of unearthly flutes. Figures were slowly moving through the crowd, blowing long, twisty pipes. It sounded like the crying of thousands of women swept up high into a windy sky, every moment louder and more inhuman, rising and falling in atonal scales.

Something new had appeared.

It was Fiona's sculpture. The twenty-foot idol looked even more savage and garish in the gray dawn than it had in Fiona's studio. Its harsh colors had nothing to do with the morning light; it was so bright and terrifying that it seemed to put the universe out of joint, like something pasted into reality from elsewhere.

The crowd rushed toward the Ichthala, their shouts fighting the screaming of the flutes. Jo was caught up in a crush of sweaty veiled bodies, all pressing toward the idol. She couldn't control where she was going, the flutes wailed so cacophonously she almost couldn't hear the mob, and she was pushed ever closer to the idol, even though she wanted nothing more than to get away from it. The idol swayed and lurched, threatening at any moment to topple onto the crowd, but Jo couldn't stop being pushed toward it, and she couldn't look away from its staring eyes. But the eyes were not vicious or cruel. They looked helpless.

The shrieking flutes became unbearable. Jo's brain throbbed. The mob was in a frenzy. Something horrible was about to happen. And no matter how loud anyone yelled, there was no noise but that from the intolerable pipes.

The mob attacked the idol. The thing swayed dangerously, dipping and tilting left and right, as hands tore at it, veiled figures climbed up it, and rocks flew at it from all directions, punching holes in its skin. A creamy blood was trickling out. The crowd parted as the idol swung toward them and the shrieking flutes blasted ever higher. Jo was pushed closer—

The idol fell.

Jo cried out as the eyes rushed at her and it crashed, exploding with milk.

She shrank back in shock. The idol was filled with some kind of milky liquid, now gurgling out of its cracks and holes. Her face was spattered with the bitter white juice. Everyone was tearing the idol apart, kicking and bashing it, sucking the milk on their hands and knees, veils ripped off. Jo had seen countless festivals in Eldritch City, but never anything like this.

Through the crowd she glimpsed Sir Festus raising a shard of the Ichthala to his mouth, sipping the last bit of milk. Dame Myra was licking it off her fingers. Daphne and Maurice were slurping puddles of milk on the street. Everywhere she looked, everyone was doing it—the Odd-Fish, the Wormbeards, people she knew from the street, strangers.

Someone tapped her shoulder.

It was Ian. He was smiling, his lips smeared with milk. He had a bowl in his hands.

"Have some!" he said.

Jo felt sick. She took the bowl from Ian.

"Go on, drink up!" said Ian, smiling with strange forcefulness.

She drank. But as soon as Ian was gone, she spat the milk out on the sidewalk and sat on the ground. She was too weak to do anything else. She had never felt more alone.

TWENTY-THREE

THE rain stopped as suddenly as if someone had switched it off. Almost immediately vegetation sprang out of hiding, wriggling through cracks and breaking out of the soil, spreading like fire throughout the city. The city became alarmingly lush, covered in wet green leaves, exploding with ferns and lurid tropical flowers, smothered in ivy, creepers, and weeds. The days were sunny but humid, and the smell of damp soil was everywhere. The rainy season was over.

Eldritch City celebrated its Founders' Festival a week after Desolation Day. There were rides, games, concerts, freaks, and parades, and the mountain was tangled up in the looping tracks of a roller coaster roaring through all the neighborhoods. Everyone dragged out of storage their traditional floats for the

Founders' Festival parade. The knights, squires, and butlers of the Odd-Fish rode on the creaky, centuries-old Odd-Fish float, waving to the crowds. The only knights missing were Sir Oliver, Colonel Korsakov, and Aunt Lily; they still hadn't returned.

Jo was miserable. The gruesome rituals of Desolation Day, the threat of the Belgian Prankster, her upcoming duel with Fiona—all of it seethed inside like a wildly boiling soup. She stood on the float, smiling and waving emptily. The awakening city, with its sunny days and flourishing plants and jubilant festival, was so contrary to her mood that Jo felt it was mocking her. Even the warm sun on her skin and the fresh air in her lungs felt wrong to her. She felt numb. Her anxiety had hit such an unsustainable pitch that it had slid into a deadened calm.

The parade was a disorderly throng of elephants, dancing bears, marching bands, acrobats, clowns, tigers, dancers, balloons, and floats. The police shot off dazzling, colorful muskets, the mayor rode a wild rhinoceros, and eelmen hauled about obscene-looking giant vegetables, shrieking and clicking in their incomprehensible language. Exotic animals were brought in from far countries, including a brontosaurus that only days ago had been contentedly munching leaves in a distant swamp; the huge beast now lumbered amiably down the street, not noticing the chaos it caused every time it flicked its tail, sending people sprawling and tents crashing to the ground.

Everyone dressed up for the parade, but the cockroaches had pulled out all the stops. Sefino sported white velvet trousers lined with gold braid, furry pink boots, a puffy blouse, and a sombrero covered in hundreds of blinking electronic lights.

"You're probably going to compliment my ensemble," said Sefino to Jo. "And I understand that at times like this, words may fail you."

Jo said, "What do the lights on your sombrero run on?"

"Secrets, I must have my secrets," smiled Sefino, waggling his finger. "Originally there was also a model train that continuously circled around the brim, but I decided that was a bit much."

"Restraint," said Jo.

"*Exactly*," said Sefino. "Artful restraint is my hallmark. Though I don't rule out including the train in the future. Chug chug chug," he said thoughtfully. "Chug chug chug. Hmmm."

"Look, there's Chatterbox!" said Jo.

Sefino swiveled his head around. The centipede journalist was strolling down the boulevard.

"Listen, Jo," whispered Sefino urgently. "The other butlers and I have something planned. After tonight, Chatterbox will never be able to ignore us again."

"What do you mean?"

"Only this. We have planned a spectacle for tonight so scandalous, so shocking, so *brazen* that Chatterbox will be forced to write about it. Look for me on the front page tomorrow, Jo. I say no more."

"I hope it's nothing obscene."

"Er . . . I say no more." Sefino held his breath; then, unable to stop himself, shouted: "Do you hear me, Chatterbox? I say no more!"

Chatterbox turned. "Oh! Good afternoon, Sefino."

"I say no more!" said Sefino. "Pry as you might, Chatterbox, use all your subtle skills to wangle the secret from me—none shall avail you! I say no more!"

Chatterbox looked pityingly at Sefino. "I told you, from now on I will only print about you that which is strictly newsworthy." He bowed to Jo. "Your zealous advocate, Miss Larouche, has seen to that."

"*Newsworthy!*" hooted Sefino. "You'll find tonight will be more than *newsworthy*, Chatterbox. Sharpen your pencil, oil your typewriter, perform whatever foul rituals you newspapermen must do before your 'big scoop,' as you would have it—tonight's escapade will be truly historic."

"My dear Sefino, I only write you fellows up if you make royal asses of yourselves. Lately you have behaved merely like silly asses."

"Well, Chatterbox, I promise you," said Sefino with rising passion, "tonight we shall make such *spectacular* asses of ourselves that—"

"Oh look," said Chatterbox. "Something shiny on the ground."

"That we shall—"

"Excuse me, I am absorbed in watching this shiny piece of paper. It is fascinating. Do you know, I think it will continue to fascinate me until you go away? Yes . . . for just about that long."

Chatterbox watched the shiny bit of paper intently. A breeze disturbed it, and Chatterbox clapped his hands in delight. "What a perfectly charming piece of shiny paper!" he exclaimed. He looked up. "You're still here?"

"I say no more, Chatterbox," growled Sefino. "Just remember—*I say no more!*"

"If only," sighed Chatterbox.

The parade ended, and the squires scrambled off the float, eager to get to the festival. Sir Alasdair called after them, "Remember, everyone meet behind the main stage at nine o'clock! I need you all for my urk-ack concert!"

Jo felt the festival's pull. Ever since Desolation Day, Fiona's threat to expose her at the duel, to kill her, had choked Jo with a paralyzing dread. Sometimes she could barely think of anything else. She needed something to distract her. And if what Fiona said was true—if the duel was the end of life as she knew it—Jo wanted at least to enjoy her last days of Eldritch City.

Jo ran over to Ian, Dugan, and Nora, then met up with Audrey. Together they plunged into the madness, passing so many surprising sights that Jo's head was constantly turning. There were the normal rides—Ferris wheels, tilt-a-whirls, and carousels—but there were also terrifying contraptions that shook and spun and flipped screaming people so carelessly and violently that it seemed certain someone would die. Jo wanted to go on all of them. Freaks slunk in the darkness between the tents and rides—a man whose body was covered with eyes leered at them, and a woman's long, slithering beard pinched Dugan's bottom. They watched twelve-foot-tall puppets reenacting stories from Eldritch City mythology, and took boat rides through slimy tunnels, where hideous creatures leaped out at them and they shrieked with laughter and fright. There were cages where they fought trained pterodactyls with wooden swords, and they took a submarine ride under the bay and saw brilliant fish and sunken ships and ruins from thousands of years ago. Surrounded by her friends, entranced by the festival, Jo almost forgot her anxieties.

But a strange thing happened at every ride or show or booth they visited. As soon as the ticket taker saw Jo's group, he immediately waved them in, even if there was a long line. And if they tried to pay, the attendant would always say, "Compliments of the house, Miss Larouche," or "Your money's no good here, Mr. Barrows," or "Go right on in, Miss McGunn."

Finally, Ian planted his feet and refused to move. "What's going on here?"

"What do you mean?" said the attendant nervously.

"Why do we get to skip every line? Why do we never have to pay?"

"Ah . . ." The attendant cleared his throat. "We can't all have friends in high places, can we?"

"What friends?" said Ian.

The attendant's face paled. "Ha, ha . . . the gentleman likes his joke."

"I'm not joking! Who is it?"

"Well . . . ah . . . you see . . . er . . . *Oona Looch*," whispered the attendant fiercely, and pushed a stunned Ian past the line and into the tent. Inside, the attendant snapped, "It's not enough we have to answer to her beck and call—you have to make it difficult? Why don't you pipe down, kid?"

Ian looked shocked. "Oona Looch is doing all this for me?"

"Well, hoo-whee. The little sweetheart can put two and two together."

"But I don't want special treatment!"

"Listen, kid, I'm just doing my job. If Oona Looch's people saw you had to wait in line at my ride—well, I'd have some unpleasant explaining to do. So cool it, loverboy, and enjoy the favor."

Ian stopped complaining. But he wasn't happy about it. Nor was he happy as Nora and Audrey speculated on how Ian might one day repay Oona Looch's favors.

The sun sank behind the trees and the sky darkened, but the festival went on. Soon every neighborhood blazed with colorful lights, and the mountain twinkled like a Christmas ornament floating in a black sea.

It was almost time for Sir Alasdair's urk-ack concert. Most of the Odd-Fish had gathered backstage, and Sir Alasdair was giving them final instructions. A sweaty man by nature, Sir Alasdair was particularly damp tonight in anticipation of his performance. He was also, to Jo's alarm, wearing nothing but a golden swimsuit, "to make it easier for me to insert myself in the urk-ack," he explained, his gut spilling over his swimsuit shamelessly.

"Keep the urk-ack calm," said Sir Alasdair. "Stroke him, reassure him. It'd be a pity if he panicked in the middle of the second movement and ran amok in the audience. Frankly, I'm afraid he might feel uncomfortable in front of so many people."

Jo said, "You know, it might also make him feel uncomfortable to have a naked man inside him, pinching his internal organs."

"Now you're just being silly," said Sir Alasdair.

In moments the curtain would open. Dame Isabel was onstage, introducing Sir Alasdair. The squires massaged the urk-ack, which grunted and shifted its huge bulk restlessly. Jo felt herself getting all twisty and tense, even though all she had to do was keep the urk-ack calm.

She hoped Sir Alasdair's concert was a success. Sir Alasdair wasn't Jo's favorite knight, but she was impressed by how hard he had practiced for this show. Far from the ridiculous farts and burps he'd forced out of the urk-ack at first, Sir Alasdair could now coax tones from the worm that, if not beautiful, were at least interesting.

Sir Alasdair nervously peeked through the curtain. "Lots of people," he whispered. "Looks like the whole city is out there."

Sir Festus took him by the shoulders. "Alasdair, you'll do splendidly."

"Thank you," said Sir Alasdair.

The audience was applauding as Dame Isabel came backstage and said, "Okay, Alasdair! This is it!" She kissed him, the curtains rose, and then Sir Alasdair stood before all of Eldritch City, bowing as the audience clapped and hooted.

Sir Alasdair gave a final bow, and then he pointed to the urk-ack. The urk-ack gurgled and obediently opened its mouth. Sir Alasdair put one foot into the monster's jaws, swung the other around, and then wriggled down its throat. The audience murmured curiously. Sir Alasdair yanked the urk-ack's tonsils, and the worm's mouth closed. For a moment nothing happened; the audience held its breath.

Then the music started.

Jo was startled at how good it was. She'd thought she had heard what Sir Alasdair was working on, but now she realized she'd only heard him play one part of his song at a time. Tonight Sir Alasdair was playing every part at once, weaving them together intricately, a dozen melodies flirting and tangling and combining and diverging again, so precisely and marvelously that it was difficult to believe the music was grunts and snorts forced out of a giant worm.

It was a clear night, warm and slightly breezy, and Jo could smell the salty tinge of the ocean, the greasy aromas of carnival food, the oily reek of the rides, and the chemical tang of the lubricant Sir Alasdair had smeared on himself. She was exhausted after a long day of running around the carnival, trying out all the rides, watching the shows, and gorging herself on weird foods. Sir Alasdair's music was beautiful and distant, but also strangely sad. Jo closed her eyes and let it wash over her. She didn't want it to end.

Someone screamed above. Jo looked up, startled. Something was falling from the rafters—a dirty ball of arms and legs and tattered scraps. It fell on the stage with a thump and immediately sprang up, limping about, waving its arms and shouting, "Stop the show! Stop the show!"

Spooked, the urk-ack reared up, knocked down the squires, and vomited out Sir Alasdair, who bounced across the stage like a blob of pink putty. The urk-ack gave a mighty squeal and broke free of the squires, bolting off the stage in panic. The Odd-Fish, shouting and running, tried to bring the urk-ack back under control, but it had gone berserk.

Jo was left alone on the stage with the ragged man. He was wild-eyed, with long gray-black hair and a scraggly beard. His once-white suit was dirty and yellowed, and he was waving around a chipped teapot, yelling, "Stop everything! I'm taking over this show! Nobody move! This teapot is a bomb! Why, *I'm* a bomb—of musical talent! This is my moment of triumph! Tonight you shall all experience MY MUSICAL!"

The man clutched ragged pages of sheet music to his chest. He threw some of it at Jo. "Sing your heart out, kid! This is your big chance to be a star!"

The police were already coming up the aisles. The ragged man saw them out of the corner of his eye, whirled, and brandished his teapot at them, waggling it threateningly.

"Not a step closer!" he shouted hoarsely. "Within this ordinary-looking teapot is enough explosive to blow this city sky-high! And," he added roguishly, pointing to himself, "inside this ordinary-looking *man* is enough top-notch musical entertainment to blow this audience sky-high—with toe-tapping delight!"

Jo suddenly recognized the man. *"Ken Kiang?"*

"Oh, yes, hello, Jo. I'm sure we'll have a lot to chat about at the cast party afterward. But now, if you would kindly not interrupt the show . . . thank you."

The rainy season had not been kind to Ken Kiang. Months of wandering the flooded streets, sleeping under bridges, and eating wet garbage from restaurant garbage bins had shriveled him into a bony shadow. But as bad as it got, Ken Kiang knew everything was going his way. He was certain his genius was holding the Belgian Prankster at bay, even as he feverishly wrote his musical on damp napkins and the backs of candy wrappers.

Ken Kiang kicked off his musical with reckless zeal. He had once envisioned a grand spectacle, but over time he had lowered his expectations. "And who needs another bloated, overproduced revue?" Ken Kiang had said to himself. "I'll just do an intimate yet edgy one-man show." Still, the more elaborate production wistfully ran through his mind as he strutted back and forth, sang off-key, and danced so frantically it seemed he was being publicly electrocuted:

> *Greetings, Eldritch City!*
> *Ken Kiang here, with a ditty*
> *That wasn't written by a committee!*
> *So sit back and enjoy, it's quite pretty! And witty.*
> *Not to listen would be a pity!*
> *I once drank the blood of a freshly strangled kitty.*

God, I'm good! thought Ken Kiang. Had there ever been a song quite so wonderful? Ken Kiang doubted it.

At first Jo was too stunned to think. Then she was furious. Who did Ken Kiang think he was, ruining Sir Alasdair's concert? She could hardly believe she had once been afraid of him. She wished someone would stop him and his horrible rhymes. Maybe, she realized, it should be her.

The audience was booing. Ken Kiang felt a wild happiness: works of genius are never understood in their own time. Rocks and food flew at him, but he flung himself into his musical with new energy, capering back and forth, bawling:

> My name is Ken Kiang!
> Listen to my harangue!
> The Belgian Prankster, I've defanged!
> He attacked me—it boomeranged!
> I ate him like meringue
> Like a dang orangutang, I sprang! Bang!

Jo couldn't take Ken Kiang's musical for another second— and she was just about to charge across the stage, and force him to stop, when a trembling glove touched her shoulder.

It was Sefino. The cockroach was on the verge of panic.

"Psst, Jo," hissed Sefino. "You must help me with my hat."

"What? No!" Jo shook Sefino off. "Don't you see what's happening?"

"I certainly do," whimpered Sefino. "He's ruining my plans."

"Ruining *your* plans?"

"Jo, remember when I said the butlers had something special planned for tonight? We were going to do it after Sir Alasdair's performance, as a kind of encore, but now . . ." Sefino gestured limply at the caterwauling Ken Kiang.

"Sefino . . . I hesitate to ask this, but what were you going to do?"

"We were all," murmured Sefino, looking around carefully, "going to wear silly hats."

"You're always wearing silly hats!"

"No. These are *extremely* silly hats." Sefino pointed to a string dangling from his sombrero. "When I pull this, my sombrero shall open, a whirling propeller shall emerge, and I shall ascend to the skies! The other butlers have similar flying sombreros." Sefino produced a bulging sack of photographs. "What's more, as we soar over the crowd in our heli-sombreros, we shall shower upon our adoring fans these autographed pictures of ourselves."

"Might that not incite a riot of enthusiastic admirers?"

"Jo, that is the risk we are willing to take."

Meanwhile, the crowd was annoying Ken Kiang. A little audience participation was nice, but the boos, jeers, and flying food were making it hard for him to perform. He also noticed the police were approaching him from either side. Ken Kiang suspected his next few moments onstage would be his last. He stopped the musical and started lecturing the audience.

"Don't you realize who I am?" shouted Ken Kiang. "I'm the savior of Eldritch City! I've defeated the Belgian Prankster! Yes, me! Not once, but many times! Single-handedly, I might add! Without breaking a sweat! You pusillanimous, ignorant, ungrateful, stupid, swinish, crass, blind, vulgar, miserable *turds,* don't you see that if it weren't for me, Eldritch City would've been destroyed long ago? Whaaaaaaaat! *Hoagland Shanks?*"

It was. Shouldering a path through the angry crowd and baffled police, Hoagland Shanks made his way toward the stage, suitcase in hand, hollering: "Consarn it, officers, lemme through! I've gotta help out my old friend Kenny. Dagnabbit, put that weapon away, officer! Doncha see that's a talented fella up there, just tryina give yuh some honest entertainment? Kenny!"

Hoagland Shanks waddled onto the stage and gave Ken Kiang a big bear hug.

"Shanks, how—what—" Ken Kiang spluttered, staring up at the handyman in disbelief. For weeks he had fantasized Hoagland Shanks was a broken man, but now here he was, as healthy and affable as ever, and "willin' to lend a helpin' hand to make sure Kenny's show goes on"!

Jo was also astonished to see Hoagland Shanks. The fat handyman had been a fixture in Dust Creek all Jo's life; seeing him here was a pleasant shock, as unexpected as seeing Mrs. Beezy, or the Cavendishes, or any of the other old patrons of the Dust Creek Café. Jo ran across the stage and gasped, "Mr. Shanks! What are *you* doing here?"

"Long story!" said Hoagland Shanks, wiping sweat from his

forehead. "Time enough for that later, Jo! Perhaps over a peach pie! Wouldn't mind! But first things first. Gotta, *gotta* make sure Kenny's musical is a big hit!"

"But Mr. Shanks, he interrupted Sir Alasdair's show! Sir Alasdair worked so hard——"

"Now, heck, Jo," said Hoagland Shanks. "Let's not rush to judge. Everyone wants their moment in the sun, I guess! Can't grudge 'em that. We've all got dreams! My dream was to eat pies, and Kenny helped me achieve that dream. Now I'm gonna do *him* a good turn."

"Oh," said Ken Kiang, disappointed. "I didn't destroy your soul?"

"Heck no! And those were some delicious pies—much obliged!" Hoagland Shanks tipped a nonexistent hat.

"What's in your suitcase?" said Ken Kiang.

Hoagland Shanks's eyes twinkled. "Special effects!" he said, tousling Ken Kiang's hair. "Now, Kenny, not another word outta yuh! Sit back and enjoy the show!"

Then an extraordinary thing happened. In a whirlwind of glittering confetti, extravagantly costumed performers floated from the sky on parachutes, singing the overture from Ken Kiang's musical! No sooner did they touch down on the stage than a full orchestra hustled out of the crowd, instruments in hand, playing Ken Kiang's music—just as he had written it!

Ken Kiang looked at Hoagland Shanks in wonder. "Shanks, how——"

"Time enough for explanations after the show!" chuckled Hoagland Shanks, punching Ken Kiang's arm. "Now let's enjoy some top-flight musical comedy! Maestro!"

The conductor struck up the band. There it was! Act one, scene one—just as Ken Kiang had written it on the back of a paper bag—the scene in which Ken Kiang arrives in Eldritch City and sings about how he will destroy the Belgian Prankster! The stage filled with a dancing chorus. Ken Kiang watched, astonished. It was going splendidly—and all according to the script! Just as he had imagined it! Better, even!

Jo had been shoved aside by the singers and dancers, and bumped into Sefino again offstage.

"Where *were* you?" fumed Sefino. "Didn't I say I needed your help?"

"Sefino, did you see what's happening out there? It's insane!"

"My hat isn't working!"

"Who cares? Where did all these singers and dancers come from?"

"The propeller is jammed," whimpered Sefino.

"What do you expect me to do?" yelled Jo.

"I expect you to fix all my problems!" said Sefino. "Blast it, Jo, stop being so self-centered!"

"There's more important—"

"Glory! Assist me to glory! Look at these!" Sefino waved a handful of crumpled papers. "These are fan letters, Jo, begging me to undertake a grand and ambitious enterprise!"

"Those aren't fan letters, Sefino, those are your own auto-graphed pictures *of yourself*!"

As the musical's first song ended, Hoagland Shanks tapped Ken Kiang's shoulder. "Now, Kenny, I hope you don't mind, but I've added something to your musical. Gave myself a cameo." He grabbed his suitcase and clambered up the stairs to the stage.

"Well, uh . . . sure . . . go ahead," said Ken Kiang numbly. Ever since Hoagland Shanks had appeared, he had felt like he was in a waking dream.

As Hoagland Shanks took the stage, the orchestra changed its tune, lurching from the sparkling musical score to a raunchy wail, horns blasting lasciviously as Shanks struggled to unbutton his shirt. Grunting and grinning, Hoagland Shanks shrugged off the shirt and let it fall to the stage. Then he started to peel off his undershirt.

"Shanks isn't stripping, is he?" said Ken Kiang. "No, no. He's not stripping."

He was. The audience howled in angry protest over the unsightly striptease. But Hoagland Shanks did not care. Bumping and grinding, he hopped around the footlights, wriggling out of his trousers. The crowd shouted for him to put his clothes back on. Hoagland Shanks winked in response, waved coyly, and waggled his hips. His voluminous pants soon floated off the stage, followed by a yellowed pair of gargantuan drawers.

Hoagland Shanks faced Eldritch City and wiggled his naked body with indecent delight.

"Okay, buddy, let's go," said a policeman, taking Hoagland Shanks by the arm.

"I'm not done!" said the nude Hoagland Shanks, shaking off the policeman. "I want to take it all off, and I'm *gonna* take it all off!"

"Sorry to break it to you, fella, but you've gone about as far as you can go."

But Hoagland Shanks went further. As the band blared, Shanks produced a knife and sliced a neat cut from his forehead to his navel. He tore off his skin, revealing the insides of his body: a throbbing, squirming mass of blubber and muscle. He ripped those away, too, until there was just a skeleton. The skeleton walked over to the suitcase, opened it, and rummaged about, picking out some new guts, and carefully stapled them onto itself. Then the skeleton retrieved a wrinkly sheath from the suitcase, and wriggled into it—the skin of a huge, gray-haired man. He then went on to put on clothes, tauntingly, in a kind of bizarre reverse striptease: first dozens of long, dirty furs and pelts; then a pair of oversized green ski goggles; and finally, a ragged rawhide diaper.

And the Belgian Prankster—for it was he—chortled.

TWENTY-FOUR

THE return of the Belgian Prankster sparked a citywide panic. The festival collapsed into an uproar, a stampede, and Jo had never before run so far, so fast, so long. When she finally stumbled to a stop, breathless and exhausted, she was lost in an unfamiliar neighborhood. The streets were deserted, but not far away she could hear hundreds of people screaming.

The next few hours were a flurry of confusion. The Belgian Prankster hadn't done anything yet, but everyone prepared for the worst. Many barricaded themselves in their homes; others fled the city; still others sat numbly on the sidewalk, awaiting catastrophe. Jo did not return to the lodge but spent all night wandering the streets. Everybody had the same panicked expression. Jo just felt empty. She listened to the jittery conversations with a dreadful calm. Everyone was sure of only one thing: that something awful was about to happen.

But nothing happened.

The headlines of the *Eldritch Snitch* for the next few days told an increasingly baffling story. The first day was an across-the-mast screamer:

BELGIAN PRANKSTER RETURNS!

But if the first headline was shocked, the next day's headline was puzzled:

BELGIAN PRANKSTER WON'T MOVE

It was true. The Belgian Prankster hadn't moved from the spot where he had first appeared. He stayed put and kept on chortling. Everyone had abandoned the neighborhood around him. No one dared venture near. But for all the terror the Belgian Prankster inspired, he wasn't doing much. He just stood there and kept up his inscrutable chortle.

The headlines became more and more bewildered:

BELGIAN PRANKSTER STILL WON'T MOVE

Then:

BELGIAN PRANKSTER SHOWS NO SIGN OF MOVING SOON

Finally:

MOVE ALREADY, BELGIAN PRANKSTER!

But not even a stern chiding from the *Eldritch Snitch* could induce the Belgian Prankster to budge. Soon the braver citizens of

Eldritch City began to approach the Belgian Prankster. At first they dared only watch him from behind barricades, fifty yards away; but as the days wore on, more and more Eldritchers regained their courage and drew closer to the enigmatic man who chortled and chortled but did not move.

Terror became bafflement; bafflement yielded to impatience; finally, impatience gave way to disappointment. The Belgian Prankster had failed to deliver an apocalypse. He had not killed a single person, or even blown up a single building. He became a figure of public ridicule. Children scampered up to the Belgian Prankster, poked him, and ran away laughing. Doctors examined him and found him to be in excellent health. Still the Belgian Prankster did not move. But he kept on chortling.

People will put up with being terrified, but no one will tolerate being bored. Now the Belgian Prankster was merely holding up traffic. Eventually some policemen picked up the Belgian Prankster and hauled him off like so much lumber. The Belgian Prankster didn't seem to notice, but continued chortling as he was carried away. But where to? He couldn't be jailed, for he had broken no law—he was just being weird. So the Belgian Prankster was declared insane and committed to the Eldritch Asylum for the Feeble of Brain.

The neighborhood where the Belgian Prankster had appeared was cleaned up. Strangely enough, it turned out that all the singers, dancers, and orchestra from Ken Kiang's musical had been nothing more than ingeniously complicated papier-mâché dolls. In any case, they were swept up, piled into trucks, and hauled away to the dump.

Life went back to normal for everyone in Eldritch City, except Jo.

It was five days after the Belgian Prankster had returned.
Jo had not slept once. Every night she lay in bed with her eyes

open. She craved sleep, but she was afraid that if she fell asleep, the Belgian Prankster would appear and take her—she had no illusions about the Belgian Prankster being locked up in the asylum. Jo drank coffee after coffee, desperately trying to stay awake, dreading sleep; but she needed to sleep; but she was terrified of sleep; but she was going crazy without sleep; but she couldn't sleep . . .

She had been *right next to* the Belgian Prankster! But if he had really wanted her (and if Hoagland Shanks had really been the Belgian Prankster all along—and that was unthinkable, what on earth, *why*?) then why hadn't he taken her long ago, back in Dust Creek?

She wanted to go to him.

It was stupid. It was suicide. Aunt Lily had specifically warned her not to. But where was Aunt Lily now? She hadn't stopped the Belgian Prankster from coming to Eldritch City—so where was she? Had the Belgian Prankster killed her? And Korsakov, and Sir Oliver? Jo was frantic. Aunt Lily, Korsakov, Oliver—they might all be dead. But that was unthinkable, impossible. Again and again Jo's mind circled back to the same question: where was Aunt Lily?

The days dragged on, and the heat beat down with a vengeance, sticky and sluggish. Nothing seemed worth doing. The city glared harshly in the day, making Jo's eyes ache. At night she writhed in bed, feeling like she was wrapped in hot wet cotton.

She couldn't stop thinking about the Belgian Prankster. Her duel was coming up in three days, but she stopped practicing. What was the point? Fiona was going to kill her, or at the very least expose her. She barely spoke to her friends anymore. Everyone assumed she was withdrawn because Aunt Lily was still missing, but they were only half right.

Jo wanted to kill him. The Belgian Prankster had practically murdered her parents, and now maybe even Aunt Lily, Colonel

Korsakov, and Sir Oliver, too. Jo ached to kill the Belgian Prankster—and with her father's message, she felt she might even know how. Furious but repulsed, fascinated but terrified, she felt herself pulled toward him.

It was time for the final ritual before the duel: a tea ceremony at the Grudge Hut in Snerdsmallow, in which Jo and Fiona were required to read hundred-line poems insulting each other. It was two hours before the ceremony, and Jo was sitting at the café with the other squires. But she felt distant from everyone around her. She told herself Aunt Lily was gone, but she felt nothing. She just felt empty, hardly even human.

"Have you written your poem yet?" said Ian.

Jo didn't even know what he was talking about at first. "Um . . . no. I haven't."

"You're kidding," said Ian. "This is serious, Jo. You can't just blow it off."

"Well, I'm not kidding," said Jo irritably.

Audrey said, "Can't Jo just say something off the top of her head?"

"No, the poem has to be in the traditional style," said Ian. "Unless Jo can improvise in iambic tetrameter, she'd better start writing now."

Jo's head was pounding. "I don't even know what iambic tetrameter is. I don't care. Why do I have to go through all this?"

Ian started to object, thought better of it, and said: "Well, here's an idea. Sefino writes five or six poems denouncing his enemies a day. I'll get him to crank something out for you."

Jo looked up. "Would you really, Ian?"

"Don't mention it. I know what it's like for your knight to go . . . missing. I hope they're all right. I'll go find him." Ian squeezed her hand and was gone.

Maurice said, "So what happened to that crazy Ken Kiang guy?"

"They threw him in jail," said Albert. "Disturbing the peace, bomb threats . . . he'll be locked up for years."

"Hey, Nora," said Daphne. "It looks like the Belgian Prankster is back, but nothing's happened. How does your theory explain that?"

"Well . . . it doesn't," said Nora. "If reality truly followed the show, the Ichthala should've appeared at the same time. That didn't happen. I guess *Teenage Ichthala* doesn't predict the future after all."

"Aren't you disappointed?" said Daphne.

Nora looked at Daphne strangely. "Disappointed that the city hasn't been devoured?"

"So you were wrong!" said Daphne.

"Yes, Daphne," sighed Nora. "Is that what you wanted to hear? I was wrong."

Daphne nodded. "Well, I'm glad you can admit it, at least."

Maurice said, "So how do you feel about the duel, Jo? You ready to fight Fiona Fuorlini?"

Jo was staring blankly into her coffee.

"Jo!"

"Huh?"

"Are you ready for the duel?"

"Oh . . . yeah, I guess."

"Are you okay?" said Nora.

"I'm fine. Just tired."

"Then drink your coffee. The tea ceremony is over an hour long," said Nora. "You don't seem so hot, Jo. Your skin almost looks green. Where's Sefino?"

"I'm here, I'm here," muttered Sefino, entering with Ian. He had been in a foul mood ever since the cockroaches' debacle at the Founders' Festival.

"All the butlers," fumed Sefino, "resplendent in our most glittering finery, majestically rocketing into the sky like so many brilliant fireworks, showering the crowd with genuine signed portraits of ourselves—free of charge, if you please—and nobody even notices!"

"The Belgian Prankster had just returned. Everyone thought the world was about to end," said Daphne. "Don't you think your timing was off?"

"Timing has nothing to do with it!" raged Sefino. "Can't people notice two things at once? Can't people say, 'Ah, there's the Belgian Prankster, we're all going to die—very nice'—and then! Behold the glamorous Odd-Fish butlers streaking across the firmament, thoughtfully distributing signed portraits to fans and collectors! I ask you: did the Belgian Prankster fly? Did he distribute signed portraits of himself? No, and no! He just sat and chortled, and *he* got all the attention! It's unfair, it's unjust, it's actually immoral . . . and nothing, *nothing* about us in the *Snitch*!"

Eventually Sefino was subdued by sympathy and a few drinks. The squires left Jo and Sefino to a booth in the back, where Sefino spread out some blank paper and licked his pencil.

"So you need help with your poem?" said Sefino. "Let's see. What rhymes with *Fiona*? Almost nothing, I'm afraid. How about *Fuorlini*? Hmmm. *Genie* . . . *meanie* . . . *fettuccine* . . . not much there, either. You should get a different opponent."

"It's too late for that."

"Then again, *Larouche* is tough to rhyme, too," mused Sefino. "But she's got you on *Jo*. Let's see, *Vertigo, overthrow, gazebo, comme il faut* . . . there's a lot to work with. Have you considered changing your name to *Orange*? Nothing rhymes with *orange*. Orange Larouche?"

"I've already changed my name, remember?" murmured Jo. "From Hazelwood?"

"Do you know, Jo, I'd almost completely forgotten."

"Of course you have."

"But it doesn't matter, does it?" said Sefino. "The Belgian Prankster came back, but he didn't touch a hair on your head!

329

You were right next to him; he could have grabbed you on the spot! And now he's safely locked up in the asylum. Everything can go back to normal, and nobody need know about your nasty little secret. . . . Seriously, though, don't you think Chatterbox should have at least written *something* about me?"

Jo stared at Sefino in disbelief. The depth of his vanity had never fully struck her until now. Sefino was the only one who knew about her secret, and Colonel Korsakov was missing, along with Aunt Lily and Sir Oliver, all whom might be dead; yet he felt his progress in the society pages was of greater importance. Jo was bewildered into silence.

"Jo? . . . Jo! Enough moping, let's get this poem done."

Jo lay in her bed, painfully awake.

She had disgraced herself at the Grudge Hut. Woozy with exhaustion, she'd spilled the tea as she poured it in Fiona's cup. When Fiona read her poem denouncing Jo, Jo couldn't keep her eyes open. When she stood up to read the poem Sefino had written, the words looked garbled, a rushing filled her ears, she felt dizzyingly empty, and she collapsed.

The Grudge Hut broke into angry shouts. Fiona's seconds demanded Jo forfeit, but Fiona calmed them down; she wanted the duel to go on. Jo could hardly look at Fiona. In three days Fiona was going to kill her, or at the very least expose her. In three days her life was going to be over, disastrously.

Ian and Nora helped Jo back to the lodge and put her to bed. Her insides felt sour and scraped-out. She watched the afternoon light shining from behind the drapes. After a few hours it faded to a mellow evening glow and then dissolved into night.

She couldn't fall asleep. She could hear activity all throughout the lodge as knights and squires and butlers came and went, slamming doors and talking and laughing; she heard them become quiet and whisper as they approached her room, thinking she was asleep, and then resume normal volume when they were almost out of earshot. Jo felt as though she had been stricken by a plague, isolated so she didn't spread her infection to others. She wasn't called down for dinner, but Ian brought up her food for her.

"Jo?" he said softly.

She pretended to be asleep. Ian laid the tray next to her bed. He gently touched her face and said something soft, something she couldn't hear. Then he was gone.

Jo watched the ceiling as another sleepless night dragged on. It was so late it was nearly morning. The sun sulked beyond the dark horizon. Jo was listless but twitching with an energy that would eat her up if she didn't do something. She felt as if she were full of squirming baby mice.

Jo got out of bed. Her head tingled with needles and ice and tiny fires. She wandered the halls of the lodge restlessly. Nobody else was up and about. The lodge felt as deserted as the very first time she had entered it. Her duel was in less than three days, but she wasn't thinking about that anymore.

She was thinking about the Belgian Prankster. She couldn't take it anymore. She couldn't spend the rest of her life awake, forever terrified of him. She burned to kill him—and her father's message may have told her how to do it. *If you cut off his stinger and turn it on him* . . . was that what her father meant? Could she trick the Belgian Prankster? Could she go to him, pretend that she *wanted* the Ichthala blood? And then . . .

Jo went to the kitchen. She opened drawer after drawer until she found a knife.

She was going to do it.

Jo opened the front door and stepped outside.

The neighborhood was deserted. Jo walked the dim streets in a daze. She rode an empty subway train for a while. The doors opened and closed, opened and closed, but all the platforms were empty. She got off in Flurd-Poffle, all the way on the other side of town, and started walking again. Here, too, the streets were empty in the dark morning.

She had come to the asylum.

Jo took a deep breath. She put her hand in her pocket and touched the knife. The Belgian Prankster had something that belonged to her. Ever since his return to Eldritch City, Jo had felt an ache, as though he had stolen part of her that night. The pull only became stronger the closer she came to him, the ache sharper. Jo pushed open the big glass doors of the asylum.

The lobby was empty, a large, cold room with glass walls. Harsh light highlighted the dark blotches in the gray carpet, the little rips in the furniture, the ashen pallor of the dead plants. It was still dark outside, and the lobby was reflected in the glass window walls like a shadow world. The only sound was an electric hum.

Jo looked for a guard or a receptionist. But nobody was there. She walked up to the door that led into the asylum proper, and entered. Nobody was there to stop her.

But she wasn't surprised. Everything was unfolding with the logic of a nightmare. She was going to kill the Belgian Prankster, and the world seemed to hold its breath in dread. She could hardly believe she was actually going to him. She watched herself climb the stairways of the asylum, as if she were watching herself on TV.

Jo searched the empty white hallways for the Belgian Prankster. The silence was eerie. There were no doctors or patients. Jo wondered where everyone had gone. She had a hollow pain throughout her body. She felt like someone had stolen her heart, her stomach, everything inside her, and she was a walking empty skin.

She came to the Belgian Prankster's cell, on the top floor of the asylum, in the maximum security section. There were no guards. The door was open.

Jo stopped. What on earth was she doing? Aunt Lily had told her to stay away from the Belgian Prankster. And the Belgian Prankster obviously expected her. Why else had it been so easy to get to him? The Belgian Prankster had probably killed all the doctors and nurses so that it would be that much easier for her to come. Why was she doing this? The Belgian Prankster had made his long-dreaded return, and hadn't hurt her. Why seek him out?

But Jo couldn't help herself. Her mind was cloudy with sleeplessness. She touched the knife in her pocket. She had to be calm.

She clenched her fists and slowly relaxed.

Jo passed through the door, and into a cocktail party.

The Belgian Prankster had redecorated his cell in the style of a swank bachelor's pad. The white room was furnished with mod plastic couches and multicolored cubes, space-age art hung on the padded walls, and the centerpiece was a groovy sculpture of aluminum cylinders. Swinging lounge music crackled from the PA system.

Jo was baffled. She had braced herself for a nightmare; a cocktail party caught her off balance. If she had entered the cell to find the Belgian Prankster howling atop a bloody heap of dead doctors and patients, she would've been frightened, but it would have made some kind of sense. But this . . .

The cocktail party was so crowded that Jo couldn't even see the Belgian Prankster. She was jostled on all sides by the asylum's doctors, nurses, and patients, who mixed freely and chatted as they sipped cocktails out of laboratory glassware. The staff and inmates of the asylum all had a happy look in their eyes, and conversed exclusively in quips. There was a robotic merriness in the room that creeped Jo out, a desperate lightheartedness; she felt she had strayed onto the set of a sitcom that was about to be canceled and was only getting worse by trying harder.

Jo heard a familiar chortle. She froze—but then she gripped the knife, breathing deeply. She forced her way through the chattering crowd, pushing past the doctors and nurses, who blithely ignored her—until, finally, in the back of the room, she found him.

The Belgian Prankster lounged in a booth, surrounded by

fawning psychoanalysts. He had just told a joke, and they were all laughing uproariously.

"Too true! Too, too true!" guffawed a venerable therapist. "Belgian Prankster, you hit the nail on the head!"

"You're the toast of the town, Belgian Prankster!" cooed a spinster nurse. "Now what you need is the love of a good woman."

"No, what he needs is a stiff drink! I'll go get him one!"

"No, I will!"

"No, me!"

"Me! Me!"

"Gentlemen, gentlemen . . . ladies," murmured the Belgian Prankster. "Take it down a notch."

"Whatever you want, Belgian Prankster!"

"You're the boss—that's what *I* always say."

"You can take *me* down a notch any time you like, Belgian Prankster," said the nurse breathlessly.

"Why, you're a regular ding-a-ling ding-dang-doodle, Belgian Prankster!" chirped a young doctor. "A first-class, blue-ribbon, dippity-doopity ding-a-ling ding-dang-doodle, and you can take that to the bank! Huh, fellas?"

The Belgian Prankster grimaced at Jo in embarrassment. Then he cleared his throat (immediately causing all the psychoanalysts to go silent) and said, "Esteemed doctors—"

"He called us 'esteemed'!" whispered a doctor excitedly—

"May I introduce you to my friend Jo Hazelwood," continued the Belgian Prankster. "Jo Hazelwood, please meet the most eminent authorities on psychology in Eldritch City. I won't introduce them individually, for they are interchangeable turds."

"Score another point for the Belgian Prankster!" said a therapist giddily. "You got us that time, I'll give you that!"

"That's what I'd call a 'zinger,' " another psychoanalyst said, nodding. "The Belgian Prankster's got a lot of 'zingers,' I assure you."

"They're funny because they're true!" added another doctor.

Jo said, "What have you done to them?"

"Oh, I host these little social mixers in the mornings," sighed the Belgian Prankster. "It loosens everyone up for the rigors of the workday. Don't worry, they won't remember a thing when they wake up. But oh, the headaches they'll have!"

The Belgian Prankster took out a cigar. At once a dozen matches and lighters blazed in front of him, held by eager hands. The Belgian Prankster picked one at random and lit his cigar, puffing contemplatively.

Jo stood before the table, uncertain. She bit her cheek, reminding herself what was real. Reality was outside this place. This was just another one of the Belgian Prankster's jokes. Wherever he went, he warped everything around him into an empty jest.

"Doctors," said the Belgian Prankster quietly. "I apologize. But please excuse me and Miss Hazelwood for a few minutes. Why don't you all refresh your drinks."

"Whatever you say, Belgian Prankster!"

"We'll be here if you need us!"

"Need anything while I'm up, Belgian Prankster?"

"No, no; that will be quite unnecessary." The Belgian Prankster smiled as the psychoanalysts drifted away, bleating compliments; and then they were gone.

The party was over.

Jo and the Belgian Prankster were alone.

Jo faced the Belgian Prankster at last. As always, he was clad in his dirty fur pelts, green ski goggles, and enormous rawhide diaper. His breathing was forced and shallow, making the fatty bulk beneath his revolting patchwork of furs rise and fall irregularly. Sweating and snuffling, slowly smacking his lips, the Belgian Prankster twitched his monstrous tongue in and out of his mouth and started to fondle his purple, runny nose.

Jo was more terrified than she had ever been. How could she have been so stupid to come here? The Belgian Prankster had her in the palm of his hand now. If he could brainwash all these doctors and patients, couldn't he force her to do whatever he wanted? With all her might Jo resisted the mad urge to run away screaming—and the even madder urge to throw herself upon the Belgian Prankster and surrender. If there was some peace in letting him have his way, she was almost tempted to give in.

But Jo held her ground with the last shred of her fingernails, even as it seemed to be crumbling away from her. She was determined not to let this loathsome man get the better of her. He would not have the satisfaction of seeing her afraid.

"Please, sit down," said the Belgian Prankster.

Jo remained standing.

"You like my little amusement?" said the Belgian Prankster.

"Subtle," said Jo.

"Why the sarcasm?" said the Belgian Prankster mildly. "Just trying to make you feel at ease. But nobody ever really appreciates me. Look at me, Jo: I'm forlorn."

"The heart breaks."

The Belgian Prankster turned his head slightly, surprised. Jo gritted her teeth. She was sure he saw through her icy attitude and would come back with a nasty insult. But the Belgian Prankster only grinned.

"Where's Aunt Lily?" said Jo, her voice close to breaking. "Did you kill her?"

The Belgian Prankster yawned, showing his enormous tongue. Jo could see it pulse grotesquely. He smacked his lips, leaned back, and spread his arms wide.

"Let's talk about why you're really here," he said. "You've come to me in the dead of morning. You don't know why you came, but you came anyway, at great risk. Who knows what I'll do? You've been frightened of me for years. But here I am, as mild as a lamb. Who could've guessed? The truth is, I'm the only one who can give you what you want. You came to me because you want to know who you are."

"I know who I am."

"Do you? Please, sit down. You make me nervous. Who are you?"

I make him *nervous?* thought Jo. But she sat down. So far, she was holding her own. At first she was just faking being brave, but now, to her surprise, Jo found she actually was almost brave. She said, "I am the All-Devouring Mother. And I am here for my blood."

The Belgian Prankster grinned. "You didn't come here for that."

"Yes, I did," said Jo, her insides scraping against each other.

The Belgian Prankster shook his head. "That's not why you came."

"I know why I'm here," said Jo, more frantically than she intended.

"No, you don't," snickered the Belgian Prankster.

"I came here for my blood!" shouted Jo.

"No!" barked the Belgian Prankster. "You came here to kill me."

A wave of dread crashed through her. Of course the Belgian Prankster knew she wanted to kill him. He knew everything. And how could she possibly fight him? The Belgian Prankster had all the powers of the Silent Sisters. She had a kitchen knife.

But she said nothing and just stared at him.

"But you don't know how to kill me," said the Belgian Prankster. "What do you have? A knife? Something small, something in your pocket?"

He took out a pistol from his diaper. Jo flinched but her eyes didn't move from his goggles.

The Belgian Prankster shot a hole in his own forehead.

"You can't kill me." He smiled as smoke drifted out of the hole in his head. "But that's not the real reason you came. You really do want the blood of the Ichthala. You couldn't admit it to yourself, so you invented another reason to come. Any excuse to come see me. Anything to get your blood back. I have waited thirteen years for this, and I am ready."

Jo forced herself to say, "I've been waiting for thirteen years, too."

"Brave girl!" sneered the Belgian Prankster, rising and coming toward Jo. "You really *do* want the power of the All-Devouring Mother? What's the matter? Eldritch City too much for you? Made an enemy? Fiona Fuorlini, I believe? When I give you this blood, none of that will matter anymore. It has ripped me up inside. But it is worth it. For thirteen years I have carried it for you, for this moment."

Jo said, "You don't really want to do it, or you would've already."

The Belgian Prankster was behind Jo now. She heard his voice, tingling in her neck—"Oh, but I *do*"—and Jo gasped as he lurched toward her.

His face was right next to hers now. In the window behind the booth, morning light was spreading throughout Eldritch City. Their faces were faintly superimposed over it, side by side in the shadowy reflection. He was breathing hard, his hairy hands gripping the edge of the table. Jo felt she would crack any second.

Finally the Belgian Prankster drew back.

"So you *do* know why you came," said the Belgian Prankster. "You do want your blood. It is part of you. It is you. I have *you* in here." The Belgian Prankster tapped his nose. "And once I give it back to you, you will remember who you are."

Jo clenched her fists. It was true. The Belgian Prankster had her true self locked up somewhere in his fat, repulsive body. She could almost sense it gurgling around inside him. But she didn't want it; she was afraid of it; she was afraid of what she would become.

"I'm ready," said Jo.

The Belgian Prankster started doing something unspeakable to his nose. Jo's heart was beating like mad. She felt the knife in her pocket. She couldn't lose her nerve. She tried to stop trembling as the Belgian Prankster furiously pulled and tore and ripped at his nose, chuckling.

"And then the Silent Sisters' monster will eat you, and your soul will take it over! You will devour! You will devour and devour and devour. You will become more than human; you will be a force. You will be an unstoppable, annihilating wave. You won't remember your life. A force does not remember. Energy cannot think. You will devour and devour and devour without even knowing it, forever, devour and devour and devour and devour . . ."

Jo stopped. She didn't know what she was feeling. It wasn't fear or hatred or even disgust.

It was a horrible tingle of joy.

Jo stared at the Belgian Prankster's reflection and tried to stand.

"No," she choked.

"You came for this," said the Belgian Prankster, ripping at his nose.

"Don't," said Jo.

The Belgian Prankster tore his nose off his face. He tossed it onto the table. The nose twitched and quivered in front of her, running juices all over the glass.

"Please," said Jo. But she didn't move. She could just barely see behind her, in the reflection, something sticking out of the Belgian Prankster's face—gray-yellow, bubbling with scabs and bristling with hairs, stabbing a yard out of his face like a hideous beak. Jo couldn't move. No, that wasn't true, the truth was worse—she *didn't want to move.*

The Belgian Prankster was behind her, leaning closer. Jo shut her eyes.

He whispered, "You are about to become a god."

The thing pricked the back of her neck.

Jo yanked out the knife. The Belgian Prankster reared back, too late. She spun and slashed at his face—black blood spurted, sizzled—

The Belgian Prankster howled, staggering backward, clutching the stinger-like thing. Jo scrambled away as he careened toward her, shrieking, and crashed into the aluminum sculpture, smashing it into pieces. She'd only scratched the Belgian Prankster—and now he was charging after her in fury, roaring.

Jo had almost made it to the door when the Belgian Prankster tackled her. All at once she was crushed under his massive body, a hell of darkness, pressure, and stinking furs. Her scream strangled in her throat, she couldn't breathe, couldn't move—and then it happened.

A twitching stinger sank into the back of her neck, and it was not pain but an icy blank feeling that shot through her. Jo felt the cold, oily blood pouring through her guts, staining her veins and dirtying her heart. She was sobbing and screaming, the world was darkening, she strained to get away but she couldn't move, and then blackness fell like an avalanche.

TWENTY-FIVE

Jo didn't remember how she got back to the lodge. She woke up crumpled in her bed. She had slept for sixteen hours. The Ichthala blood boiled furiously inside her, twisting up her guts, but Jo was too exhausted to fight it. She drifted in and out of nightmares.

Every couple of hours Jo woke up and felt a buzzing in the back of her neck, a cold prickling in her ears. Her brain itched with needles and worms and fizzing sparks, and then suddenly a shrieking noise blasted into her head all at once—she couldn't control it, she couldn't shut it out.

Jo staggered to the bathroom. The light filled the white tiled room with a harsh glow. She had a glass of water, and then another. She was suddenly short of breath. She grabbed the sink, breathing in as deeply as she could, but it wasn't enough. Her heart beat faster. She looked in the mirror and her skin took on a yellow tinge in the light. Her eyes seemed as though they were far away, some other person's eyes.

She stepped out of the bathroom. She lost her breath again, sank to the ground—she couldn't stand up or she'd get dizzy and fall. She crawled the rest of the way to her bed.

She couldn't understand herself. Why had she gone to the Belgian Prankster? She had felt emptiness chewing away inside her before—as if the Belgian Prankster had something that belonged to her. Now she had it back, but it was far worse than any emptiness. It was busily working inside her now, weaving her veins into different patterns, shuffling her organs, reshaping her into something new and strange.

Jo crawled up into her bed. Was the world really going to end? She was so delirious, she felt it already had. Everything in her was fighting the blood and losing. The duel was only a day away. Aunt Lily was nowhere to be found. Jo reached behind her neck and touched the wound, the raw hole where he had gouged her, the sticky Ichthala blood clotted around the rim. It was all the worse because she couldn't see it. She was getting dizzy again. She couldn't hold off the fog and confusion any longer. It rushed in with a vengeance of lights, sounds, colors, and chills.

The next day Jo had to fight Fiona Fuorlini.

Jo knew she was going to be killed. She hadn't trained at all since the Belgian Prankster had arrived. At first Dame Delia had sternly ordered Jo to get back into training—then threatened her, then cajoled her, and finally even pleaded with her. It was no use. Her body felt locked up, paralyzed.

Jo, Ian, and Nora rode the subway down to Lower Brondo in anxious silence. Ian and Nora knew that Jo was in no condition to fight, but they had no idea how bad she really was. Jo felt the Ichthala blood slosh around inside her as the subway rattled and bounced. She didn't feel in control of her own body—as if she were up to her lip in slime, and only by exhausting, continuous effort could she keep from being sucked under.

They arrived at the Dome of Doom early, before the crowds. It didn't seem as exciting as last time. The glamour of night was gone in the afternoon gloom. All the floors were empty, all the lights on. The enticing darkness, the exuberant crowd, the wild fashions and violent scenes were gone. There was a stench of stale smoke and disinfectant. Janitors mopped the floors as bartenders restocked the bars.

Fiona and her seconds were already there. Jo, Ian, and Nora crossed the cavernous space, their footsteps clicking loudly, and settled in a booth in the opposite corner.

Oona Looch was right on time. She wasn't carried in on a throne, and her tough-looking daughters stayed in the shadows. She ran over the rules of the duel.

"No guns," she said. "No endangering the crowd. No leaving the arena until someone's been knocked in the water. That's all. If you die, too bad. I don't care if you both get killed, as long as it's got some razzle-dazzle! *Razzle-dazzle,*" she sang throatily. "As far as I'm concerned, it's all show business. Give 'em some flash, give 'em some pizzazz! The crowd paid good money to see you fight. Give 'em something to remember. *Razzle-dazzle!* Surprise 'em! Got it?"

"Oh, there'll be plenty of surprises tonight," said Fiona.

"That's the spirit," said Oona Looch. "Let's wrap this up. Which gods are you representing? Larouche?"

Jo had chosen her god carefully. "I'm Aznath, the Silver Kitten of Deceit."

"A fine god. We've had plenty of good Aznaths. Fuorlini?"

Fiona said, "Ichthala, the All-Devouring Mother."

There was a tense silence.

"An unconventional choice, Fuorlini," said Oona Looch finally. "We haven't had an Ichthala since, well, since thirteen years ago. Look, I don't care which god you choose, but I can guarantee the crowd will *hate* you for choosing that one."

Fiona bowed. "All due respect, but I think it's very appropriate."

Oona Looch shrugged. "Of course, you have a perfect right to make a damned fool of yourself. You're dismissed to your ready rooms," she said, and stuck out her left big toe.

Oona Looch's toe was as thick as Jo's thigh. In a traditional show of respect, everyone had to approach Oona Looch on their knees, kiss her gold toe ring, and retreat on their knees.

Ian went last. As he kissed her toe ring, she cooed, "You don't have to stop there, loverboy."

Ian reddened.

"I like this kid," said Oona Looch fondling Ian's chin with her toe. "Modest, almost a prude. Stout, pure-hearted lad. I'll dirty you yet, son."

"Thank you very much, Mrs. Looch," mumbled Ian shakily. Oona Looch leered at him as he scooted backward on his knees.

Jo's ready room was a moldy locker area that it seemed had never been cleaned. It stank of old sweat and urine, the tiles were dirty and chipped, and the rusty plumbing dripped with mysterious juices.

Ethelred was waiting for them when they entered, fresh from the duel officials' inspection. The ostrich was overjoyed to be reunited with Jo, and nearly knocked her down with affectionate pecks.

After Ethelred calmed down, Nora said, "Oona won't give up, will she, Ian?"

Ian winced. "Every time I see her, I swear she's going to pick me up and eat me."

"You took a suspiciously long time kissing her toe ring," said Nora. "It was almost as if you . . . enjoyed it?"

"Ha," said Ian.

Jo was feeling too ill to join in Nora's teasing. It took everything in her just to keep standing up. She watched Ian and Nora with unexpected tenderness. These were the last hours she would ever have with them, even if she did survive.

But she didn't have time for thoughts like this. There was much to do. Before the duel, Jo and Fiona were allowed time to practice flying their ostriches around the empty arena, in full armor, to get a feel for the space. But as Jo, Ian, and Nora were busying themselves in putting on Ethelred's armor, Jo remembered something.

"I forgot to make costume armor for myself!" said Jo.

Ian and Nora smiled at each other, and Nora said, "Actually, that's not a problem, Jo. Sefino gave us this before we left the lodge." She gave Jo a box wrapped in lavender foil. A little card said, *To Jo. Good luck! From the butlers.*

Jo opened it and gave a little gasp. The butlers had made her beautiful ceremonial armor, woven with swaths of silver fur, complete with claws and a tail. There was also a furry cat's-head helmet with silver whiskers and pointed ears. Sefino also included suggested insults for Jo to use during the insult stage of the fight. Jo's heart softened; she felt guilty about how severely she had judged him before.

Ian said, "Hey, what's up with Fiona fighting as Ichthala? Tasteless."

"Oh, I see through that," said Nora. "Fiona's just trying to prove how hard-core she is. But think about it—how tough *is* it, really? The Belgian Prankster came back, but the Ichthala didn't appear. The city still stands. Either the prophecies were wrong or I'd say Ichthala is a pretty weak god. So the joke's on Fiona, right, Jo?"

Jo felt the Ichthala blood rise in her, but she fought it down and said, "We'll settle it at the Dome."

"Atta girl," said Nora.

There was one last ritual Jo and Fiona had to perform—to eat a final dinner together. Nobody but Jo and Fiona was allowed in the dining room, and neither was allowed to speak a word during the meal.

Jo had been underground for hours. *The sun must have gone down by now*, she realized. *I'm going to die without ever seeing it again.* Even if Fiona didn't kill her, she would tell everyone who Jo really was. Every passing second rushed her closer to that moment.

She sipped her soup and glanced across the table at Fiona.

Fiona stared back at her with pure hatred.

At first Jo tried to return the stare, but soon she had to look away. Fiona's righteous anger was too strong for her to endure—and Fiona *was* righteous. Jo was the liar. It was her birth that had destroyed half the city; it was she who had secretly met the Belgian Prankster; and now she was full of the Ichthala's blood. It struck Jo that if this was a story, then Fiona was the hero. Jo was the dangerous dragon that had to be slain.

The black blood hissed and bubbled wildly through Jo's body, tickling her veins.

It was now just a half hour to the duel. Jo heard the crowd roaring down the hall as Nora and Ian helped Jo strap on her armor. Everything inside her was writhing and twisting.

Suddenly Nora said, "Jo, what's wrong with your neck?"

Jo saw her neck in the mirror. The wound had blackened and spread. She quickly jerked her armor over it. "Bruise I got training. It looks worse than it is. Help me with this, will you?"

A couple of minutes later Audrey dropped by, starry-eyed at all the backstage machinations of the duel. "I can't believe I'm actually in a ready room at the Dome of Doom," she said, and took a deep breath of the putrid air. "Heavenly. Better than I'd imagined! You're *so lucky* to be dueling, Jo. You're living my dream. Look at that armor! It's fabulous. You're gonna demolish her! Woo!"

After a few minutes of Audrey's pep talk, Jo almost felt as if she had a fighting chance. Then, with a last kiss and a shout of "Good luck!" Audrey left for her seat.

With just five minutes to go, Oona Looch knocked on the door. "Almost time, kid," she said to Jo. She turned to Ian. "And you and I have a *date* afterward, sweet stuff. Don't speak! I won't take no for an answer. After the festivities I'm gonna whisk you to my love hideaway and make a man out of you. Something to look forward to!"

Then, after slapping Ian's butt (and nearly swatting him across the room), Oona Looch departed down the hall, whistling.

Jo and Ian traded glances. It was hard to say who looked more alarmed.

An usher came to the door. "Okay, Aznath. Let's go."

Jo mounted Ethelred, put her feet in the stirrups, and received her lance from Nora. Ian and Nora went out first, bearing banners emblazoned with the traditional symbol of Aznath, the Silver Kitten of Deceit. Jo followed, gently urging a nervous Ethelred on. They made their way down the dark hallway, and into the chaos of the main floor.

Jo rode Ethelred out into the tumultuous crowd, at once dazzled by popping flashbulbs and nearly deafened by the screaming fans and shouting reporters. She saw Chatterbox waving a pencil, yelling questions at her over the din, jostling with the other journalists. Ushers just barely held the mob back so Jo could approach the arena. The Ichthala blood quickened in her, stirring up and rising; she almost spit it up. She heard the announcer's voice boom somewhere. Daphne and Maurice were sitting at a table together, cheering her on—she also spied Albert muddling through the crowd, and Phil chatting up some girl in the back. The Ichthala blood raced through her arteries, threading through the secret corners of her body and tying her up, tightening and squeezing. There was Dugan, taking last-minute bets at a corner booth, and Oona Looch lolled on her throne, roaring with laughter as her daughters looked on stonily. Drums rumbled faster and faster. The crash of cymbals and gongs made the air shake. Sefino and the rest of the butlers flung flowers at her. The Wormbeard squires were there, too, sitting all in a row, in identical purple cloaks, steel goggles, and long yellow scarves. Audrey was whooping it up with her show business friends in the premium seats. A convention of eelmen were right next to them, gurgling and spitting and wolfing down heaps of spicy jellyfish. Dame Delia, Sir Festus, and Sir Oort were there, too—the Odd-Fish knights couldn't wish Jo luck personally before the fight, for that would imply they knew she was illegally dueling, but Dame Delia winked, and Sir Festus gave Jo a hearty thumbs-up. It was a sellout crowd.

In a storm of glitter, confetti, and streamers, Jo rode Ethelred into the Dome of Doom, Ian and Nora at her side. They walked out onto a little platform that poked out into the arena. Fiona was entering on a similar perch, far away on the other side.

Jo glanced at the lake of black water, far below. She looked up and swallowed. This was it.

Fiona had already dismounted and started the threats: "Aznath! Silver Kitten of Deceit!" she bellowed across the arena. "Gaze upon my dread mouth, and know the terror of your doom! For I am Ichthala, the All-Devouring Mother—and tonight your deceits shall be overthrown, your silver fur gnashed between my all-masticating jaws!"

The crowd exploded with boos. Oona Looch was right: the crowd didn't like an Ichthala duelist. Jo gripped her lance tightly and shouted Sefino's recommended response:

"So, Ichthala! Boasting in speech, yet paltry in deed! I *am* Aznath, Silver Kitten of Deceit, and my meow is your death sentence; my purr, your despair; my litter box, your grave! Let fly your thrashing tongue, your gnawing teeth, your gulping throat; I choke your esophagus with the foodstuffs of destruction; I fill your greedy maw with the meal of dishonor! Devour it, Ichthala; taste it well; savor your doom; for that is all you shall ever devour again!"

The crowd went wild. The chant of "Aznath! Aznath!" started up. Fiona sneered from within her Ichthala costume (a smaller, wearable version of the idol she'd made for Desolation Day) and yelled over the chanting:

"Who can take seriously this idle braggadocio, from a weakling both vile and pusillanimous? Do you not know, Aznath, that I, Ichthala, the All-Devouring Mother, shall gather unto myself a thousand living scorpions and sew them into a pair of scorpion underwear? And do you not know that I shall force you to wear this underwear? For I *shall* do this, Aznath; and as you howl, stung in the most unmentionable places by your own writhing, poisonous underwear, I shall also set that underwear on fire. And then I'll kick you. I have spoken!"

"Can it be, Ichthala?" retorted Jo. "Have you dishonored even your own dishonorable self, and stooped to stitching disgraceful undergarments in your diseased fantasies? Do such whimsies allow you escape from your nauseous existence, and your ignominious fate? For your fate is this: I, Aznath, Silver Kitten of Deceit, shall cut you into narrow strips, and stretch your entrails into a thin twine, and then string a guitar with them. And then I will play your *second* least favorite song on that guitar, for to play your *least* favorite song would be too good for you, and frankly, a bit much. *I have spoken!*"

Fiona was enraged. "I'm going to rip off your fingernails, Aznath, and feed them back to you in a spicy gumbo of your own blood!"

"I'm going to eat your children!" countered Jo. "I don't care if you don't have any yet! When you're in labor, I'll be waiting outside the delivery room with a knife and a fork!"

"I'm going to tear out your intestines!" foamed Fiona. "Then I'll make a rodeo lariat out of those intestines, and then I'll lasso you with those intestines, and then *hang you with your own intestines!*"

"I'm going to cut off all your fingers," shouted Jo, "and then I'm going to cut off your mother's fingers, and your father's fingers, and the fingers of everyone you love! Then I'm going to build hundreds of dollhouses out of these severed fingers! *Then* I'm going to put rats in all these houses, and then, after the rats get comfortable, *I will kill all the rats;* and then I will *burn* down the city; and then will I kill *you,* with a diamond dagger plunged deep in your dark, unholy, malformed, unnatural, godless, nauseating, cancerous, wretched, crap-spackled *heart!* I HAVE SPOKEN!"

The crowd roared and screamed and stamped their feet in glee.

"Avaunt!" said Fiona.

"Hark!" said Jo.

"Fie!" said Fiona.

"Alack!" said Jo.

"Egad!" said Fiona.

"Forsooth!" said Jo.

"Aaaaaaaagh!" said Fiona, and jumped onto her ostrich. Jo swung her leg over Ethelred, and the ostrich sprang to its feet. Fiona reared back and launched into the arena, dipping and climbing toward Jo. Ethelred scampered back, spun, hunched, and charged into the air, diving toward Fiona.

Jo brandished her lance, flicked the trigger so that fire blossomed out either side, and spun it around. Fiona flipped her flaming lance back and forth, the flames zigzagging blindingly. Then they were on top of each other, clashing and scrabbling in midair, as their ostriches shrieked and clawed.

Everything went black. The screams and noise of the Dome of Doom were gone. The Ichthala blood boiled over in her, pulsing so violently that Jo felt it was nearly bleeding out of her eyes. Far away, deep in the distant darkness, there was a tiny, colorful man, dancing.

She was back in the Dome of Doom. She gasped for air. Fiona was driving her back to the wall. Jo almost fumbled away her lance. Feebly she tried to counter Fiona's attacks, but Fiona whacked her parries aside. Jo was overwhelmed. She was going to lose. It took everything in her to fend off Fiona, but Fiona was hardly trying. Fiona held back, puzzled, searching for trickery in Jo's apparent weakness, casually bashing her around, surprised, even disappointed, at how easy she was.

Again Jo blacked out, sucked down into darkness and silence. The little glowing man was still dancing. She strained to force her way out, but the Dome of Doom came back only in one-second snatches, and she was always pulled back down into the darkness and the dancing man, rapidly coming closer, a crumb of color in a black ocean.

Fiona was flying away from her. Round one was over. The crowd was booing at Jo's inept fighting. She wheeled Ethelred around and flew back to her perch, where Ian and Nora waited to adjust Ethelred's armor and give Jo water.

"I'm getting killed out there," said Jo.

"First-round jitters," said Ian. "Now go back out there and show her what you've really got!"

"I'm blacking out!" said Jo, but nobody heard her over the noise. Ian and Nora shouted encouragement, but Jo saw the worry in their faces. Ethelred squawked and dived back into the arena. Fiona swooped toward her. Round two had begun.

This time Fiona didn't mess around. Every time Jo attacked, Fiona swatted her aside and came back with a furious combination of ripostes that battered her so hard she could barely stay in her saddle. Fiona's lance stabbed, slashed, bashed, and skewered her, biting into her armor, tearing at the fur, burning her skin, pummeling her.

Jo wasn't good enough. No amount of practicing could have prepared her for Fiona. The ostriches fluttered and circled each other, growling and snapping. Jo struggled to keep just out of Fiona's striking range. It took all of her skill just to hold Fiona at bay. The crowd groaned and booed. They didn't want defense; they wanted action.

Fiona lost her patience. Snarling with contempt, she drove her attack forward with new force. Jo couldn't block it. With a blinding series of feints, stabs, thrusts, and slashes, Fiona broke

Jo's defenses and battered her, whacking her shoulders and arms, spearing her in the chest, and finally walloping her over the head. The crowd cheered wildly.

Once again Jo blacked out. The Ichthala blood gushed and tingled through her, oily and full of seething power. She was drowning in it, swallowing lungfuls of black, sticky blood. The dancing man was closer now. It was the Belgian Prankster. He was saying something.

Jo screamed and shook herself, breaking out of the nightmare, but just barely. At any moment it could absorb her again. She tried to flee Fiona, but she was panicking now, making mistakes. Fiona saw her chance and whacked Jo from behind, bashing the back of her head.

The Dome of Doom flickered. She was going to die. She could hardly even defend herself, and inside she was drowning, sucked into a furious undertow of Ichthala blood. Fiona was bringing her lance around in a flaming sweep—Jo mounted a desperate defense, but Fiona shattered it, knocking her clear off her ostrich.

Jo was falling. She had lost. Her mind blinked back and forth between the arena and darkness. She was falling in the arena and she was falling through miles of blackness, into the lap of the Belgian Prankster. The water was rushing up to swallow her, and the Belgian Prankster's face filled her vision, whispering: "I'm right here to help. Let me help you."

Jo hit something. It wasn't water.

She grabbed whatever it was and held on for dear life.

Ethelred had dived down and caught her.

The crowd went nuts. It was a beautiful move. Fiona flitted above in a victory swoop, thinking the applause was for her, and Jo saw her chance. Spurring Ethelred upward, she aimed her lance straight up, and just as Fiona noticed her—too late—Jo speared the underside of Fiona's ostrich's wing.

The ostrich squealed. Jo yanked her lance out. Ostrich blood spattered on her. Her lance was gory with blood and burnt feathers. The crowd shrieked and roared. Fiona's ostrich could hardly keep in the air, and she retreated, looping and zigzagging back to her perch. Jo just barely made it back to her own perch.

"Brilliant move, Jo," yelled Nora. "Absolutely brilliant!"

"I can't go back out there," wheezed Jo.

"You have to!" shouted Ian. "You own this now! Go out there and finish her off!"

"I'm blacking out!" protested Jo. "I'm dizzy, I can't!"

"Finish her!" said Ian and Nora, shoving Jo back into the fray.

Fiona's seconds had patched up her ostrich as best they could, but it was no use—the ostrich could barely keep aloft. Still Fiona whipped her ostrich toward Jo, half flying, half falling—

And then Fiona *leaped off.*

Fiona crashed on top of Jo, and now they were both on Ethelred.

The crowd couldn't believe their eyes. It was an audacious move. Jo and Fiona struggled in the saddle, each trying to push the other off, but Jo couldn't twist around enough to fight. They scrabbled and grappled as Ethelred squealed in confused outrage, and just when Jo thought she was forcing Fiona off, Fiona got an unexpected grip on Jo and chucked her off entirely.

Somersaulting through the air, Jo flailed her arms and grabbed the leg of Fiona's much-abused ostrich. Jo clung on as it shook its leg, shrieked, and tried to bite her; finally, with a ferocious kick, the ostrich flung her across the arena, and Jo hit the cage wall.

Jo grabbed the bars of the cage, hanging on. It wasn't over until she fell in the water. But she had lost her ostrich, she had lost her lance, she was bruised, bloody, and broken—and then she blacked out again. The Belgian Prankster gibbered to himself in the darkness. She felt the Ichthala blood build up, brimming behind her eyes, a black, sludgy gelatin, foaming out of control inside her. It was power.

Jo knew what the Belgian Prankster wanted. He wanted her

to use the Ichthala's powers. But she knew that once she did that, she would unlock the All-Devouring Mother inside her, and the Silent Sisters would come, and then . . . Jo could feel the shape of the power, stronger than nature, so strong that if she used it, the universe itself might unravel. It was almost unraveling her now.

Jo opened her eyes. She was still clinging to the side of the cage. She saw the faces of the crowd, just beyond the bars, bestial and ugly, screaming for blood. She twisted around, looking down into the arena. Fiona could hardly control Ethelred—the angry, loyal ostrich bucked fiercely under her, turning around to bite Fiona every chance he got.

Jo scrambled up the bars of the cage. Somehow Ian and Nora had gotten a new ostrich and lance and were waving her over. Jo started to cross the ceiling, hand over hand, toward her perch on the opposite side.

The crowd was on its feet, stamping and hollering and pressing their faces against the cage as Jo hung from the dome. Some hooted encouragement, others screamed abuse, still others tried to stamp on Jo's fingers or pry them from the bars. Jo looked down—far below, Fiona was riding Ethelred hard, breaking him. It wouldn't be long before she'd broken him enough to come after Jo.

At last Jo made it down to her perch. Ian and Nora were yelling something, but Jo hardly heard them. She grabbed the extra lance from Ian and mounted the ostrich—Dame Delia's bird—and looked down at Fiona, just in time to see that Fiona had drawn a gun.

With an echoing blast Fiona fired.

The bullet nicked a cage bar just inches from Jo's head, ricocheting off with a spark.

The crowd heard the blast, saw the gun and flew into a panic. If bullets were flying around, anyone could be shot. Suddenly the spectators' area was thrown into a tumult of screams, elbows, and shoves, everyone stampeding to get out of the Dome of Doom.

Jo was astonished Fiona had brought a gun. Fiona probably hoped Oona Looch would understand why, once she revealed what Jo was—she was already shouting it now:

"Do you know who Jo really is? I'll tell you! She's—she's—"

But nobody was listening. The crowd was charging for the exits, trampling each other underfoot, clogging the doors and hallways. More bullets zipped past Jo, cracking into the bars and walls nearby. Dame Delia's ostrich was spooked by the gunfire; it whirled and fled into the spectators' area, knocking down Ian and Nora on the way out. Moments later Fiona came in pursuit, squeezing Ethelred through the same exit.

For a duelist to fire a gun was unprecedented, but for the duelists to fight in the spectators' area was unheard-of. Fiona rampaged after Jo, firing wildly, overturning tables and breaking the furniture. Jo just barely kept a dozen yards ahead, as Dame Delia's ostrich awkwardly fluttered through the debris and panicking mob. People tried to keep out of the way of the huge, flapping ostriches as they crashed through the tables and bars and couches, scattering chairs and toppling cabinets of bottles that shattered with mighty crashes, sloshing the floor with gallons of expensive drinks. Oona Looch's daughters ran after the ostriches, trying to bring them under control, but even they were kicked, trampled, and flung aside.

Jo wheeled around and ducked back into the Dome of Doom. Fiona charged after her. Jo heard the blast of a gun, and once again she blacked out.

The Ichthala blood seethed smoothly through her, from the corners of her heart to the tips of her fingernails, threading its way to exactly where it needed to be. The Belgian Prankster said, "It's your power. You took it, just like you had to. Now use it! It belongs to you!"

But Jo felt like *she* belonged to *it*. The blood was welling up, squirting out of her eyes, running out her nose, gurgling in the back of her throat, seeping from under her fingernails. She tasted it in the back of her throat, like motor oil.

Jo shook herself awake—she and Fiona were back in the arena, their ostriches clashing at close range, Ethelred squealing piteously as Fiona forced him to fight against Jo. She brandished her lance, but Fiona had one bullet left.

Fiona shot Jo point-blank.

The bullet turned aside in midair.

Jo stretched out her hand and blasted Fiona across the arena. A black flower opened up inside her, dark and angry. She was using the power, using the Ichthala blood—she felt the All-Devouring Mother grow wildly inside her, calling out to the Silent Sisters as she smashed Fiona against the cage, again and again and again.

She looked into the crowd and saw Aunt Lily staring at her in horror.

Blankness rippled through Jo like a cold poison. She let Fiona fall, and the unconscious girl dropped into the water.

Jo had won.

A thunderous cheer went up from all sides, intolerably loud. Jo clutched Dame Delia's ostrich, hovering in the center of the ring, staring around at the fans, at everyone screaming her name. It was over.

She had betrayed them all.

TWENTY-SIX

Jo landed and was overwhelmed. Pressed in by shouting fans, she couldn't even dismount her ostrich, and was forced to ride it through the crowd. It was the wildest duel ever at the Dome of Doom. Everyone was exhilarated to be there, and everyone wanted to be near the winner.

Jo was in a daze. Nobody knew she'd used the Ichthala's powers, but she knew something horrible would soon follow. Her dread mounted as she waited for the other shoe to drop. It reminded her of when she was six, living at Aunt Lily's ruby palace, and her bedroom doorknob had unexpectedly come off in her hand. For an instant Jo had almost expected the rest of the palace to fall apart, too, a chain reaction bringing ceilings, walls, and floors crashing down.

Jo felt that way about everything now. If she could send bullets careening away from her and fling Fiona across the arena with a wave of her hand, then anything was possible. It made the universe seem flimsy, as if one wrong move could send it all flying apart.

Ian and Nora led Jo through the back passages of the Dome of Doom. Fans jammed the tunnels, so loud that Jo had to scream when she asked Ian, "Where are you taking me?"

Ian yelled back, but she couldn't hear him. A door opened, and she rode her ostrich into a grand ballroom.

It was a victory party. Jo dismounted and was mobbed. Everyone was slapping her on the back, kissing her, shouting congratulations in her ear, lifting her up on their shoulders—she tried to draw the line at that, but nobody cared what she thought, and up she went. After they lowered her, Phil Snurr pumped her arm and declared, "What a fight! You nailed her, *nailed her*!"

"And she had it coming," said Daphne. "I still can't believe Fiona shot at you! Oona Looch is going to eat her for breakfast."

"If Fiona's not already dead," said Albert. "Laid it on a bit thick, didn't you, Jo?"

"Had it coming," said Daphne again.

Jo said, "Have any of you seen Dame Lily?"

"Uh, no," said Maurice. "Sir Oliver and Colonel Korsakov haven't come back, either. Sorry, Jo. I'm sure Dame Lily would have loved to see that fight, though."

"But I thought I saw Lily."

There was a respectful silence. Maurice coughed in embarrassment.

"I don't think she came, Jo," said Daphne. "But if Lily was still with us, she would've loved this victory party, wouldn't she?"

"But I could've sworn I saw her," said Jo. The image of Aunt Lily staring at her was burned in her eyes. She knew what that stare meant—Aunt Lily understood what she had done.

"Just relax, have fun," said Daphne. "This is your night. By the way, don't you have a change of clothes? You're kind of nasty right now."

Jo went back to her ready room to shower and change. Luckily, her dress had a high neck that covered up her wound. Jo hoped it hadn't worsened, but there was no time to check—Nora and Ian were already knocking on the door, yelling for her to come back out into the party.

Jo had to accept congratulations from a hundred different well-wishers, and then the band cranked up, and music drowned out further conversation. People started to dance, and Jo was sucked into the frantic merriment. She didn't want to dance; she was battered and weary, scared of what the night had in store for her. Time after time she tried to get away, but someone always shouted, "Hey! The lady of the hour is escaping!" and good-naturedly shoved Jo back among the dancers.

Finally she gave in. She began to dance, and soon she forgot her bruises and cuts and aches. Her exhaustion fell away and to her surprise, out of nowhere, she felt brilliant.

Jo spun past the eelmen, thrashing around in a traditional jig, and wove in and out of a high-kicking line of Oona Looch's daughters. It hit her: she'd really won. She hadn't been killed. She hadn't been exposed. She was giddy and flushed, and she felt violently alive. She shook off her fear, forgot her guilt. She didn't care anymore. She had used the Ichthala's power, but the world hadn't collapsed. She hadn't turned into a monster. The Silent Sisters hadn't come to get her. Jo felt as though she'd awakened from a long nightmare. And even if what everyone had said was true and the world was about to end, she didn't care anymore. She'd go out with a bang.

She looked for Ian. He was pushing through the crowd, Oona Looch not far behind, her arms outstretched, shouting, "I can't wait anymore! I must have you, Ian!"

Jo crossed the room, grabbed Ian's waist and arm, and started to dance.

"Hey! What are you doing?" said Ian.

"We're dancing," said Jo.

"Why?"

"I'm helping you escape Oona Looch," said Jo. "Dance with me, and she'll get the hint."

"Oh, I get it. Thanks, Jo. I owe you one," said Ian. "But, as you can see, I can't dance."

"Let me lead."

"Hey, you're good at this!"

"Aunt Lily was grooming me for vaudeville," said Jo. Then: "I can't see Oona Looch. Has she given up?"

"No. She's still coming . . . she's almost right behind you," said Ian.

"We need to drop more hints," said Jo.

"These subtle hints aren't working," said Ian.

"This isn't subtle," said Jo, and kissed him.

Ian's eyes stayed open the whole time. Jo drew it out for as long as possible, her lips mashed up awkwardly against his teeth. She didn't know what she was doing but she didn't care.

Oona Looch stopped in her tracks.

Jo turned. "Yes? Can I help you?"

"I never knew . . . I never . . . ohhh," said Oona Looch in a small voice. "I thought Ian and me were going to my love hideaway . . . it was going to be all swell, and . . . I had surprises, like a . . . Are you two . . . are you . . . boyfriend and girlfriend?"

"Yes," said Jo. "We are."

"Well, do I have egg on my face," said Oona Looch. "You could've told me! And now I've gone and made a darned fool of myself. Fair's fair, I suppose, to the victor go the spoils. Imagine, me trying to seduce your boyfriend on your victory night! My apologies, Miss Larouche." She turned to Ian. "But you . . . you broke my heart, Ian. *You broke my heart.*"

Oona Looch's face darkened with pent-up emotion, and her body quivered; for a moment it seemed she might burst into frustrated violence; and then she started blubbering. Oona Looch waved away the dozens of handkerchiefs suddenly offered by her daughters—like a sudden display of a hundred flags of surrender—and trudged out of the room, sniffling.

Jo and Ian kept dancing. They danced closer, and her hand was sweating in his. They didn't speak, but danced for the next song. Jo felt they were walking on thin ice. But she wanted the ice to break. She didn't know where they would fall, but she wanted to find out.

The band stopped playing, and a bell rang for the midnight feast. Jo and Ian stopped dancing and looked at each other uncertainly.

"So, thanks for getting Oona off my back," said Ian.

"Did you mind that I kissed you?" said Jo.

"No . . . no," said Ian.

They were still holding each other, and neither knew what to do. Slowly they let each other's hands go and went up to the victor's table, where Nora and Audrey and the rest of the squires and some of the butlers were already waiting.

Nobody had seen that Jo and Ian had kissed. But as dinner went on, they exchanged glances, and Jo felt something unfamiliar open up inside her. She wondered how it would be different with Ian after tonight.

Nora said, "Hey, does anyone know how Fiona is doing?"

"Still unconscious, but she's alive," said Albert. "Jo just knocked her out, that's all. Say, how did you finally beat her, Jo? Everything was too crazy for me to see."

Jo looked away. "Just a lucky hit."

Nora said, "Hey, Jo. Chatterbox kept nagging me while you were dancing. Says he wants an interview."

"How can Chatterbox sleep?" thundered Sefino. "Now he's twisting the arms of my *friends* to dig up dirt about me! Jo, don't do the interview. He'll take advantage of your generosity in the afterglow of victory, and wrangle all manner of scuttlebutt from you."

"Sefino," said Jo patiently, "do you think it's possible Chatterbox might really want to ask about the duel and not just you?"

"Jo, Jo. Always the naive crumpet. He'll start with the duel, of course, but before you know it, you'll be deluged with shameless inquires such as 'What manner of scandalous underclothes does Sefino wear?' or 'What unnatural vices does Sefino practice when alone?' "

"Fortunately I can't answer those questions."

"Jo, he's diabolical. Beware his perfidious machinations."

"I thought Chatterbox didn't even write about you anymore."

"Undoubtedly Chatterbox is conserving his resources for a final, all-out onslaught of libel," said Sefino. "What can I do, other than wait for the inevitable slander? It is widely claimed that I have the patience of a saint. I do not necessarily dispute such claims."

"By the way, thanks for making the armor."

"Further proof of my virtue," said Sefino. "Needless to say, the *Snitch* never publishes anything about my tireless charity work."

Audrey suddenly stood up, her eyes narrowed.

"What's wrong?" said Jo.

"Um . . . nothing." Audrey gazed around the room as though searching for someone. "I'll be back in a second." She dropped her napkin on her plate and walked quickly away.

Jo didn't have time to wonder, for she saw a familiar friend across the ballroom. With a shout of joy she leaped up and dashed toward Ethelred, who had just been brought in by some of the Dome of Doom's ostrich doctors, freshly bandaged and cleaned up.

"Are you all right, Ethelred?" said Jo, hugging him and burying her nose in his feathers. "Fiona didn't hurt you, did she?"

The doctor said, "He's banged around, but he's not seriously injured. He's probably more upset that Fiona forced him to fight against you."

Ethelred gurgled and sheepishly looked away. Jo whispered in his ear: "It's okay, Ethelred. I understand. Look at me. I'm proud of you."

Ethelred peeped back up at Jo, making little squawks,

and seemed to smile. Then he carefully nipped Jo's shoulder. Ethelred was given a place of honor at Jo's table, with all the lizards and weeds he could eat. (The ostrich had impeccable table manners.)

It was a half hour later, during dessert, that Jo saw Dame Isabel and Sir Alasdair out of the corner of her eye, entering the ballroom with grim faces. Then a dozen policemen came in after them. Jo put down her fork, her hand trembling. She looked around the room for Dame Delia, Sir Festus, Sir Oort, any of the knights who had supported her duel.

They were gone.

"Attention!" shouted Dame Isabel. "Quiet, all! We are here to make an arrest!"

Everyone saw the policemen. The buzz of conversation died.

"Aw, Isabel, what gives?" shouted someone. "Okay, Jo Larouche dueled, it was illegal, but big deal—why rain on her parade now?"

"Dueling is the least of Jo Larouche's crimes!" shouted Dame Isabel. "I knew about the duel, of course. You'd have to be deaf and blind and an idiot not to! But that's not why I'm here. Ever since Jo Larouche arrived among us," she growled, pointing at Jo and approaching her, "she has lied to, endangered, and bamboozled all of Eldritch City. But tonight she will be exposed!"

"What are you talking about?" yelled someone else.

"I could mention the *ring* we found in Jo's room," said Dame Isabel, and Jo's stomach dropped. "I could even mention that, by order of the mayor, all Odd-Fish knights are now under arrest. Sir Alasdair and I volunteered to go to jail as well. I thought I'd never say this, but today I am ashamed to be an Odd-Fish. But I won't bother listing all the evidence. I just want to hear Jo deny it and add one more lie to her *mountain* of lies! Go ahead, Jo. Tell everyone you're not the Hazelwood baby. Tell them you're not the Ichthala—tell them you're not the All-Devouring Mother!"

Jo tried to force words out of her mouth. Nothing came.

"Do you deny it?" said Dame Isabel. "Go on, deny it! Why stop lying now?"

Jo turned to Ian. "Ian . . ."

Ian shrank away, shaking his head in shock.

"You won't admit it?" said Dame Isabel, standing over Jo. "Well, here's what we found in *Dame Lily's* room! It turns out it was *she* who had cut that hole from the tapestry. And why?"

Dame Isabel unfurled a ragged piece of tapestry for all to see. It was a picture of the Silent Sisters, standing in a circle, bowing to a girl in the center.

The girl was unmistakably Jo.

Jo said, "I'm—don't—it's not—"

"You *still* deny it?" shrieked Dame Isabel. "Then let's show everyone the final proof!"

Dame Isabel grabbed Jo roughly and turned her around. Jo shut her eyes tight as Dame Isabel tore open the back of her dress, exposing her neck. The room broke into screams.

"Look, Ichthala!" said Dame Isabel, pushing a mirror into Jo's hand. "Look at what you're turning into!"

Jo took the mirror in her shaking hand and forced herself to look. The wound had become much worse—scaly and reptilian now, oozing with black blood, bristling with hair, its lips trembling, gasping like a small gray mouth.

It was true. She was turning into a monster.

"What more proof do you need?" shouted Dame Isabel hoarsely. "You see the wound. She went to the Belgian Prankster in secret, she did it willingly! She is already half monster! *Jo is the All-Devouring Mother!*"

Jo looked around in desperation. Everyone was edging away from her. Nora screamed and hid her face. Ian stared at Jo with uncomprehending terror. Jo looked for Audrey, but Audrey had disappeared.

"Arrest her!" ordered Dame Isabel, and the policemen approached Jo as everyone else scrambled away.

"But I'm not bad!" said Jo. "I don't want to hurt anyone!"

"More lies!" screamed Dame Isabel. "We can't take a chance with a liar! Arrest her, lock her up, expel her from the city, anything—do something before it's too late!"

"I'm not evil!" said Jo, and then the policemen seized her.

The mountain lurched. All the lights went out. The Dome of Doom went black, a tumult of rumbles, scrapes, and cracks shot through the mountain, echoing all around the cavern, and the floor swayed and jolted, upsetting tables and chairs, knocking everyone to the floor. Jo felt the blood oozing out of her wound. She was making the earthquake happen. The All-Devouring Mother was shrieking inside her, all of the Ichthala's rage was spraying out, and she was helpless against it. And yet it was her. Every tremble of her stomach shook the mountain; every heartbeat made the city quake.

Jo staggered away into the darkness, trying to avoid being trampled as the party broke into mayhem. The policemen spread out, trying to restore order, and Jo heard Dame Isabel shouting over the crowd's roar, "Get her! Don't let her escape!"

Jo felt her way along the wall and bumped into someone in the darkness.

Ian's voice: "Who are you?"

"It's Jo. Help me, Ian. I don't—"

"Get away from me. Get away from me or I'll shout and everyone will know where you are."

"Ian, please don't—"

"You killed my mother. You lied to me!"

"Ian—"

He pushed her to the ground. "Get away from me!"

Jo scrambled away and ran into the darkness. She blundered out of the ballroom, running into people, tripping over them, but she didn't slow down. She remembered talking with Ian, riding on the elephant together, on their way to the Municipal Squires Authority, when he'd said that even if Aunt Lily was arrested, Jo could rely on him.

It hadn't meant anything.

A little thing she didn't even know was inside her, that some part of her had been secretly tending, was ripped out, and part of her came with it. Jo didn't know where she was going. She didn't care. She ran blindly into the stadium area of the Dome of Doom.

The Silent Sisters were waiting for her.

They glowed blue in the darkness, veils and gowns rippling in an invisible wind, holding out their clutching bony hands. Jo screamed but couldn't hear anything—all sound was gone except for an old woman's voice, itching deep inside her brain. Jo spun, ran—toward more shimmering blue Silent Sisters, gliding from the opposite hallway, reaching out for her.

Jo turned and sprinted toward the elevator room. She found and jabbed the button in the darkness. Nothing happened. She hit it. Again nothing. The blue light down the hall grew stronger. She felt around tremblingly, looking for the door to the stairs. The blue was getting brighter, looming behind her, starting to light up the room.

A chilly fingertip touched her shoulder.

Jo yelled and tore up the stairs, three at a time. She didn't have the strength to run, but she couldn't stop. She couldn't look back, but she knew the Silent Sisters were right behind her, fluttering up the stairs, shimmering in the darkness like jets of gas flame—Jo burst through a door and suddenly she was out on the streets of Lower Brondo.

It was three in the morning. The city was in a pandemonium. The earthquake had jolted buildings out of their foundations, and they slumped against each other, knocking each other down like dominoes. Flames leaped out of windows, smoke billowed in dirty dark clouds, and the streets were full of people running around in panic.

A glimmering blue Silent Sister was skimming down the street—everyone scattered before her, screaming, not looking back. Then the Silent Sister saw Jo and spread her arms wide, bobbing and sailing toward her.

"There she is!" said someone. "The Hazelwood monster!"

"I'm not a monster!" shouted Jo.

A mob was coming toward her, too, their faces ugly with rage, ready to tear her apart. Two more Silent Sisters appeared from opposite directions, floating and fluttering toward Jo, their arms outstretched. Jo was trapped.

A yellow sedan skidded around the corner, crashing through the mob, roaring straight toward Jo. It spun to a stop, the door flew open, and Audrey yelled, "Get in!"

Jo dived into the backseat, bricks and rocks thunked against the car, and Audrey floored it, screeching away, veering onto the sidewalk, nearly running over people in the mob.

"Since when do you have a car?" shouted Jo.

"I just stole it. Keep your head down!"

Jo ducked below the window. "Where did you go? What happened to you?"

"I saw the knights were being escorted out of the party," said Audrey. "When they didn't come back I got suspicious. I slipped away and found out what Dame Isabel had planned. By then the police weren't letting anyone back down into the Dome of Doom, so I couldn't warn you. Then the earthquake happened, so I stole this car and started driving around looking for you. I knew you'd find a way out."

"How did you know?" said Jo.

"Because it's true, isn't it," said Audrey, her hands tightening on the wheel. "You are who they say you are."

Jo curled up. "You know who I am?"

"Yes."

"Don't you hate me, too?"

"No. I guess I identify with your character?" Audrey grimaced. "I wish you'd told me. You could've trusted me."

"Do you really think I'm . . . the All-Devouring Mother?"

"You know I never bought that Silent Sisters nonsense. Look, I don't care who they say you are—I'm not going to let a bunch of crazy people kill you."

Jo felt she could hardly breathe. "Can you get me out of the city?"

"All the city gates are locked and guarded. Nobody's getting out. You're going to have to hide somewhere in the city."

"Where could I possibly hide?" said Jo.

Audrey paused. Then she said, "Nobody would expect you to hide in the lodge, would they? It's big, and there's lots of hidden rooms—I won't tell anyone, I swear! Not even Ian. I could visit you secretly, bring you food, and a few months later, after this blows over, I'll help you escape for real. Good plan?"

It sounded like a terrible plan. "Thanks, Audrey. You're a good friend."

They drove a while in silence.

"Actually, you're my only friend," Jo added at last.

"What?"

"Ian and Nora—when they found out—"

"Put it out of your mind," said Audrey firmly. "Forget about it. They were shocked. Whatever they said or did, it's not what they really feel."

"But Ian blames me for killing his mom, Nora's obsessed with crazy myths about me. I never told them who I really am, and they were my—"

"One day it'll be all right," said Audrey. "You have to believe that. But today, no. Today you have to stay away from them."

Jo held herself tight, rocking on the floor of the backseat as Audrey yanked the steering wheel, stepped on the gas, and zig-zagged down the streets. Finally Jo said, "Why are you the only one who doesn't mind that I've been lying all this time?"

"I'm a liar myself," said Audrey. "Look—we're here."

Audrey drove past the lodge and then pulled around into the empty alley. "Hurry up, let's get inside before anyone sees you," she said quickly.

The lodge was deserted and in shambles. Audrey had to kick open the front door, which had become wedged into the twisted door frame. Inside the furniture was thrown around and broken, windows were shattered, and some of the ceilings had fallen in the earthquake.

"Where am I supposed to hide?" said Jo.

"This way," said Audrey, pulling Jo up the half-collapsed staircase. On the fourth floor Audrey led her down a hallway Jo had never seen before, pressed a panel in the wall, and opened a hidden door. There was a narrow hallway leading into darkness.

Jo looked at Audrey in astonishment. "How do you know about these things?"

"You know—poking around. I had a feeling this might be useful. C'mon, get in."

Jo and Audrey squeezed down the hallway, which narrowed into a crawl space, and finally dropped into a tiny closet, hardly large enough to stand up in. It was dark except for a trickle of light coming from a hole in the bricks.

"Leave everything to me," said Audrey. "I'm going to go fetch you some supplies, check the situation outside. Ditch that car, too."

Jo grabbed Audrey's arm. "You're leaving?"

"I can't do any good sitting here with you," said Audrey. "Come on, I've gotta go."

Jo slowly let go. "But . . . you'll come back, right?"

"As soon as I can."

"I don't know what I'd do without you."

"We'll get you through this," said Audrey. "Oh, and—uh—give me your dress."

"What?"

"Don't ask! Here's some other clothes for you to wear."

Jo reluctantly took off her dress and gave it to Audrey, who shoved some street clothes at her. Then Audrey pulled herself up into the crawl space and was gone.

Jo waited, shivering. When Audrey was with her, it seemed possible that she just might get out of this alive. But now despair came rushing back. She couldn't bear to think about her wound. She could feel it sending roots into her body, sucking up her blood and converting it into something nastier, spreading its tentacles all over her back.

Jo stared out the crack in the wall, out at the chaotic street and the crumbling city. It was all because of her. Maybe Dame Isabel had been right. Maybe she was born evil.

An hour later Audrey came back. Jo could hear her voice on the other side of the wall.

"It's getting worse out there," she said. "The Belgian Prankster escaped from the asylum. Nobody knows where he is. The Silent Sisters are tearing the city apart searching for you. Nobody can stop them. Every time someone comes near the Silent Sisters or even looks at them too long, they lose their mind, or faint, or just start crying. Everyone just wants to find you and hand you over to them. And there's something else."

Jo couldn't stop shaking. "What?"

"The earthquake cracked open the top of the mountain," said Audrey. "City hall, the mayor's mansion—it's all destroyed. And there's a *new* building on top of the mountain. It used to be underground. It's like the earthquake made it bubble up to the surface. It's—it looks like—"

Jo whispered, "It's the temple we visited. It's temple of the Silent Sisters."

Audrey paused for a long moment. "Yes."

"They're going to find me," said Jo.

"But I've got a plan for you to escape!"

From outside there came the angry shouts of a mob. Jo turned away from Audrey's voice, tremblingly got on her hands and knees, squinted through the peephole—then jerked back as if something had poked her eye.

The Silent Sisters were in front of the lodge, all twelve of them, standing absolutely still, shimmering pale blue in the gray dawn. Behind them, a mob was waving torches, stomping and shoving, screaming at the lodge.

"Audrey, the Silent Sisters are here," whispered Jo. "They're *here!*"

"Calm down! I've got a plan, okay?"

Audrey's footsteps pattered away, leaving Jo alone. Jo made herself put her eye back in the peephole. The Silent Sisters hadn't moved. They were standing around a veiled palanquin. Jo squinted closer, straining to see what was inside the elaborately draped tent.

Then she realized: the palanquin was for *her*.

The mob was swelling in size, growing more violent. A burly man with shaggy black hair and beard stood on a car, whipping the crowd into a frenzy, gesticulating and screaming. The crowd threw bottles and bricks at the lodge, answering his shouts with angry chants.

"Come out, Hazelwood!" said the man. "We know you're in there! Go to your Silent Sisters, just as you should've thirteen years ago! Go back to your own, Ichthala—or we'll burn you out!"

"Burn, burn, Ichthala!" roared the crowd, shaking their torches up and down. "Burn, burn!"

"Your plan isn't working," said Jo. "Audrey, whatever your plan is—they're going to burn down the lodge! Audrey! Why don't you answer me?"

Footsteps, and then Audrey's voice again: "I'm going out there."

"It's me they want, Audrey, not you!"

"They won't know the difference until it's too late."

"Audrey *what*—"

Audrey dropped down into the closet. Jo staggered backward, stunned—for a moment she didn't believe it was her. Audrey was wearing Jo's dress, and her veiled face was covered with Ichthala makeup, including a fake wound on her neck.

"I got my makeup from the show," said Audrey. "I'll go out there disguised as the Ichthala and lead them away from the lodge. By the time they realize it's not you, you'll have escaped!"

"What . . . I can't let you do that, Audrey!"

"Come out *now,* Ichthala!" thundered the bearded man. "We're tired of waiting, of your lies! You have one minute to give yourself up to the Silent Sisters or we'll burn you out!"

The crowd roared: "Sixty! Fifty-nine! Fifty-eight!"

"I'm going." Audrey climbed up out the trapdoor.

"No!" Jo scrambled after her. "It's not going to work! The Silent Sisters won't be fooled. I have to face them myself. Only I can stop this!"

"Fifty-two! Fifty-one! Fifty!"

"You, alone, against the Silent Sisters?" said Audrey. "You can stop this on your own? They've got you cornered. They've got the whole city against you!"

"That's why I have to face them!" said Jo, running after her. "You've played me well until now, but this last time, it has to be me!"

Audrey turned around. "If we substitute me for you, it'll at least give you time to escape."

"Escape *where,* Audrey?" said Jo. "Where can I go that's safe? The Silent Sisters will kill you, then they'll track me down again!"

"Twenty-nine! Twenty-eight! Twenty-seven!"

"Do you *want* the Silent Sisters to get you?" said Audrey. "I'm on *your* side, Jo. I'm trying to help!"

"But I can't keep running away," said Jo. "I'm the only one who can stop this!"

Audrey stood blocking the front door, her eyes desperate; but then she sagged, her energy and enterprise gone.

"Four! Three! Two . . ."

The lodge door opened. The crowd faltered, broke into gasps and whispers.

Jo stepped out onto the porch. The mob began to back away.

She walked down the stairs and into the street. The crowd parted before her. The Silent Sisters fell to their knees. She approached the palanquin and opened the curtain. Inside was a dark tent of perfumed pillows and jeweled drapery. Incense burned in a little gold pot.

Jo took a deep breath. She climbed up into the tent, closed the curtain, and lay down on the pillows. She felt the palanquin rise.

They had her.

TWENTY-SEVEN

THE tent bounced and jiggled as the Silent Sisters carried it up the mountain. Surrounded by swaying red and purple curtains, cut off from the world, Jo felt as if she was tucked inside a pulsing heart. The gold pot steamed sweet smoke, blurring the jewels sewn into the overlapping layers of drapes, spiraling and blossoming into dizzying patterns; muddled by the incense, dazzled by the gems, Jo's head grew fuzzy and huge, and she tried to look away, but the maddening jewels were everywhere, blinking and swirling, receding . . . fading . . .

Jo bit her cheek, dug her nails into the flesh of her legs, strained her eyes open, but everything was slipping away. Invisible voices whispered, thickening and slowing as the world grew heavier, dissolving in the dreamy smoke and curtains.

The palanquin bumped on the ground. Jo tried to sit up. She couldn't. Her body wouldn't move. She saw a dribble of gray light—and the Silent Sisters gathering around, opening the curtains. Gray veils crowded on every side, trembling fingers touching her all over. A nauseous chill slithered under Jo's skin. The fingers clutched her arms, slipped under her back, and lifted her out into the cold morning.

They were on the peak of the mountain. The cathedral of the Silent Sisters towered out of the fog, dwarfing the wrecked buildings all around, its crooked spires and spiraling towers crusted with lurid coral, pink and aqua and gold. The cathedral looked like a huge prehistoric insect, panting and heaving, waiting for her.

The Silent Sisters carried Jo up the cathedral steps. Her body felt as limp and delicate as wet paper. With each step, she felt as if she might tear into pieces. A jewel-toothed slit loomed all around her, glinting dully, and she was inside.

The world disintegrated into disconnected colors. The incense had scrambled her mind into a foggy blur. The Silent Sisters took off her clothes and laid her in a jade basin of water, washing her with bony fingers. The only sound was the gurgle of the bath, distant and dwindling. The hands dried her, rubbed oils into her, massaged her until she felt like jelly. Then they wrapped her up in shrouds and carried her deeper.

Dim figures moved all around Jo, holding up chalices, waving scepters, whirling in solemn, incomprehensible dances. The wound on her neck was opening wider, twisting in on itself. She was losing her body. Her mind was a flickering match. A whispered chant swirled all around, a freezing calm spread through her. The match went out. She didn't know who she was. She was dead all over.

The Silent Sisters carried her deeper, spiraling down through a corkscrew of crumbling black stone, cramped coiled tunnels like the inside of a wasp's nest, hundreds of coffins packed in stacked rings, circling down to the bottom of the cathedral.

The golden mouth smiled.

Jo was too far gone to do anything. The jaws grinned wider, emeralds and rubies blinked, swarmed, silver glyphs uncurled, danced, and swirled away. She tried to twist around, but her body was slack. She passed into the golden mouth and its glittering lips closed behind her.

Jo lay on a stone floor. Her mind was poured out and lost, too vague and blank to think or feel or even be afraid. The darkness around her trembled and flowed and she felt a slow thump in her bones—the heartbeat of the All-Devouring Mother. The wound had spread all over Jo now, shooting roots deep into her. The wound opened and gave a tiny screech.

A blast of gurgling thunder answered. Then Jo saw it, brooding in the shadows: shockingly enormous, a looming blob of sagging, scabbed, sewn gray flesh, a spider with countless arms, legs, and tentacles wriggling all around a moaning mouth. The mouth crouched back on a hundred legs, a row of furious eyes along its side, a mountain of chewed-up flaps, twitching snakes, crinkled sacs crisscrossed with veins and stitches hanging off, bubbling over—a gigantic, misshapen mouth, snuffling and groaning.

The gigantic thing was hissing toward her, but Jo's heart was slow, her mind empty. Dozens of tentacles came slithering toward her, wrapping around her, and suddenly she was lifted high in the air, dangling above the steaming mouth. The mouth opened wider, wider, cracking open scabs. It exhaled a blast of hot rotten air—

And Jo was flung into the All-Devouring Mother.

She plunged into a lake of spit. The saliva burned her skin, sizzled down her throat. A whale-sized tongue swept everything toward a row of gnashing teeth. There was a tremendous gurgle, a drain opened under her, and Jo was flushed down into the All-Devouring Mother.

A dense stew of organs and arteries churned past, yanking,

sucking, jerking Jo in every direction——and suddenly she was spit out of a tube and into the stomach.

It was a quivering funnel descending into a pool of glowing brown-green juices, foaming and throwing wildly shifting shadows, seething with dirty heat. She was steadily sliding toward the sizzling pool. She couldn't move. In a panic she strained every muscle to get away. Nothing. She kept sliding toward the frothing acid.

A rumble came from the tube. The stomach heaved, shook, there was a great gurgling blast——and smashed timbers, blocks of stone, metal girders, and millions of bricks sprayed into the stomach, splashing and dissolving into the pool. The All-Devouring Mother was already devouring Eldritch City. The air swirled with sour gases, the ghastly brown light grew brighter, and the stomach began to expand.

Jo realized she could move her arms a little. Her legs were coming back to life. But it was too late, she was slipping faster and faster, caught up in a river of wrecked buildings, ripped-up roads and trees——she scrabbled, she couldn't stop——Jo twisted, turned around, clawed for something to hold on to, the stomach convulsed and dropped——the pool rushed up and she plunged in.

The world fell away.

It came roaring back, too fast, too hot, too painful. Jo reversed, exploded, grew obscenely huge.

She wasn't herself anymore. She was outside. There was too much daylight; it smashed her open, cut to her heart. She blinked with ten thousand eyes. She had too many eyes, she saw too many things. Ten thousand Eldritch Cities kaleidoscoped around her. She had too many mouths, gasping and shrieking, stretched sideways, puckered too tight, crammed with too many teeth shoved in the wrong way. She didn't have enough skin. Someone had stitched her together, backward and inside-out and *wrong*—— every stitch sang with pain, threads pulling and straining and tearing. She couldn't move, it hurt too much, she had to move, she had to eat. She was starving. There was a building in front of her. She smashed it. She ate it. She needed more. She oozed, staggered, threw herself forward. Another building. It was in her mouth. She needed more. She was huge, she was getting huger, eating, swelling, eating Eldritch City, skewered with pain but boiling over with wild shrieking power. She recognized it all. It was hers. The Belgian Prankster was right. The Silent Sisters were right.

They had brought her back.

She was the All-Devouring Mother.

Jo screamed.

The world wavered, blurred, popped like a bubble. Suddenly she was back in her old body, back inside the monster, thrashing and drowning in sizzling juices, swirling down into a dark, sucking hole—and then she grabbed something solid.

Jo clutched at it desperately, holding on hard against the juices rushing downward all around her. Inch by agonizing inch she pulled herself upward, even as more and more of her tore off, sinking away into the hole far below. At last her head broke the surface and she heaved herself out of the pool.

She was holding a gold thread.

Jo stared at it. Her father's message: *Follow the gold thread*—

She collapsed into a puddle of bubbling gravy, panting. *I can't go on,* she thought. But the All-Devouring Mother was already tearing Eldritch City apart. At any second she might lose her consciousness to it again. She could feel the world starting to flicker again. Tears streamed out of her cut-up eyes. *I can't go on,* she said to herself. *I can't.*

Jo crawled, feeling her way along the gold thread into a throbbing tunnel. She felt like she was made of scrambled eggs, melting into the ground, getting sucked into the walls, falling apart in chunks. The gold thread dipped, looped, swerved, reversed, tangled with other threads, red, black, blue, orange, white, and green, crisscrossed and knotted. Jo held tight, following the gold thread with her hands, tremblingly, an inch at a time—

To the All-Devouring Mother's heart.

Jo stopped. The heart loomed overhead, as huge as a house, a pounding, squirting, gray and purple mountain of bulges, valves, and tubes. Every pulse shook the entire body, sprayed a blast of yellow blood into the air, flooded the mammoth arteries, slurped the blood back in through the veins, ran down the heart's side in sheets. Jo stared at the heart, terrified. If she went any closer, the heart would suck her in, tear her apart, pump her out in a hundred pieces. Jo stood still, hopeless. Everything wobbled—

The world disintegrated, streaming backward into darkness.

Then it expanded into stabbing daylight. She was the All-Devouring Mother again, huge and hungry and angry, bloated far larger than before, her hundreds of mouths full, overflowing with Eldritch City. Her eyes swiveled, spun around, saw people running—

She screamed and the world whirled, broke, glittered away. Jo gasped, her head pounding, back under the rhythmically exploding heart, still holding the gold thread. She couldn't stop moving. Every time she stopped she lost her consciousness to the All-Devouring Mother. Jo climbed the swaying gold thread, twisting out of the way of the pulsing, sucking tubes, following it into a twisty little valve, into the All-Devouring Mother's heart.

Inside the heart was a throbbing chaos. Jo couldn't keep her balance, falling down and getting thrown against the walls as everything shivered and lurched around her as the heart exploded and shrank, exploded and shrank, with deafening thumps. The gold thread ended here, dangling from a knot of gold, red, blue, orange, white, and green, swinging in the ceiling of the quaking chamber.

Jo jumped and grabbed the end of the thread.

The thread strained, pulled back.

Jo pulled again, harder. A section of the heart's lining split. She swallowed, pulled more. A whole wall of entrails collapsed, and the room flooded with steaming yellow blood.

Black hisses crept up all around, yanking her inside out. She exploded outward and was the All-Devouring Mother again, stomping and slithering around Eldritch City, the sunlight ripping through her skin. Little flying things were buzzing all around her, driving steel pins into her, hacking holes in her—tiny people on tiny ostriches. She swatted them away and rolled forward, opened her huge hot mouth for another building—

Jo screamed and yanked the gold thread with all her might. The heart ripped, zigzagged, tore apart, and suddenly she was back inside, squirming out of the heart, the gold thread tight in her fist, dashing through a swamp of guts, crashing through a jungle of bones, the gold thread pulling hard, ripping the monster apart behind her.

She was wild with pain and desperation; she wasn't thinking, she was just running, climbing up the esophagus, back into the mouth, and suddenly the mammoth tongue rushed at her. Jo yanked the thread and the tongue split, collapsed, and sank away. She sloshed blindly through the spit, the world reeling around her red and black, pounding on all sides. For the first time she had hope. She was still in the monster's mouth, but she had the gold thread. She could feel its tug. All she had to do was somehow get out, climb out of this mouth, and keep pulling the thread as far out as she could, unstitching the whole monster—

"Silly," whispered the Belgian Prankster. "Did you think it would be that easy?"

Jo choked. The Belgian Prankster was on her before she could move. She couldn't even see him, but his blubbery arms picked her up, crushing her. The world reeled dizzyingly around.

"We're going back down," he said. "And this time you'll *stay down*."

Jo kicked and screamed, mashed against his naked chest, swallowed in his ragged fur coat. He was squeezing her to death. Her bones were cracking; he was killing her. She looked up—

Just as Aunt Lily's ostrich came hurtling out of the sky and kicked the Belgian Prankster in the face.

Jo fell from his scrabbling hands, collapsed into the bubbling spit, and saw them, high up in the air: the knights and squires of the Odd-Fish, all mounted on ostriches, flying down toward the All-Devouring Mother. Jo's heart leaped. She didn't know how, she didn't care how—they'd come for her. Aunt Lily had come. Her friends had come.

The All-Devouring Mother roared, and a wormy army of tentacles exploded out, entangling the knights and squires. The Odd-Fish wheeled, darted, and streaked in, flashing their weapons—Dame Myra felled three tentacles with a slash of her axe, Sir Oort plunged his lance into a bulging sac, and Sir Alasdair and Dame Isabel fought side by side, dipping and swooping and skewering the monster with spears. The squires fluttered and dived, firing arrows at the All-Devouring Mother, and even the Schwenk was there, frolicking about, playfully plucking out the monster's eyes and tearing off its ears. And Jo also saw—she couldn't understand it—riding the Schwenk: Ken Kiang?

But everything was dimming, wobbling. Her eyes were mashed, full of blood, her body was full of holes, leaking out. She could hardly hold on to the gold thread—and suddenly the Belgian Prankster loomed up like a huge, monstrously beaked bird in the black red haze, coming for her.

In a flash of feathers and armor, Aunt Lily swung back around on her ostrich, leaped off, ignited her lance in midair, and landed in front of the Belgian Prankster, slicing and slashing at him with sizzling double arcs of flame, as rapid and merciless as a machine. The Belgian Prankster fell back, meeting her lance with his beaklike stinger. Aunt Lily ducked, danced away, lunged, and locked her lance against the stinger. They swayed, pressing against each other.

"Run, Jo!" Aunt Lily shouted. "Get out, get out!"

Jo tried to push herself up—and collapsed.

The Belgian Prankster lunged forward, forcing Aunt Lily back. Her shoulders heaved, her body swayed. "Jo, I can't hold him! *Run!*"

Jo tried, but it hurt too much. Her body didn't even make sense anymore—she didn't know where her arms or legs were. She was just a chewed-up, half-melted mass. The world was flickering; any second, it might fall away again.

"Jo, *get out!*" screamed Aunt Lily.

Jo just barely saw, out of her crushed and bloody eyes, the Belgian Prankster lunging with his stinger, thrusting, forcing Aunt Lily back, back—

The Belgian Prankster knocked her lance away.

Aunt Lily stood shocked, empty-handed.

The Belgian Prankster drove his stinger into her chest.

Jo screamed.

Aunt Lily shivered, her arms and legs twitching, and fell. Jo was still shrieking. The Belgian Prankster stopped for a moment and lifted his head to make a peculiar noise—a long, mournful wail, like a snuffling foghorn—as he swayed back and forth.

Then he turned to Jo and grinned.

He started coming for her.

The All-Devouring Mother screamed, its entire enormous body lurching. Everything in the mouth churned up in a sloshing gurgle, surprising even the Belgian Prankster, who slid away from her, startled and off balance, and tumbled down the All-Devouring Mother's throat—along with Aunt Lily.

Aunt Lily's eyes fluttered open. "Jo . . ."

The Belgian Prankster and Aunt Lily swirled down the dark hole and were gone. The throat was angling downward all around Jo, every second becoming more slippery and steep. Jo slipped, but scrambled and grabbed a tooth to hold on as the throat fell away. She looked up and saw Ian staring over the edge of the mouth.

Ian took a terrified step back. Jo pulled him close and pressed the gold thread in his hands.

"Take this," gurgled Jo. "And run!"

Ian stammered, "I—I—"

"Trust me, Ian! Run! RUN!"

Then the esophagus opened up, the All-Devouring Mother howled, and Jo was sucked down in a flood of spit and gristle.

Jo churned down through a tunnel of jelly and cartilage and was spat down into the All-Devouring Mother's stomach—now hugely bloated with hunks of buildings and streets and trees, all of it sliding into the shimmering pool.

Aunt Lily was crumpled in the corner.

Jo tried to shout. Her throat wouldn't work. Little by little she pulled herself over to where Aunt Lily lay. It seemed impossibly far. The world was blacking out, rushing in, flashing and flickering, stabbing her behind her eyes. She fell to her knees, out of breath, next to Aunt Lily.

"Aunt Lily?" rasped Jo. "Can you hear me?"

Aunt Lily's eyelids twitched and her lips moved.

"We've got to get out of here, do you think you can . . . can you . . ." Jo looked at Aunt Lily's gashed chest, her glassy eyes. She didn't know what to do.

Aunt Lily whispered: "Jo?"

Jo gathered Aunt Lily up and cradled her head. "It's me."

"I can't see."

"That's okay, I've looked better. Oh no, no, no—" Jo felt her shiver in her arms. Aunt Lily's breathing became shallower. Jo tried to move her so she would be comfortable, but she didn't know what to do.

"Everything's dark," said Aunt Lily distantly. "I just feel like . . . I had the strangest dream."

"I don't . . . What?"

"It was marvelous," said Aunt Lily. "We were together. Some old friends took us in a plane, we went to a city . . . We had so many friends, and . . . and . . . Jo?"

Jo swallowed. "Tell me more."

"I've never had a dream like that," said Aunt Lily. "It was such a good dream."

Jo managed to say, "Close your eyes. Maybe you'll dream about it again."

Aunt Lily closed her eyes. Jo held her in the flickering light, long after she stopped moving. She clutched Aunt Lily and rocked and didn't know what to do. Aunt Lily was dead.

When she heard the Belgian Prankster coming up behind her she didn't move. She felt him, a faint tingle in the small of her back, electricity crawling up her spine. The stinger appeared over her shoulder, and she closed her eyes tight.

The Belgian Prankster put his arms around her. Aunt Lily slipped away and was gone. He was carrying Jo away. She beat him with her arms, but she was weak, exhausted.

The Belgian Prankster whispered in her ear: "I know. I know."

Jo was crying, but she didn't feel anything. Her body shook, her mouth made noises, tears streamed from her eyes, but she couldn't feel anything. He was carrying her toward the glowing pool. Jo stopped fighting and clung to him, burying her head in his furs.

"Soon it'll be over," said the Belgian Prankster. "You won't hurt anymore. Nobody will, when we are all inside you again."

The pool was right before them, gurgling and bubbling. Jo took her head out of the Belgian Prankster's furs and stared at it with something like craving.

"Now you know," he whispered. "Now you understand what we want."

He was lowering her into the pool. It felt cool and smooth and tingly. Every tension in her slackened, and a tremendous relief stole through her.

"It's all over now. It's almost over. It's like falling asleep."

The world sank away into watery darkness, and her mind was flowering outward, swelling and unfolding into a vast, complicated consciousness, filling up the All-Devouring Mother, clicking into place in a thousand little points, locking.

She opened her ten thousand eyes.

She glared at Eldritch City all around. She howled—buildings flew apart, the mountain shook, trees were torn from the roots, flung into the sky.

"Now finish what you have started," said the Belgian Prankster, "Ichthala."

She lumbered forward, smashed, and ate. She screamed, stomped, chomped, tore, and gobbled blindly. She couldn't stop. She was feverish, bloated, too fat and disgusting to move, but burning inside, filled with a sucking emptiness that needed more, more, more.

But pain tore through her—someone was pulling her apart. The thread holding her together was straining and ripping loose, pulling further and further out.

"Someone is trying to kill you, Ichthala!" whispered the Belgian Prankster.

Tiny nuisances were flying around, pricking her—fat men with mustaches and beards, some bony old women, boys and girls flapping about on shabby-looking birds—she snatched them out of the air, squeezing them as they struggled against her.

"Who are they?" said the Belgian Prankster.

She didn't recognize them.

"They are trying to kill you! Take them, crush them!"

She stared dimly, puzzled. Now she remembered them vaguely. But it was worlds ago, when she had a different name . . . what was her name?

She stopped, confused. What *was* her name?

"Your name is Ichthala!" said the Belgian Prankster.

No, no, something else. The little things were wriggling free—

"That name no longer exists, Ichthala! Kill them!"

Claws snapped, jaws chomped shut. She grabbed the little flying things, tied them up in knots. There was only one left, darting and looping away from her. It had the gold thread, pulling faster and faster, popping open her stitches, yanking the life out of her.

"That's the one, that one!" said the Belgian Prankster. "Get that one, kill *that* one!"

Her tentacles ran out, snaking and twisting, and caught it.

She could feel its tiny heartbeat—a boy on a bird. The boy was still pulling on the gold thread, as taut as a wire. Her vast, bubbling, bulging body trembled, the last stitches straining, stretching with agony. The boy kept pulling the thread, his bird bleating. She focused her ten thousand eyes on him. He was shouting something.

"He's going to kill you!" screeched the Belgian Prankster. "He, all of them, they want you dead! They're not your friends, they never were! Now finish it, crush it, kill it, finish it all!"

In a hot haze, she tightened—

And a sudden searing agony shot through her entire body, further out and deeper inside than anything she'd ever known. The last stitch popped open, the last bit of gold thread loosened, the last knot untangled, and the gold thread flew out of her and was gone.

Everything dropped away. She plunged down, tore upward, ripped in half. A rush of stars pulsed, reversed, flourished into a million-spined, burning white snowflake and shattered away.

The All-Devouring Mother fell.

Jo's eyes flipped open.

She was awake. Someone was holding her under cold slime. She grabbed its hands. They crumbled, burst into fire. Someone was howling. Jo stood up and saw the Belgian Prankster staggering away, stumbling as fast as he could away from her, his goggles off and his eyes wild with terror. Jo was white-hot, pure flames licking all around her—and in a dazzling flash she was upon him, burning him, shredding him, boiling higher and hotter every second, radiating blinding light everywhere.

She grabbed his stinger with fiery hands.

"No! No! No! Don't do that! Anything but that!"

Jo flared up into a perfect incandescence, scorching lightning rushing through her—and tore the stinger off his face.

The Belgian Prankster screeched, scrambling away, holding his hands to his nose. A whirl of sparks, and Jo flew at him in a streak of lightning, bringing the stinger down.

And then the stomach collapsed; the esophagus collapsed; the heart collapsed; the mouth collapsed; the intestines collapsed; somewhere outside, the All-Devouring Mother collapsed, crashing down on Jo, the Belgian Prankster, everything, everything, and then there was nothing.

TWENTY-EIGHT

FOR Ken Kiang it was the final indignity.

Not prison; no, actually Ken Kiang had quite liked prison. He had his little cell, his hour of exercise, his three squares a day—really, what more did a man need?

No, the indignities had started when Ken Kiang was sitting in his cell and heard a screech outside. Ken Kiang ran to the window and was astonished to see a great, four-winged, yellow, purple, and red feathered beast attacking the prison, its talons shredding the walls as if they were cardboard.

The Schwenk (for that was what it was) was accompanied by a flock of armored ostriches, flapping and fluttering around, swooping into the demolished walls; moments later they burst out, each ostrich with a knight, and they all flew away.

The Schwenk started flying away, too. But it hesitated—and with a mischievous glint in its eye whirled and flew straight at Ken Kiang.

Ken Kiang yelped, scrambling across his cell—and the Schwenk came crashing through in an exploding spray of bricks, snatched him up with its monstrous beak, and tossed him on its back.

After that, all Ken Kiang could do was hang on.

Ken Kiang hung on as the Schwenk and the ostriches flew to the cathedral on top of the mountain; hung on as they all dived down to attack a vast, incomprehensible monster, all mouth and teeth and eyes and tentacles; held on when the Schwenk was caught and squeezed by the monster's claws; held on as a gold thread stretched farther and farther out from the monster, drawn out by a boy on an ostrich, until the boy gave a final yank and the monster fell, unfolding into a melting pile of meat.

And even this was not the final indignity.

It was the congratulations.

"Outstanding Schwenkmanship, old boy!" roared Colonel Korsakov, slapping Ken Kiang on the back. "Never knew you had it in you! A top-drawer Schwenkrider, eh? You must tell me your secret!"

"Thank you, Mr.—*Kiang*, is it?" said Dame Delia. "I don't know what we would've done without your help. I've rarely seen such valor in battle."

"Breathtaking," agreed Sir Oort. "You are clearly a warrior of exceptional prowess."

"No I'm not!" protested Ken Kiang.

"Oh, come now," said Sir Festus.

"Really, I didn't do anything," Ken Kiang tried to explain. "I still don't even know what happened."

"A modest man." Dame Isabel nodded.

"But most ferocious when roused to battle," squeaked Dame Myra.

"I like this man's face," declared Sir Alasdair. "He possesses a quiet nobility."

"Are you blind?" said Ken Kiang. "*Look* at me—I'm the idiot who interrupted your concert!"

"Oh well, it would've been interrupted by the Belgian Prankster anyway, right?" said Sir Alasdair cheerfully. "Come upstairs, I want to show you my smells organ."

"No, no!" interrupted Sir Festus. "Before Mr. Kiang goes anywhere, I move that the Order of Odd-Fish present him with an honorary knighthood!"

The applause, and Ken Kiang's protests, subsided when Sir Oliver cleared his throat.

"I will not have it," said Sir Oliver quietly. "I will not allow this . . . *Ken Kiang* to be given such a preposterous recognition. Honorary knighthood, indeed."

"Finally," said Ken Kiang. "The voice of reason."

"The only suitable reward," continued Sir Oliver, "is a proper, *full-fledged* knighthood! Therefore I, Sir Oliver Mulcahy, Grand Bebisoy, dub you Sir Kenneth Kiang of the Order of Odd-Fish!"

"Isn't anyone *listening* to me?" shouted Ken Kiang. But the cheering of the knights drowned him out, and soon he was silenced entirely when the cockroaches dumped the Hat of Honor onto his head.

Jo opened her eyes.

Everything was blurry. Her throat was dry, she couldn't move. She was in a bed. Her eyes struggled to focus. She saw a chipped wood desk, a wardrobe, a little leaded-glass window . . .

A lean, spindly man sat at her beside, watching her closely. His dark skin was peppered with freckles, and his round spectacles were perched askew, almost diagonally on his nose. He was saying something to her, but her ears felt sealed with wax. She tried to speak but her tongue was as dry as paper.

The man held a glass of water to her lips. She could hardly open her mouth. The glass tipped and water trickled down her throat, cold and delicious. The fog began to lift. Jo blinked. It was her bedroom. She was at the lodge of the Order of Odd-Fish. And this man . . .

"Don't speak," said Sir Oliver. "It would be too much for you. You've been through enough. And Jo . . . you did brilliantly."

Jo looked at herself—and her heart, though fragile, managed a feeble leap.

She wasn't a monster.

Sir Oliver saw Jo's reaction. "Yes, you're okay, mostly," he said. "The gold thread that held the All-Devouring Mother together also bound you to it. Once the monster fell apart, the metamorphosis started working backward. We almost didn't recognize you when we first found you. But you've been coming back to your old self, little by little."

Sir Oliver paused, weighing his words. Then he said:

"Except for your wound from the Belgian Prankster. That you will always have."

Jo almost couldn't hear him. But she could move a bit. The more she tried, the more blood seemed to flow back to her limbs, and she felt like a statue coming to life. She managed to lift her arm. Slowly, with difficulty, she reached behind her neck and felt around. The wound was there, but barely there, a tiny closed mouth.

Then darkness crept in the corners of her vision, stars blinked and swirled—she fell back, her breath shallow and painful.

"Don't strain yourself." Sir Oliver gently put her arm back, adjusting her pillow to a more comfortable position. "You'll be able to move eventually. For now, just rest. Although . . . there is something I must tell you."

Jo stared at him blankly.

Sir Oliver took a deep breath. "Lily is dead."

The fact hit Jo like a hammer. In a dim corner of her mind she'd hoped that Aunt Lily might come barging into her room with some wild, hilarous story of how she survived—the kind of thing that only happened to Aunt Lily, some crazy combination of chutzpah and ludicrousness. Jo would laugh till her ribs hurt, Aunt Lily would already be planning their next adventure, and . . .

Jo's face crinkled, but her body was so drained she couldn't cry. She tried to speak, but all that came was a dry croak. She closed her eyes, all the breath came out of her, and she lay very still.

For a long time Sir Oliver did not speak. When Jo finally opened her eyes, he was dabbing his eyes with a handkerchief. He looked at Jo and gave a small, lopsided smile.

"As for the rest of us, the knights and squires . . . we're the worse for wear, but all alive, fortunately. And perhaps a bit wiser. Sir Festus, at least, no longer talks so enthusiastically about dying in the glory of battle." Sir Oliver paused. "A sprained nose has that effect."

A noise involuntarily came out of Jo, something more like a cough than a laugh.

"Seems you're coming around." Sir Oliver peered carefully at her. "I admit there were days we lost hope. A couple of times we almost lost you. I don't mean to shock you, but . . . you've been unconscious for about a month."

Jo's eyes widened.

Sir Oliver nodded. "Thirty-eight and a half days, to be precise. In fact, today's the day of the Grand Feast. That means you have been in Eldritch City for one year exactly."

Jo could hardly comprehend it.

"It's been a nerve-wracking month." Sir Oliver looked at Jo with concern. "We brought doctors in, but it seems modern medical science is ignorant on how to treat a half-digested ex-goddess. When we found you, you weren't much more than a glob of burnt skin, teeth, bones, inside-out guts, strings of carti-lage, and . . . feathers?" Sir Oliver looked genuinely puzzled. "Why on earth had you sprouted feathers?"

Jo answered by drooling.

"I'm going to call that progress." Sir Oliver wiped away the drool with his handkerchief. "We ransacked the archives for what to do. The best research we could find was from a certain Dame Zulinda, who specialized in avant-garde hypochondria. But even Dame Zulinda, in her most extravagant fantasies, never envisaged an affliction like yours. In the end, we had to accept the inevitable and use the tools we had at hand. Yes," said Sir Oliver gravely. "I was obliged to dither."

For the first time, Jo was glad she couldn't speak.

"At first I merely fudged, I hedged," said Sir Oliver, his eyes growing distant. "Then I floundered, I waffled, I malingered . . . I noodled about, I loafed . . ."

The door opened and Daphne came in with a stack of blankets. At the sight of Jo awake Daphne's eyes widened, she gave an involuntary "eep!" and threw the blankets down, running back out the door.

Sir Oliver watched Daphne run away with a faint smile. "Everyone's been taking turns watching at your bedside," he explained. "There's a betting pool over who'd be with you when you woke up. I'm happy to say that you have made me a moderately wealthy man."

Jo could hear Daphne shouting downstairs, and a murmur of voices answering. She looked up at Sir Oliver, her eyes frightened and questioning.

Sir Oliver nodded. "Don't worry, Jo. Nobody blames you for what happened. Some buildings were destroyed, but it could've been much worse. Very few people were killed. The city knows they owe their lives to you. The Silent Sisters gave you a terrible fate—we know. And you handled it better than anyone could have asked."

All around the lodge, the mumble of voices rose to a roar as doors slammed and feet ran up and down the hallways.

"But I have to apologize to you." Sir Oliver sighed, and for once there was no twinkle in his eyes. "We were wrong, Jo. Me, and Lily, and Korsakov—we didn't want to believe you were the Ichthala. We thought all you needed was to be protected from the Silent Sisters. But we should have told you more. We should've trusted you. Still, Lily said that even if we were wrong . . . even if you *were* carrying the soul of the All-Devouring Mother . . . she assured us you'd never do what the Belgian Prankster wanted. And in that, at least, she was right."

Jo hardly heard the last sentence; the words *Belgian Prankster* made her body go cold. In her bedroom, in the cozy haze of being half awake, she had almost forgotten about him. Her heart pounded against her fragile chest.

Sir Oliver saw the panicked look in her eyes. "It's okay. You don't need to worry about him anymore. We didn't find the Belgian Prankster's body, but . . ." Sir Oliver hesitated, then stood up and held out his hand. "Actually, Jo, let me help you up. I have something you need to see."

At first Jo thought she couldn't possibly. But Sir Oliver helped her put her feet on the floor, and with difficulty, she was able to stand. He held her up, and Jo took one step, and then another, and together they inched out of the room, out into the hallway.

Step by hobbling step, Sir Oliver helped Jo around the corner, and they made their unsteady way to the staircase, and down into the common room. Jo squinted around: it was just as she remembered, with Sir Festus's and Colonel Korsakov's favorite overstuffed chairs, the fireplace, the huge head of the Prancing Gobbler, the ranks of bookcases and portraits, and . . .

Something new was on the wall: a withered tube mounted over a dirty scrap of paper. At first Jo didn't understand what she was looking at—and then she gasped.

It was the Belgian Prankster's stinger, nailed to the wall, right above a ragged note that Jo had forgotten about:

This is Jo. Please take care of her.
But beware.
This is a DANGEROUS baby.

Sir Oliver turned to Jo and shrugged. "A slapdash memorial, I know, but we were in a hurry and . . ."

But he never finished. A great happy shout went up, and Jo turned and saw that the room had filled with the knights, squires, and butlers of the Order of Odd-Fish. She couldn't hold it in anymore, and collapsed into a sob of relief. Sir Oliver held Jo up as everyone gathered around her, cheering. She remembered her first morning at the lodge, the first time she had walked down these stairs, when she wished there was something she could do, something to make her feel like she belonged in the Odd-Fish.

Jo closed her eyes. She had done it.

The cocktail party before the Grand Feast was supposed to be subdued, but it quickly got out of hand. Even though the lodge was still draped in black in mourning for Aunt Lily, everyone was so happy and relieved for Jo that all somberness was swept away by a giddy hilarity.

The faces and voices passed by Jo in a whirl. Somewhere inside, she had given up any hope of ever seeing any of the knights or squires again, so even the sight of Albert stuffing his face with cheese and crackers made her unexpectedly emotional.

"What?" said Albert, crumbs falling from his lips.

Everyone wanted to hear Jo's story, but she could still hardly manage a whisper, so she had to be content to sit while everyone came and went, talking to her. Only one thing bothered her—Ian. He was nowhere to be found, and she was afraid to ask after him.

Meanwhile, Nora and Audrey had swooped down on Jo and,

after hugging her so hard that she felt her bones might break, immediately plunged into a frenzied dialogue that Jo could barely understand.

"You should've seen yourself the past couple of weeks!" said Nora in her high-pitched gasp. "Every time I came into your room you had changed into something else! One day you looked like you were made out of, I don't know, a billion crumpled-up little squids! Then a couple days later you had become like a . . . what . . . a kind of . . . what, Audrey?"

"A fish monkey?" said Audrey.

"*Exactly!* A slime-leaking fish monkey! We had to change your sheets, like, once an hour or so! You smelled like rotten cheese and gasoline! Dame Isabel was in heaven! What did it feel like, Jo, huh?" Nora shook away her long tangled hair and her eyes emerged, huge and bright. "What happened?"

"Give her a break, she can barely speak," said Audrey. "By the way, Jo, they asked me to act in another drama about you, about your adventures in Eldritch City. Like a *Teenage Ichthala—the Sequel.*"

Nora looked confused. "But who would play *you* then, Audrey?" A bolt of pleased surprise went through her face. "Wait . . . who would play *me?*"

"But I told them no," said Audrey. "Anyway, I'm not an actress anymore. As of last week . . ."

"Audrey's an Odd-Fish!" said Nora.

Jo stared at Audrey, her mouth open.

"Yep, I'm Dame Myra's squire now," said Audrey. "Turns out she's wanted a squire for years and was just too shy to request one. I'm moving into the lodge tomorrow!"

Audrey and Nora were soon shoved aside by other squires and knights who wanted to see Jo—Phil and Daphne wanted to tell a long story about flying their ostriches against the All-Devouring Mother, Maurice was smiling and continually saying "good work, good work," even after everyone had stopped listening to him, and Dugan kept running back and forth with drinks and appetizers for her. There were so many questions Jo wanted to ask, but it hurt to speak; she felt like someone had scoured her throat with sandpaper. Still, her strength was coming back, bit by bit, and soon she found she could even hobble around the room.

Meanwhile, Sir Alasdair hauled out the urk-ack and played it for a couple of songs, with the cockroaches' band accompanying him, but it was so bad that everyone shouted at them to stop, especially when Sir Festus started singing. At one point Dame Isabel approached Jo and stiffly conceded, "I can't say I approve of all the lies, but then again you did save the world, so I suppose it evens out in the end." Dame Myra had strewn the lodge with curling ivy with luminous berries, and Sir Oort was hanging from them like a white-furred monkey, hiccupping and swinging from vine to vine, as Dame Delia chased him with a broom; Jo noticed that even Ken Kiang was there, although he seemed somewhat befuddled, trapped under the colossal Hat of Honor.

"I'm not quite sure what's going on," said Ken Kiang, who was barely visible under the hat, his voice muffled. "Apparently I am now a knight. I suspect somebody, somewhere has made a tremendous error, and I have a creeping feeling it might be me. Er . . . I can't move."

Just then Sir Oliver, Colonel Korsakov, and Sir Festus came roaring and singing around the corner, knocking Ken Kiang over. After hasty apologies Sir Oliver said, "By the way, Jo, I forgot. I have something that belongs to you." He fished in his pocket and took out a silver ring. "I think you can wear this openly in Eldritch City now."

Jo held the ring in her trembling hand, turning it over, looking where it said JO HAZELWOOD on the inside. She remembered how she had felt when she first saw the ring, back in the ruby palace, when the ring had felt like a promise. It seemed like a hundred years ago.

"By the way, Jo," whispered Colonel Korsakov with childlike wonder, "what was it like inside the All-Devouring Mother's digestion?"

Sir Oliver said, "Time enough for that later, Colonel. The girl can hardly speak."

"Of course . . . but one day, over a roast beef and plum pudding, I'd love to hear the tale . . ."

Sir Festus cut in. "And for my part, I'll tell Jo about how I fought against the All-Devouring Mother! It's a heroic yarn, of course, with plenty of derring-do, such as when I—"

"Wait," rasped Jo with difficulty. "How *did* you all get to fight? Dame Isabel said you had all been locked up in prison."

"Quite so," said Sir Festus. "But it seems someone in the Order of Odd-Fish was owed a favor by Oona Looch. No sooner were we incarcerated than Oona Looch herself came around, bringing all our weapons and armor, demanding our release. Raised quite a fury. I recall her holding the police chief up by his ear, five feet off the ground, when—"

"When the Schwenk came." Sir Oliver glanced over at Korsakov. "For some reason the Schwenk came blasting out of nowhere, with all the ostriches flapping after it, and broke us out of jail. Very inspiring."

"Of all the unutterable cheek," fumed Colonel Korsakov. "Now I'm in debt to the beast."

Sir Festus said, "Funny thing about the Schwenk. I think it *likes* being hunted."

As Sir Festus and Colonel Korsakov began a loud, boozy debate about the psychology of the Schwenk, Jo glanced around— and happened to spot Ian, creeping past a hallway on the other side of the room, skirting the edges of the party.

Jo felt her heart twist. Why wasn't he celebrating? She tottered across the room toward him, holding herself steady on couches or tables, passing Maurice and Phil, who were trying to wake up an already unconscious Sir Oort, and a group of cockroaches excitedly passing around copies of the *Eldritch Snitch*. After a long, painful trek to the opposite hall, she finally made it to where Ian had been—but he wasn't there. Jo turned around in a painful circle, confused and hurt. Was he avoiding her?

Then she glimpsed Ian again, on the other side of the room, jogging down the opposite hallway. Jo groaned, heaved herself up, and staggered back into the party, stumbling and weaving through the knights and squires, her legs numb and clumsy.

Just then Sefino climbed on top of the piano, clearing his throat and taking huge gulps from a suspicious-looking bottle. Jo winced, for she knew what that throat clearing meant: he was going to make a speech.

"Ladies and gentlemen!" proclaimed Sefino. "I hold in my hand a newspaper—"

"You hold in your hand a bottle of whiskey," Albert pointed out.

"I hold in my *other* hand a newspaper," continued Sefino, waving it about. "And I am gratified to announce that we butlers of the Order of Odd-Fish have finally received our just due from the *Eldritch Snitch*. Though I once doubted I would ever say this, Chatterbox has redeemed himself, and I can confidently declare that our epic feud with the *Eldritch Snitch* has at last reached a happy resolution."

"What did they write?" said Daphne.

"It's at the end of the article detailing Jo's little misadventure with the All-Devouring Mother," said Sefino. "I direct you to the final paragraph. I shall allow Sir Oliver the privilege of reading it aloud."

"Honored, I'm sure," murmured Sir Oliver. He put on his glasses and read, "*During the battle between the All-Devouring Mother and the Order of Odd-Fish, the Odd-Fish butlers were to be found in a local tavern, carousing, capering, and consuming to excess, according to eyewitnesses. The butlers were reprimanded for disorderly conduct by the Eldritch constabulary, and Sefino was charged with public indecency.*" Sir Oliver looked at Sefino. "This doesn't seem quite so . . ."

"Read on, read on," said Sefino airily.

"Ah . . . yes, the last sentence. *Although a disgrace to Eldritch City in general, and the Order of Odd-Fish in particular, it will be noted the butlers all wore irreproachable ascots.*"

"Vindication!" roared Sefino. "There *is* such a thing as justice, after all."

By this time Jo had managed to hobble across the common room to the hallway where she had seen Ian. Again he was gone. Jo leaned up against a banister, breathing hard. She could hear the babble of the party, she even heard Nora asking where she had gone to, but she was too tired to make it back. She sat on the floor in the dim hallway, alone, and then the bell rang for everyone to change into their feast robes and come to the banquet room. Footsteps pattered up and down the halls, and she only heard the squires coming and going from the closet where they changed into dining gowns. She could hardly summon the energy to make it there.

The bell rang again, far away, in the banquet hall. Jo picked herself up; she couldn't spend the rest of the night lying in a dark corner while everyone else was whooping it up in the banquet hall, and soon the knights and squires would start to worry. Her body aching all over, she started toward the squires' closet to change into her own dining gown. The last few steps, and she grabbed the doorway, pulling herself into the closet.

Ian was in the shadows.

Jo stopped, too surprised to speak. Shouts and hoots buzzed down the hall, but in the closet it was silent. It was almost too dim to see. Jo couldn't even tell what was in Ian's eyes.

"Where have you been?" said Jo, out of breath.

Ian did not speak for a few seconds; then he said, very quietly, "I was out of the lodge when you woke up."

They stood in the dark and Jo had no idea what to say. She couldn't see his face, couldn't read him.

Finally Ian said, "I heard about your aunt, Jo. I'm sorry."

Jo stared into the darkness. He sounded like he was sorry.

She wanted more than anything to touch him, to make up with him, but she couldn't find the words, couldn't find the energy.

"Ian, are you still . . . ?"

Ian didn't say anything.

Jo came closer to Ian. "You don't . . . still blame . . ."

She saw, in the darkness, Ian's lip curl. Too late, she saw he had a gun.

Ian shot her.

There was an ear-breaking POW and Jo reeled away through a haze of blue smoke, staggering backward.

She blinked, startled. She was still standing. She looked around, then down, and through the swirling blue dust she saw what had struck her: a little rolled-up piece of paper.

Ian said, "I set it for maximum sincer—"

With a hilarious shriek Jo flew at Ian and knocked him down, crushing the Apology Gun as they tumbled backward together. She hit him until her arms couldn't hit anymore, and Ian lay back, laughing, and she stopped trying to beat Ian up and just collapsed on him, out of breath.

A minute later Jo got off him, embarrassed but still smiling. Ian got up and offered his arm. She took it, and together they went back into the party. She couldn't stop smiling.

Ken Kiang stepped outside.

It was all too much for him. The smoke, the lights, the laughter, the dancing . . . he had to breathe some cold night air and clear his head.

He was finished with Eldritch City. It was time to go back. He'd done what he'd meant to do—he had fought against the Belgian Prankster—and even if he wasn't the one who had defeated him, well, at least he had helped, or . . .

But no. Ken Kiang knew he was deluding himself. He had to admit that *everything* he attempted had ended in failure. He couldn't pull off being evil; he couldn't kill the Belgian Prankster;

his musical was horrible; he had even been fired from the Municipal Squires Authority. And yet here he was, unexpectedly at the happy ending, and why? Ken Kiang knew he didn't deserve it. The whole thing was infuriating.

And yet Ken Kiang had to admit he liked this place. Despite himself, he liked the knights. He was happy. He could almost imagine being happy here for some time.

Many times, Ken Kiang had heard the saying "The road to hell is paved with good intentions." It would be too tidy to say that for Ken Kiang, the road to heaven was paved with bad intentions. Still, his intentions had always been the worst; yet now he was as close to happiness as he was ever likely to get.

Ken Kiang hesitated. He took a breath.

And then Ken Kiang—no; Sir Ken—walked back inside.

The lights at the Odd-Fish lodge stayed on late that night. The feast went on and on, nobody wanted it to end; course after course came out, borne by troops of dancing cockroaches, and as the wine was poured around, Sir Oliver proposed a toast to Aunt Lily, and Dame Delia quickly followed with a salute to Sir Oliver, and another toast to Aunt Lily; whereupon Colonel Korsakov leaped up and bellowed an emotional toast of his own to Aunt Lily's memory, along with affectionate respects to Dame Delia and Sir Oliver, and indeed all the Odd-Fish, which was received with warm applause—Jo was certain there was no group of people in the world so fond of toasting each other. It seemed everyone had a favorite story about Aunt Lily, told to laughter, applause, and some tears, and for the first time Jo understood how much the Odd-Fish had loved Aunt Lily and already missed her. Then Audrey stood up, her blond hair glowing and her droopy eyes sweeping mischievously around the room, and proposed a toast to Jo, which was immediately seconded by Nora's breathless squeak, and the rest of the squires, who shouted "Hear! Hear!" and banged their silverware against their glasses. And just when Jo thought she might die of embarrassment,

Ian rose and quietly proposed a toast to the entire Hazelwood family, Sir Martin and Dame Evelyn included. The table broke into applause, and the toasting knights and squires became more and more extravagant and violent, crashing their glasses together, sloshing their drinks, pounding their silverware and leaping on chairs in transports of sentiment. Drinking songs started up, raucous and incomprehensible, with Sir Festus standing on the table and conducting the Odd-Fish with broad, slashing sweeps of his arm while Cicero vainly protested and tugged on his robe. Then the cockroaches' band cranked up, chairs scraped back and clattered to the floor, and all the knights and squires were suddenly dancing, and Jo whirled and weaved through the capering knights and squires, flung from Maurice to Nora, and from Nora to Dugan. The knights snaked past, arms locked in high-kicking rows of purple-stockinged legs, and Jo grabbed Audrey and threw her at Phil, hooting and ducking a glass just before it smashed on the wall behind her.

Later that night, after everyone else had gone to sleep and the lodge was silent, Jo would quietly slip out of bed and wander around the empty halls of the lodge, alone. She would creak down the stairs to the basement and Aunt Lily's old workroom, where the torn-up machines were already gathering dust, never to be tinkered with again; she would wander up to Aunt Lily's old bedroom and stand on the balcony, looking out over the city; she would climb up to the roof, where she had clung to Aunt Lily as the lodge was carried into Eldritch City and Aunt Lily first looked at the city and said to herself, "I'm finally home. We're home."

Jo spun into Ian's arms, laughing; they looked at each other, and Jo spun back into the dancing. It was true. She was home.